WAR ANGELS MC
Winnipeg:
Carter's Cache

Table of Contents

CHAPTER 1

Carol

Twenty years ago

"Karl, I just need you to listen to me," I said. I was exhausted and I had been busy getting my life in order for the past three days. This was the last thing I needed to do before I was deployed and I'd purposefully left it to the last because I knew Karl was going to be difficult.

"I don't know what you want me to do, Carol, she's a five-year-old girl, she needs her mother." Karl insisted and I shook my head.

Karl and I had separated a year ago and while I was happier, and Paige, our daughter was happier, life was still difficult.

"Karl, I'm not asking you to take her full-time," I continued, rubbing my forehead with a heavy sigh. "Seriously, I don't really even want you to take Paige more time, I'm only asking that you stick to the schedule, show up on time, drop her off on time and make your child support cheques out to my mom and not me. Is that really a big deal?"

"Well, I kind of think it is a big deal, Carol," Karl scoffed, and I could just see him rolling his eyes.

I carded my hand into my hair and almost whined when I hit a knot in the curls. I tipped my head and held my phone between my ear and my shoulder to work the knot out and untangle my fingers.

3

SLADE

"Why is that such a big deal?" I mumbled, only half listening to my ex-husband now.

"Because, I start making cheques out to your mother and not to you and you have reason to tell the courts that I'm not paying child support, I've got your number Carol."

"Karl, that's ridiculous," I sighed just as heavily as the last time, only two minutes ago. "I'm not going to do that, I'm only going to take you to court if you don't pay the support at all. Honestly I would be just as happy if you paid with cash but we need to keep a paper trail."

"And why can't I just write these cheques to you and not your mother?"

"Because I'm going to be deployed and I won't be able to sign the cheques so mom can cash them." I said, finally getting to the point of this entire conversation.

"What? Why the hell are you deploying? I thought you worked in a damn office?"

"I do work in an office, but the opportunity came up and I was asked to go."

"Women shouldn't be fighting in combat roles, your place is in the kitchen or at worst in the office answering phones." Karl muttered and now I rolled my eyes. "Why are you doing this now?"

"I've always wanted to do this, Karl," I reminded him. "You're the reason I didn't before, you and Paige -"

"Oh so that's what this separation is about? You wanted to go to Iraq and shoot some terrorists so you kicked me out? Ended our marriage?"

"No Karl, you ended our marriage when you lost all of our money on VLTs and had sex with some random stranger and gave me gonorrhea." I replied dryly.

"That was a mistake, it was an accident and I've apologized for it, over and over again, when are you going to let it go?"

"I'm probably not going to let it go, Karl, you gave me gonorrhea!" I shouted into the phone. "And you're still gambling!"

"What I do with my money is my business!"

"Karl, I don't care what you do with your money, as long as you pay your child support before you stick it all into a machine." I told him and he scoffed again.

"Yeah right."

"Karl, will you please just do what I asked and pay your support on time, pay it to my mother and I swear I will not take you to court over missed payments."

"I'm going to hold you to that, you know." Karl insisted and I sighed, nodding my head even though he couldn't see him. "I'm recording this conversation, so you can't back out of it."

"Karl, that's illegal," I said, trying to sound reasonable even though I knew Karl wasn't really capable of reasonable. "If you use that recording for anything I will take you to court for recording me without my permission."

"I'm not really recording Carol, don't get your panties all twisted in a knot." Karl sneered and I sighed.

"Whatever, Karl, will you please just do what I asked, it's not a big deal, it's just writing my mother's name on the cheque instead of mine."

"I've already written the next four cheques with your name, what, I'm just supposed to throw those away and waste them?"

"Cross off my name, initial it and write in my mom's, not a big deal."

"Sure, for you." He snapped and I shook my head.

"All right Karl, thanks for being so understanding and helpful, I really appreciate it. I leave tomorrow morning, really early so I won't see you when you pick Paige up in a couple of days at your regular visit, talk to you soon, buh bye."

I hung up the phone and groaned, rubbing my forehead with my fingertips.

"Is he coming?" I turned to see my five-year-old daughter Paige standing in the doorway, her raggedy stuffed rabbit tucked under her arm.

"You bet he is sweetheart," I said, crouching down so she could step into my arms. "Just like always on Wednesday he'll be here."

"'Kay," she said and cuddled up on my shoulder. "It's okay you're going mommy, I understand."

"You do?" I asked, cautiously, never sure what my girl was going to come up with.

"Yep, you gotta go and take care of other kids as good as you take care of me." She said, nodding and I smiled. I smoothed her blonde waves out of her face and sighed.

"I won't be gone very long," I told her and kissed her forehead. "Just a couple of months, I'll be back before you know it."

"I know, but I'm still gonna miss you."

"I'm gonna miss you like crazy." I sighed, wrapping my arms around her tightly.

"You should take Rabbit with you," Paige said, holding up her stuffed toy.

"Oh no, who will keep you company if I take Rabbit?" I asked, my heart breaking that my little girl wanted me to take her stuffed animal so I wouldn't be lonely.

"I have grandma, she'll keep me company." Paige insisted and I smiled even though my eyes filled with tears.

"You keep Rabbit, okay? The first chance I get I'll get another Rabbit and then we can both have one."

"Then if you go away again we can switch Rabbits, then we really won't be lonely!"

"That is a fantastic idea!" I agreed, making my sweet girl beam happily. "Why don't you go and get your pajamas on and we'll watch a movie in my bed?"

"Yay!" Paige cried and rushed from my room. I looked up to see my mom standing in the doorway with tears in her eyes.

"Oh mom, stop," I said gently, standing up and walking over to hug her. "I'm going to be fine."

"I know you are," she sighed and hugged me back. "And you know I would never ask you not to go, you need to do this and I stand behind you one hundred percent."

"Thanks mom."

"But I'm still going to miss you and so is that sweet girl."

"Yeah I know," I chuckled sadly and leaned back laughing when I saw we both had tears running down our cheeks. "I'm not sure if I'm doing the right thing."

"You most definitely *are* doing the right thing." Mom insisted, shaking me slightly. "Don't ever doubt that this is what you should do. You're a strong woman and you have a drive to make the world a better place for your daughter and other little girls in the world.

"Don't ever doubt that you're doing the right thing."

"I know all that," I sighed and sniffed, reaching up and wiping away the tears that were still gathered in my eyes. "I just will miss her so much."

"And she'll miss you, but she'll also write you letters and you'll write her back and maybe you can still call her and you're only deploying for four months."

"She's going to change so much in that time."

"She is, but you bought me that fancy camera and I even know how to use it now so I'll be taking lots and lots of pictures."

"Thank you, mom. I don't know what I'd do without you."

"Oh sweetheart," mom said, hugging me again. "What would I do without you? I've loved having you and Paige here for the last eighteen months. Since your father died I've been so lonely."

"I know, mom. You know, dad's been gone almost six years, it wouldn't be horrible if you decided to date again." I murmured and she scoffed.

"Forget about it," she pulled away and left my room. Calling over her shoulder she said, "I'm quite happy being single, I definitely don't need a man for anything."

I laughed, remembering how contentious my parents marriage had been. They loved each other endlessly but there was always an argument around every corner.

"I'm ready!" Paige exclaimed, hopping from her room with Rabbit.

"Okay, I need to put on my pajamas," I told her, looking down at the sweatpants and ratty t-shirt I was wearing. "You go get the movie ready and crawl into my bed and I'll be right there."

"'Kay!" Paige squealed and rushed over. "Can we watch Ariel

again?"

"Sure sweetheart," I said with a smile. "We can watch what-ever you want."

CHAPTER 2

Carter

"Private Carter!"

"Sir, yes sir!" I snapped to attention when my commanding officer called my name.

"You're shipping out, son!"

"Yes sir!" I said, because that's what you do when your CO tells you to do something. You agree and then go and do what you're damn well told and you do it better than anyone else.

"You're going to Afghanistan, son." My CO said then continued to explain exactly what I would be doing in Afghanistan. I could feel my heart rate speeding up as he spoke and I had to really fight to stay standing at attention. This was my dream come true! To serve my country, to serve with distinction, to fight for freedom and peace. "You leave at oh-five-hundred tomorrow, go get packed."

"Yes sir!" I said, snapping a salute then leaving the COs office. I walked sedately, but quickly out of the building and when the coast was clear I took off for the barracks. I burst inside, looking for my best friend, Marty.

Marty and I had joined together, we had gone to school together since we were kids and had grown up together. When I told him I wanted to join the CAF he said he wanted to as well. I wasn't sure he actually wanted to, I think it was more like basic training was better than staying home with his abusive alcoholic father and his alcoholic mother. Marty spent a lot of time at my house growing up, trying to keep away from his parents. He swore to me when we were kids they weren't always like that, it was only after his older brother was killed in a car accident that they started drinking and fighting.

I didn't know the difference so I believed him. My parents had moved into the house two doors down from Marty when we were in grade four, a year after Marty's brother died. James, Marty's brother was ten years older than Marty and he had been a hockey star. James had been going places apparently but he'd had too much to drink one night with his buddies and had gotten into a car after a game and all four of them had died.

It was considered a tragedy but no one really talked about the family who was killed by four drunk kids going for a joy ride. They only talked about the kids and their promising future hockey careers gone to waste.

I found Marty sitting on his bunk reading a book. I honestly wasn't surprised, Marty was a bookworm and I wouldn't be surprised if he was deployed he left his C7 behind because he'd filled his duffle with books.

"Hey, hey!" I exclaimed, standing at the end of his bed with a huge smile on my face. Marty held up a finger, telling me to wait while he finished the page he was on then looked up at me expectantly. "I'm being deployed!"

"Shit man, that's awesome!" Marty exclaimed and jumped off the bed. He stepped over and gave me a high five then punched me in the chest, shaking his fist out. Marty and I were exact opposites, at least physically. At twenty-one I was already six foot five and well over two hundred pounds of muscle. Marty is what one would call compact. He was lucky if he made it to five ten with his arms in the air and was one sixty soaking wet. Thing was, Marty was a fuckin' genius and his most used muscle was his brain.

I never knew why Marty joined with me, especially not in a combat role but it looked like he would be shifting his focus to intelligence.

"When do you leave?"

"Oh-five hundred," I told him with a proud smile. "I gotta go pack."

"Awesome, one last night to party a bit before you go." Marty exclaimed and I snorted. Considering his brother died drinking and driving and his parents were alcoholics Marty loved his beer. He was always wanting to get on the beer, but he never got drunk. Or if he did he hid it well.

"Let me get my shit together before we go," I chuckled, clapping him on the back then headed to my own bunk and went through all of my stuff, packing what I would need, making sure it was all there and all ready. An hour later I was packed and ready to go.

Wearing civvies, civilian clothes, Marty and I left the base and headed to the bar most of us grunts frequented. There, the booze flowed, for a price, and the chicks were easy because they wanted to say they'd banged a military guy. Whatever their reasons the groupies were a good time and I certainly wasn't going to pass one up. Or two or three.

Marty had a regular girl he hung out with on these nights and while he wasn't her regular guy it was a system that worked for them. We met her in a dark corner and they immediately started making out, which was fine with me. I went to the bar and grabbed a drink then turned around to survey the crowd.

"Looks like your friend ditched you," I looked down to see a pretty blond with far too much makeup blinking up at me. I'm sure the batting eyelashes were meant to be sexy or coy but it just looked like she had a twitch or something stuck in her eyes. Still, she had lips that would look fantastic around my dick and huge tits that I hoped were real.

"No biggie," I shrugged, smiling down at her. "Looks like I've got a new friend."

"You sure have," she smiled, biting her lip and stepping closer, sliding her hand up my chest. Glad that I'd stuck a couple of condoms in my pocket I bent to nibble her ear, making her giggle. "How do you feel about PDA?"

"Isn't that what we were just doing?" I chuckled and she shrugged. The coy act was getting old but those lips were seriously a mind fuck.

"I've been here for about an hour already," she explained, trailing her long red nail over my chest, between my pecs. "And I've had enough to drink that I really need something long and hard."

This chick's breathy voice was sending all the blood flowing through my body straight to my dick. Of course her words were helping with that, too.

"How do you feel about men's rooms?" I asked her, growling slightly and pushing my hips into hers. She gasped and smiled.

"I like them better than dark alleyways," she purred and reached down to grab my dick through my jeans. I laughed but her words gave me the idea that she did this often. I was most definitely not the first guy she'd propositioned in a bar and probably not tonight even.

"How much is this gonna cost me?" I asked, leaning back to look down at her. Instead of becoming insulted she smiled, showing off a little jewel glued to her tooth. She opened her eyes wide, pretending innocence but not quite making it with her fake eyelashes so heavy she could barely keep her eyes open.

"Just an orgasm and a drink," she promised and squeezed my dick harder. Even the idea of her being a prostitute hadn't softened me up any so I mentally shrugged. Reaching down I took her hand off my crotch and pulled her behind me to the bathroom. She could barely keep up in her way too high heeled shoes but I didn't care, pretty soon she'd be on her knees anyway.

I was right about her mouth, it looked amazing stretched around my cock. Just before I came in her mouth, though she pulled back and stood up.

"My turn," she simpered and I growled. She slid up onto the counter and lifted her short skirt, spreading her legs. She wasn't wearing any underwear and I grunted at the sight. She leaned back against the mirror and plumped her tits in her hands. Slowly I pulled a condom out of my pocket and tore open the package, fitting the rubber to the tip of my dick. "You don't need that, I'm on the pill."

"Good to know sweetheart," I grunted, fitting the condom down my length. "I always go gloved, no matter what."

"Aww, I wanted to feel you with nothing between us." She whined, pinching her nipple with one hand and sliding her other hand between her legs.

"Trust me sweetheart," I growled and pulled her off the counter. I spun her around and pulled her top down to expose her breasts. "You'll feel me."

I pushed her shoulders so she was leaning over the counter then spread her ass cheeks and pushed myself into her pussy. She widened her stance with a gasp and tilted her ass up, changing the angle I thrust into her. With her breasts hanging loose they swung with every one of my hard, fast thrusts.

"Oh, I'm coming . . . I'm so close . . . oh baby, come in my cunt!" This chick was crazy and even with a condom on and with her saying she was on the pill I didn't think it was a good idea to come while I was buried deep inside her. Pulling my cock out at the last second I shoved three fingers inside her as I came in the condom. The girl screamed and cried out as though she were orgasming but her pussy did nothing around my fingers.

If she wasn't watching my face in the mirror I would have rolled my eyes. She was barely even wet. With a heavy sigh I pulled my fingers from between her legs as she pretended to pant then washed my hands in the sink. When I'd washed her off my hand I pulled off the condom and flushed it down the toilet just as someone started pounding on the door.

"Uh oh," the girl said, shimmying her skirt down over her hips and turning to face me. "We've been found out."

"Christie! You better not be in there!" The guy pounding on the door yelled. The girl's eyes got wide as she bit her thumb nail and looked up at me.

"Christie?" I asked and she shrugged.

"Nice to meet you," she murmured

"Is that your boyfriend or your dad?" I asked, pointing to the door.

"Neither," she shrugged again.

"Pimp?"

"Husband."

"Fuck," I growled and reached over to unlock the door just as the husband threatened to kill me.

"You -"

"Stop!" I said, holding my hand up, stopping him in his tracks.

He looked up, way up cause this guy couldn't have been any taller than six feet if he was lucky and his eyes got wide.

"Look Kelly, we're through," Christie said from behind me, her claws digging into my sides. "You and me, we're done and I'm with him now."

"Whoa!" I said, holding my hands up in surrender. I moved around Kelly, pulling Christie's hands from my sides and holding her back away from me. "We are not together, if you're through then you guys discuss that between you, I had no idea she was married, she came onto me and asked me to fuck her. Sorry, next time I'll make sure the chick who sucks me off in the mens at the bar isn't married."

I turned and walked away down the hall, shaking my head while the two of them screamed at each other behind me.

"Fuckin' crazy," I muttered to myself. I stepped up to the bar and ordered another beer as Marty stepped up beside me, clapping me on the back.

"So, you've met Christie?" He asked, chuckling.

"You know that crazy chick?" I asked, glaring down at him.

"Yeah, her and her guy do this every weekend." Marty explained and I rolled my eyes. "I don't think she's ever gone all the way with her mark, though. Kelly usually interrupts before it gets too far."

"Yeah well, it got too far this time," I muttered and ordered a shot of tequila, slamming it back then drinking my beer.

"Oh fuck, no way," Marty chuckled and I nodded, lifting my eyebrows at him as Kelly and Christie walking out behind us, arm in arm. She looked up at me and winked then disappeared out the door with her husband.

"Thanks for the heads up, fucker," I mumbled and relaxed onto a stool. Marty just laughed so hard he snorted, shaking his head.

"Hey, at least you got off, you're not shipping out with blue balls."

Marty was not wrong. I would not be shipping out so fucking horny I wanted to die. Instead I was shipping out with a different kind of headache from too much tequila and too many beer chasers. Luckily the flight to Afghanistan was a long one and no one was expected to stay awake for it.

When the plane touched down in Afghanistan I stood and flipped my pack onto my back, waiting for my turn to disembark. I could feel the heat all the way at the back of the plane and knew I was in for the long haul. This was gonna suck. We were directed to our barracks and bunks then told to meet in the personnel tent to receive our orders. It wasn't really a tent so much as a long warehouse with a curved top.

I stood at parade rest with the rest of the personnel off the plane and waited to hear my name. Only my name didn't get called. I stood while the rest of the soldiers filed out and went where they had been directed and waited.

"Private Carter," the Major giving orders said quietly as he read a file he had been holding in his hands. "You've just arrived here in the sand box."

"Yes sir," I replied, thinking it was a supid thing for him to say. The room had just been full of people who had just arrived in the sand box.

"You have a specialty in explosives, Private Carter."

"Sir, I have a specialty in weapons however explosives are my favourite." I told him and he nodded.

"Your expertise will come in handy while you're here," the Major agreed. "Are you ready to get to work?"

"Yes sir, I am."

"Excellent, follow me," he said and left the building. Quickly I turned and followed him, staying one step behind him just to his left. "We have a rather unorthodox position for you. This never happens so you'd better pay attention. Our weapons officer was injured and will not be returning to active duty."

"I'm sorry to hear that, sir."

"Don't be too sorry," the Major said and flung a door to another building open and walking inside. "At ease."

I followed him in and stood to the side at parade rest. I saw five men lounging on bunks and watching the Major expectantly. Each of their gazes flicked to me but none of them said anything.

"You could at least pretend to have moved to stand at attention." The Major mumbled, shaking his head.

"Sorry Maje, maybe next time." The oldest man in the room said and the others chuckled.

"This is Private Sean Carter," the Major said with a heavy sigh. "He's taking the place of Sergeant Smith for the time being."

Then the Major turned and left the building. I stood frozen, frowning and confused.

"Where you from Carter?" The guy who'd spoken before asked.

"Edmonton, sir," I said, not breaking parade rest.

"Relax kid," the man said and waved me over. I blinked then slowly walked over to stand closer to his bunk. "This your first deploy?"

"Yes sir."

"Not sir, just Hunt," the man said and I nodded. "We're a little less formal here than you're probably used to, we don't bother with rank so much as long as you're willing to work with us we all work together."

"Of course," I nodded, looking around the room at the other men.

"That," Hunt pointed at the man sitting on the next bunk cleaning his rifle. Well, caressing more than cleaning. "Is Jag, short for Jagged Edge, he's our sniper. That," Hunt pointed to another guy who was much smaller than the rest of the men in the room. "Is Tongue, he's our linguistics expert."

"Is that cause you speak in tongues or cause the ladies love you?" I asked, eyeing the man who just smirked.

"Bit of both," he smiled and Jag snorted.

"That's cause what you got in your pants won't do it, gotta use your tongue." Another huge guy laughed from the far corner of the room.

"Haven't heard no ladies complain about what I'm carrying." Tongue laughed, shaking his head.

"That's cause they don't beg you to fuck them after you're done like they do me." The big guy said, grabbing his crotch.

"That," Hunt continued, pointing to the guy, "is Ghost, not because of what he's got in his pants."

"You got any sisters kid?" Ghost asked and I shook my head, making him sigh. "Too bad."

"What does Ghost do?" I asked, turning back to Hunt who just smiled.

"Whatever the fuck he wants." Hunt said, making everyone else in the room laugh. "Believe it or not that giant fucker can get in or out of anywhere," Hunt told me, keeping his eyes on me and I'm sure I was supposed to be impressed but I had seen Ghost move out of the corner of my eye so when I turned back to him and found him with his nose practically in my ear I didn't so much as blink, let alone flinch like he had been hoping for. "He's stealthy like."

"He should practice that more," I said, locking my eyes with his crazy ones. That got all the other guys hooting and laughing and Ghost smirked then moved away slowly.

"And last, but not least is Speed," Hunt said pointing at a big guy sitting in a corner with ear buds in his ears. He seemed to be ignoring everyone but I could tell he was totally paying attention. That and even though his music was on so loud that I could hear it across the room he knew exactly what was being said by everyone. "He's our driver."

"Got it." I nodded and planted my hands on my hips, looking around before focusing on Hunt again. "And what do they call you?"

"Why, I'm the Hunter of course," He snickered and I nodded.

"Right, so what am I doing here then?"

"See," Hunt said, moving off the bunk and standing in front of me. "Smitty was our bomb tech, that is until he blew three of his fingers off, the Major said you're an explosives expert. Your job is to blow shit up."

"That I can do," I said, smiling for the first time since getting onto the damn plane in Ottawa.

CHAPTER 3

Carol

Seventeen Years ago . . .

"How long are you going for this time?" Paige asked as she helped me pack my duffle. I smiled at her when she gave Rabbit a kiss and tucked him beside my fatigues.

"Shouldn't be for more than four months, like last time," I said, reaching out and tucking her crazy hair behind her ear. The older Paige got the more her hair looked like mine. It had started out just thick and wavy, but the wave was getting tighter and less manageable. My hair was always tight curls, no matter what I did with it but it was much darker than Paige's light blonde.

"Are you gonna fight again?"

"Probably," I shrugged, turning back to my closet. The last time I'd been deployed hadn't been as scary as I'd thought it would be. Mostly we patrolled safe areas and kept the peace. It was actually kind of boring but I was happy to do it. I had been deployed three times now and I loved it. I had made some pretty amazing friends during that four months, friendships I would never lose. One such was a man who had retired after that tour.

We'd hit it off and become more than friends. John wanted more of a relationship than the Wednesday night, every other weekend booty calls but I wasn't willing to go there. We'd been 'seeing' each other for two years when he'd told me he wanted more. I'd apologized profusely and told him I couldn't commit to more than what we already had. I still saw him every so often but it was more in passing in the grocery store. Just to say hi as he walked past with his wife. A woman I'd met briefly and really actually liked.

I didn't mind being single and while I missed sex, I didn't exactly need a man who make me orgasm.

Paige and I were still living with my mother because it was convenient and she liked having us there. Mom still refused to date so I didn't pressure her, thinking she would do it when she was ready. If she never did then that was her choice.

"You're gone for my birthday this time, though," Paige said sadly and I smiled.

"Then it's a good thing we had your party last weekend so I didn't miss anything, hey?" I said and dropped a few more pairs of fatigues into my duffle before zipping it up. "I'll be back before you know it."

Paige nodded but still sighed sadly.

"What are we going to watch tonight?" I asked her, knowing she would want to curl up in my bed again and watch a movie like we did when either of us left for any amount of time. When she spent weekends with her dad and his latest girlfriend she would crawl into my bed and we'd watch. It was always the same movie, so I don't know why I bothered to ask, but I always did.

"Little Mermaid," she said with a smile. I'd had to buy the disc three times since we started our tradition because she watched it so much.

"All right," I chuckled and lifted my duffle off my bed. "Go get ready for bed while I take this to the door."

"'Kay!" Paige ran off and I carried my bag to the front door.

When I woke up at oh-dark-stupid I didn't want to wake Paige by rummaging around looking for things. It was easier if I moved all the things I would need in the morning out of my room.

Paige came running back wearing her pajamas just as I was pulling on my own pajama shirt and we crawled into bed, starting the movie.

The next morning, I silenced my alarm and slid out of bed, kissing my little girl on the forehead and leaving the letter I'd written her on the nightstand. I walked out of my room and got dressed in the bathroom then met mom in the kitchen where she held a to-go cup of coffee for me. I kissed her cheek and grabbed my duffle and slid into the cab waiting at the curb.

"Awfully early isn't it?" The driver asked as I closed the door.

"Yeah but I deploy back to Afghanistan tomorrow and I still have to report to Ottawa for briefing today," I explained and he nodded.

"Well, then this trip is on the house," he said, reaching to turn off the meter. "Or the car, as it were."

"Oh, you don't have to do that," I insisted, shaking my head.

"Ma'am, it is the least I can do to say thank you for your service," the driver told me, locking his gaze with mine in the rear view mirror. I smiled and nodded my thanks, overcome with emotion.

"Thank you." I said softly and he nodded again.

"You leaving anyone home?"

"Yeah, my little girl and my mom," I said, thinking I probably shouldn't tell a stranger that I'd left my mom and daughter alone in the house while I was away for an undetermined amount of time. The driver seemed to read my mind though and chuckled.

"Don't worry about me," he said, shaking his head and holding up his left arm which was actually a hook. "Got one of these more or less on my leg, too. I won't be doing anyone any harm and your secret is safe with me."

"Thank you," I said again, chuckling. The rest of the trip to the airport was quiet and the driver pulled right up to the departures door, putting the car into park and turning to look at me over the back of the seat.

"Here you go," he said with a smile. "You be safe, be smart, I expect you to come home to that little girl."

"Yes sir," I told him with a smile then pushed my duffle out of the car and slid out after it. He stayed until I was inside then drove away and I smiled again. My flight was only about four hours and luckily the plane was pretty empty so I was able to sleep most of the way. When I got to Ottawa I was taken directly into a meeting with other personnel to explain the situation.

"You'll be going back to the same refugee camp as you were in before," the CO said sternly. I looked around the room and saw a lot of the same faces I had worked with on my last deployment. "Things have changed, though. No longer is this a peaceful area, it's much more dangerous. You will still be keeping the peace but you will be in teams of six instead of four. The situation has changed drastically with the political climate."

I sighed, wishing that wasn't the case, but like everyone else affected by what was going on in Afghanistan, I had been watching the news. I had known before my CO had called that I would be shipping out soon and had prepared accordingly.

"Get some rest, your flight leaves in," the CO looked at his watch and nodded. "Seven hours, dismissed."

"Hey, Carol!" I turned once I was out of the meeting room to see who had called my name.

"Becky," I smiled and hugged my friend. We had been on the same team the last time I was deployed and I missed her in the last few years.

"How are you?" She asked as we turned and started walking toward the mess hall.

"I'm good, missing my girl already," I told her and she nodded.

"I know what you mean, Jeff is pissed that I'm going out again," she said, rolling her eyes over her husband.

"He misses you," I said chuckling. "And he's worried."

"Sure, he misses that I do everything around the house and chase the kids and he's worried I'm not going to be back to keep doing it." Becky scoffed and I shook my head.

"That's not it!"

"It totally is!" She insisted as we got into line for food. "So, how's John?"

"John is just fine," I told her, laughing. "He's happily married to a lovely woman, they make a great couple."

"What?" Becky demanded, picking up her tray and walking over to a table. "You can't be serious!"

"I'm totally serious," I shrugged. "John wanted serious and I didn't. When he told me our casual thing wasn't enough I broke it off so he could go and find what he was looking for."

"Carol, you're barely twenty-six, you're way too young to give up on love and marriage."

"Who says I am?" I asked, shrugging. "I'm not giving up on it,

I'm just not into it right now."

"Excuse us, ladies?" Becky and I looked up to see a giant of a man, probably a couple of years older than us and another much smaller man, a couple of years older than the first. "Mind if we sit?"

I blinked and looked around the hall, seeing multiple empty tables then looked at Becky who was rubbing her forehead with her left hand, showing off her wedding ring.

"No," I said shrugging, barely making eye contact with the man who kept staring at me. "Have a seat."

I continued to eat while Becky tried to hide her laughter unsuccessfully.

"Hopefully we end up on the same team for this," Becky said, ignoring the two guys. "Last time was horrible being the only two women over there on opposite shifts."

"Where are you ladies headed?" The big guy asked, butting into our conversation. I blinked and looked at him and he smiled. "Sorry, I'm Chief Warrant Officer David Parsons but people call me Ghost, that's Master Warrant Officer Mike Harder but everyone calls him Tongue."

"Uh huh," I said, blinking at him. "Master Corporal Carol Wilson, Sergeant Rebecca Downey."

"Ma'am," Ghost said with a nod in my direction, then another towards Becky. "We just got back from the sandbox, is that where you're headed?"

"Yes, Chief, it is where we're going," I replied, not liking the way this guy was watching me.

"What will you be doing over there, MC?" Ghost asked and slid his fork full of food into his mouth. He did it slowly, closing his lips over the tines of the fork before pulling it out slowly, his eyes on mine. I'm sure he intended it to be sexy but I wasn't feeling it.

"We'll be peacekeeping and patrolling a refugee camp," I told him, turning back to Becky and continuing to eat.

"Well," Ghost said slowly, turning to me once he'd chewed and swallowed, slipping his arm over the back of my chair. "Maybe we'll see you there. We just got home but we're scheduled to go back in a week or so."

"That's great," I said, pushing my chair back to stand. I lifted my tray and looked at Becky. "I'm finished eating -"

"Me too," she said and stood as well. I turned to carry my tray half full of food to the garbage, pausing only slightly when I heard Ghost call me a frigid bitch. I scoffed but kept going, so angry I almost threw the entire tray into the garbage. Becky laughed and shook her head. "What a dick."

"No shit," I muttered and we walked to the barracks to relax until we shipped out. It wasn't long, apparently the plane we were taking was just waiting for the wings to be de-iced and then we were headed out. As much as the heat in Afghanistan was oppressive it would be nice compared to the snow and ice around here.

The quick nap I had in a bunk assigned to me for the time being wasn't enough but the flight to Afghanistan was a long one I would definitely get to sleep then.

This time when we arrived at the base Becky and I were bunking together as well as assigned to the same team. We didn't get a chance to get comfortable and were sent out first thing in the morning. We ate breakfast on the go then climbed into the Humvee and got ready for the rocky ride to the refugee camp.

Everything we'd been told was true. The people we passed looked more desperate and the road was rockier, as though the

27

potholes were divots blown out of it by bombs and not by the passage of time or vehicles.

"Shit," I muttered as I held on to the holy shit handle, rocking back and forth in the back of the truck. "I was just here less than a year ago, it's gotten this bad already?"

"This is calm," the corporal driving us shouted over the noise of the diesel engine. "It was much worse a couple of months ago. Still, you should be extra careful, keep your heads on a swivel."

"You betch, Corporal," I murmured with a nod. He dropped us off at the gates of the camp and picked up the team we were replacing then was gone again. We patrolled for the eight hours we were there for and while nothing came up it wasn't exactly relaxed. For three months of our four month deployment we did this, moving in and out and around the camp, making friends and connections with the people living there. It wasn't until our second last patrol that shit hit the fan.

"Becks," I said softly in my comms and she glanced at me but said nothing. We were both watching a man and woman arguing in the middle of what passed for the street between rows of tents. "This feels worse than just two people having a marital spat."

"I hear ya," Becky said and held her C7 low but at the ready. "Be cool, she's pissed that he was out with his buddies last night while she was home with their sick kid."

"So marital bliss is the same all over the word. Where the hell is he hanging out with buddies?" I asked, glancing around to see if anyone else was paying attention. I had no doubt that Becks could understand what the couple was saying, she was a language specialist and had learned three different languages just since being deployed to this camp a few years ago.

"That's a good fuckin' question," Becky said and thumbed her mic, sending a call for assistance to the rest of the team. They should have all been pretty close since we were a team of six and I looked up just as our team leader strolled around another tent. Chief Warrant Officer Pettman was a good man, one I trusted with my life but right now he looked harried and that freaked me out.

"We're gettin' the fuck outta here," he said sharply but quietly.

"Yes sir," I murmured, nudging Becky's elbow.

"Oh fuck," she said turning to look at the both of us. "He just said there's a plan to attack the next patrol, tonight's patrol."

"Let's get back and report what you heard," Pettman said grimly and we both nodded. Leisurely so we didn't draw attention to ourselves we turned and walked back to the front gates of the camp. No one said anything to us, no one tried to get our attention. Just as we reached the last line of tents we were met by the remaining three members of our time who turned just ahead of us and headed towards the Humvee that was waiting.

We never would have seen the attack coming, though. Before we knew what was happening a burst of gunfire echoed through the valley as dirt bounced up around our feet.

"What the fuck?" I yelled as Pettman yelled beside me, arching backward. I turned just in time to see blood splatter from his back and before he could fall I managed to get my shoulder under his chest to keep him upright. Letting him fall to the ground would mean wasted time and effort to get him up again to move him.

"Becks!" I screamed and she turned with her C7 up and fired two rounds, ending the life of the man standing behind us with his own assault rifle falling to the ground with him. "Let's go!"

With the help of one of the other men in our team I carried

Pettman to the Humvee and dumped him groaning in the back then crawled in behind him. I slid my hands under his shoulders and pulled him all the way in while another team member pushed.

In all we took maybe two minutes from the time the first shot was fired to when the corporal was speeding away with us all in the Humvee but it felt like time had slowed.

"Pettman!" I yelled in his face but the man had passed out. With help I rolled him to his side and stuck my fingers in the holes the bullets had made in his uniform, tearing the shirt so I could see the damage. "Son of a bitch!"

Two holes, bleeding profusely on either side of his spine just below his ribs.

"No exit wounds," Davies, one of the privates on our team said and I nodded.

"Let's see if we can at least slow the blood down. Be careful though, we don't know where those bullets hit."

"Yuh," Davies said and started pulling gauze pads and bandages out of his med pack.

"Fucking hell," Ryker, another corporal said from the seat in front of us. Becky had taken the front passenger seat and Ryker and Mitchell were in the middle while Davies and I were in the back with Pettman. "This is fucked up, man."

"There's something going on in that camp," I told them quietly and they all locked gazes with me. "Becks heard a couple fighting, the husband said there was going to be an attack tonight."

"Well, they moved it up then," Mitchell mumbled and I nodded.

"I don't think this was it, though." I said, shaking my head. "I think this was just the beginning."

Unfortunately I was right and Pettman wouldn't be the last man or woman injured in whatever the refugees had cooked up. Pettman would be the worst, though and while he lived he would never walk again. The two bullets damaged his spine to the point that his legs would never work properly again. While he wasn't exactly paralyzed feeling in his legs was intermittent and he was never sure when the feeling would disappear and he'd collapse to the ground.

That had been our worst deployment to date and Becky and I sat in the mess hall for long hours waiting to hear about Pettman and whether or not he would make it.

"Hey ladies!" I looked up to see Ghost, Tongue and another guy strolling into the mess hall.

"Aw fuck," I groaned and dropped my head with a heavy sigh.

"Heard you had some excitement today," Tongue said with a smile as he sat beside Becky who glared at him.

"Yup, watching my CO get shot in the back then killing the kid who did it, awfully exciting," she grumbled as Ghost sat beside me and the other guy stood at the end of the table with his arms folded over his chest. I looked up to find he had earbuds in his ears and his music was obnoxiously loud.

"Who gives a shit," Ghost smirked, shaking his head. "We heard your CO is gonna make it and that kid was a terrorist, kill or be killed right?"

"That kid was fifteen," I told him incredulously at his cavalier attitude.

"Get 'em while they're young," he shrugged then smiled again. "What are you ladies planning for tonight?"

"Gonna go to bed and try not to dream about blood splatter

then head out in the morning for home."

"Aw, I can keep your mind off of that," Ghost murmured and shifted so he was facing me, his arm on the back of my chair and sitting far too close for my liking. I sneered at him and tried to lean away but the body of his friend standing beside me was too close and I couldn't move very far.

"No, thanks, I'm good." My tone was dry and most definitely unwilling. "Excuse us."

I grabbed my coffee cup and stood, Becky following me then turned to leave.

"You know," Ghost said, tsking and shaking his head. "That's the second time now that you've disrespected a superior. Didn't they teach you to wait to be dismissed?"

"How about we forget about this and I won't file a complaint against you for harassment?" I asked and turned, walking away. Becky followed me, her shorter legs almost running to keep up with my much longer strides.

"Let's hope that doesn't backfire and bite you in the ass," she murmured as I slammed out the door of the mess.

"He's not going to complain," I told her confidently. "If he did he would have to explain his own behavior and it hasn't exactly been complimentary. I'm sure I could talk to any number of women in this barracks and get the same story."

Fortunately Becky and I shipped out the next day, heading home and using two weeks of the last month of our deployment to debrief on what we had seen and heard while we were at the camp. We were sent home two weeks early and no one was more happy about that than I was.

Unfortunately that would not be the last time we encountered Ghost and his friends.

CHAPTER 4

Carter

"Aw hell," Marty said beside me and immediately locked his gaze on his beer. We were sitting in the same dingy bar we always went to. The same bar I had been dragged into the mens room to have sex in. Okay, I totally went willingly into that bathroom, but that wasn't the point. I had been deployed for two full years, working with Hunt and his team until they'd been moved somewhere else and I'd been put on another team. This was the first time I'd been back home and I was greatly enjoying my vacation.

"What?" I asked him and he shook his head.

"Don't look now, but your fuck buddy just waltzed in the door," he muttered and took a pull off his beer.

"Mine? Dude, I haven't been here in three years, how do you know she's mine?" I demanded, not looking over at the door.

"I know because she's been coming in here at least twice a month looking for you since about six months after you shipped out the morning after," Marty snorted and I frowned.

"Why the fuck would she be looking for me?" I asked just as someone tapped me on the shoulder. I turned to see Christie standing in front of me with a toddler on her hip. "What the fuck? You can't bring a kid in here!"

"Well how else was I supposed to find you?" She demanded then immediately started to cry. Like big crocodile tears that made her ton of makeup run. Christie was not a pretty crier.

"Why the hell would you want to find me anyway?"

"Because! She's yours!" Christie wailed and I blinked.

"Who's mine? The kid?" I demanded, holding my hands up in surrender. "No fuckin' way is that kid mine!"

"We had sex that night and nine months later she was born!" Christie insisted but I shook my head.

"Nope, no way," I said, standing my ground. "There's no way she's mine -"

"You sure?" Marty asked behind me and I turned to glare at him. "She's pretty cute."

"Fuck you man," I said turning back to Christie. "You said you were on the pill, I wrapped up *and* I pulled out before I came, there is no way in hell that kid is mine."

Marty was right though, she was cute. All bright blonde curls and big blue eyes, but definitely not mine.

"What?" Christie demanded, her tears drying almost immediately. "Are you sure?"

"Positive," I assured her and she frowned.

"That dick head, I told Kelly she was his! Even told him to do a paternity test but he refused." Christie snarled and I shook my head.

"You should get the courts to order one anyway," I told her and she scoffed then turned on her heel and stormed out of the bar. I turned to find Marty laughing his ass off. "Laugh harder and I won't have to push you off the fuckin' stool."

"Sorry man, that was priceless," he chuckled and shook his head. "I told her the kid wasn't yours."

"You could have warned me!"

"Dude, neither you nor Christie have a dimple in your chin, that kid does, there is no way that kid is yours. It's simple genetics. I've seen Kelly, he's been in here multiple times since that kid was born. It's obvious he's her father."

"Whatever," I muttered and drank my beer. "No more fucking in the mens for me."

"Aw, that's too bad," a voice said beside me where Christie had just left. I looked down to find yet another base bunny smiling up at me with 'come fuck me' eyes. I sighed and shook my head.

"For real honey, not interested," I said and turned to Marty who leaned back to look at the girl.

"I'm interested."

"Marty we've been through this, once was enough," she mumbled, rolling her eyes.

"That good, huh?" I scoffed and she rolled her eyes.

"Who'd have thought a guy that big was *that big*, ya know? I was sore for days after that." With that announcement she turned and hobbled away, her too high shoes looking dangerous. I laughed and turned to Marty who just shrugged.

We spent the next couple of hours in the bar then poured ourselves into a cab and went back to the barracks. Marty had to work in the morning but I was well and truly on vacation for the next few weeks, two of them at least.

It was kind of a boring existence since I didn't have any family to visit and Marty was still working. My parents had been older and had passed away shortly after I graduated high school. I considered looking at buying a small house to work on but I didn't really plan on being in the country much. I was young and I had no attachments, I might as well deploy and make as much money as I could. Eventually I would have to retire, I might as well have a nice nest egg when I did.

A week into my vacation I was walking through the base when I ran into Ghost, Tongue, Speed and Hunt.

"Hey, Carter!" Ghost exclaimed a la John Travolta in Welcome Back Cotter.

"What's up guys?" I asked with a huge smile, clasping hands with the four older guys and giving them fist bumps. "You hanging round or you heading out again?"

"We just got back," Hunt said smoothly and I nodded. The man still made me slightly uncomfortable, even though we'd saved each other's lives a few times over the couple of years we worked together. "We were lucky enough to be around when that refugee camp imploded."

"No shit," I murmured nodding then sighed. "I just got back from Yemen about a week ago, got another week to relax then I'm shipped out again."

"Scary shit man," Tongue murmured, and Speed nodded.

"You ever work with Pettman?" I asked but they all shook their heads. "I worked with him for a week last year, good guy."

"Well, now he's a good guy with a fancy chair," Ghost smirked and I rolled my eyes. Ghost was such a dick. "Heard Master Corporal Carol Wilson was around, you seen her?"

"Don't know her," I shrugged, shaking my head.

"Too bad, she is seriously fine, would not mind getting between those long legs," Ghost sneered, thrusting his hips and laughing. I rolled my eyes but ignored him.

"Shut up, Ghost," Hunt mumbled and Ghost chuckled. "Where

you headed now?"

"Just headed to the mess then the gym, you?"

"Debrief," Hunt sighed and I nodded.

"Where's Jag?" I asked, not seeing the team's sniper anywhere.

"Uh, Jag didn't make it out of the last mission," Tongue murmured and I blinked, surprised.

"No shit," I murmured back. "I'm sorry to hear that."

"Yeah, it was pretty fucked up." Ghost agreed with a nod, sobering quickly.

"We'll talk to you soon," Hunt said, clapping on the shoulder and the four men walked away, leaving me standing alone in the middle of the base. No longer hungry I forgot about the mess hall and went straight to the gym. I worked out for a few hours then went to find Marty.

"Hey Carter," he said when I found him at the bar.

"You ever do anything else?" I asked him, sitting on the stool beside him.

"Like what? Cause there's so much to do around here?" He asked and sipped his beer.

"Just heard Jag didn't make it back," I sighed and signalled the bartender for a beer.

"Yeah, I heard that, too. Fuckin' sucks," Marty mumbled, scrubbing a hand over his face.

"What's wrong with you?"

"I don't know, man. Just a shitty day I guess." We sat quietly at the bar for a little while longer before we left the bar. I couldn't sleep that night and ended up in my CO's office the next morning, begging to be sent out again.

"Carter, why can't you just enjoy your vacation? Go visit family?"

"What family? It's the middle of winter, not like there's beaches or anything to go to. I've been to Niagara Falls, seriously sir, I just want to get back to work."

"You're going to get injured and then you're no good to us," my CO sighed heavily but agreed to send me back overseas. "Jag's death was not your fault."

"Yes sir," I nodded then waited to be dismissed. The CO sighed again and sent me on my way and I went to find Marty. "I'm shipping out again," I told him when I found him in his office and he nodded.

"I figured, I'm going this time, too."

"Seriously?" I asked, smiling and excited. "We going to the same place?"

"Bahrain, there's some shit going on over there they need an intelligence guy for," Marty shrugged.

"Aren't you excited?"

"For what? I'm going to be doing the same thing there that I do here, no excitement at all to be had except this time I might get shot at."

"Oh come on," I said unfolding my deployment papers. "Look, Bahrain," I said pointing to the paper and showing him. "We'll be in the same place at the same time. Think of all the fun we can have!"

"Yeah, in a dry country, and by dry I don't mean the desert -"

"Bahrain doesn't have a desert."

"- with women in burkas, how is this exciting?" Marty asked dryly from behind his desk. "The US Navy's Fifth Fleet is there, we're gonna have to deal with asshole American's the whole time. I really don't get your excitement."

"I'm excited because we'll be together for a while, come on, you're not excited for that?" I asked, nudging his chair with my foot.

"Yeah, all right, that's kind of exciting," Marty agreed, reluctantly. I chuckled at him and smirked.

"It's gonna be great, I promise."

It wasn't great. In fact it was so far from great I can't imagine it getting any worse.

Marty didn't just sit behind a desk, he was sent out in the field to find intelligence on a smuggling ring that had been digging up Bahrain's ancient artifacts and selling them on the black market. Marty had a knack for seeing pieces of the puzzle that no one else saw and while we were working with American soldiers we were actually doing something besides sitting behind a desk.

Marty hated it and honestly I didn't blame him. The American soldiers treated him like shit and there was only so much I could do to stick up for him. Plus the climate of Bahrain was hot and miserable and while Ottawa can get pretty hot it's nothing like Bahrain's humidity.

After a week on one of Bahrain's smaller islands we found absolutely no signs of smuggling and Marty was frustrated beyond belief. I think he was also drying out and having some trouble not having any alcohol for the last three weeks. I learned a lot about my best friend on that deployment. I hoped that after this he'd stay sober but I had a feeling he'd just drink more when he got home.

"Well thanks for nothing," the American commander said when we finally arrived back at the Embassy. He shoved past

Marty, hitting him so hard with his shoulder he almost fell.

"Like it's my fault your intel was useless as fuck?" Marty demanded, shaking his head.

"You better watch it, smart mouth," the American snapped, turning and shoving his nose in Mary's face.

"Or what?" Marty demanded, scowling, his hands on his hips. The American was easily as big as I was but Marty wasn't backing down. He'd done everything he could to find what the American's needed but it just wasn't there. "I told you it was the wrong fucking island but you refused to listen to me."

"Hey, hey, guys," I said getting between the two men and pushing the American back. "There was nothing there and that sucks, but it was no one's fault."

"Whatever," the American snapped and turned away. His team followed him and Marty glared at them the entire time.

"I need a fuckin' beer," he muttered when they were all gone.

"Yeah," I sighed. "I know what you mean."

After that Marty flew home and I stayed in Bahrain. I worked with the American's again and found signs of smuggling but not on the island they'd had us on before. Turned out their intel had been wrong, so wrong that we were on the wrong fucking island, just like Marty had told them. I shook my head, scoffing, staring at the commander. He knew exactly what I was saying and I didn't even have to utter a word.

I worked with the American team for another four months before I was shipped back to Yemen. I kept in touch with Marty through email but his messages were getting fewer and farther between. When I did get a message it was pretty random and didn't really make sense. I didn't want to let his CO know in case he got in trouble but I also didn't want him getting into shit he shouldn't be into.

Finally after a month of not hearing from him I sent his CO a message, asking him to check on Marty just to make sure he was all right.

The message I got back tore my heart out. Marty was no longer a part of the Canadian Armed Forces. If he showed up to work he was usually late and always drunk or drinking on the job. It was disheartening to say the least that Marty ended up just like his parents.

CHAPTER 5

Carol

Twelve Years ago...

"Wilson! Lay down cover fire!"

"Light 'em up!"

"Son of a bitch! Where'd they come from?"

We were pinned down with no way to get out. Behind us were a network of caves that we didn't know where the end was and in front of us was a group of insurgents who were looking for blood. Our blood.

"What about the caves?" I shouted over the gunfire.

"We'd get caught, they're a dead end!"

"We got incoming! Friendlies with transportation!"

"Thank fuck!"

"Just keep us alive until the Griffon gets here!" We kept firing and within minutes the CH-146 Griffon was hovering not far from our position.

"They can't land!" Our CO called out to us, "we're gonna have to rope climb! The gunner is gonna lay down cover fire so we can all get the fuck outta here!"

"Wilson, you go first!"

"No, Beck's injured, she should go first!"

"Downey'll need help once she gets to the top, you get up there and help her get in!"

"Yes sir!" The second I saw a rope fall from the Griffon I jumped up and ran, leaping to catch the rope and climbing up. I was just reaching for the handle to pull myself up when my arm started to burn. I screamed and looked down at my arm and saw a strip of burned skin across my shoulder. "Shit!"

"Come on, Sergeant!" The gunner yelled, grabbing the front of my tactical vest and hauling me into the Griffon.

"Son of a bitch!" I yelled again then tapped my comms. "I'm in, send her up!"

Slowly Becky was moved to the ropes hanging down from the helo. Our team members tied the ropes around her waist and I hit the lever to bring the ropes back up.

"Keep shooting!" The gunner yelled and I lifted my C7. It hurt like hell but I had to keep shooting. When Becky was close enough I reached out and grabbed her hand and yanked her into the helo. She groaned and collapsed at my feet and I quickly untied her then hit the lever to let the ropes down again. I dragged Becky farther into the helo and started doing first aid on her wounds.

"Son of a bitch, Becks!"

"Oh I know!" Becky moaned and panted. I lifted her shirt to find the bullet wound on her hip and pressed more gauze, trying to at least slow the blood flow.

"I can't believe you of all people got shot!" Becky groaned again as one after another of the rest of our team climbed up into the helo.

"We're outta here!" The pilot yelled and the helo lifted higher into the air, taking off quickly. Half an hour later we were touching down within the walls of the base and the rotors of the helicopter started to slow. Medical staff rushed forward with a gurney and we helped move Becky onto it so she could be rushed away for surgery.

"How about you?" I looked up at our CO and shrugged.

"It's just a scratch," I told him and he nodded towards the med tent.

"Go on, have it looked at, it might actually need stitches."

"Yes sir." I said and turned away.

"Hey, Wilson," I turned back and looked up at him. "Good work out there."

"Thank you, sir." I nodded grimly then followed the nurses and doctor pushing Becky's gurney. I dropped my pack at the doors of the clinic and stepped inside, smiling at a nurse who looked like she was far too busy.

"Hey, give me a minute?" She called and I smiled, then sat on a gurney. Ten minutes later she hurried towards me and stopped, looking down at me. "What can I do for you?"

I turned and showed her my wound and she grimaced.

"That looks painful."

"It actually is, it burns." I agreed with her.

"No shit, eh?" She lifted the sleeve of my t-shirt and got to work cleaning the wound. "Well, lucky for you it doesn't need stitches, just a bandage."

"Hooray!" I snorted and she chuckled.

"Yeah, yeah," she smiled and finished cleaning my wound then wrapping a bandage around it. Once she'd taped it up she stood back and pulled her gloves off. "All right, keep that dry and clean and if anything is off or you have a fever or the pain gets worse then come on back."

"Thanks," I said and hopped off the gurney. I grabbed my stuff at the door and headed over to my barracks to get changed and shower. I was just leaving mine and Becky's room to go and find something to eat then go and check on her when the members of our teams hollered for me to join them.

"Come on, Downey's still in surgery, she'll be there after we have a beer!"

"Ugh, yeah all right but I gotta eat something first!" I called back and they laughed.

"Bring it with you!" I shrugged and grabbed a sandwich then took it with me to the building where a makeshift bar was set up. All it served was light beer but at this point I'd take it. It was cold and refreshing and my arm hurt like hell.

Unfortunately when I got there my team was drinking with another team that I wanted nothing to do with.

"Well, if it isn't Mater Corporal Carol Wilson!" Ghost yelled from the bar and I rolled my eyes.

"It's Sergeant now, Chief." I said, sitting on a stool and unwrapping my sandwich.

"Heard you had a little excitement today." Tongue said and I shrugged. He put a beer on the bar, his hand on top of the can and popped the top before pushing it towards me. "Have a beer on me."

"I think I'll take one I've opened myself, thank you very much," I told him and bit into my sandwich. He watched me for a long second then shrugged and handed me a cold unopened beer, leaving the other sitting on the bar. I pointed at it as I chewed. "Feel free to have that one."

Tongue said nothing and I turned my back on Ghost and

Tongue to talk to my team.

"Any word on Becky?" I asked my CO but he shook his head.

"Nothing yet, depending on where that bullet hit this could be it for her." He replied and I nodded.

"I know, which would suck, she loves this shit." I agreed. We talked for a few more minutes and I had another beer then switched to water. Slowly I began to feel dizzy and I patted my CO on the shoulder. "I'm out."

"You feeling alright, Sergeant?" He asked, concerned and I nodded.

"I'm good, nothing a good sleep won't fix." I slid off the stool and stumbled slightly before righting myself.

"Let me help you get to your room."

"No, you stay, seriously, I'm fine." I left the bar but was still dizzy and now I felt nauseous. I grimaced and figured it was the meds I was given for my arm and I probably hadn't eaten enough. As quickly as I could I made my way to the women's barracks.

"Hey, Sergeant!" I stopped and sighed heavily, looking up at the night sky. "You're not lookin' so good."

"I'm fine, Ghost," I slurred and kept walking, feeling like I was floating.

"Let me help you at least get to your barracks."

"Nope," I insisted, shaking my head and stumbling again. I held my hand up to hold him off but he laughed and wrapped his arm around my waist anyway.

"Come on, I'll just get you inside."

"Nope, no, no, no, no, not happenin'," I slurred again but that was the last thing I remembered. At least until I woke up the next morning feeling like I'd been hit by a damn freight train. "What the ever loving fuck?"

I sat up slowly, holding my hand to my head and frowned. My head was killing me, and I felt super fuzzy and dizzy. My stomach was rolling and I thought I was going to throw up.

"Why the hell am I naked?" I murmured, looking down at myself. Not only was I naked, which I never slept naked, but I wasn't even under the blankets. I looked at my lap and found the insides of my thighs covered in blood. "What the ever loving fuck?"

I jumped up and almost fell over from the dizziness then slowly threw some clothes on, finding my panties from the night before torn on the floor. I thought hard about what had happened but the last thing I could remember was Ghost walking me back to the barracks. I stopped, pulling a shirt on over my head and frowned, trying to remember anything after that but it was all a blank. There was nothing.

"Holy fucking hell, that son of a bitch raped me!" I gasped and rushed out of the barracks, barely pulling my boots on and doing my best not to throw up. I rushed to the medical building and burst through the doors, finding the nurse I'd talked to the day before.

"Whoa, Sergeant," she said as I held her arms, gasping for breath. "What's the rush?"

"I think I was raped."

"What?" She demanded and I nodded, the movement almost bringing me to my knees.

After that everything moved so fast my head spun, and not just from the dizziness. I was still confused and even a little dizzy from whatever I'd been given the night before but I still couldn't remember anything.

Quickly the doctor did a rape kit and while he was very gentle everything hurt. My vagina, my legs, my pelvis, my stomach. There was pain everywhere and I couldn't remember anything. I didn't feel like I was being traumatized again because I didn't remember the initial trauma. I couldn't decide if that was worse or not.

Fucking Ghost.

I had blood drawn because the doctor thought my symptoms sounded like I'd been drugged and I thought back, trying to remember.

"Tongue, he tried to hand me a beer, he'd opened it with his hand over the top of the can but I refused to drink it. I made him give me one that wasn't opened." I sat with the base counsellor after that, but I just ended up more confused. "I need to go, I ship home tomorrow, I can't stay here, I'm done."

"Carol -"

"No, I can't do this anymore," I sobbed then took a deep breath, trying to control myself. "I just can't. My little girl is at home waiting for me, I need to get home, I'm retiring or I don't know what."

I jumped up and rushed out of the counsellor's office. I hit the dusty path just outside and stopped, breathing heavily, bent at the waist trying to catch my breath.

"Hey, Sergeant," Ghost. I stood straight and looked up at the man I knew had raped me, my eyes impossibly wide. "You're lookin' a little better than last night, how're you feelin'?"

"You sick son of a bitch!" I screamed at him. Lashing out with my fists and feet I kicked and punched.

"Stop! What the hell!?" He demanded, trying to protect himself.

"You raped me!" I screamed at him just as he got his hands around my wrists. He held me tight and stared down at me like I had lost my mind. He also looked more shocked than anything but I didn't believe it. He raped me.

"What the fuck are you talking about?" He demanded, breathing heavy as I struggled. "I didn't fuckin' touch you!"

"You drugged me and the last thing I remember is you *helping* me to my room!" I sneered at him as I fought still. "Then I wake up this morning in pain and covered in blood! You raped me!"

"I didn't rape you, Sergeant," Ghost insisted, shaking his head. "I swear to you, I laid you down on your bed and walked out."

"Liar!" I screamed at him then lifted my knee and slammed it into his balls. With a groan he slid to the ground and I shoved him away from me. As he crouched on the ground I spit on him then turned and stormed away.

Remembering what the doctor had said. There was no semen present, whoever had raped me, and I had been raped, had worn a condom. There would never be any proof and since I couldn't remember anything because I had definitely been drugged, there was nothing anyone could do.

With tears flowing down my cheeks I stormed into mine and Becky's barracks and started tearing the sheets off my bed. I couldn't stand to look at the mess. I wasn't thinking, I should have put the blanket into a bag and taken it to be processed. Maybe there were skin cells or something on it, something that could be used to stop Ghost. Instead I carried the sheets and blanket to the garbage can and was about to throw them in. Something inside caught my eye, though and I stopped.

There on top of the trash in the basket was a condom. A used condom. Was Ghost really that stupid? He used a condom to rape me with then left the damn thing in *my* garbage bin? It couldn't be, he couldn't be *that* stupid.

I dropped the blankets on the floor and rushed around my room. I found the ziploc bag I used for my shampoo and conditioner so they didn't explode in my bag and emptied it out. I grabbed a pair of tweezers and carefully lifted the condom out of the garbage. Disgusted I dropped it and the tweezers into the ziploc and sealed it. I stormed out of the barracks, my evidence in my hand and hurried to the medical building.

"Here," I said to the nurse and shoved the ziploc in her face. "The stupid dick left this in my room."

"That is so gross," the nurse grumbled but took the ziploc, holding it between her finger and thumb like touching just the bag disgusted her. "We'll have it tested." She assured me and I took a deep breath, my eyes filling with tears. "Chief Downey was asking about you, she's awake right now if you'd like to go and sit with her."

Grateful for the distraction I nodded and walked over to the beds soldiers used until they could be flown out to Germany or Canada. Becky was at the far end, away from the main doors and I pulled a stool over to her bed.

"Hey," she said when she saw me, groggy from the meds. "I heard last night was quite the party."

"Sure, for Ghost," I snorted and she frowned.

"Ghost? What about Ghost? I heard from the Lieutenant that you drank too much and had to be helped back to the barracks."

"Oh no, someone drugged me then raped me," I stated then couldn't hold the tears back. I lifted my hands to my face and hid.

"No shit," Becky gasped and tried to sit up.

"Don't," I said, shaking my head. "I don't remember it, I just, I woke up sore and there was blood everywhere." I sniffed again and swallowed hard. "I came in and the doctor did a rape kit but the fucker wore a condom."

"What now?"

"Well," I scoffed, smiling even though I really didn't feel like it. "See, that's where it gets interesting. He was so smart to wear a condom but he wasn't smart enough to take it with him. The idiot dropped the used condom in our garbage can."

"Oh my God, you can't be serious," Becky gasped, falling back on the bed. I nodded and swallowed hard again then sighed.

"I'm done," I murmured. "I'm not coming back here, I can't."

"I don't blame you, who do you think it was?"

"Ghost, I know it was him. He helped me to bed, he even said so, then he helped me out of my clothes."

"He said that? He actually admitted to raping you?"

"No, he definitely denied that part," I muttered darkly, swallowing hard and wiping the tears from my face again.

"Oh God, Carol," Becky sighed, shaking her head. "I'm so sorry."

"Yeah," I sniffed again. "Me too. But tomorrow we're flying out of here and I will never have to see those assholes again."

That night I didn't go back to our room. I slept in the hospital on the bed beside Becky and because of the situation the nurses took pity on me and left me there. Someone said Ghost tried to find me and talk to me but I didn't care, it's not like I had any more to say to him. The next day I shipped out to Germany with Becky.

I saw another counsellor while I was in Germany but I still

couldn't remember anything. I didn't know what to do. My memory of that night was a total blank, my mind just was not cooperating. The counsellor couldn't help me, but told me, in fact, ordered me to see the base counsellor when I got back to Ottawa.

I did, and when she said she would need to see me once a week for the foreseeable future and prescribed antidepressants I went straight to the Commander's office and began my Release Administration. It took time, and it was more time that I was away from Paige but it was something that had to be done.

CHAPTER 6

Carter

"Hey," I looked up to see Speed walking towards me. I had been in Yemen for six months now and had just applied for JTF 2. Special Operations Forces, I realize now that's what Hunt and his team did but at the time when I'd first worked with them I was too green to know. Now I knew and I wanted a part of that.

"What's up Speed?" I asked, giving him a chin lift. I would be heading back to Canada in the next couple of weeks to perform the physical tests for JTF 2 and I was excited as fuck. I hadn't expected to find Speed or any of Hunt's team here in Yemen, though. There wasn't really a lot going on here.

"You hear the news?" He asked, sitting beside me on the ground where I was relaxing after a long day. Yes I was sitting in the dirt, and yes I was sitting against an outside wall, but it was actually in the shade and my bottle of water might stay cold ish long enough for me to actually drink it.

"What news? The Taliban surrender?" I smiled at him and took a long drink. I was surprised to see for the first time since I'd met the man years ago that he didn't have earbuds in his ears and he wasn't listening to music.

"I wish, but even if they did what would I do? This is my life you know?"

"Yeah, I hear ya, this is kind of it for me, too," I agreed, squinting as I looked around as soldiers doing PT around us or throwing a football around. A couple even had baseball gloves and were tossing a baseball back and forth. "So what's this amazing news?"

"I don't know if it's amazing," Speed scoffed, shaking his head. "It's shocking, that's for sure."

"Holy fuck Speed, just spit it out. Seriously, you don't talk for like ten years then all of a sudden you talk so much without saying shit."

"Tongue was arrested for rape." He said and he was right, it was shocking, as in I just about choked on my mouthful of water and had to spit it out on the ground beside me.

"What the fuck?" I demanded, wiping my mouth with the back of my hand and staring at the man beside me. "When the hell was this?"

"I know!" He agreed, throwing his hands in the air. "I've worked with Tongue the entire time I've been enlisted and I never would have suspected. They have proof and everything, you think you know a guy."

"What kind of proof? Are they sure it's for real? The chick's not just talkin' out her ass?"

"Oh no, it's for real. We've known this woman for a few years now. Ghost was always trying to get her to go out with him but you know how smooth Ghost is."

"Yeah, like the coarsest fuckin' sandpaper."

"Right, but one night about five months ago this woman is in the bar tent and Ghost and Tongue are there with her team. They had just come in from shooting up some terrorists on a mountain side and one of her team had been shot and she'd been grazed. Ghost says Tongue tries to hand her a beer and he opens it and she pretty much tells him to go fuck himself and get her one that's unopened."

"This is unreal man," I said, shaking my head and drinking the last of my water.

"Yeah well, Ghost helped her to her place but Tongue's the one who raped her, drugged her and raped her and the stupid idiot left the used condom in her garbage can."

"What's Ghost doing?"

"He told Tongue to go fuck himself, he really liked this woman and his best friend goes and does this? Then more women start coming out of the woodwork you know?"

"That is seriously fucked up. I hope they throw the book at him and he gets ass fucked in prison for the rest of his fucking life."

"You and me both man." Speed said, despondently, shaking his head. After a few minutes of watching the activity around us Speed sighed. "So what's next for you?"

"I just finished my application for JTF 2, thanks for the heads up that's what you guys were by the way." I told him and he snickered, shaking his head. "What's Hunt up to? And where's Ghost?"

"Uh, Ghost is tied up with Tongue's thing, waiting for them to clear him completely which shouldn't take too much longer because he really and truly wasn't involved. And Hunt is heading up some new super secret darker than black ops group."

"No shit?"

"Yeah."

"You gonna get on that team?"

"Not if I can fuckin' help it, those guys are pretty much mercs for hire."

"Seriously?"

"Yeah, Hunt has got a bee up his ass about something."

"Huh, well maybe we'll end up on the same team when I finish training."

"Oh, you think it's that easy do you?"

"Fuck man, it's gotta be if you made it through!" I told him laughing and ended up getting punched in the arm even though Speed was laughing with me.

For the rest of my deployment in Yemen Speed and I never actually worked together, but when we had free time we were often hanging out. I learned a lot from Speed, both about life and the military. He also told me about the tests for JTF 2 and helped me prepare for those. I knew it wasn't going to be a walk in the park but holy shit it was intense. Three weeks later I found out just how intense.

The pre-screening physical test was nothing really, fewer reps and less weight than I usually lifted but the seven days of hell once I was accepted were just that, hell. Thankfully I was in peak physical condition and while hell week was far from easy, worst week of my life, I made it through. I would like to say I made it through with flying colours, I know that would be a lie.

While I was working on the academic side of the JTF 2 training I tried to find Marty but he had been kicked out of his apartment and of course there was no forwarding address. I went to the bar we'd always gone to and the bartender said Marty was often there but he never drank.

"Why would an alcoholic come to a bar and not drink?" I asked, confused.

"Because he shows up completely tanked and has no money so we don't let him in," the bartender explained with a shrug and I rolled my eyes.

"Is there a night that he usually shows up?"

"Yeah, every day that ends in 'y'," the bartender smirked and walked away.

"Ugh," I groaned and dropped my head to the counter, or almost did. I stopped when I realized it was sticky and I definitely did not want to put my face there.

"He's here," the bartender said and I looked up just as he nodded towards the door. I turned to see Marty stumble in the door and sighed. "Hey, Marty, I already told you, you can't be in here."

"Says who?" Marty slurred belligerently.

"Says me, I just said so."

"Hey Marty," I said getting off my stool and walking over the door.

"Who are you?" Marty asked, glaring up at me then his face cleared and he smiled. "Sean! How the hell are ya?"

Marty clapped me on the shoulder then turned to the bartender.

"Hey, hey, a pitcher of beer for my friend here," he called across the bar and I looked over, shaking my head.

"I'll have water, but get him a beer," I told the guy who didn't move.

"He's not allowed in here man."

"I'll be responsible for him, I swear he won't do anything but drink his beer, catch up with his best friend and then we'll be out of here." I told the bartender who finally relented with a heavy sigh.

"Fine," he reached below the bar and grabbed a clean glass,

filled it with beer and grabbed a bottle of water from the fridge, putting both on the bar for me. I took them both over to a table and sat down, waiting for Marty to join me.

"Man, I owe ya," Marty said and started chugging his beer.

"Hey, slow down, that's the only one you're getting tonight," I told him, holding my hand out to him.

"Yeah, sure," Marty said and set his glass down, extra careful none of the beer spilled.

"How have you been, Marty?" I asked, watching him as he stared into his glass.

"You know, pretty great, workin' hard and all. The commander keeps us busy."

"Marty, I know you're not working, at least not at the base." I told him gently and he scoffed at me. "Seriously Marty, why don't you let me get you into a rehab place?"

"Nah, those places are for quitters," Marty said then laughed at his horrible joke. "I ain't no quitter!"

"Marty, you're an alcoholic."

"No, I'm not!"

"You're going to get someone killed just like your brother did."

"What the fuck do you know about it?" He demanded and pushed out of the booth. The angry look on his face was a surprise. He reached for the glass of beer but he was so drunk I easily grabbed it before he did.

"Come on, man, this isn't you."

"What do you know? You don't know me! You go off to all corners of the world, you have no idea who I am!"

"Marty -"

"Fuck you, I'm outta here!"

"At least let me call you a cab!"

"Fuck off!" Marty yelled and fingered me over his shoulder as he stumbled out the door.

"Fuck!" I swore, staring at the door with my hands on my hips.

"Told ya," the bartender said as he walked past me to wipe down the table. "The guy's a lost cause."

"He's been my best friend since we were kids, man, I couldn't just forget about him."

"I hear ya, but people gotta want to get better and he doesn't want to. Maybe one day he will and I'll hope for that, but he's made his choice, what's yours gonna be?"

"Yeah," I sighed and pulled out my wallet then handed the guy a twenty. "Thanks man."

I left the bar and started walking. It wasn't far to the barracks where I was living so I didn't bother calling a cab. I hadn't bothered buying a car since I was out of the country so often it didn't make sense to pay for insurance or parking. Maybe it was time for that to change.

Now that I was JTF 2 I wouldn't be out of the country quite as often. As special forces we were often sent out for a week or two at a time, maybe a month, then brought back to train more. I was almost thirty, only four more years, maybe it was time to look for a house. It's not like I didn't have the money saved up for a down payment and it's not like I needed any-thing huge. It would also be nice to sleep in a regular bed for a change instead of the bunks at the barracks.

My mind made up, I walked onto the base and up to my room.

I looked around the space and grimaced. Everything about it was temporary. Most often I kept my things in storage because I was deployed so often I couldn't always store my shit in my room. Someone else was assigned to it when I was gone and more often than not I got a different room every time I came home.

I could have stayed with Marty those times but he had a tiny one bedroom apartment that he barely fit in. Another person would just be too much. And now that space was gone anyway.

Knowing I had PT early in the morning I should have gone straight to bed but I knew I wouldn't be able to sleep. Instead I pulled out my laptop and started looking at real estate and what it would take to get a mortgage. I even found a couple of places I liked and sent emails to the realtors, making appointments for the next day.

For once I was excited for something that wasn't me being deployed to a new place. I actually went to bed with a smile on my face.

It didn't hurt that the next afternoon I met the realtor at the first house I'd chosen and liked it right away. It was a small place with two bedrooms and two bathrooms. The kitchen and living room were open concept and the backyard was huge.

"I might have to get a dog to fill this yard." I said, absently, staring out at the space.

"You're actually very lucky to have this space," Jenna, the realtor said. She was very pretty, long, thick red hair and green hazel eyes. "Most of the houses in this neighbourhood don't have this kind of yard because they're newer builds. The owners either added onto the house or they tore down the original and built bigger."

"What a waste," I mumbled then smiled and winked down at her. She blushed, the pink on her cheeks making her freckles stand out just a bit more. "So what's next?"

"Well, we have other houses to see -"

"No, I want this one," I said, shaking my head and turning to go back inside. "What do I have to do now to buy it?"

"Oh, are you pre-approved for the mortgage?"

"Nope, haven't even been to the bank yet."

"Do you have a down payment?"

"Yeah, all I've done the last few years is work and when I was in the country I lived at the barracks so it's not like I was paying rent."

"How's your credit?"

"Good I guess," I shrugged. "I always pay my credit card bill but that's about all I've got."

"Well, because you're military you shouldn't have a problem getting a mortgage." Jenna said with a smile and a shrug. "Let's go back to my office and I'll write the contract, let the sellers know about the offer and tomorrow you'll have to go to the bank and look into a mortgage."

"All right, let's do that then," I smiled and a week later I was a homeowner. The night Jenna called me to tell me that I had bought the house, the sellers had accepted my offer and all the conditions were lifted, we celebrated.

Holy shit did we celebrate. Jenna was wild in bed and she liked that I wasn't around all the time. That night began a years long friends with benefits relationship that made both of us very happy. She even helped me pick out furniture for the house then helped me break in my new king sized bed.

And my couch.

And my shower, both of them.

And my kitchen counter.

I also got a dog to fill my backyard and the few times that I was deployed Jenna would stay at my house to watch Klaus.

Yeah, I know, Klaus wasn't a typical dog's name but she was a doberman pinscher and she was already named when I found her at the pound. And yes, Klaus wasn't a girl's name but it fit her so it stayed. There was no point in me changing it after she'd already gotten used to it.

Her previous owners had gotten rid of her when they couldn't make her a killer. She had been trained to be a guard dog but because she didn't have the killer instinct they didn't want her. I was just happy that she was trained, I definitely didn't want her killing anyone.

Klaus was loyal and loving and she always forgave me when I had to go away for work.

My life was just perfect and I hoped nothing changed.

CHAPTER 7

Carol

Ten Years Ago . . .

"Hey Carol, how are you feeling today?" I looked up as my counsellor, Brooke stepped into the room. I sighed and shook my head at her.

"How am I supposed to feel?"

"Angry, depressed, stressed, paranoid," Brooke began then shrugged and shocked me. "Happy, elated, relaxed, excited for the future." She stopped and looked at me with a smile. "That's just it, Carol, there isn't any one way you're supposed to feel."

"Well, I am still angry."

"Why?"

"Because I was raped? And I can't remember it?" I asked her, frowning as though that answer were obvious. "And it was three years ago and I can't forget about it?"

"Would it be better if you could remember it?"

"In some ways I kind of think so," I sighed and shrugged. "At least then I'd know why I was paranoid, then I'd know what exactly I was angry about, I'd just, I'd know."

"I can see that," Brooke said nodding. "Who are you angry at?"

"Tongue, Ghost, myself."

"I can certainly understand why you're angry with Tongue, why are you angry with Ghost?"

"Because he died before I could apologize for accusing him of raping me and kicking him in the balls."

"Why are you angry with yourself?"

"Because I accused an innocent man of rape and kicked him in the balls and never apologized," I shrugged then sighed heavily. "And because I'm too scared to try to have a relationship with a man."

"Are you afraid of the man? Or where you would have to go to meet the man?"

"Maybe a little of both I guess," I shrugged, considering Brooke's words.

"Do you believe in God, Heaven?"

"I suppose," I shrugged again. "I don't have any reason not to."

"Is it possible that Ghost went there? Is it possible that if there is a God and a Heaven that Ghost can hear you?"

"I don't see why not."

"So you can still apologize to him then. Because what I see is that your anger at Ghost is the same as your anger at yourself, you just don't feel strong enough to take it all so you're dividing it between the two of you. Apologize to Ghost, I highly doubt he's holding a grudge and I highly doubt even if he was alive that he'd not forgive you."

"I know you're right."

"So then what you need to work on is forgiving yourself."

"Yeah." I agreed, nodding.

"Did you go to the trial?"

"Parts of it."

"I read all the transcripts, were you there when Ghost testified?"

"No, I couldn't handle it."

"Hmm," Brooke nodded then took a deep breath. "Ghost testified against Tongue."

"I heard."

"He broke down on the stand, he said if he could apologize to you and make it right he would have. He even said he didn't blame you for accusing him, he understood that you were distraught and given that you were drugged had to make assumptions based on what you knew at the time."

"He said that?" I whispered, my eyes jumping to Brooke who nodded and smiled.

"He did. So, I would think that he's already forgiven you, you just have to forgive yourself."

"Yeah, you're right," I mused, frowning, actually beginning to feel lighter. Brooke smiled and looked at her cell phone that had just buzzed on her desk. She frowned and looked up at me.

"Carol, Lo says he needs you in his office right now."

"Right now? Or right fucking now?" I asked with a smile as I stood.

"The second one."

"Oh, well I'm on my way then." I hurried to the door then stopped and turned back to look at Brooke. "Thanks for today."

"My pleasure, hon," she said with a smile. "I hope everything is okay."

"Me too," I hurried out of the clinic and ran into the main building of the MC. After getting nowhere with my therapist at home someone had suggested I come here, to Kamloops. A couple of guys had started an MC, a motorcycle club, where they helped veterans dealing with PTSD and reintegrating into society after leaving the Armed Forces. I figured what the hell, it couldn't hurt.

The only problem was leaving Paige behind. Even worse was that she had to spend so much time with Karl. He wasn't a horrible person exactly, unless you were married to him, but he wasn't the best role model either. My mom wasn't all that young anymore and she had a hard time keeping up with a fifteen year old girl. Now Karl kept Paige the majority of the time and mom got her every other weekend and Wednesday evenings.

It worked for us and Karl was happy that I was paying him child support for a change. Unlike Karl, though I paid it without complaining.

I walked across the main room of the clubhouse and knocked on the door of Lo's office.

"Yeah!" Lo called and I stepped in. "Carol, come sit down."

Lo did not look good, in fact he looked horrible and I had to wonder what was going on.

"What's up, Lo?" I asked and sat in one of the chairs in front of his desk. All his guys were sitting around in their usual spots looking worried and upset.

"I've got some bad news," he began then sighed and scratched his forehead. "Uh, your daughter Paige, she's staying with your ex husband?"

"Yeah, Karl and my mom are sort of sharing custody, why?" I asked, frowning.

"Your mom called, your daughter was supposed to be there last night?"

"Yeah, it was Wednesday." I said, looking around again. "Did Paige not make it? Did mom call Karl?"

"She called Karl and he told her to leave it alone, that what's done is done and she should just forget about it."

"What the fuck is that supposed to mean?" I demanded angrily.

"Your mom called here obviously looking for you, you were in a group session so I took it upon myself to figure out what the hell was going on." Lo sighed and scrubbed his hands over his face. "I had Siobhan call the Winnipeg police and get as much information as she could. It's not good, Carol."

"Lo, just tell me, please."

"Karl got involved with some seriously bad guys," Seether said, taking over the story. "He borrowed more money than he could ever pay back."

"Karl's a gambler, that's why we split up ultimately, that and the other women."

"Well, he's still a gambler, I'm sure like most gamblers he thought he could borrow a shit load of money, play the VLTs or whatever and win it all back and then some. Of course it doesn't work that way and he couldn't pay his bills." Axle murmured and I blinked.

"The people Karl borrowed the money from took Paige as payment." Lo murmured softly and I started to feel like I had been drugged again. I started feeling dizzy and nauseous and my vision began to tunnel.

"Where is she?"

"We're not sure, yet, but we're going to get her back."

"How?"

"We just opened an MC in Winnipeg," Lo said, scrubbing his hand over his face again. "I've been in touch with Razz, the president, he's got his guys on it."

"I have to go."

"Of course you do," Seether said nodding. "You've got a flight out in the morning, you just have to go and pack."

"When you get home one of the guys from the MC, possibly Razz himself, will be at the airport to meet you."

"I'm going to kill Karl," I vowed and all seven guys in the room nodded.

"You want help with that just let us know." Lo said and I actually kind of smiled. It didn't last long, though.

"I'm gonna go start to pack and call my mom."

"That's a good idea, I told her you would call her as soon as possible. It's been a couple of hours, she's probably freaking out."

"Thanks Lo," I said quietly, standing in the doorway of the office and looking around the room at all the guys there. "For everything."

Before any of them could say anything I rushed out of the room and up to the room I had been assigned while I was here. I grabbed my cell phone off the charger and dialed my mom's number.

"Carol?"

"Mom," I sighed and sat on the edge of the bed. "Have you heard anything?"

"No, and Karl refuses to cooperate with the police." My mom whimpered and sniffed. "There are some large men here who say they're going to help us find Paige."

"Mom, they're from the same group I'm staying with here," I told her, trying to stay positive. "These guys are trained, mom, they'll find Paige, probably before the police do."

"There's a man here named Razz, he wants to talk to you."

"Put him on, mom. Listen, I'll be home tomorrow, my flight leaves here first thing in the morning."

"Okay, dear, be safe." She sniffed and sighed. "Here he is."

"Carol?" The voice was gruff but not unfriendly.

"Yeah, Razz?"

"Yeah Darlin', look don't worry about your girl, we'll get her back for you," Razz said and cleared his throat before inhaling deeply. "Maybe even by the time you get off that plane tomorrow."

"Razz you're not smoking in my house are you?" I asked and Razz chuckled.

"Does your back porch count as in your house?"

"No, thank you for that."

"Hey sweetheart, my pleasure."

"Razz, can you promise me you'll get Paige back? Like swear on your own kid's life?" I asked, knowing I sounded desperate but that's how I was feeling. "Or your wife or someone?"

"I swear on my brother's grave that we will find your daughter." Razz assured me and I sighed. "Techie, our computer expert, has already started looking and he's found a few threads to pull. I can't guarantee what condition she's going to be in though, so prepare yourself for that. The guys who have her are not known for being gentle or kind."

"If she's alive she can be saved, she just needs to get home." I insisted and he 'mmhmmed' in agreement.

"All right, I'm gonna let you go. Tell Lo I said hi and get your butt back here all right?"

"Yeah, I will, thanks Razz." I swallowed hard and rubbed my forehead. "Lo said one of your guys would be picking me up at the airport?"

"Yeah, probably me, I'll meet you by baggage claim."

"Okay, thank you, Razz."

"See you tomorrow, Carol." Razz hung up and I was left sitting on the edge of the bed, staring into space.

"I should have told Razz to kill Karl." I muttered to myself then jumped up and started to pack. I wasn't exactly careful about it either and ended up having a hard time closing my suitcase because I just piled everything inside. It was done quickly though and then I was at loose ends. I figured I should probably eat and get to bed, even though it wasn't late.

I went down to the kitchen and found one of my favourite people in the kitchen.

"Willis, what are you doing here?" I asked and he shrugged. Willis was the sixteen year old son of a former JTF 2 member. Ethan wasn't a member of the MC but his brother-in-law was and they spent a lot of time here. Plus his youngest brother worked as a bartender here as well, or used to until he opened the MC's youth club.

"Aunt Casey came to see Uncle Nick and I was helping her with stuff at their house so I came with her." He replied and I nodded. I really liked Willis. He was a good kid who had a good head on his shoulders. He was set to graduate a year early from high school and he wasn't sure if he wanted to go into the armed forces or not. He was only a year older than Paige and I actually enjoyed talking to him.

"Right on, you want something to eat? I was just gonna make myself something." I said to him and he nodded.

"Sure." He got up and started pulling stuff for sandwiches out of the fridge and I smiled. He always seemed to know exactly what I wanted. "How's Paige? Have you talked to her lately?"

"Well, see that's the thing," I began then lifted my hand to wipe fresh tears from my eyes.

"Carol, what's wrong?"

"Paige has been kidnapped -"

"No shit!"

"Yeah," I chuckled and sniffed. "The MC in Winnipeg is out looking for her but I'm going home tomorrow. Razz said he'd have her back by then."

"Knowing Razz he probably will."

"You know Razz?" I asked, smiling at Willis and realized I was actually taller than me, and I wasn't short.

"I probably know most of the guys that go through here," Willis shrugged and I nodded. "Razz will find Paige."

"I like how positive you are."

"Eh," Willis shrugged again.

"So you gonna join up when you graduate?"

"I don't know, Kris did and so did Ryker but I don't know if that's what I want to do."

"What else would you do?"

"Police work?"

"So, military lite?"

"That's not what the RCMP is!" Willis insisted and I chuckled.

"Why would you not go into the military?"

"Mom freaks out whenever I talk about it?"

"Sure but all mom's do that, why would you go into the military?"

"Because it's the right thing to do, because I want to help people, because there's a lot of injustice in the world and I can help."

I nudged his shoulder with mine and smiled.

"Yeah all right," he smirked and together we put together a couple of huge sandwiches.

"Thanks, kid," I said and we walked to the table to eat. I was still worried like crazy about Paige, I was stressing out about my daughter but talking with Willis always made me feel better. He was a year or so older than Paige but talking to him made me feel like I was talking to her.

Eventually Willis' Aunt Casey came in to get him and Saint raced in the kitchen and wrapped his arms around his wife. She squealed then laughed as he lifted her and swung her around in a circle.

"Missed you baby," Saint growled into her neck while she laughed. "Come on kid, your dad is waiting for you."

"See ya later, Carol," Willis said, carrying his plate to the sink and finishing his glass of milk quickly. "Good luck with Paige."

"Thanks kid," I smiled as the three of them left the room. I quickly finished my sandwich and cleaned up after myself and

Willis then went up to my room. I cleaned the bathroom and fixed my packing then crawled into bed and tried to sleep. It didn't happen, though and I laid awake for hours.

The next morning I slid out of bed and carried all of my stuff downstairs then waited for someone to drive me to the airport. I couldn't eat, I was too nervous, worried about Paige. Lo drove me to the airport and said nothing the entire way, not that the trip was a long one. When we pulled up in front of the departures door he put the SUV into park and turned to look at me.

"Carol," Lo said with a heavy sigh. "I don't know what happened on your last deployment, Brooke didn't and wouldn't tell me. We've all heard rumours, though -"

"Lo -"

"Carol, listen, it doesn't matter what the rumours are. It doesn't matter if those rumours are true, what matters is you're here now, you're strong and you *will* get past the pain. I also know because you're strong you'll get your daughter back and you'll help her get past what she's dealing with. I don't know if you had planned on staying with the MC past your treatment here -"

"I hadn't decided." I shrugged and he nodded.

"That's what I figured, and Winnipeg is much different than here, Razz is . . . well he's different, but he's a good man. Him and Techie will find Paige and the men who took her will pay for taking her."

"It's Karl who needs to pay."

"I agree, just know that no matter what you decide about the MC you'll always be protected. Whether you're a member or not any time you need help or Paige needs help you go to Razz or you call me, got it?"

"Yeah Lo, thanks," I said with a sharp nod and a sniff. Neither of us were exactly free with our emotions but I appreciated what Lo had said.

"Get in there before you miss your flight," Lo said, nodding to the doors of the airport. "Tell Razz to keep me up to date about Paige, all right?"

"You bet." I left the vehicle, dragging my suitcase behind me and hurried to the check in desk. It didn't take long and while I waited for the flight to board I called my mom to let her know I was about to get on the plane. She said there was nothing new but the large man who was in charge said they were close.

I breathed a sigh of relief then told mom I had to go. I got on the plane and got comfortable, settling in for a good eight hour flight, okay, not a good one.

When I got off the plane in Winnipeg I hurried to baggage claim, hoping I would find Razz standing and waiting for me with Paige beside him. I wasn't so lucky. I did find Razz, and I was surprised by what I saw but disappointed that Paige wasn't there with him.

"Carol," Razz said as I looked around. I had no idea what the man looked like but he walked up to me like we were best friends. He even pulled me into his arms in a big hug and I had to admit it was comforting. Razz was a big man with kind eyes and a head full of thick, dark hair that was graying at the temples. His square jaw was clean shaven except for a patch under his jaw that he must have missed.

"She's not here?" I asked, pulling back and looking up at him.

"No, sorry sweetheart," he said, shaking his head. "Techie got a lead though and the guys were going to be checking it out. I hadn't heard by the time I had to leave to come and get you."

"Do you think she's okay?" I asked, looking up at him with

desperation in my eyes.

"Honestly I really think she is," he sighed with a nod. "I don't think these guys really want to hurt her, they just want their money. I think if they don't get it from your ex then they'll sell Paige -"

"Sell her?"

"Shhh."

"Sell her?" I repeated much quieter. "Like human trafficking sell her?"

"Yeah that is what I meant, but they haven't had time to do it. Karl promised them their money and they gave him forty-eight hours to get it to them."

"Yeah, but it's been at least that hasn't it?"

"Yeah, but they're not going to have a buyer set up already," Razz insisted and I nodded, sighing and shifting from one foot to the other. "Let's grab your bags and see if they've made contact yet."

"Okay," I nodded, swallowing hard. Razz walked me over to the baggage carousel and we waited for my suitcase. Me impatiently and him with his arm slung across my shoulders as though he were trying to keep me from running away.

I pointed out my suitcase and Razz grabbed it then took my hand and led me out of the terminal. He helped me into an older model pickup truck and tossed my suitcase into the back. We went straight to my mom's house and when we pulled up she rushed out the front door and straight at me.

"I'm so sorry, I'm so sorry, I should have kept a closer eye on her!" My mom sobbed into my shoulder as we hugged.

"It's not your fault mom," I told her, hugging her back and swaying side to side. "You didn't do anything, you couldn't have stopped this. This is all Karl's fault."

"He asked me for some money, I should have given it to him."

"No mom, you shouldn't have, you did the right thing," I assured her, pulling back to look in her face. "Karl shouldn't have gambled and he shouldn't have borrowed from dangerous guys and he shouldn't have told them they could have his daughter as collateral. That's all on him."

As we were standing in the yard talking and hugging another SUV pulled up to the curb. The back door opened as we watched and a big man slid out then jumped out of the way as Paige pushed past him and ran for me.

"Mom!" She cried and barrelled into me, wrapping her arms around me and sobbing.

"Oh my God, Paige!" I exclaimed and cradled my baby girl against my chest.

"Oh my baby girl," mom said, echoing my thoughts. I pulled her into our hug and the three of us stood crying on mom's front lawn as five giant men stood around us in a semicircle watching us. Eventually I looked up at all of them and smiled through my tears.

"Thank you, all of you, so much," I sobbed and they all nodded.

"No thanks are necessary," one of the guys said with a shrug. "You're one of us, we'd do anything for you."

"The police will be here soon to take Paige's statement, I don't know when she ate last," the oldest of the men said, shoving his hands in his pockets.

"Come on sweetheart," my mom said, pulling Paige away from me and into the house. "Let's get you something to eat. How about a hot shower?"

"Will you all come inside?" I asked the men standing around

me on the lawn. "The least I can do is make you something to eat as thanks."

"We'd like that sweetheart," Razz said, walking towards me. "Grinder can you grab the suitcase from my truck?"

"Yes boss." One of the younger men said and walked over to Razz's truck and grabbed my bag.

That night after all the bikers and all the police and all the extra people were gone I helped Paige to bed.

"Mom," she said softly as I left the room, my hand on the light switch. "Will you stay with me?

"Why don't we sleep in my bed? It's bigger, we'll watch Little Mermaid," I suggested and she hurried to follow me out of the room.

She might have been fifteen but that night she was my little girl again and she let me cuddle her up in my arms. She had a couple of nightmares but nothing too bad. She hadn't been assaulted and she hadn't been beaten but she had been told she was going to be sold and that her father had sold her to them to pay his debt.

It was enough for me to take him to court again and have his rights revoked.

CHAPTER 8

Carter

"We're close," Speed said in my ear and I tapped my comms so he knew I heard him. We were sneaking through the deserted streets of a bombed out village looking for an HVT - high value target. Not one that we planned on taking back with us, either.

The rest of our team was spread out through the village, checking for any signs that people were still here. We had been told there was no one, that everyone had been either killed or had run to the refugee camp. Intel could be wrong, though.

"Slow," I said softly, looking around the openings of buildings.

"This is the house," Speed said and I nodded.

"No door," I murmured, checking around the opening. Explosives were my expertise and the HVT we were looking for was the leader of a group known for their imaginatively wired explosives that caused huge numbers of casualties. "Clear."

Slowly Speed and I moved through the doorway and continued down a dark, narrow hallway. I looked up and was actually grateful that there wasn't a lot of space above us. Insurgents couldn't sneak attack from above if there was no space for them. The hallway was just wide enough for me to stand with an inch on either side of my shoulders.

"Door," Speed said behind me and I held my fist up. This opening had an actual door in it and I could easily see wires stuck to the wall around the doorway with small pieces of what looked like clay.

"It's C4," I said softly and traced the wires with my eyes.

"Can you disarm it?" Speed asked and I shook my head.

"I don't know," I replied, looking around me on the floor. "I need to see the device, I'm afraid if I pull these wires it'll set it off. I'm afraid if we open the door it'll trip a wire and blow us all to hell."

"I'm not ready for that yet," Speed murmured and I nodded.

"Ditto, is there another way into that room?" I asked through the mic but got a negative response.

"There are no windows at all, just that one door." Mic said in my ear. Mic was another teammate who had been assigned to the same team as me and Speed when Mic, Taze and I finished JTF 2 training. I had respectfully asked that Speed be on our team since he hadn't been assigned to a new one since Tongue had been convicted and Ghost had died a few months after.

"Taze, what do you think? We know for sure this guy is in this room?" I asked, leaning against the wall of the hallway.

"We were told by more than one very reliable source that Al-Badai is in that room." Taze said into my ear. "Heat signature is still there."

"Then I say we get out of here and blow the building with him in it." I said looking up at Speed who smiled and nodded. I immediately started pulling blocks of C4 and wire out of my vest. "I don't think we'll need a lot," I explained quickly as I worked. "I'm pretty sure a decent sized explosion will set off the bomb that's already here and blow the place to hell and back."

"Works for me," Speed chuckled. I attached the C4 to the door and ran a long lead of wire from the block. When we were at the end of the hallway I lit it and we ran like hell.

I had been right, the explosion I'd set had set off a chain reaction that set up another much larger one that made the building we'd just been in disappear. Speed and I sat behind a wall, using it as cover, and waited.

"What do you see, Taze?" I asked, getting comfortable, knowing it could take some time for the dust to settle.

"Not a whole fuck of a lot," Taze replied on a growl. "Heat signature is gone, though."

"Well, let's take a look then, shall we?" Speed asked and I smiled. Slowly we sat up and turned to look over the wall and saw - dust. I pulled my sunglasses down over my eyes and we started moving around the end of the wall, my C7 rifle at the ready. Speed did the same with his and we made our way back across the street.

"I see nothing," I murmured as we went through the dust. I lifted my handkerchief to cover my mouth and nose so I didn't inhale the fine dust and kept going.

"Just rubble, looks like all we did was add to it." Speed mumbled and I agreed.

"We're sure one hundred percent that Al-Babai was in this room?" I asked as we walked around the perimeter of where the room should have been.

"Maybe not a hundred percent," Mic said in my ear and I grunted.

"Well, let's get back to base," I said and we turned, right into the muzzle of a pistol. "Whoa."

I stopped and held my hands up, blinking and taking a step back.

"Horshack, what's up?" Speed asked when I stepped back into him. The guys had started calling me Horshack after Ron Palillo's character from Welcome Back Kotter since Speed had started calling me Kott-er after the title character. Not exactly my last name, but close.

"Uh, we got a little girl with a pistol pointed at my head," I said gently through my teeth, trying to smile reassuringly.

"You sure that's a girl?" Speed asked, looking around me.

"Nope, just keep smiling," I said, taking another step back. "All I know is this kid has a gun pointed at my head and he or she looks very nervous, I'd rather not get shot."

"Nooo shit," Speed murmured and backed up with me. "Did you see if the safety was still on?"

"You didn't see the gun?" I asked, frowning.

"No, your big head was in the way."

"Yeah, we're talkin' a Colt single action six-shooter, buddy, no safety and that sucker was cocked."

"Fuck," Speed gasped and I nodded.

"Just take the kid out!" Taze yelled in my ear.

"Did you seriously just say that?" Speed asked incredulously. "That's the kind of shit I transferred out of Hunt's team for."

"Are you shittin' me right now?" I asked, glancing over my shoulder at Speed.

"Not now," Speed singsonged and I looked back at the kid.

"Okay, kid, let's put the gun down," I said, trying to sound soothing, trying to convince this kid who didn't speak a word of English to put his gun down. "Mic, I need some help here."

"Say: ln nuwdhiak , dae almsadas min fadlik," Mic said in my

81

ear. I repeated it as best as I could and saw the kid second guess her intent.

"She's not putting the gun down, Mic," Speed said quietly.

"Yeah well, Horshack's pronunciation was a little off," Mic murmured and we watched as the kid crouched and slowly set the gun on the ground. Both Speed and I breathed a sigh of relief, until the kid jerked at a noise and dropped the gun the last few inches to the ground, causing it to fire.

"Shit!" I yelled and fell back against Speed, knocking him backwards on his ass. "Son of a bitch!"

I looked down at the blood blossoming on my pants.

"Asaf!" the kid cried, jumping back, skittering away. "Asaf! Asaf!"

"Oh holy fuck," I groaned, looking down at my thigh.

"Mic! Call a helo!" Speed yelled in my ear. "We need a medic! Horshack's been shot!"

"Exfil is just outside of town!" Mic yelled back a minute later.

"We're comin' to you!" Taze yelled as Speed pulled some bandages and gauze out of his pack and wrapped my leg, trying to stop the bleeding, or at least slow it down. Just as he tied off the bandage as tightly as he could Mic slid to my other side and together they lifted me to my feet.

"Let's go!" Mic yelled over my scream of pain and we were hustling to the far edge of the town. "Helo's ten out."

"Stay with us, man," Speed muttered, one hand holding my wrist slung around his neck and the other gripping the back of my pants. Him and Mic almost carried me out of that little village and by the time we got to the exfil point the helo was just touching down.

"Where's he hit?" Taze asked as he added more bandages and gauze to my leg, tying the bandage tighter than before.

"Inside of the thigh," Speed guessed and I nodded. "Bullet's still in there."

"Fuck," Taze mumbled. "Try not to move him, it could've hit his artery and moving him could cause more damage. Get the leg up in the air."

The ten minute flight to the base was harrowing to say the least. When the helo landed I was barely holding on to consciousness and the pain in my leg unbearable. I passed out just as I was moved to a gurney and wheeled to the medical tent. Okay, it wasn't a tent, it was a large warehouse type building that was constructed for emergency purposes like this. I didn't think I would ever be in need of those emergency purposes, though.

I woke up again just as I was jolted, hard. Taking a deep breath I turned my head and found a nurse beside me, checking my vital signs. I continued to look around and realized I wasn't in a hospital and I was strapped to the bed I was on.

"Where are we?" I croaked, confused.

"Just landed in Germany," the nurse, an army lieutenant said with a smile. "You're very lucky to be alive, Chief. That bullet nicked your femoral artery, you almost bled out."

"That why I hurt so fuckin' much?"

"Probably part of it, yup." I grunted at her chirpy tone and went back to sleep.

"Hey, you're back," I'm not sure how this person knew I was awake since I hadn't opened my eyes and neither my breathing or heart rate had changed but reluctantly I blinked my eyes open and looked around. "There he is, how does it feel to be alive?"

"Not sure I am alive," I grumbled then cleared my throat. I immediately started to cough then groaned at the pain throughout my entire body. "On second thought, I must be if I hurt this much."

"You are alive, though it's been touch and go for a while now."

"Where am I?"

"Germany, you came in three weeks ago after being shot in the field." I blinked up at the guy standing next to my bed. I frowned since he didn't look like a nurse but he was wearing scrubs and had no name tag or badge to identify him. "I'm Dr. Arnold. You were shot in the upper thigh, the bullet entered your leg and nicked your femoral artery then lodged itself in the muscle just behind it."

I looked down at my legs and saw they were both still there, thankfully.

"Can you move your toes?" I did then groaned because it hurt like hell. "Excellent."

"You said three weeks," I reminded him and he nodded.

"Yeah, you must have picked something up while you were being transported or there was something on the bullet we don't know but you contracted an infection." Dr. Arnold explained and I groaned again. "Yeah, it was touch and go for sure. You've been in and out of consciousness but mostly out and we've been pumping you full of antibiotics. We think we've got it now for the most part but there was a time about a week ago we thought we'd have to take your leg."

"You can do that without my consent?" I asked, confused.

"If it means saving your life you bet your ass we can." He scoffed and I grunted. "Anyway, once you're up to it, I'd say about another week, you'll be shipped home and you'll have an appointment with your career manager about what's next. Of course there will be tons more doctors appointments and physio and all sorts of shit and it's going to take time."

"Where's my team?"

"From the sounds of it already deployed again."

"What are my chances of getting back out? Is this career ending?"

"Normally I would say no, but with the infection I can't honestly say. A lot will depend on how you rehab and how that infection goes." The doctor paused and took a deep breath. "I should warn you, this infection was really bad, especially because of where it started. We've been running tests regularly but you should know there's a chance it caused you to be sterile."

"Thank you doctor," I said with a sigh then closed my eyes, exhausted, and fell back asleep.

A week later I was on another plane headed home. My infection was under control and I would keep my leg, thankfully. Unfortunately I wouldn't be keeping my job, though I didn't find that out for another few weeks. Instead I found out that my life had imploded and it would take a few years to get it straightened out.

The minute I stepped off the plane in Ottawa I went straight to my career manager's office. He explained what would happen next. I couldn't go back into the field but I wasn't exactly on holiday. I had to go to physio for my leg but I was also expected to be in the office every single day to do paperwork or whatever was necessary. I ended up becoming a handler for my team and while I enjoyed working with my team again it just wasn't the same.

"There's more," Captain Rush said grimly. We had just finished discussing my new duties until my leg was better and I was about to head home and get some sleep. "Martin Fischer was killed last week."

"What? Marty's dead?" I demanded, confused. "How?"

"Driving drunk, hit a tree," Rush explained and I sighed heavily, scrubbing a hand over my face. "He was the only one in the accident, the only one in the car. An autopsy was done and his blood alcohol level was three times the legal limit. If he had blown on a breathalyzer he'd have blown 0.24, possibly more."

"Fuck," I sighed and sat forward, my elbows on my knees and my chin rested on clasped hands.

"His funeral is tomorrow," I nodded but only vaguely heard what else the Captain said. I knew what church the funeral was at and what time. I thanked the Captain for his time and left his office. I jumped into a cab and went home.

Home, my home. It was nice not to have to go to the barracks. Instead I would be going to my house, my bed and my dog. I decided on the ride over I would text Jenna the next day and let her know I was home. She often watched Klaus for me and checked on the house while I was away but this time I had been gone a lot longer than usual. Since she wasn't even my girlfriend, Jenna wouldn't have been notified of my injury.

Pulling up to the front of the house the cab driver turned to me, confused.

"You sure this is the right place?" He asked and I nodded, just as confused. There was a for sale sign on my front lawn and blocking the driveway was a sign proclaiming an open house taking place at that moment. As we sat watching the house a smiling couple stepped out of the front door with Jenna holding the door for them and waving goodbye.

"It's the right house," I growled and handed the driver his money. I grabbed my duffle and stormed as quickly as I could with my cane across the lawn to the front door.

"Oh, please use the walkway," Jenna said with a smile then looked up at me. Her face went ashen when she realized it was me she was talking to.

"What the fuck is going on, Jenna?" I demanded and she squeaked, turning and rushing into the house, trying to slam the door in my face. Quickly I stuck my cane out and stopped the door from closing then shouldered it open, pushing her back a few steps.

I walked into the house and dropped my duffle just inside the door, glaring at her.

"Tell me what the hell is going on!" I bellowed at her and she bit her lip.

"You were supposed to be dead," she insisted, swallowing hard.

"What?"

"I was told you were dead!" She insisted, shrilly.

"Who told you I was dead?" I demanded and she shook her head.

"I don't know his name, he called me, was a captain or lieu-tenant or something. Said you had died in the field and they needed your house sold." Jenna explained, swallowing hard. "You've been gone for over a month, Sean! How was I supposed to know you were alive?"

"You could have called me! I still had my cell phone!" Of course I was in and out of consciousness for three weeks and my phone had been at the base in Afghanistan so that wouldn't have worked either, but that wasn't the point. Plus, she had met Speed, she could have called him and asked.

"You were dead!"

"Where's Klaus?"

"She's at my house, when you didn't come back I couldn't very well leave her here."

"I want her back," I told Jenna and limped through the house to the kitchen.

"You can't have her back, she's mine now."

"Wrong, Jenna, that dog is mine."

"Possession is nine tenths of the law, Sean, Klaus is mine."

"You're quoting the law to me now? When we're standing in my house that you're trying to sell illegally?"

"You were dead!" She yelled again, throwing her hands in the air.

"You could have called!"

"So could you have!"

"You're right, in between getting shot in the leg, almost bleeding out when the bullet hit my femoral artery, getting some infection that kept me in a coma for three weeks, almost losing my leg to that infection then a week of getting healthy enough just to travel, I definitely should have called you. You're right, next time I'll remember to call my fuck buddy slash house sitter."

"You're an ass!"

"And you're a liar!" I yelled angrily. "There's no way anyone from the base called *you* to sell my house! Bring me back my damn dog or I'm calling the police. Get that sign off my lawn and cancel any sales contract you might have started."

"There's already an offer on the house," she mumbled sullenly.

"Then you'd better call those people up and tell them they aren't getting it. Conditions have *not* been met since the house isn't FOR SALE!"

Jenna whimpered as though she were actually afraid of me but she knew damn well she wasn't in any danger from me, and not just because I could barely move and she was all the way on the other side of the room.

"Get over yourself, Jenna," I sneered at her, shaking my head. "Get out of my house, get that sign off my lawn and get my dog back here by tonight."

"Klaus is mine now," Jenna insisted, shaking her head. I stared at her for a quick moment then pulled my phone out and called the police. "Who are you calling?"

"The police," I told her just as someone answered on the other end. "Yes, I'd like to report my dog stolen."

"Oh, are you sure your dog has been stolen and not just run away?" The woman on the other end asked, confused.

"I'm sure, the woman who stole her is standing in my living room. She's admitted to taking my dog while I was deployed and is refusing to give her back. She also tried to sell my house without my permission."

"Sean!" Jenna screeched.

"Okay," the woman on the phone said slowly. "I will direct your call to one of our constables, please hold."

"Thank you," I said into the phone then stood watching Jenna as she fumed in front of me.

"Fine!" Jenna seethed and snatched her purse off the kitchen counter then stomped to the front door.

"Go get Klaus first, then take your stupid sign." I called after her, hearing her scream just before she slammed the door.

"This is Constable Holdway," I heard once I was taken off hold. I explained the situation and told the man I didn't want to press charges at this time, only wanted a file with the details of the situation just in case I needed to press charges in the future.

Holdway and I spoke for a few more minutes as I slumped on my couch drinking a beer. Holdway was a veteran as well and we commiserated over the shit we saw and the shit we came home to. At least I didn't come home to find Jenna fuckin' some dude in my bed like he did. I was laughing over something Holdway had said when I heard a car pull up and a door slam.

"I think she's back," I said with a groan as I pushed myself slowly off the couch. Of course, as slow as I was moving, by the time I got to the door Klaus was already there and scratching to get in. "There's my Klaus," I smiled and opened the door, stepping out of the dog's way so she didn't knock me on my ass. "Hey Holdway, thanks for the chat, if I need to I'll be in touch."

"Hey man, anything for you, just ask for me if you need me." I hung up the phone and slowly sat on the floor and hugged Klaus as she climbed into my lap, wagging her stub of a tail so hard her whole body shivered and wiggled.

"I know, girl," I told her, scratching her ears and rubbing her sleek body. "I missed you, too."

I sat there with my dog in my lap and the front door wide open as Jenna fought to pull the for sale sign out of the ground. I could have gotten up to help her but my leg hurt and my dog missed me. And she tried to sell my fucking house out from under me, fuck her.

Eventually I got off my ass because my leg was killing me and Klaus had fallen asleep in my lap, having worn herself out. Jenna didn't bring any of Klaus's things, like food, so I put in a call to the local grocery store and had them bring a big bag as well as a few other things. I made myself something to eat then made sure my dress uniform was pressed and clean for the funeral the next day.

I hadn't been cleared to drive so my truck sat useless in the garage. I'm lucky Jenna didn't try to sell that, too. I called a cab and went to the church. I don't know what I expected but it wasn't a large space full of people. Marty was a good guy, he was my best friend and I loved him but he had changed, his life had gone in a direction I couldn't follow him. I was surprised that he had this many people who cared if he lived or died, though. He had to have an entire life that I knew nothing about.

I walked into the church and stood at the back for a long time, watching and waiting until my leg hurt too much and I had to sit. The service was touching and my heart was breaking for my friend. It wasn't until the procession to leave the church that I saw anyone I recognized. Walking slowly behind the casket and the priest were Marty's parents. And they looked rough.

I don't mean they looked heart broken that their last child was dead, though I have no doubt that was part of it. No, this roughness came from a life of over indulgence in alcohol and other substances.

Using my cane I pushed to my feet just as Mr. and Mrs. Fischer came to my row. My black uniform, though not as eye catching as the white Navy uniform was still a sight to see. Especially with the multiple medals and bars on my left breast and my size. My movement caught Mrs. Fischer's eyes and she stopped to stare at me.

"How could you?" She rasped, glaring up at me with tears in her eyes.

"Ma'am, I am so sorry for your loss," I tried but she was having nothing to do with it.

"You're sorry?" She asked, deceptively quiet.

"Maggie," Mr. Fischer tried, wrapping his hands around his wife's upper arms.

"No, Bill, this bastard is the reason Martin is dead!" She screeched and reached for me. I wasn't sure if she was going to push me, hit me or grab me but I took a step back and lost my balance. My injured leg gave out under me and I fell back into the pew. "It's your fault!"

"Ma'am," I started and tried to push myself up again. "I didn't know Marty was this bad," I said, thinking it was only kind of a lie. "I haven't seen Marty in years."

"Because you left him behind! He was your best friend! He did everything for you and you dropped him like a hot minute the second it suited you!"

"No ma'am," I tried, shaking my head.

"Bill," she sobbed then lashed out and slapped me across the face. It was so quiet in the huge church the sound of the slap and then the resulting gasp of the people in the building echoed around us. "Get me away from this garbage."

Mrs. Fischer spit at me and I stood frozen, looking down at the nastiness that was dripping down the front of my uniform. I blinked, dumbfounded as the people around me shuffled along, leaving the church. When I was alone I sat back down and stared blankly at the front of the church.

"Son?" I looked up to see an older gentleman walking towards me from the front of the church. He was wearing the black clothes of a priest or reverend and he was small in stature. "Were you here for the funeral?"

"I was, yes," I replied, blinking at the empty, quiet building. I don't know how long I had been sitting in that pew but it was long enough for the flowers and pictures and other things to be cleaned away.

"Son, the funeral ended over two hours ago, you looked like you needed some time alone with Our Lord. Are you doing all right?"

"No, Father, but I will be," I sighed and used my cane to push myself to my feet again. I barely bit back the groan as I stretched the stiff muscles in my leg.

"Are you sure, even if you're not religious I am a good listener."

"Thank you Father, but I need to get back home. I've only just gotten back from overseas and my dog is probably going crazy thinking I've left her again." I reached out to shake the man's hand and he smiled up at me. His face was craggy and he was probably older than dirt.

"Anytime you need to talk you come right back." He said and I thanked him for his kindness.

I left that church feeling like my life had finally come to a head. All my choices and decisions had brought me to this point and I had one more decision to make.

It would be the hardest one yet but it would be the one that made the most difference and be the most life altering.

CHAPTER 9

Carol

Seven Years Ago

"Razz, thank you so much for everything," I sighed, sitting at the table in my mom's kitchen. My kitchen, at least it had been for six months or so until I ran out of money and had to sell the house.

Mom had passed away six months ago after a massive stroke. She had left everything she owned to me and Paige. Her funeral had been taken care of and she'd paid for it long before she'd even died. The mortgage was paid off and we really only had to pay the taxes and utilities and while I didn't make a whole lot of money working for the MC, I made more than enough to cover expenses. Even with an eighteen year old daughter.

That is until I went to the doctor because my chest hurt. She hadn't been sure what was going on so she sent me for a ton of tests. The only one that showed anything definitive was the mammogram. I had a large lump in my left breast that so far hadn't spread to my lymph nodes but needed to be removed as soon as possible. With the surgery and the chemo and radiation I wouldn't be able to work and I couldn't keep the house and pay for all of that.

My health insurance would cover most of my medical bills, but without a steady income I couldn't pay for the remainder. I had sat in Razz's office a week before and cried my eyes out, telling him everything that was going on. Karl refused to pay child support after his visitation was revoked and he wasn't working so even maintenance enforcement couldn't make him pay.

"Carol, darlin', you know the MC will do anything for you," Razz told me, leaning back in his chair and sipping his coffee. Over the last few years Razz and I had become friends. He was a good man but he wasn't available for a relationship. He'd made that clear right up front and I promised him it wouldn't be an issue since I wasn't looking for a relationship and probably never would.

"I know Razz, it's just really amazing that you guys are stepping up for Paige and me and her father can't even pay for a new pair of shoes." I grumbled and Razz snorted.

"When do you go into hospital?" He asked and I sighed again, scrubbing a hand over my face then pushed the hair back that had fallen into my face.

"Next week," I told him and dropped my forehead to the table top.

"You decided what you're gonna do?" I rolled my head from side to side, telling him no. I had a few options, I could have just the lump removed, have treatment and hope for the best. I could have a unilateral mastectomy and remove only the breast with the lump, have treatment and hope for the best or I could have a bilateral mastectomy, remove every little bit of breast tissue, have treatment and hope for the best.

"I have no idea," I mumbled and sat back in my chair.

"Have you talked to Paige about it all?"

"Yeah, she said I should do whatever would keep me alive longer." I sighed again, locking my gaze with Razz's. "She made the point that even if I have a complete mastectomy and I hate not having breasts I can always get plastic surgery."

"True, do you care if you have breasts?"

"Right now? No, maybe if I had a man in my life I would consider it but right now I want to not have to deal with it all. And really, it's not like I'm ever looking to have a man in my life."

"I think you've got your answer," Razz murmured, rubbing his hand over his mouth.

"Yeah, I do," I sighed and whined. "The house is sold, you guys have given us an apartment, everything is packed to either move to the apartment or be taken to Goodwill. There isn't really anything left to do but move. And cut my boobs off."

"Carol," Razz scolded and I scoffed a laugh. "Your breasts do not make you a woman and not having them does not detract from how beautiful you are."

"Razz, you don't have to remind me, though I really do appreciate you saying so. You know I would do anything for you," I said, staring into his eyes, trying to make him see that I didn't care about his orientation or who he loved or desired. He sighed and I knew he was remembering the night I made a fool of myself, even after he'd made his position clear.

"Razz," I sighed, blinking back tears. I leaned towards him and kissed him. My mom had just died and for the first time in years I actually wanted to feel something more than cold. Except Razz didn't kiss me back. He had always been thoughtful and caring and while he'd never made a move, what man would say no to a woman who wanted him?

"Carol," he said gently, wrapping his hands around my upper arms and held me away from him.

"Oh, I'm sorry, I just . . . never mind," I said and jumped off the couch, wringing my hands and feeling stupid. "Um, s-stay as long as you want, I-I'm going to bed."

"Carol," Razz said, standing from the couch. He was older than me, but not by much, ten years, maybe fifteen, and he was still in incredible shape. "Wait, it's not what you think."

"Really, Razz, it's fine -"

"Carol, stop!" Razz said sharply and scrubbed his hand over his face. "No one knows this -"

"It's fine, Razz, I won't do it again, you're not attracted to me and that's fine -"

"I'm not attracted to you Carol, but not because you're not attractive -"

"Seriously Razz, don't worry about it, I'm fine -"

"I'm gay!" We both froze and stood staring at each other, me completely stunned as understanding dawned and him shocked and worried about what my reaction would be. "I haven't told anyone, no one knows except for Matt's mom and she didn't care because she didn't want me anyway. Matt doesn't know either and I'd rather he not know."

"I won't say a word, to anyone, I swear," I assured him, stepping towards him. I made the effort to snap my teeth closed and pick my jaw up from the floor. "You know no one will care, right?"

"I don't know that," Razz said, shaking his head. "The Canadian government may not have ever had a don't ask don't tell policy but you've served, you know the shit that's said."

"Yeah, Razz, I do," I sighed and hugged him, resting my head on his thick chest. Eventually he sighed and wrapped his arms around me and hugged me back. "Your secret's safe, Razz. Friends?"

"Absolutely, darlin'."

"Don't start, Carol."

"I'm just saying, I don't mind being your cover if that's what you want." I shrugged and he shook his head, scoffing.

"No, that is not what I want. One day you're going to find a man to love and you'll be stuck with me. I'm not gonna be the one to stand in your way."

"Razz, you know that's not going to happen."

"What I know is that you are going to find a man to love and he's going to help you heal. We're not all bad guys, Carol."

"I know, Razz." And I did know, I just didn't think there would ever come a time when I would want to be intimate with a man, ever again.

I missed it, though. I missed being held by a lover, I missed feeling secure in a man's arms. Hell, I missed sex and there was nothing my BOB could do to help relieve that. It could help give me orgasms but it was cold and impersonal and there was nothing intimate about it. Unfortunately for me, without knowing what had happened, what Tongue had actually done to me, I couldn't move past the attack.

I still didn't remember that night, and I knew I never would, but it still ate at me and made me crazy.

A week later I was sitting in a hospital bed being prepped for surgery. I had made a decision and it was not an easy one. Paige had agreed, though that she would rather have a mom without boobs than no mom at all. So, the bilateral mastectomy it was.

"We'll be here waiting when you're finished," Razz assured me, patting my shoulder and holding Paige against his side.

"I know," I sighed with a smile.

"You'll be fine mom," Paige said, sniffing and smiling through her tears.

"I should be telling you that," I smiled at her and held my hand out for hers. She gave me one last hug and kiss then I was wheeled out of the room and down the hall to the OR. I chose to not bother with either nipple- or skin-sparing since I had no plans for reconstructive surgery at any point in time. I'd discussed all the options with the pros and cons of each with my doctor and that was my choice.

The surgery took just over two hours and I was taken back to recovery to wait for the anesthesia to wear off. Another thing I don't remember a thing about, this time, though I was okay with that. After about an hour, still feeling good from the pain relievers, I was taken to my hospital room. About half an hour after that Paige and Razz came in and sat beside my bed.

"How're you feelin' darlin'?" Razz asked softly, smoothing his big hand over my forehead and pushing my hair back from my face. Smiling sleepily I blinked up at him.

"These drugs are great, Razz," I whispered and he chuckled.

"Mom, you're feeling okay?" Paige asked from the other side of my bed and I smiled up at her, too.

"Yeah, baby, I'm good. Just tired. I'm sure I'll be feeling the pain soon, though." I told her and she nodded. "You have classes tomorrow?"

Paige had started taking business admin classes at a local college and so far was loving it. I didn't care what she did as long as she was happy.

"Yeah but I already talked to my profs so they're okay with me taking the day off." She shrugged and I nodded. Paige was smart, missing one day of classes wasn't going to hurt and if all went well I would be getting out of here on a Saturday so she wouldn't be missing any other classes since she was determined to be the one to take me home.

"Okay everyone," a nurse said as she walked through the door of my room and stopped at the end of my bed. "Visiting hours are over for today," she looked at Paige with a reassuring smile. "Don't worry, we'll take good care of her."

"I know," Paige said and bent to kiss my cheek. Then Razz did the same and they were both gone.

The nurse asked a few questions, explained a few things then left me to sleep. It didn't take long before my body relaxed into sleep and I was out cold again. I slept so hard I didn't even notice when the nurses came in to check on me. I wished I could sleep this soundly all the time. The next thing I remember was the nurse coming in first thing in the morning. It was probably shift change because this nurse was new, and she was angry.

"What the hell are you doing here?" I took a deep breath and blinked because as far as I knew I belonged here. It took me a second to completely wake up and notice the nurse wasn't looking at me. She was glaring across the room and I followed her gaze to find Karl standing by the window.

"I came to check on my wife," Karl said and I frowned.

"Ex wife, Karl," I mumbled then turned to the nurse. "Please call security, I don't want him here."

Thankfully instead of leaving the room to call security and leaving me alone with Karl the woman walked over to the phone beside my bed. I didn't think Karl would actually hurt me, he wasn't that kind of guy, but I was not in good enough shape at the moment to defend myself if he'd changed over the last few years. Okay, I wasn't feeling good enough at the moment to breathe let alone defend myself against a man who was much bigger than me.

It had been a few hours since I'd had any pain meds and I was definitely feeling it now. The nurse must have seen my distress because she reached across me while she spoke on the phone and pressed the button on the morphine pump, sending glorious numbness into my veins.

The next time I woke up Paige and Razz were in the room and another guy I had never seen before.

"Hey sweetheart," Razz said and kissed my forehead again. "How're you feeling?"

"Karl," I whispered and swallowed hard.

"I know," Razz said and grabbed a cup of water with a straw for me. "He's gone, he won't be back and if he tries you'll be guarded."

"K," I whispered and blinked.

"You in pain?"

"Yeah," I murmured and cleared my throat. "It hurts, worse than when I got shot."

"Mom," Paige gasped and Razz and the new guy chuckled. I smiled and winked at Paige then looked over at the new guy. He was handsome, like really handsome, and tall. He had to stand a few inches over Razz's six foot three inch frame. He was also muscled, completely ripped and bald. I'd never really been attracted to bald men before, but this guy pulled it off easily.

"Carol honey, this is Chief Warrant Officer Sean Carter, formerly of the Canadian Armed Forces. Lo sent him out a couple of days ago." Razz said, his gaze shifting from me to Chief Warrant Officer Sean Carter and back to me again.

"Nice to meet you, sir," I said softly and he smirked.

"None of that, just Carter is fine," the big man said and I nodded.

"Carter's gonna be here at night until you're released, make sure Karl doesn't come back," Razz explained and I nodded.

"Thank you," I said and blinked but Carter just shrugged.

"No thanks necessary," he replied then looked to Razz. "I'm gonna head back to the clubhouse and get some sleep before tonight, you all good here?"

"Yeah, we're good, aren't we girls?" Razz asked and I smiled but Paige rolled her eyes.

"Of course we are Razz," she smiled. "It's not like you're leaving, and even if you were all that self defense you've taught me I'm pretty sure I could take dad down pretty easily if I had to."

"Glad to hear it girl," Razz chuckled as Carter said goodbye and left the room.

"What's his story?" I asked, my eyes following Carter out the door then jumping back to Razz. Razz, who smiled knowingly and I rolled my eyes at him. "It's not like that."

"Sure it's not." Razz agreed with a nod.

"Mom, he's super hot, you should go for him." Paige said with a nod and I rolled my eyes. "You're both single and the way he was looking at you he obviously doesn't care about this," she said waving at my chest, or what was left of it. "You haven't dated in so long, he'd be a good place to start."

"Enough Paige," I chuckled lightly then winced at the pain in my chest.

"Come on darlin'," Razz said, sliding his arm behind my back. "The nurses said they want to get you moving around a bit today."

"Oh great," I mumbled, making Razz and Paige chuckle. "Actually, I think I have to pee."

"Excellent," Razz murmured as he helped me out of the bed.

"I'll help you get there and back but if you need help in there you're on your own."

"I'll help." Paige muttered, rolling her eyes.

The rest of the day was spent eating when I could, sleeping most of the rest of the time, chatting with Paige and Razz when I was awake and talking to nurses and doctors. At five when Carter came back, Paige and Razz kissed my cheek and left.

"Do you mind if I eat?" Carter asked, sitting in the corner with a bag of food. Unable to stop myself I took a deep breath and groaned.

"That's just cruel," I mumbled and he smirked. Slowly he reached into the paper bag and walked over to the bed with a small container of fries.

"Still cruel?" He asked, chuckling.

"No, now you're a saint." I sighed and thanked him for the fries. "How did you know these were my favourite?"

"Asked around," he shrugged as he sat down again and started to eat. "I've never been to Winnipeg so I've been spending my free time exploring and since I knew I was coming up here and I've spent time in the hospital I know the food sucks. Everyone said this was your favourite place so I hit it up on my way over."

"Well, I've lived in Winnipeg my entire life except for a few deployments and it took me years to find this place," I replied, munching on a fry.

"Where were you deployed?" Carter asked, sipping his drink.

"Mostly Afghanistan, patrolling refugee camps."

"That where you were shot?"

"How did you know about that?" I asked, suspiciously, frowning at him.

"You mentioned earlier that your chest hurt more than getting shot." He shrugged and I nodded.

"No, we were patrolling out in the field that time. A good friend was shot in the hip and as I was roping into the helo to help her up and in I was shot in the arm. It was just a graze though so it's not like I really know what it's like to be shot," I shrugged then grimaced, regretting the movement.

"Well, I've been shot and I can tell you it hurts like hell."

"When were you shot? Where were you hit?" I asked and watched him hesitate. "Let me guess, you could tell me but then you'd have to kill me."

"Something like that," he chuckled and I smiled, he really was good looking. Even though his head was shaved he still had a beard and full facial hair and it should have looked silly but it was actually very appealing. "I was shot in the upper thigh, nicked my artery, spent time in the hospital in Germany with a raging infection, almost lost my leg."

"Well hell, that's way worse than my little graze," I said, pointing to the slight scar on my upper arm. Blinking he stood and stepped closer to the bed to get a closer look at my arm.

"Mm mm mm," he hummed, shaking his head. "That looks like it was a terribly horrible injury. That coulda' killed ya. Coulda' lost your arm."

I scoffed at him and shook my head. We ate in silence for a little while and then he shoved all his garbage in the paper bag and tossed it in the garbage can by the door. He walked over to me and held his hand out for my garbage then threw it out for me.

"You need anything? Gotta get up for anything?" He asked and I considered it. Yeah, I had to pee.

"This is gonna be awkward," I told him, peering at him through my eyelashes.

"Gotta pee?"

"Yup."

"All right," he said, looking down at my blanket covered legs. "We can do this one of two ways. I can help you to the bathroom, you can do your thing and I can help you back. Or, I can go get a nurse to help."

"Ugh, they're so busy, it could be an hour before they get in here to help."

"All right then," Carter said and helped me toss the blanket off my legs. Slowly and painfully I turned so my legs were hanging off the side of the bed. I stopped, leaning over and breathing hard through the pain. "Maybe you should have taken some meds before attempting this."

"Too late now," I groaned and held my hand out. Carter wrapped his big palm around my hand and wrapped his other arm around my waist, helping me slide slowly to the floor.

"You know, I could just carry you there and back." He murmured and I snorted.

"Doesn't help me get better." I mumbled and this time he snorted. Carter helped me to the bathroom then waited just outside the door while I did my thing. He stood beside me, keeping me steady while I washed my hands then helped me back to the bed. After that I was so damn tired I passed out cold.

Two days later, with no more visits from Karl, Razz and Paige came to take me home. I signed all the release papers, got all of my stuff gathered and made follow up appointments with the doctor. Then Paige helped me get dressed and Razz helped me into a wheelchair and we left the hospital.

The drive to the compound was slow through city traffic and painful but we made it and Carter was there to help out of the truck.

"Should I carry you? Or can you walk?" He asked, looking down at me

"I'll walk," I murmured and he nodded, his big hand warm on my lower back. "Slowly."

We made our way into the clubhouse, an old hotel that Razz had found when he'd first been sent to Winnipeg to open the chapter for Lo. It was absolutely spectacular what he'd done, turning the hotel into an apartment building and adding storefronts in a strip mall in front of the hotel.

I walked through the front doors of the hotel and froze.

"Carol!" Was shouted when I stepped inside and I laughed.

"What is this, Cheers?" I asked with a huge smile.

"Hey sweetheart," Mason said, stepping forward and kissing my forehead. "You're lookin' good."

"Thanks Mason," I whispered, closing my eyes. Mason was a young guy, probably ten years younger than me and he'd been through something truly horrible on his last deployment. He didn't talk about it, ever, with anyone. I'm sure Razz knew about it but only because he was the president.

"Hey Carol, got a surprise for you," Techie, the computer genius of the club said as he lumbered across the room. I blinked up at him and smiled. He had been career military, never married, had no children and only retired because of his health. Techie liked his cigars, whiskey and steak too much. After a couple of minor heart attacks he was advised to retire early. Despondent over losing what he considered his life he went to Kamloops and Lo gave him a new purpose.

"Can you tell me the surprise after I sit down, Techie?" I asked, smiling up at him.

"Oh, of course, Doll," he said and moved so I could shuffle forward. Apparently I was moving too slowly because someone brought an armchair over for me to sit in then pushed me closer to where everyone else was gathered. I laughed but didn't complain.

"All right Techie, lay it on me." I said and yawned.

"Look at this," he said, handing me some papers. I looked but all I saw was a bank statement with no name and a very large balance.

"What is this Techie?" I asked, frowning at him where he sat on the coffee table.

"That is Karl's secret bank account," Techie replied gleefully.

"What?" Paige and I said at the same time, looking back at the paper.

"Where the hell did he get all this money?" I demanded.

"We haven't figured that out yet," Mason said, slouching on the end of the couch beside me. "We're thinking though since we didn't exactly get this information legally we could use it to make him pay your child support. Or at least pay for Paige's college."

"How exactly are you going to do that?" I asked and Mason just shook his head.

"Plausible deniability, sweetheart," Razz said, patting my shoulder. "Come on, you yawn any wider than that and I'll be able to fit my whole fist in your mouth."

"Ugh, Razz, not funny," I mumbled. He chuckled and leaned down, lifting me out of the chair.

"Paige honey, come open your door for me so I can put your mom to bed." Razz said, walking towards the elevator. I snuggled into his chest and sighed. Razz and I might not be anything but friends but everything about him was still comforting.

We stepped off the elevator and he carried me down the hall to mine and Paige's apartment. Just as she unlocked the door a dog barked.

"Who's dog is that?" I mumbled sleepily.

"Carter's, her name is Klaus," Paige said with a smile. "He got the apartment across the hall from us."

"Paige honey can you go tell Carter Klaus wants out?" Razz asked and she hurried away.

"Thank you, Razz," I said, stretching up to kiss the underside of his jaw.

"You know I'd do anything for you, girl."

"I know," I whispered as he set me on the bed.

"Your pills are here beside you, the bottle is open so be careful. Bottle of water right beside the pills, also open, don't spill it." He said and kissed my forehead.

"'K," I sighed and fell asleep.

CHAPTER 10

Carter

I was just coming out of my apartment with Klaus on her leash as Razz came out of Carol's apartment.

"She all right?" I asked, pulling my door closed and pulling Klaus to heel.

"She will be," Razz sighed and scrubbed his hand over his head. I was bald by choice, Razz was steadily losing his hair and it looked like he was having trouble accepting it. What he had left was pretty thick around his ears.

"What's her story?" I asked, wanting to know more about the intriguing woman.

"What do you mean?" Razz asked, frowning up at me.

"She's interesting," I shrugged. "Just wanted to get to know her better."

"She's had it tough, and not just from the ex, keep your distance, she's not looking for anything." Razz warned.

"Not even friendship?" I scoffed and he shook his head. "Oh wait, you're together," I said holding my hands up in surrender. "I'm sorry man, I didn't mean it like that, she really is interesting, I really just wanted to be her friend."

"Whatever," Razz mumbled, shaking his head. "Just be careful with her."

"Absolutely," I told his back as he walked away. "Come on

Klaus, let's go for a run."

Klaus whined and grumbled, telling me she was more than ready for a run.

It had taken me two years to get shit figured out with the armed forces and my injury and physio and so much more. It took months before I could even walk without the cane and even then I still had a lot of pain when I stepped on my left leg. It was frustrating as hell, for me and for Klaus. I had to hire some kid to take her on walks and runs just so she didn't tear my house apart from boredom.

It helped that the dog walker was young and pretty and not actually a kid but a full grown, legally consenting adult. Not only did she not mind me sharing showers with her but she begged me to. Who am I to say no to a pretty lady? Thankfully she wasn't nearly as crazy as Jenna the realtor and didn't try to steal my dog.

She just sicced her wife on me and I ended up being their marriage counsellor. That had been a tense afternoon to say the least. Trying to get dog walker Tracy to explain to her wife Beth that she wasn't satisfied with their sex life and she wanted to try something new. Not the worst day of my life and it ended up with the two of them kissing and making up. Unfortunately they went home for the make up sex and I was alone in the shower once again.

Once I'd finally gotten my discharge papers, sold my house and headed for Kamloops I was so done with Ottawa. Life had been good there, and like had seriously sucked ass there. I was ready for something else.

When my career manager had mentioned the War Angels MC I was intrigued. A group of vets who started a group to help more vets. My career manager had given me the number for the mother chapter and sent me on my way. I'd gone home and called Lo immediately and after talking to him for five minutes I was ready to put my house up for sale and move.

After six months in sunny, pretty Kamloops I was ready to move on. Not because I didn't love it there, but because it was already established. All the important roles had been filled, I wasn't needed there or in Vernon. Lo had given me the choice of any city that had an MC and I thought long and hard about those choices. Calgary, Saskatoon, Winnipeg or Collingwood.

Collingwood was back in Ontario, didn't want that. Calgary was closer but too country western for me. Saskatoon was smack dab in the middle of farm country and they didn't have either a hockey or football team. Important reasons.

Winnipeg it was. I'd never been to Winnipeg and Lo had said for the most part this was a pretty new chapter. The roles were mostly established but there was still some movement in the ranks so to speak. I've been here a week and so far I fucking loved it. I'd been given a job right away and while it wasn't super exciting, sitting in a hospital room watching someone sleep, it was still a job. There was the chance that I could kick someone's ass.

Also, there was something about Carol that piqued my interest. I don't know what it was, her name was familiar but I couldn't figure out why. I knew I hadn't met her anywhere, in all the years the two of us had been in the military we had never worked together but I couldn't put my finger on why I knew her, or at least of her.

Out behind the hotel I threw a ball for Klaus until she brought it back and collapsed at my feet. I laughed at her and crouched down, giving her a rub down. She groaned and rolled onto her back as she panted, showing me her belly.

"She's beautiful," I looked up to see Mason standing beside me. "You train her?"

"Nah," I said, standing. "I got her from the pound but she'd been trained to be a protection dog. She didn't have the killer instinct though so her owners surrendered her. She'll still protect, though, and take down an assailant, she just won't go for the throat."

"Huh," Mason nodded, watching her lay in the grass at my feet. "You like it here so far?"

"Yeah, it's actually pretty great." I said and he nodded again.

"Well, welcome," he said, holding his hand out and I shook it. "Razz said you were interested in Carol."

"Uh, no?" I said, confused. "Her name is familiar is all. I feel like I know her but can't figure out from where."

"Hm," Mason nodded, staring out over the yard. "She's special, you know? We're all pretty protective of her."

"Yeah, I can see that," I mumbled and Mason looked up at me with a smirk.

"It's not like that."

"Not like what?"

"She's not special because she puts out for everyone, she's special like everyone's sister."

"Whoa," I muttered, holding my hands up. "I never said that and I never assumed it. She's with Razz, I get it, I'm not about to over step, like I said, her name is familiar but it's not a big deal."

"All right man," Mason said, clapping me on the shoulder and walking away.

Sighing I shook my head and bent down, clipping Klaus' leash on her collar.

"Let's get to bed, girl." I said and took my dog inside. The party in the main room was still going pretty strong, another difference between here and Kamloops. There was a party almost every night here.

"Hey, Carter! Come have a drink!" Someone yelled but I just waved over my shoulder. I wasn't feelin' it tonight. Klaus and I took the stairs up to our floor and I was just about to go into my place when Klaus started sniffing and scratching at Carol's door.

"Come on, girl," I said, tugging gently on her leash. Then she started barking and jumping up on the door. She grabbed the leash in her teeth and pulled me towards the door. "What the hell, Klaus?"

She barked high and sharp in reply so I knocked on the door. There was no answer but Klaus was not letting it go. Slowly I opened the door and just stuck my head in.

"Hello?" I really didn't expect a reply but the one I got worried me. A low groan sounded from somewhere inside and I slowly pushed the door open farther. "Carol? You okay?"

Klaus yipped and pulled on her leash. Not expecting it I let the leather strap go and Klaus barrelled across the apartment.

"Klaus!" I called softly and went to find her. What I found was Carol sitting on the floor in the bathroom looking pale. She was sitting against the wall across from the toilet and she was curled into a ball, her arms wrapped around her protectively. "Oh hey, you're not looking so good."

"It hurts," she whispered and swallowed hard. I crouched beside her and reached out to brush her hair off her forehead. I was surprised by how soft the curls were and how they bounced back like springs.

"I'm sure it does, sweetheart," I murmured and shifted closer.

"What do you want first? Should I go get your pills then carry you to bed? Or the other way around?"

"I don't know," she moaned and I smiled slightly.

"Well, I'm here now," I said and reached for her. "This is gonna hurt more and I'm sorry, I'll try not to make it any worse than it has to be."

Carol nodded and stayed curled up in her ball. I didn't want to uncurl her so I picked her up and wrapped my arms around her legs and back. She groaned as I stood and I hated the sound.

"Shh, sweetheart, I'm sorry," I whispered into her hair. I carried her into her bedroom and sat on the edge of the bed with her on my lap. I reached over and grabbed the open pill bottle and tipped two into my hand. I put the bottle down and grabbed the water. "Here."

I held the two pills to her lips and waited until she opened her mouth then slipped them onto her tongue. I held the water bottle to her mouth and held it while she drank, swallowing the pills. When she moaned and lifted her hand slightly I pulled the water away and set it on the table again. I held her for a few more minutes as she panted in my arms, slowly relaxing as the meds took effect and her pain lessened a little at a time.

I stood and settled her on the bed, pulling the blankets up and over her then walked out to the living room. Klaus refused to follow me so I left her with Carol and texted Razz. He didn't answer quickly enough though so I called him.

"What?" He barked into the phone and I pulled it away, glaring at it. When I put it back to my ear it was another man's voice I heard in the background.

"Uh, I'm at Carol's, I just wanted to let you know I found her on the floor of her bathroom."

"What the fuck are you doing in Carol's place?" Razz demanded and I heard the other man's voice again. I couldn't hear exactly what he was saying but it didn't sound like this was a drinking buddy. The tone of his voice was softer, gentler.

"I hadn't planned on it," I snapped back, scrubbing my hand over my head. "I was bringing Klaus in from her run and she wouldn't come into my place. She kept scratching and barking at Carol's door. I opened the door and stuck my head in and heard Carol moan, painfully."

"Fuck, where's Paige?" Razz asked and I heard rustling in the background.

"Downstairs, the party is still going strong."

"Go get her, I'm on my way," Razz said and just before he ended the call I heard another man say 'babe'. I blinked down at my phone then shook my head. I didn't care what Razz did in his free time, it was none of my damn business. I went back into Carol's room and found her sound asleep with Klaus laying beside her on the bed, her snout on Carol's stomach as she blinked at me.

"Stay Klaus," I said and she groaned and crawled farther up the bed so her nose was tucked under Carol's ear on the pillow.

Positive that Carol was in good hands, or paws as it were, I left her apartment and hurried downstairs to find Paige. I found her sitting on a member's lap, laughing with a beer in her hand. I stopped in front of them and glared down at the guy who had his hands far too close to where they shouldn't be.

"You old enough to be drinking?" I asked Paige as she looked up at me and sipped her beer.

"Yeah," she laughed then finished her beer. "Legal age is eighteen in Manitoba. Besides, it's only one and it's not like I'm not safe here."

"Right," I grunted and looked down at the guy she was with. He just raised his eyebrows at me and waited. "Your mom needs you."

"Oh shit," Paige exclaimed, jumping off the guy's lap, or at least trying to but he held onto her.

"Wait, where you going?" He asked, and she winced as his fingers dug into her hips harder than was necessary.

"Let go Grinder, my mom needs me." Paige said, pushing his hands away.

"You're coming back though, right?"

"Not tonight," she said, shaking her head but Grinder wouldn't let her go.

"She said to let go," I growled and Grinder scowled up at me but didn't let her go. At least not long enough for her to stand up. Instead he reached up with a hand and cupped the back of her head and turned her face towards him, covering her mouth with his and kissing her deeply. He watched me the entire time as she fought him and the other members whistled and cheered behind me.

"Grinder!" Paige yelled when she finally got free. She hit his chest and smacked his face while he laughed and she hurried away. I glared down at him, not moving to follow her as Grinder smirked up at me. When he turned to fist bump with another member, gloating I struck. Reaching out faster than he could see I grabbed the collar of his shirt and yanked him out of his chair and slammed my fist into his face.

"What the fuck man!" Grinder yelled and a bunch of other guys jumped to their feet.

"You don't fuckin' touch her," I growled in his face. "She told you to let her go you get your fuckin' hands off her."

"I never heard her say no, man!" Grinder complained and I shook him hard.

"She said to let her go!" I bellowed in his face then hit him again and again until he was groaning and limp in my hands. I tossed him back into his chair and turned to face the rest of the members.

"What the fuck is your problem man?" One of the other guys asked and I growled at him, too.

"You think that shit is okay?"

"She didn't say no," the guy shrugged and I saw red.

"She doesn't have to say the word 'no'! She said to let her go, she said she was leaving, she fought him. That's the same as saying the word 'no'!" Holy fuck I was angry, that kind of shit was never okay with me, especially not after hearing about Tongue and the shit he'd pulled and it finally dawned on me how I knew Carol's name. "Next one of you dumb fucks I hear about pulling shit like that with any woman is getting his ass kicked! If you see it and don't step in I'll kick your ass, too."

I turned and stormed away, finding Mason standing across the room with his arms crossed over his chest. He gave me a chin lift and as I passed he clapped me on the back. I hurried up the stairs and pushed my way into Carol's apartment again. I didn't go find Paige yet, though, knowing I needed to calm down before I did. Seeing Carol had a balcony I went outside and leaned on the railing for a few minutes, letting the cool air calm me down.

"Hey," I turned to see Paige stepping out onto the balcony, her arms wrapped around her. "Thank you for coming to get me."

"She all right?" I asked, turning and leaning back against the railing, my arms crossed over my chest.

"Yeah, she's sleeping. Your dog won't leave her, though."

"That's fine, Klaus can stay as long as Carol wants her." I shrugged.

"Klaus?" Paige chuckled. "I thought she was a girl?"

"She is," I shrugged again. "She was already named when I got her."

"I feel so bad, I thought she'd just sleep."

"You don't have to feel bad, Carol should have taken her meds before she went to sleep when she first got back." I told Paige and she nodded. "Those guys down there always act like that?"

"Usually, they don't usually get aggressive like that, though." She shrugged and sat on one of the chairs behind her. "Razz is usually there to make sure things don't get too out of hand, though."

"Hm, yeah I called Razz when I first found Carol. He was - indisposed."

"Hm, Razz has a friend he goes to see sometimes. Never brings her here, though. Always goes to see her and no one has ever met her, not even his son." Paige shrugged. She said 'her' not 'him'. So it was a secret that Razz was gay. Well, I sure as hell wasn't letting that cat out of the bag. Razz was keeping it a secret for a reason, that's all I needed to know.

Paige and I talked on the balcony for a little while longer until Razz appeared in the doorway. He gave me a look I couldn't decipher and gave Paige a head nod. She smiled at him then stood and went inside.

"You gonna take your mutt?" Razz asked me as I followed the two of them inside.

"I doubt she'll come. If Carol's okay with her there just send her over to my place in the morning." I replied and left the apartment. I heard Razz grunt and Paige call goodnight and then I was in my own place. I got ready for bed, flexing my hand and knowing it would probably hurt in the morning but I didn't care.

Now that I remembered why Carol's name was familiar to me that's all that seemed to matter. Speed had mentioned her when he told me about Tongue being charged and found guilty of rape. Carol was one of the women he'd raped. She was the woman Ghost had the hots for, the one who wouldn't give him the time of day.

Knowing that, I understood her relationship with Razz a little better. I had thought at first when I'd realized he was gay and hiding his relationship that he was hiding it from his girlfriend. That him and Carol were in a relationship. The way he doted on her and Paige I thought they were together. Then he'd warned me away from her and I figured for sure they were together. Now though, knowing her history I could see he was no threat to her. She probably knew he was gay, or understood on some level that there was no chance that he would want more than friendship from her.

Either way, my interest in Carol didn't wane. She was a beautiful woman, and obviously strong. Still, I wouldn't be pressuring her into anything, ever. I would never push her to be more than my friend. If she ever wanted more than that I was ready and willing, but any part of our relationship was on her terms.

I went to bed and the next morning opened my door to find Klaus sitting in the hallway panting.

"I took her out," Paige said from across the hall and I smiled at the girl.

"Awesome, thanks hon," I said and rubbed Klaus down. "Was

she good last night?"

"Oh yeah, she never left mom's side until this morning." Paige smiled. "Razz was sleeping in the living room and Klaus went and got him when mom got restless but other than that she was so amazing."

"That's good," I let Klaus into the apartment and she trotted over to get a drink of water then flopped onto her bed by the couch with a groan. I smiled and was just closing my door when Razz came out of Paige and Carol's place.

"Come to my office," he said with a chin lift then walked away. I looked at Paige with wide eyes and she giggled then disappeared into her apartment. Razz went into his own apartment instead of going downstairs so I figured I had time to go to the kitchen and grab some coffee and maybe breakfast. No breakfast, but I did get coffee and an apple then headed around the strip mall to the MC's office.

Carol had been the receptionist until she went for her surgery and her desk was covered in papers and folders and it was a mess. After seeing how spotless her apartment was I knew she'd hate to see her desk like this when she came back. Quickly I scanned through the files and started putting them away in the filing cabinet.

I was just putting the last few papers in order when Razz and Techie walked in with Mason and Grinder.

"You want a job?" Razz asked and I shrugged.

"Figured Carol wouldn't want to come back to work to a mess," I said and he nodded then waved for me to follow him into his office. Techie and Mason followed without a sound but Grinder scowled at me and I was happy to see he had a large bruise on his cheek and jaw. I waited for Grinder to pass then followed them all into Razz's office.

"Sit," Razz said, pointing to an empty chair in front of his desk. When no one else sat I shook my head.

"Rather stand, thanks." I stood with my arms crossed over my chest and my feet shoulder width apart. Razz sighed and nodded to the other three who then sat in chairs around the room. After a moment, my gaze locked on Razz's I, too sat but certainly didn't relax.

"I heard there was an issue last night." Razz began and I shrugged, acting like I didn't know what he was talking about. "We don't allow fighting here between members, unless it's sparing or in the ring."

I shrugged again because there was no way I would have done anything different last night.

"I don't recall a fight," I said clearly.

"Grinder's face says differently." Razz muttered and I shrugged.

"A fight would imply that punches were thrown by both parties. Punches were only thrown by one party. That's not a fight, that's a beat down." I explained and almost laughed when I saw Mason's lips tip up on the corner.

"You fucker!" Grinder snarled and moved to stand.

"Sit!" Razz barked, sticking Grinder to his chair. "Why did you feel the need for a beat down?"

"After I called you about Carol I did what you asked and went to find Paige." I began, knowing I was not in the wrong and having no problem explaining what exactly happened. "She was sitting in Grinder's lap. I told her Carol needed her and she moved to get up. Grinder gripped her hips and wouldn't let her stand. She asked him to let her go and he refused then forced her to kiss him. She shoved him away and jumped up, running to the elevator. Grinder and everyone else in the room thought it was hilarious. I did not. I grabbed Grinder and showed him the error of his ways."

"Is that so?" Razz asked but I just shrugged and he looked at Techie who also shrugged.

"Wasn't there, Prez," he said and Razz looked at Mason.

"It's true."

"That bitch sat on my lap for over an hour, grinding her ass on my dick then thinks she can just run off without following through? So what if I kissed her, after all the teasing I deserved a fuck more than that!" Grinder insisted angrily.

"Grinder you're on probation," Razz sighed heavily. "No parties for a month -"

"What the fuck for?" Grinder demanded, jumping to his feet.

"Don't make me lock you down for that month!" Razz bellowed, silencing Grinder's complaint. "Right now you are still able to go to work and use the common rooms. You keep this shit up and you'll be locked in your apartment for that month with no income."

"I didn't do anything wrong!" Grinder insisted, throwing his hands in the air.

"When a girl says let go you let the fuck go, dude," Mason insisted and Grinder levelled a glare at the other man.

"Get to work," Razz continued. "And stay away from Paige."

Grinder stormed out of the office and I stayed where I was. I'm sure that wasn't the only thing Razz wanted to talk about but I sure as hell wasn't going to start talking first. It didn't take long for the older man to lean back in his chair with a sigh, his bulk making the chair creak.

"That's not how we do shit around here," he said, looking at me with a grim expression. He probably thought he could intimidate me but I'd met much scarier men than him in my time and not backed down.

"No, the way you do shit around here is for the fifteen other men in the room to watch and laugh and do not a fucking thing while a young girl is practically molested right in front of them." I said, sounding lazy even to my own ears. Mason snorted and out of the corner of my eye I saw Techie's eyebrows rise up to his hairline.

"Paige knows what these guys are like," Razz began and I lost my shit.

"Paige is an eighteen year old child!" I bellowed, jumping up from my chair so fast it flew back against the wall by the door. "A child who is a third the size of Grinder! She told him to let her go! That's all that matters!"

"He's right," Mason mumbled and Razz grunted.

"This about Carol? You got your eye on the mother so you protect the daughter?"

"Fuck you!" I spat, breathing heavily. "This has nothing to do with Carol, this has to do with a young girl who should be protected by every single man here, no matter what. Unless this is a 'like mother like daughter' thing for you."

"What the fuck does that mean?" Razz demanded and I smiled, knowing it wasn't a nice smile.

"I remembered why Carol's name was so familiar to me," I told him, leaning over his desk with my fists pressed to the surface. "I remember exactly who Carol is."

"Mase, Tech, get the fuck out," Razz said slowly, glaring up at me. Once the two men were gone and the door was closed

Razz continued. "What the fuck do you know?"

"I was on the same team as the fucker who raped her," I told him slowly. "My first deployment I was teamed up with Ghost and Tongue and their team when their explosives expert was injured. Speed told me about it months later, after Ghost got himself dead. So you tell me, Razz. Why should Paige know what those men are like? Why should she have to worry about those men? Isn't this her home? Isn't she safe here?"

"Sit down," Razz said finally, sounding exhausted. He scrubbed his hands over his face and sighed. I righted my chair and sat back down in it, slouching, no longer tense. "She doesn't want anyone to know, Paige doesn't even know. Me and now you are the only ones who do."

"I doubt that," I shook my head. "The court proceedings were public, are public because it wasn't just CAF members Tongue targeted."

"No one else here knows about it."

"I'll give you that," I shrugged then looked him right in the eye and held his gaze. "I'm very good at keeping secrets."

"What the fuck does that mean?" Razz rasped harshly.

"Not a fuckin' thing Razz."

"So what, you're gonna black mail me now?"

"Nope, I seriously don't give a fuck. I'm letting you know I don't give a fuck and I won't say a word to anyone. It's none of my business and it's none of anyone else's business. If you don't want people to know I won't say a word."

Razz watched me for a few more minutes then sighed heavily.

"Where are you working this week?"

"Where do you want me?"

"Nowhere near Grinder," he muttered and I grunted. "Do you want to work in the mechanic's shop? That's where Grinder is and he's damn good at his job, I'd rather not move him out of there if I don't have to."

"I don't not want to work there but I'm not about to upset the status quo."

"Anymore than you already have."

"True." I consented with a nod. "But that needed to be upset."

"All right, check out the other businesses, see what you like. Can you teach self defense?"

"Yeah," I nodded and he nodded back.

"Do that, for any of the women and men who want it. Most here are trained but not all. Some of them will just want to spar but for some of them getting taken down by a woman will be good for them." I snorted and he nodded again. "That receptionist position is gonna be available soon."

"Why? You firing Carol?"

"No, promoting her to VP, you want that desk out there?"

"Not a chance in hell," I chuckled, shaking my head. "Give it to Paige, isn't that what she's going to school for?"

"More or less," he nodded and seemed to like the idea. "You'd be doing me a favour if you looked after it for the time being, though."

"I can do that," I shrugged, not thinking I was even slightly above doing paperwork or filing. A job was a job, even if I thought it would be boring. Plus, I could talk to Carol more so she could tell me how she did things and I didn't mess up her system.

"Good, now get out of my office."

I snickered but did as he said, going out to Carol's desk and seeing what other work needed to be done. It didn't look like there was much and I figured Carol had probably gotten everything straightened away and cleaned up before she went to the hospital.

I guess now was as good a time as any to get a little on the job training from the woman I was temping for.

I smiled to myself and left the office, jogging around the strip mall and into the hotel.

I probably shouldn't be so excited to talk to a woman with Carol's past and having just had surgery, especially that type of surgery, but I couldn't help it. I'd only known her a week and I could easily see why Ghost was attracted to her.

Now was also probably a good time to come clean about knowing the men from her past.

Just before I knocked on Carol's door I turned back to my place and called Klaus. Klaus was always good at buttering people up and I figured for this conversation we would all need a little buttering.

CHAPTER 11

Carol

Five Years ago . . .

"Carol," Razz said, shuffling past my office on his way to his.

Two years ago he'd made me his VP at the MC and while I'm sure Grinder wanted the job I knew there was no way Razz would give it to him. Not after what had happened with Paige, Grinder was too volatile, Techie didn't want the position and neither did Mason but both agreed I was perfect for the job.

"Come to my office please."

"Sure Razz," I said, jumping up and rushing after him. As I passed Paige sitting at my old desk I raised a questioning eyebrow at her but she just shrugged. Bridge, our accountant was just coming in for the meeting I'd set up with her. "Hey, can we reschedule?"

"Oh, sure," she said with a shrug and a smile. Bridget had just gotten to the MC about six months before. Razz had called Lo in Kamloops and asked him if he had anyone with accounting experience or knowledge since neither him nor I could make complete sense of our books.

Paige had tried, too but there were too many businesses for any of us to do that as well as our other jobs. Within a week Bridge was here ready to take over the money.

"I'll just leave these on your desk."

"Sure, thanks," I said, patting her arm as she set the account books on my desk. I hurried into Razz's office and was suddenly worried.

He didn't look good, he suddenly looked much older than his fifty years. I knew he'd had a doctor's appointment today but he said it was nothing serious.

"Razz?"

"Close the door, Carol." He said gently and I quickly did as he asked. When he pointed at the chair in front of his desk I sat quickly.

"What's going on, Razz?" I asked, sitting on the edge of the chair.

"I, uh, got some test results today," he said gruffly and sniffed and he actually looked like he might cry.

"What kind of test results?"

"You know Robert and I, uh parted ways?"

"Yeah, you told me that a while ago," I said softly, heartbroken that Robert and Razz couldn't still be together. They obviously loved each other and I couldn't think of a single reason why they wouldn't still be together. If Razz understood it he didn't explain it to me.

"I didn't want that, you know? I was ready to stay with him no matter what, no matter how sick he got, no matter who found out -"

"What are you talking about? Robert is sick?"

"AIDS," Razz whispered as a tear slipped from his eye and slid down his cheek. "Or," he sniffed hard, "I guess HIV."

"Oh my God, Razz!" I gasped and jumped up, rushing around his desk and hugging him hard.

Slowly as Razz cried into my stomach he told me about Robert breaking up with him months ago and why. He told me that Robert had advised him to get tested as well, how crushed Robert was that he might have given Razz AIDS or HIV.

Razz told me he'd gone and gotten tested and his results had come back today.

"I'm positive, Carol," he whispered hoarsely into my shirt.

His big hands gripped my hips, hard and I figured I'd have bruises but I wouldn't complain now. My best friend was in unimaginable pain and I wasn't about to step away from him now.

"Razz?" I asked, leaning back to look down at his tear streaked face. "Your tests are positive? As in you're positive for HIV?"

The only response I got was a small nod and more tears.

"Oh God, Razz, I'm so sorry." I whispered and held his head to me again, rubbing his shoulders and petting the top of his head.

"Hey - Whoa, sorry," Carter said as he stepped in the door. I looked up at him as he froze then stepped all the way in and closed the door, locking it.

"Carter," I warned but he shook his head.

"I know the truth, Carol," he said, putting his hands on his hips. "I found out right after your surgery."

"You didn't say anything."

"Why would I?" He scowled down at me and I actually felt like he was disappointed in me. "It's no business of mine who the man loves."

"Sorry," I murmured and curled myself over Razz. "He just got really bad news."

"Yeah, I can see that."

"Razz?"

"Yeah," he grumbled, sitting back and pulling away from me, wiping the tears off his face and clearing his throat. "Fuck, tell him."

"Uh, Razz's partner found out he has HIV, that's why they're not together anymore, Razz just found out he has it, too." I murmured, my hand still on Razz's shoulder.

"Fuck man, I'm so sorry." Carter sighed, shaking his head as he sat in the chair I had jumped out of earlier. "There's treatment though, man. It's not a death sentence anymore. You can still live a long life."

"Matt doesn't know," Razz murmured, refusing to make eye contact with anyone.

"What doesn't Matt know?" Carter asked, frowning. "That you're gay? Or about your diagnosis?"

"Either." Razz growled.

"Jeez, you two really do know how to keep the biggest, life altering secrets from your kids, don't you?" Carter scoffed, sitting back in his chair.

"Carter," I scolded and he rolled his eyes. A couple of years ago Carter had told me he knew Ghost, Tongue and Speed.

He'd told me Speed had told him about what Tongue had done to me and he'd been shocked, not because he didn't think Tongue had actually done it, just that he hid his shit well from the rest of the world.

After that night Carter and I had become good friends and I respected the man immensely. I was also still insanely attracted to him but too scared to act on it. Me not telling Paige about

Tongue was a common discussion for us.

"Sorry," he muttered, rubbing the back of his neck. Carter had also been brought into Razz's inner circle and I guess now I knew why. Between the three of us and Mason and Techie and sometimes Bridge, we were a tight group.

"You've gotta tell Matt," I told Razz, crouching in front of him, holding his hand in mine. "He needs to know."

"I can't tell him," Razz said, shaking his head.

"Why not?" Carter demanded angrily. "You don't think you've kept enough secrets from him?"

"You mean besides the fact he's my nephew and not my son?" Razz demanded, just as angry, his words shocking the hell out of me. "Or maybe I should tell my overly homophobic kid that I'm gay and I have AIDS, you think that'll go over all right?"

"How is he your nephew and not your kid?" I demanded, dropping my knees to the floor. "He looks exactly like you!"

"His dad was my twin brother. He died and Matt's mom asked me to move into their house and help her raise him." Razz explained with a heavy sigh. "Matt knew something was weird but he'd never met me before because my brother and I were estranged because I'm -"

"Gay," Carter supplied for him and he sighed, nodding.

"When Matt's dad died his mom Judith asked me to move in with the understanding that we would pretend I was James but we wouldn't act like a married couple."

"And you were okay with that?" I gasped and Razz shrugged.

"She needed help, at that point I was willing to do anything she needed. She was willing to give me the chance to know my nephew, I never thought I'd ever get that."

"Where is she now?" Carter asked, frowning and Razz sighed.

"A few years later she met a guy and took off. Haven't seen or heard from her since. Tried looking for her at one point but didn't get very far." He shrugged and I looked over at Carter with wide eyes.

"Holy fuck, it's like a fuckin' soap opera," Carter mumbled, shaking his head.

"Carter!" I scolded again and he sighed.

"Sorry," he mumbled and scratched his forehead. "What are you gonna do?"

"I'm gonna die, Carter!" Razz snapped, shocking me and I blinked.

"We're all gonna die eventually Razz," Carter snapped back. "Like I said before, there's treatment for this, and does Matt really have to know all of it? I mean seriously, can't you tell him you're sick and not tell him with what? Hell, does he even need to know you're sick? I know there's a lot of medications involved in the treatment but does he need to see them?"

"Carter, what are you talking about?" I asked, confused.

"Oh come on," Carter scoffed, shaking his head. "You two are the best at keeping secrets from the people you love. You don't think you can keep a lid on this, too?"

"Fuck off, man," Razz mumbled and Carter sighed.

"Just think about it," he said standing and walking over to the door. "It doesn't have to be an immediate death sentence, man. You're stronger than that, better than that. You know I'll do whatever you need me to.

"Hell, you wanna do it and keep it a secret you can hide your shit at my place, ain't gonna bother me none. What will bother me is if you just give up."

With that, Carter unlocked the door and walked out of the office, closing the door behind him with a soft click.

"If AIDS doesn't kill me, Carter will." Razz grumbled and I laughed.

"He's right, Razz," I said gently, my hand tightening around his, resting on his knee. "You can't give up. We'd be lost without you."

"No you wouldn't, Carol," he said softly, reaching out and cupping my cheek, wiping away the tear that had fallen from my eye with his thumb. "You would be just fine."

I turned my cheek into his hand and closed my eyes, sighing at the feel of the calluses on his palm.

"Hey Carol - shit, sorry," Bridge squeaked and backed out of Razz's office, slamming the door.

I looked up at Razz and laughed, knowing exactly what it looked like we were doing with me kneeling behind his desk between his knees and him facing me.

I dropped my forehead to his knee and sighed before turning my cheek and looking up at him.

"I'll make you a deal," Razz said, sliding my hair from my forehead. "I won't give up if you give Carter a chance."

"Razz -" I began and sat up but he shook his head and gripped my hair, holding me still, looking up at him.

"Listen to me. You've been alone too long. I see how you look at him, it's the same way he looks at you. Only difference is his eyes don't hold fear, too."

"That's because I'm scared, Razz." I muttered and stood up, walking around his desk and dropping into a chair. "For good reason."

"Sure," he agreed, nodding. "I know there's a good reason for it, but it's been how long, Carol?"

"I don't know, Razz."

"Don't give me that horse shit," he scoffed at me. "I'm pretty sure you know to the day how long it's been."

"Let's just say it's been about five years," I shrugged and he nodded.

"When are you gonna let it go?"

"How about you promise to fight and I'll promise to think about giving Carter a chance, though I'm not sure why it has to be Carter, why not Mason?"

"Eh, he's too young for you," Razz said, waving his hand in the air and making me snort.

"Thanks a lot," I mumbled. "Now I'm too old for a hottie like Mason? Carter's younger than me, too you know."

"Yeah, but not ten years younger than you, only five."

"Four."

"Whatever," Razz mumbled. "You better go straighten Bridge out, explain our compromising position."

I snorted a laugh and left his office with a smile. I didn't really feel like smiling, but I was.

"Oh stop," Bridget hissed as I walked into my office.

"What?" I asked, confused. I walked around my desk and sat in my chair, grabbing one of the account books.

"Stop!" She exclaimed, reaching for the books. "Maybe you should go and wash your hands first."

"Bridget," I scoffed, rolling my eyes. "That's not what you saw."

"Hey, what you and Razz do in your private time is between you and Razz," she insisted, holding her hands up in surrender. "I'd just rather not have jizz all over my books."

"Stop it," I snapped at her, shaking my head. "That's not what happened. Razz was telling me something sad and I was consoling him, that's all. We're friends, only friends."

"Okay," Bridge said, drawing the word out, obviously not believing me.

"Ugh," I scoffed and rolled my eyes. "Let's just get this done."

Two days later I was walking up the stairs to my apartment, Carter beside me with Klaus, panting at our heels.

"You talked to Razz lately?" Carter asked quietly and I shook my head.

"Not about that anyway." I said with a sigh. "He seems to have decided that it's no longer up for discussion. We made a deal and as long as he's keeping his end of it that's all that matters to me."

"What was the deal?" Carter asked as we got to the landing for our floor. He reached ahead of me and pulled the door open for me.

"He said he would fight and not give up and I would seriously consider something."

"Oh yeah? What are you seriously considering?" He asked with a smirk and I rolled my eyes at him. "Oh come on, tell me _"

BANG!

"Was that -?"

"Gun shot," Carter agreed and rushed up the hall, all joking gone. Klaus barked and jumped around Carter's feet as he tried to get into Razz's apartment but the door was locked. "Fuck! Call 9-1-1!"

I pulled my phone out of my pocket as Carter started kicking the door, trying to get it open.

"9-1-1, what is your emergency?" A woman answered as Carter pulled his own phone out of his pocket and I heard him talking to Mason as he panted heavy breaths. "Hello?"

"Yeah, this is Carol Wilson, VP of the War Angels MC, there was a gun shot here in our president's apartment. We're trying to get inside but the door is locked. Please send police and ambulance right away.

"They're on the way, who should they talk to when they get there?" The operator asked as Carter started kicking the door again.

"Um, Paige, I'll make sure she's at the door waiting for them when they get here. She can show them where to go."

"All right, stay on the line with me -"

"No," I said, swallowing hard. "I'll leave the line open but I'm putting the phone in my pocket."

"Ma'am -" I ignored her and put my phone in the pocket of my shirt as Mason, Techie and Grinder slammed through the stairwell door.

Both Grinder and Mason had sledge hammers in their hands and pushed Carter out of the way. Both men went to work on breaking the lock and the door frame so we could get through the door.

I pulled Carter's phone out of his pocket and called Paige to let her know to expect police and EMTs.

I stood back, breathing heavily as I watched then looked over to Carter who was bent in half, his hands on his knees. I stepped closer to him and put my hand on his back, handing him back his phone.

After a second he stood and wrapped me up in his arms, his chin resting on the top of my head as he swayed us back and forth.

"It's okay baby," he whispered to me over and over again. "It's okay."

Finally the door of Razz's apartment flew open just as the elevator doors slid open and Razz's son Matt stepped off the elevators. I left the guys to hold Matt off and rushed into the apartment just as Razz pushed the blade of his KABAR into his throat.

"NOOOO!!!!!" I screamed at him and rushed forward, sliding to my knees, soaking my jeans in his blood. "No you bastard! You promised! You promised me!"

Razz stared at me as the light disappeared from his eyes.

"Dad?" Matt asked, stepping into the apartment and seeing his dad. He rushed forward and dropped his forehead to Razz's shoulder, crying. "Dad, no!"

"Carol!" I looked up and saw the police and EMTs at the door.

"Come here, Matt," I said, pulling him away from his dad and wrapping my arms around him as he cried. "Carter, tell the EMTs what they need to know."

I said it softly but I'm sure more than just Carter heard me. He nodded though as I pulled Matt with me out of the apartment and down the hall to mine and Paige's place.

My daughter was standing in the hall, her hands over her mouth, tears streaming down her face.

"Come on girl," I said to her, pulling her along with us. She stepped up to the other side of Matt and wrapped her arm around his back, comforting the much bigger boy. Matt may only be sixteen but he was big for his size.

When we got to our apartment I sat Matt on the couch and asked Paige to make a pot of coffee. It wasn't long before Carter walked into our apartment with Mason, Grinder and Techie right behind him.

"Carol, you gotta call Lo," someone said and I jumped up, pulling my phone out of my pocket.

"Shit, hello?" I had forgotten about the 9-1-1 operator.

"Hi, I take it EMTs and police are there?"

"Yes, sorry, thank you for your help." I didn't bother waiting for her response and just hung up the phone.

I quickly dialed Lo in Kamloops and stepped into my bedroom while Paige took my place on the couch. Carter and Techie followed me and I motioned for them to close the door so I could put the phone on speaker.

"Yeah?" Lo said once he'd answered.

"Lo, it's Carol in Winnipeg."

"Got caller ID hon, know who you are."

"Right, I've got some bad news." I said then froze, tears filling my eyes, unable to continue.

"What's going on?" Lo demanded, shifting as his chair creaked.

"Lo, Razz is dead," Carter said, taking over for me. He stepped closer and wrapped his arms around me, holding me tight as Techie took my phone to hold it for me.

"What the fuck do you mean Razz is dead? Is there shit going on there no one told me about? What the fuck are you guys into?"

"It's not like that, Lo." I insisted, sniffing, wiping the tears off my face. I went on to explain to Lo what had happened and what Razz had told us last week. Lo groaned and it sounded like he was hitting the phone receiver against his forehead.

"His kid didn't know?" Lo asked gently with a heavy sigh.

"No."

"I'll be out by tomorrow night." He said and hung up.

"Well that went well," I mumbled and stepped away from Carter, taking my phone from Techie.

"He didn't tell me he had HIV," Techie said sadly, shaking his head.

"You knew he was gay?" Carter asked, watching the older man.

"We served together from basic training on up, hard not to know something like that about your best friend." Techie shrugged.

"It didn't bother you?"

"Why would it? He was still Razz, he was solid, worked hard, always had my back. Best wingman you could ever ask for."

"Did you ever meet Robert?" I asked softly and Techie shook his head.

"Wish I had, though. Razz loved him," Techie sighed and I nodded.

"Carol," Mason said on the other side of the door with a gentle knock. "The police would like to talk to everyone."

"Let's go," I murmured and led the way out of my room.

"Wait," Carter said, touching my arm. "The police need to

know everything, but Razz didn't want Matt to know. I think he needs to know but right now is not the time to find out."

"You're right," I nodded, biting my lip. "Can you take one of the constables out to the hall, or even in here and tell him what happened and why?"

"Yeah, Carol, I'll do that for you." He said and smoothed his knuckle down my cheek. I reached up and wrapped my hand around his wrist and squeezed gently.

Carter smiled slightly, his eyes full of sadness then took my hand and led me out of the room. If Techie saw the moment he didn't say anything.

When we got to the living room I left Carter and went to sit with Matt and Paige on the couch.

"Constables," Carter said, getting their attention. Both men looked up expectantly and Carter pointed to my room. "Can I speak to you both here in the bedroom, please?"

They looked at each other confused but followed Carter into my bedroom.

"Matt honey, how are you doing?" I asked him, gently rubbing his back.

"Fine," he snarled, his hands curled into tight fists. I looked up at Mason who shook his head once and I sighed, not sure what to do or say.

Matt refused to speak after that and because he was still considered a minor the police couldn't really speak to him about his dad's death.

After that the constables spoke to each one of us separately, including Paige who actually knew nothing. Razz's body was taken away and we started planning his funeral.

We had no idea what to do about the MC but since I was the

VP I took over a lot of Razz's work, at least until Lo arrived the next evening.

I called a meeting in the main room and told everyone what had happened. I was surrounded by shocked and sad faces.

"What now?" Someone at the back of the room demanded and I sighed.

"Lo is on his way, he'll be here tomorrow and we'll go from there. We're planning Razz's funeral and we'll let you know details when we have them."

"What about Matt?"

"For now Matt stays here, he's sixteen so as long as he's going to school he doesn't need to be living with a parent or guardian. I'm sure Lo will have more information about that, though." I looked around the room then locked eyes with Carter who winked slowly, letting me know he was there for me.

"Anyway, tomorrow I'm going to call a counsellor for anyone who would like to talk to one."

"What the fuck for?" Someone asked and I sighed heavily.

"It's just for anyone who would like to talk, you don't have to go, it's not mandatory. It is there for anyone who wants it, no judgement, no pressure." I insisted, holding my hands up then walking away, ignoring the grumbling of some of the members.

I knew there were still a lot of people out there who thought mental health was a joke, but there were so many people who needed help. I was the last person to say they couldn't have it and I was the first to make sure they all had what they needed, no matter what.

We were all sitting around my office the next evening when Lo walked in the building. Carter had gone to the airport to pick him up but it wasn't Lo who surprised me, it was the young guy who followed behind him.

"Carol," he said and held his arms out for me. I jumped up and rushed into his arms, letting him hug me tightly. He murmured in my ear how sorry he was for our loss and if there was anything we needed to just let him know. I nodded and sniffed then looked up at the big man with a smile. "I brought you a present."

"Is that so?" I laughed and stepped back, sniffing and wiping my tears away.

"This is Joe Kirkman," Lo said pointing to the young guy standing behind him. I looked the guy over and was kind of surprised. He could not be former military.

The excessive amount of tattoos made that more than apparent. He had that haircut most young guys were getting now, shaved on the sides and much longer on the top and back but the sides of his head were tattooed were swirling silver designs.

Even his knuckles were tattooed and I was sure the ink travelled all the way up his arms under his leather jacket.

"Ma'am," Joe said respectfully, nodding to me.

"Joe came through our youth program and needed a change of scenery." Lo explained and I nodded but I didn't think that was the entire story.

"Welcome Joe, I'll just call Paige so she can show you to a room." I pulled my cell phone out of my pocket and called my daughter, telling her we needed a one bedroom apartment for Joe and a suite for Lo.

The members, of which Joe was now one, lived in apartments on the upper floors if they were living on the compound. Visitors, even important ones like Lo stayed in the hotel suites on the second floor.

"I know it's getting late," Lo said, looking around. "But there are some things I want to get out of the way as soon as possible."

"Of course Lo," I nodded. "You can have my chair or you can have Razz's office."

"I actually need Razz's office, but Techie can you hook up with Seether?"

"Absolutely," Techie said, hefting his bulk off his chair and hurrying into his own office. Lo turned to Bridge and she handed him the accounts books she had sitting her lap. He smiled at her and turned to go into Razz's office. We all followed slowly and sat in chairs around the desk.

"All right, how are you all really doing?" Lo asked, leaning back in the chair and rubbing his fingers over his chin.

"Been better, Lo," Mason mumbled and cleared his throat.

"Yeah," Lo nodded and sighed. "After Carol called I sat down with my guys and we had a discussion. You guys need a president and we didn't want to bring in someone from outside. We agreed that would probably not go over well with your guys."

"I think that's an understatement," Techie rumbled, rolling his office chair into the room.

He tapped a few buttons on the keyboard of Razz's computer and a monitor lit up on the wall. We didn't use it often but it was handy to have. Lo's team in Kamloops appeared on the monitor and they all looked as grim as we felt.

"That's part of the reason I brought Joe." Lo continued but it was just more confusing. "We thought, and we want your input, but we thought one of the people in this room would be best as president."

"What?" We all said at once, looking at each other.

"Not me," Bridge said, holding up her hands and shaking her head.

"Uh, no, Bridge not you." Lo chuckled. "Sorry, I think you would probably make a great president one day but we need you to keep doing what you're doing."

"Oh thank God," she sighed, relieved.

"No, the names put forward were Techie, Mason, Carter and Carol." Lo said with a smile, looking at each of us.

"What?" The four of us demanded, frowning at Lo.

"Techie and Carol, you've been here the longest of the four of you. Techie you already know all the ins and outs and you and Razz were good friends -"

"Don't want it," Techie insisted, shaking his head.

"I know you're still grieving Razz -"

"No, that's not it. He asked me before he died about becoming VP and I refused that, too. He said it was fine since I wasn't his first choice but he had to ask me first out of respect. I told Razz then Carol was the best choice -"

"Techie -" I began but he shook his head.

"Nope, I don't want it," he insisted still more adamantly. "Don't even put my name out there, Lo."

"Okay, well, Razz called and asked who he should have as his VP and I told him one of you four but he said he wanted Carol. I agreed." Lo said with a shrug.

"I don't want it either," Carter said, shaking his head and Mason agreed with him.

"We worked closely with Razz here in the office and he used us as sounding boards but we're not president material." Mason muttered.

"Actually you are but I'm not going to force it." Lo grumbled. "Look, we have to have a vote and we can't have just one name on the ballot."

"Wait, I would make a horrible president!" I insisted, looking around the room.

"Carol, you already run this MC, you ran the MC when you were the receptionist," Lo murmured and my teeth clacked closed. Well hell, that made me sound like a horrible bossy bitch. "It was a good thing, plus Razz was grooming you to take over for him. It was his plan all along."

"What?" I demanded and Lo shrugged.

"I don't think he planned on it happening this soon but that was his plan, him and I talked about it all the time." Lo looked around the room again. "Anyway, I've already had the ballots drawn up. I'm expecting some blow back over this, not because Carol's on the ballot or that she's the best option but because I know there's a small group here who will be backing Grinder."

"Oohhh," Bridget mumbled and Lo nodded as she bit her lip.

"That gonna be a problem for you?" He asked her and she shook her head quickly.

"Grinder is a great guy," she said then looked up at Carter when he snorted. "He really is, he told me about what happened between him and you over Paige, he's changed a lot since then, he told me he was in the wrong and he even stopped drinking after that, but you're right, Lo. He would not make a good president.

"He's a spectacular mechanic and a good person but leading an MC is not where his strengths lie."

"Agreed," Lo said and Techie and Mason nodded. "I saw that when Grinder was in Kamloops and there's nothing wrong with that and as far as I know Grinder doesn't want the position but someone called me and nominated him so I need to put his name on the ballot."

"Someone called you about this already?" I demanded angrily. "It's been a day!"

"I know," Lo said, holding his hand up in a placating manner. Up to this point the guys in Kamloops had been silent.

"There was another nomination you should warn them about, Lo," Axle said, his voice coming through loud and clear on the speakers.

"Yeah, at some point last night, I don't even remember what time because it was the middle of the fucking night and he woke me up, then Matt called me and asked me what he needed to do as president of the club." Lo explained, scrubbing a hand over his face.

"I'm sorry, what?" I demanded, dumbfounded. "He's sixteen!"

"I know," Lo sighed and looked up at the screen. "Even if he was of legal age he wouldn't be considered as president. He's not former military, he didn't go through our youth center or our rehab facility. He's a wild card but he wants that position and seems to think he should inherit it as Razz's closest living relative."

"Is he on the ballot?" Carter asked, incredulously.

"No," Lo said, shaking his head. "I explained to him it wasn't possible for the very reason I told you. He wasn't happy about it and hung up on me."

"Fantastic," I sighed, rubbing my fingers over my eyes and slumping in my chair.

"Carter, Mason, Carol and Grinder are on the ballot and I had Seether print the ballots on special paper so they can't be manipulated or forged. Only members get a vote, so Paige and Matt and other employees or the like don't get a vote. We'll do it in the morning and we should have the results by afternoon."

"All right, Lo," I sighed, shaking my head.

"Go get some sleep you guys," Lo said and we all stood. "We'll discuss the rest tomorrow."

"Of course," we all filed out of the office and I went back into mine. I slumped in my chair and laid my forehead on the desk.

I didn't expect Carter to walk in right after me and close the door behind him. When I looked up he was walking around my desk and pulling me out of my chair.

"Carter," I sighed, shaking my head.

"Shut up, Carol, I need to hold you."

"Mmm," I sighed and dropped my forehead to his chest, resting my hands on his sides as he stood and held me tightly.

"Tell me," he said after a moment and I binked.

"Tell you what?"

"Tell me what your end of the deal with Razz was?"

"Doesn't matter, he didn't hold up his end of it."

"Tell me." Carter insisted and I sighed.

"He made me agree to think about giving you a chance."

"Giving me a chance for what?" Carter asked, holding my

cheek to his chest so I couldn't look up at him. I don't know if that was for me or for him.

"For more than, this. More than friendship." I whispered, biting my lip.

"And, have you been thinking about it?"

"Carter, I haven't stopped thinking about it since you first walked into my hospital room." I told him, pulling back to look up into his eyes.

"Have you come up with anything?"

"Just that I'm scared as hell."

"Hm," he hummed and pulled me back into his arms. "We'll just start here then."

"What do you mean?" I asked, confused.

"I'm a patient man, Carol. I want you, I've wanted you since I first saw you in that hospital bed -"

"Carter, that's ridiculous, I'd just had my breasts removed and I looked and felt like shit."

"Shut up, Carol. I don't care about your breasts, I care about you."

"You won't be saying that when you see the scars." I muttered and he grunted.

"You just said when, not if. So you have come to a decision, that's good. I plan on this seduction of mine to take a few years. Don't worry Prez, I'm not going anywhere."

Carter bent and kissed my forehead then left the room as quickly as he'd come, leaving me even more confused, and scared, than before. But he also left me feeling warm and safe and secure.

As if I wasn't confused enough.

CHAPTER 12

Carter

Today was Razz's funeral. Razz had stipulated in his will that he did not want to be buried in the National Military Cemetery but he did want a CAF presence at his funeral. A military chaplain came to Winnipeg as well as a bugler, and a bagpiper. There was also a seven man escort available but Razz chose to have MC members as his pallbearers, or at least as the escort for his cremains.

There was a large group standing around Razz's grave, all former and current military members wearing dress uniforms. It was a sea of black, white and blue uniforms as well as suits and women in dresses. Razz had been cremated and the box that was his urn sat on a pedestal in front of his tombstone. Because the tombstone had military information on it the military escort had brought it with them.

I stood by Carol, my new president, as she tried her hardest not to cry. I wanted to put my arm around her but I knew she wouldn't appreciate it, that she would prefer to be consoled in private, especially now as president she wouldn't want to show any kind of weakness. On her other side was Paige who held her hand and cried freely and held handfuls of tissues.

It was a week since the vote and Carol had won by a landslide. Lo had been right to put the ballots on special paper. There had been quite a few added that were not on the special paper that had Grinder's name selected. When asked about it, Grinder himself said he had voted for Carol and didn't know about the extra ballots. Mason and I got a few votes each but nowhere near as many as Carol did. It was a bittersweet victory and one that I knew Carol wasn't so confident she should have won, or wanted to win.

When the funeral was over we all stood at attention and saluted Razz one last time. Afterwards Carol and I turned to face each other and sighed. She sniffed and I nodded, reaching out to pat her shoulder. She blinked and looked around then froze. Only because I was so focused on her did I notice the change and followed her gaze.

Across the cemetery, on the edge by the parking lot was a man, standing all alone. Carol looked up at me with a question in her eyes and I shrugged.

"Go," I said, urging her to go and talk to who I was sure was Robert. "I'll get Techie."

Carol nodded and turned, walking slowly towards the lone figure. By the time I got Techie's attention Carol was standing in front of the man. We walked up just as she hugged him and he cried on her shoulder as they held each other. Robert noticed as Techie and I stepped up behind Carol and he stepped back, wiping the tears from his eyes.

I held my hand out to shake his and he blinked at me for a moment.

"Sean Carter," I said as Robert reluctantly shook my hand.

"Lyle Connor," Techie said, also shaking Robert's hand.

"John spoke of you all fondly," Robert said, sniffing again. "He loved you all so much."

Robert was not what I had expected. He was obviously well off, probably very successful. He was dressed like a businessman who was very comfortable wearing suits and ties on a regular basis. I had expected that Razz's lover would be rougher around the edges, more like Razz himself had been.

"You should have come over," I said gently and Robert shook his head.

"Matt," Robert said with a sniff and shook his head again. "John said he didn't know, about a lot of things."

"You were important to Razz, Robert," Techie said with a shrug. "Matt didn't need to know why or how."

"I appreciate that," Robert nodded, his eyes filling with tears again.

"How are you feeling?" Carol asked gently and Robert shrugged.

"As well as can be expected I suppose," he sighed. "Sometimes the treatment is worse than the illness, you know?"

"Yeah I do," she whispered and reached out to hold his hand. "Will you please keep in touch? Let us know how you're doing?"

"Yeah," he said with another nod and a sniff.

"What's your number?" I asked, pulling out my phone. He told me and I sent him a quick message. When I saw him smile I knew he'd gotten it, probably felt his phone vibrate in his pocket.

"I appreciate this you know," he whispered, swallowing hard. "You should be angry with me, you should all hate me. I killed him."

"You didn't kill him," Carol insisted, shaking her head as her eyes filled with tears again. "Razz had a chance but he was scared. This wasn't your fault, please understand that."

"He was just so - big, like larger than life," Robert scoffed and wiped another tear from his cheek. "When he, when we first started dating I thought he was insane. How could the big rough biker be into me, you know? I was just me."

"How long were you and Razz together?" Techie asked gently and Robert smiled.

"We met right after he moved here to run the MC." Robert nodded, his lips thinning. "I'm sorry he kept you all in the dark."

"We knew, Robert," Carol said softly, still holding the other man's hand.

"I've known Razz going on thirty years, I've known for at least twenty-five of those years that he was gay." Techie explained with a shrug. "I knew about you but Razz didn't want you to feel uncomfortable with a bunch of asshole bikers and vets. He was more worried about you and Matt than he was about any of us."

"How is Matt?" Robert asked, looking at each of us.

"Angry," we all said at the same time and Robert nodded.

"Well, I'm sure you're all busy," he said and reached to shake all our hands again. "Thank you for coming to talk to me."

"Razz was family," I said, reaching out to grip the man's shoulder. "And he loved you, that makes you family."

"We understand that you wouldn't feel comfortable at the MC," Carol said nodding, agreeing with me. "But please keep in touch with us, please let us know how you're doing. And if there's anything you need, at all please let us know."

"I will," Robert said sadly, nodding again. We were doing a lot of nodding. "I haven't had family in a long time, John was my family. I really do appreciate this."

None of us said anything more as Robert turned and walked back to his car. Carol lifted her hands and wiped a few stray tears from her cheeks then turned back to the group still standing by Razz's grave.

"Holy fuck, today sucks," I sighed and Carol chuckled. She reached out and slid her hands into mine and Techie's and then we walked back to the grave. We stood beside Lo as he talked to Mason and a few other guys, Joe standing silently next to him, looking pretty good in his suit, even with his copious amounts of ink. His eyes though were locked on Paige where she was standing a few feet away talking to Bridge. Interesting.

As I watched Joe he turned his gaze to mine but the expression on his face didn't change and I began to wonder what his story was. I also resolved never to play poker with him.

That night, after the party to celebrate Razz's life and I had taken Klaus out to run off her excessive amount of energy I went up to my apartment, planning on getting some sleep. I had a shower and pulled on some underwear just as there was a knock on my door. Sighing I pulled some sleep pants out of my drawer and pulled them on, too. When I opened my door I was surprised to find Carol standing in the hall.

"Uh, I couldn't sleep," she said, looking up at me then held up a bottle of Jack Daniels. "Drink?"

I didn't answer, just stepped back and held my hand out, giving her room to step past me. She walked into the kitchen, looking around at my place as she went. I wondered what she saw. My place wasn't homey and warm like hers. She had decorated her and Paige's apartment making it comfortable and welcoming. I just had a leather couch and a huge ass tv, not even a kitchen table and my bedroom had a bed and a dresser. Spartan, utilitarian, military chic.

"Glasses?" She asked and I pointed to a cupboard behind her. She turned and pulled down two glasses, not small ones, either but I mostly had beer glasses because that's usually what

I drank. She opened the bottle of Jack and poured three fingers in each glass and handed me one. "To Razz."

"To Razz," I agreed, speaking for the first time since she knocked on my door as I tapped the rim of my glass to hers then took a drink, swallowing it all in one gulp. Carol hissed and gasped as the fiery liquid slid down her throat then set her glass carefully on the counter. "How're you holding up?"

"Uh, definitely been better," she sighed, not making eye contact. I poured a little more Jack in each of our glasses then took both to the couch, knowing eventually she would follow me. She might still prefer to have the counter between us but I wasn't giving her a choice this time. I set her glass on the coffee table and sat on one end of the couch.

She did follow and sat on the far end of the couch but didn't reach for her drink. I sipped my whiskey for a few minutes, watching her but she seemed content to wait me out.

"What's going on Carol?" I said finally and she swallowed hard then reached for her glass and slammed back three fingers of whiskey in one gulp.

"Gah!" She gasped, panting as she gripped the glass until the alcohol settled. Sniffing and sighing she set the glass back on the table and slumped back into the couch. "I looked in the mirror today."

She'd whispered it so quietly I almost didn't hear what she said.

"Carol, you wear makeup, you do your hair, you look in the mirror everyday." I murmured, confused and she shook her head.

"I look at my face in the mirror, I look at my hair in the mirror, once I'm dressed I look at my clothes in the mirror," she explained and shifted on the couch, pushing up to sit again and leaning her elbows on her knees, her hands buried in her hair. While she sat there, fighting with something I really looked at her. I loved looking at Carol but this time was different. I loved seeing her shiny brown curls, the way they floated around her face and no matter how many times she tucked her hair behind her ears it wouldn't stay off her face.

I loved that even at forty she had a smattering of freckles across the bridge of her nose and how her gray eyes sparkled when she was smiling or laughing. Even when she was angry her eyes flashed. Even when she was in pain after her surgery her eyes were never dull. Her skin was completely unblemished except for those cute freckles that I wanted to connect, kissing each one. Carol was a beautiful woman and I loved that she was taller than average, standing probably close to five foot ten.

I loved that when I held her in my arms, against my chest, she fit against me seamlessly.

"What did you look at in the mirror, Carol?" I asked gently. I stayed frozen, not daring to move in case I spooked her and she stopped talking.

"I stood in my bathroom," she began again, her face still hidden from me. I'd give her that for now. "On the back of the door is a full length mirror. I almost had it taken down and taken away. I don't know why I didn't but it was still there. I stood there with my eyes closed and took my shirt off."

"Carol," I said, confused. "It's been years since your surgery, you haven't looked at your scars at all since then?"

"Not like this," she sniffed, shaking her head. She sat back and rested her head on the couch, closing her eyes. "I looked at the drain, I made sure the scars weren't infected, I did first aid type stuff but it wasn't on myself."

"It was on you."

"It was on someone else," she insisted, shaking her head. "I looked today, I saw it all today."

"What did you see, Carol?"

"Scars," she gasped, sniffing again as tears tracked down her cheeks, slipping from the corners of her closed eyes. "I'm not..."

"What are you not?"

"There's nothing feminine left," she whispered harshly then began to sob quietly, pulling her knees up and curling around her legs, burying her face in her knees. I let her cry for a second then couldn't take it anymore. I put my glass down and moved, lifting her into my arms and sitting with her in my lap. "Carter -"

"Shut up, Carol," I muttered and held her tight. I didn't relax my hold until she had relaxed and then she couldn't stop the tears. Eventually the tears slowed and she relaxed even more.

"You're always telling me to shut up," she murmured thickly.

"That's cause I don't want to hear you say stupid shit," I told her, gripping her hip. Thankfully she laughed and didn't hit me but the laughter didn't last. "Why now?"

"I don't know," she shrugged and sniffed and I smacked my hand on her thigh.

"Don't lie to me, tell me why."

"Razz told me I had to give you a chance," she began, swallowing hard. "How can I expect you to accept this when I can't?"

"Carol, I accepted all of you, missing parts and all, years ago." I told her roughly. "I don't care about that, but if it matters to you then do something about it."

"You say that now," she scoffed, pulling away and standing up.

She walked around the coffee table and glared at me. "You say that now when it's covered up and you can't see what it really is, but what about when we're in bed. When we're naked and there's nothing there? You're telling me it won't bother you? That you won't look down at my chest, expecting to see tits and getting scars instead?"

"You said when," I said, pointing at her.

"Carter!" She growled and I smiled.

"If you think it's going to bother me so much then take your shirt off."

"What?"

"Seriously, take it off."

"No!"

"Carol, the only way to not be surprised is to prepare. So prepare me for this so that when you and I are naked in bed I won't be surprised when I look down expecting to see tits."

"Carter that's just ridiculous!"

"No it's not!" I insisted, pushing up from the couch. I walked around and took her hand. "Let me show you something." I wrapped her hand around my hard, aching cock and stared into her eyes. "Feel that? That has nothing to do with your tits. Take your shirt off."

"I need my hand back," she mumbled and swallowed hard. I let her go and waited, not quite as patiently as she watched me then slowly started to lift the heavy sweatshirt she was wearing. She pulled it over her head and dropped it to the floor, leaving her completely bare from the waist up.

I won't lie and say her scars were beautiful, because they weren't. They were scars, but they didn't detract from Carol's beauty. I stared into her eyes for a long moment as she panted in front of me then slid to my knees, resting my hands on her waist. Carol quivered in front of me but I wouldn't let her go, even though I could tell she wanted to bolt.

Reaching up I kissed first one scar, then slowly the other. I slid my hands up her back, forcing her to bend slightly so I could reach more and I licked across one of her scars before drifting down the center of her torso to her flat belly. I flicked her belly button with my tongue then nipped it with my teeth and stood up again.

I took Carol's hand again and wrapped it around my still hard and aching dick, smiling slightly when she gasped and her eyes widened in shock.

"It's not your breasts I want, Carol, it's you." I rasped and bent, covering her mouth with mine, kissing her roughly, sliding my tongue into her mouth. It took her a second but soon she was kissing me back, her hands gripping my biceps. I kept one hand spread on her upper back while the other tickled down her spine, causing her to shiver until I was cupping her ass and pulling her harder against my cock.

Carol whimpered and lifted a hand, cupping the back of my head and holding me to her.

"Carter," she whispered and I shushed her.

"Relax, Carol," I told her and kissed her again. "We're not making love tonight, but we will, when you're ready."

"Carter," she sighed and reached up to kiss me again. I obliged, happily, holding her naked chest against mine, her small hands on my scalp making me shudder.

"We're taking this really, really slowly," I told her as she frowned. "There's more going on here than just your scars and your mastectomy. You might have forgotten, but I didn't. I know about your past and I won't rush you into anything

159

you're not ready for."

"You might be incredibly disappointed because I don't know if I'll ever be ready for anything if you don't take the lead." She whispered, swallowing hard.

"Then I'll wait," I promised her and her eyes slid closed. "Come on."

I took Carol's hand and pulled her to my room.

"Carter -"

"It's okay, Carol." I told her and kept walking. When she was standing beside my dresser I opened a drawer and pulled out a t-shirt then slid it over her head, covering her. I unbuttoned and lowered the zipper on her jeans then pushed them down her legs and crouched in front of her, helping her step out of them. "Just sleep, Carol."

"Just sleep," she murmured and followed me to my bed. I pulled the comforter down and she crawled in then lay flat on her back, staring at the ceiling. If she wasn't so nervous I would have laughed but I didn't want to hurt her feelings.

I slid in beside her and lay on my side, staring at her. She turned her head to look at me and blinked.

"Can I hold you?" I asked gently and after a second she nodded. "Turn on your side and move back into me."

Carol did as I said, facing away from me and scooting back until her ass was pressed into the cradle of my hips. And yes, my still hard as fuck dick. She froze slightly but didn't move away.

"Lift your head a bit," I said and once she had I slipped my arm under her so she could use my bicep as a pillow and slid my other arm around her waist, pressing my palm flat over her stomach and chest. She froze again but quickly relaxed. "Go to sleep, Carol, I got you."

She nodded and her hair tickled my nose a bit but then she settled even more. Wrapping her arms around mine across her chest she relaxed even more until she was breathing heavily and deeply.

I knew the exact moment the next morning when she woke up. She tensed slightly and her breathing changed. I kept my breathing steady and my muscles relaxed as she slid out of my bed. I listened as she grabbed her jeans off my floor and pulled them on then rushed out of the room. When I heard the door of my apartment open and close I rolled on my back with a heavy sigh and stared up at the ceiling.

One step forward, two steps back.

Knowing I would never get back to sleep after that I got up and went to have a shower. When I left my room I found Carol's sweatshirt on the floor where I had dropped it. I picked it up and smelled it, inhaling her unique scent then sighing heavily. I folded the sweatshirt and put it on the arm of my couch to give it back later.

I went and had a shower then got dressed and went down to the kitchen. I had some food and coffee in my apartment but it was just easier to eat downstairs. When I got there, Lo was sitting at the table drinking his own coffee.

"Mornin'," I said and poured myself some coffee. He grunted a response and I sat across from him.

"My flight leaves in a few hours."

"I'll drive you to the airport." I said and Lo nodded.

"Now that Carol is president, who do you think her VP should be?"

"Mason -"

"I don't want it," Mason grumbled, walking into the kitchen behind me. I scoffed a laugh and shook my head.

"Why him?" Lo asked, ignoring Mason's denial.

"He's been here longer than me, he knows this place a little better. He's an officer, I'm a grunt."

"You served longer, you were deployed more often, you're smarter -" Mason began.

"You have a closer relationship with Carol." Lo finished and I scowled at him.

"Carol and I are friends." I insisted.

"No," Mason said, shaking his head as he sat at the table with his own coffee. "Carol and I are friends. You and Carol have a deeper connection, like she had with Razz."

"What about Grinder?" I asked, desperate for anyone else to take the job. "Or Techie."

"I've spoken to Techie," Lo said with a sigh. "The same reasons he didn't want to be president still apply. And the same reasons Grinder couldn't be president still apply."

"Mason's still the best option," I insisted but both men shook their heads.

"Are you resistant because of your relationship with Carol?" Lo asked gently and I bit my lip, watching him closely.

"Carol and I are friends." I insisted again.

"At the risk of growing a vagina," Lo grumbled, shifting in his seat, "We're going to talk about relationships here. Are you in love with Carol?"

"I love Carol, yes," I said with a shrug because that was true. "Could be in love with Carol if given the chance."

"Are you dating?"

"Not at this time."

"Sleeping together?"

"Define sleeping together."

"Sex."

"Not at this time."

"But you've slept together."

"Once, she was upset, we shared a bed." I reached up and scratched the scruff on my jaw. "I don't feel comfortable discussing Carol like this."

"This won't get back to her," Lo promised, shaking his head. "I don't consider her weak because she gets upset or cries or needs a shoulder to lean on. She's human, we all need that once in a while. But I understand that she will feel the need to put forth a strong front."

"It's not a front," I declared sharply and Lo nodded.

"Carol is one of the strongest people I know," he told me and I relaxed a little, knowing he had her back as much as I did. "She'll do an excellent job here but she needs someone who will support her and not undermine her."

"Mason."

"Yeah," Lo chuckled, shaking his head as Mason rolled his eyes. "Mason will do that, what I meant was Grinder won't work because he'll listen to his buddies at least on some level and undermine her even if it's not on purpose."

"What you want is someone who wants the MC to succeed as much as they want Carol to succeed." I told Lo and he nodded. "Then you want Mason, because I don't give a shit about the majority of the people here anywhere near as much as I care about Carol."

"I can see that, however, in order for Carol to succeed the entire MC needs to succeed. You're a team player, you had to be if you were JTF 2. Carol only succeeds if the team succeeds and you will make that happen."

"What if Carol doesn't want me for her VP?"

"That's up to her," Lo shrugged, tapping his fingertips on the table. "But you're who I'm going to suggest."

"Is this an order?"

"Does it have to be?"

"Fuck," I swore and scrubbed a hand over my head. Growling I pushed to my feet. "I gotta go walk my dog."

I left the kitchen and stormed up to my apartment, slamming inside. Klaus jumped off her bed, completely ready to come to the rescue.

"C'mon, Klaus, let's go outside," I grumbled and she hopped forward, nudging me with her head. I chuckled at her and grabbed her leash. Whether I was thinking ahead or not, I had put on sweatpants and running shoes so instead of throwing a ball for her in the back yard I took her for a run. It was still early and the streets were deserted. The coffee shop in our strip mall was just opening for early commuters but I didn't stop to chat.

Klaus and I ran past and while I had her leash in my hand I didn't bother snapping it on her collar. She was too well trained to run off and she didn't like wearing it anyway. We ran for a good hour before my mind started to wander, telling me I had worked through what it was that was bothering me. I would stay focused on whatever the issue was long enough for me to work through it then my brain would move on.

My biggest issue was if I was VP and Carol was President there would be no chance for a relationship between us. I hadn't come to a conclusion. I didn't know if we could be more than friends if we had to work so closely. I didn't know if she would allow that, but I knew I would do anything for her. I knew that if she wanted me as her VP but not as her lover, boyfriend, husband, paramour, consort, whatever, I would give her that but I wasn't sure I could ever move on.

I would have to have that discussion with Carol and only Carol.

As I ran I saw a flash of black fur and knew that Klaus was checking something out in the trees along the side of the road. I heard her bark just as I was ready to turn and go back.

"Klaus! Come on girl!" I called and heard her bark again. This time I whistled sharply through my teeth and called her again. She still didn't come so I stepped into the tree line and called her again. "Klaus!"

Another step past the treeline and I called her name again, but this time I was answered with the snarling and barking of multiple dogs. There was some yipping and then a dog cried out in pain.

"Klaus!" I bellowed and ran through the trees. It didn't take long before I was in a clearing, surrounded by coyotes. "Fuck!"

Making as much noise as I could I ran towards Klaus where she was laying on her side. My size and the noise I was making, yelling and waving my arms, frightened the small pack away. I knelt beside Klaus as she whimpered, her breathing laboured.

"Oh baby," I whispered and petted her head. I bent and kissed her then as carefully as I could I lifted her into my arms. "Come on girl, let's get you to a vet."

I stupidly hadn't brought my phone with me. I hadn't

bothered to take it down to the kitchen and then after talking to Lo I had been distracted and had forgotten it. I'd gotten soft apparently because that was something I never would have forgotten before knowing I'd be this far from home.

Klaus whimpered and cried the entire way back to the club-house. Running for an hour meant close to twice that walking quickly with a heavy dog in my arms, bleeding all over me. When I finally got to the MC I pushed into the office and found Paige at her desk.

"Paige, I need your help!"

"Holy shit, Carter," she exclaimed, jumping up from her chair.

"I need a ride to an emergency vet, Klaus was attacked by coy-otes," I panted and stood waiting as Paige grabbed her keys, phone and purse. She led me to her SUV and I slid into the pas-senger seat. We drove through the city until we came to a vet she trusted and parked in the lot.

I jumped out of her SUV and rushed inside, not even bothering to close the car door.

"Help me, please!" I begged as I pushed into the clinic. After that things moved quickly. Klaus was put on a gurney and wheeled away and I was left in the waiting room. Paige came in after texting Carol and letting her know why she'd disap-peared so quickly then sat with me and helped me fill out the paperwork.

It was an hour before the vet finally came out, a tortured, sad look on her face. The second I saw her I knew Klaus was gone.

"I'm so sorry," she said softly, tears gathering in her eyes. "She'd just lost too much blood and there were too many injur-ies for me to close up before she'd bled out."

"Aw fuck," I sighed and leaned forward, resting my elbows on my knees and burying my face in my hands.

"I'm really sorry I have to ask this now, but you said this was a coyote attack? Could you tell me where it happened? The city needs to keep track of the wild animal population, especially when something like this happens." The vet said, wringing her hands.

"Uh, I ran for about an hour," I mumbled, inhaling deeply and sitting back in my chair. I cleared my throat as I thought about my run. "I wasn't running full out, it was more a job for Klaus to have a run and me to clear my head so, maybe five, six kilometers north of the compound."

"Compound?"

"The War Angels MC clubhouse." Paige answered for me and the vet nodded in understanding.

"I noticed Klaus had run off into the trees -"

"She wasn't on a leash?"

"Not then because there were no people around and she's really well trained. If she takes off into the trees she pops back out again within a couple of feet." I explained, swallowing hard and the vet nodded again. She sat beside me and I could tell he wanted to hold my hand but I didn't want that from her. "Uh, when Klaus wouldn't come back I went looking for her, I walked maybe a hundred feet into the tree line and came to a clearing. When the pack saw and heard me they took off. By then Klaus was almost gone."

"All right, I'll let the appropriate people know." The vet said, patting my arm. "Again, I really am sorry about Klaus, she was a beautiful dog and you obviously loved her and took care of her."

I nodded, because I really didn't know what else to say.

"Um, I'm really sorry, but there is a charge for Klaus today." A very quiet little woman said from the desk.

"Fuck, I forgot my wallet," I sighed, and rubbed my hand over my head.

"I got it," Paige said, grabbing her purse. "I'll put it on my credit card and you can pay me back when we get back to the clubhouse."

"Thanks Paige," I said and she squeezed my shoulder then walked to the desk. Within minutes we were back in Paige's SUV. Thankfully Paige chose to stay quiet as she drove and soon we were back at the clubhouse. I didn't speak to anyone, I just ran up the stairs to my apartment. I hadn't noticed before but I was covered in Klaus's blood.

I stripped and threw my clothes in the garbage and stepped into the shower, turning the water on as hot as it would go. I stayed there as long as I could, letting the hot water soak into my stiff muscles. I leaned my elbows on the wall and let the water splash down my back.

"Carter?" I didn't turn, I didn't move, I didn't even open my eyes. It was the feel of her hands on my back that made me move. I turned, blocking the too hot spray from her and blinking down at her.

"What -?"

"I'm so sorry," she whispered and stepped against my chest. She wrapped her arms around my waist and pressed a kiss to my chest and then my throat.

Groaning I wrapped my arms around her and held her tightly, burying my mouth against her shoulder. I shuddered against her as her hands smoothed up and down my back.

"I'm so sorry, I'm so, so sorry," Carol murmured. I was trying so hard not to cry but dammit I couldn't stop the tears that slipped to her shoulder. I just hoped she didn't notice with the heat of the shower. "Come on, you clean?"

"Yeah," I whispered and sniffed.

"Let's get you to bed." I nodded and turned, flipping the water off then reaching out and grabbing a towel. I turned to dry Carol off but she wasn't even wet so I used to towel to dry myself and wrap it around my hips. I took her hand and helped her out of the bathtub and bent, grabbing her t-shirt I pulled it over her head then took her hand again and led her to my room.

I pointed to the bed and Carol slid into the bed. I pulled on a pair of underwear, tossing the towel into the hamper then turning to the bed.

"It's barely noon," I told her and she just held her hands out to me. Sighing I slid into the bed with her and pulled her into my arms again.

"We don't have to sleep, we can just lay here together." She said, kissing my chest and my throat. I hugged her so tight that she groaned but didn't make me let go. "Tell me about her."

For the next three hours we laid in my bed and talked about Klaus. Carol let me lay there with her and talk about my dog.

"I have to ask you something else," I said softly as her fingertips traced my abs.

"I talked to Lo, I know he wants you to be my VP," she said, cutting me off. I sighed heavily and tipped my head to kiss the top of hers. "I agree with him, you would make the best VP, for me and for the MC."

"I disagree but if that's really what you want I'll do my best."

"But you still have reservations."

"I'm worried that if you want me as your VP you won't also want a relationship," I sighed, combing her hair back from her face with my fingertips. "That's why I was on that run, I needed to think it through and I had just come to the decision that I needed to come and talk to you about it. I can't be your VP if it means you won't give me a chance."

"Are you able to keep those two positions separate? Can we be lovers without messing up our working relationship?"

"People do it all the time, Carol."

"This is a strange situation though, this isn't just a regular job." Carol insisted and I sighed. "If I look weak these guys will kick my ass. I won't be able to keep control."

"Loving someone doesn't make you weak," I told her gently. I wrapped her up tighter and rolled to my side, burying my nose in her throat. "I can help you be strong, I can support you in any and every way you need."

"If it doesn't work? If we don't work?"

"We can't tell the future, baby. All I know is that I will do everything to make us work, both of our lives, and I will do whatever you need me to."

"Even keep us a secret for a little while?"

"For as long as we have to, as long as you don't shut me out."

"Ditto."

"Ditto," I whispered and kissed the top of her head again.

CHAPTER 13

Carol

It was hard to believe it had been five years. When I looked up and saw Lo's boys walk into my office I was hit with the shock of five years. Five years as president of the War Angels Winnipeg MC, five years with Carter as my VP and more, so much more. More importantly he was my friend, my love, my everything.

He was the most patient, kind, wonderful man I knew. He never pressured me or pushed for more than I was ready to give him and if he was frustrated with me he never showed it. We didn't spend every night together, most nights yes, but some nights I couldn't sneak down to his place or he couldn't sneak up to mine. We were still keeping our relationship a secret and only partly because I thought it was necessary. Now it was as much routine as it was necessary.

Unfortunately Lo's boys weren't here for a happy reason. When the boys had been here before they had come with information about a missing family member. Bexton, the niece of a member in Kamloops had disappeared, only she wasn't just a niece of one member. She was the niece of the club's doctor and the club's attorney. She was the step-daughter of another member and the ex-girlfriend of Drew Winters, Lo's youngest son.

Bexton was found, pregnant and unconscious, laying in our hospital in a coma. When they'd found Bexton they'd also found Jordyn. She'd been here for a few weeks and the only person she really talked to was Elli, Bexton's sister. It was pretty obvious that Jordyn had been through a lot and she was traumatized completely. Mason was trying to make friends with her but so far she was only interested in his kids.

Kids he didn't even know he had until they were dumped on our doorstep not quite a year ago. Their mother had been a one night stand and she hadn't told him she was pregnant. He also didn't know she was barely legal and when she got into an accident on the way to the hospital while in labour, she ended up hemorrhaging and dying during surgery. Her parents tried to raise her twins but they were older and couldn't keep up any longer. The twins were a year old when they were brought to the MC.

It had been a crazy five years to say the least.

Now Jack was back with Hank and Bull and a new guy, Trick. A new computer genius to take over where Techie left off. Because Techie had died, been killed and we were trying to find his killer. That's why Jack had brought Trick. The plan was for Trick to stay, hopefully, and take his place with us here in Winnipeg. Unfortunately Trick was making me crazy. He called me on all sorts of things, making me question myself and every decision I had made and after being here just a month I wasn't sure him staying was what was best for me even if it was best for him and the MC.

"Hey, Caro," Carter said, walking into my office, frowning down at his phone. He had started calling me Caro a few years ago because he couldn't call me baby or babe or honey, sweetheart. I liked it but of course everyone else had picked it up as well so it wasn't really just ours anymore. Still, I didn't really mind that because in important moments he still called me Carol. I blinked up at him and waited for him to continue. "Have you heard from Robert lately?"

"Oh," I hummed and picked up my phone. I actually couldn't

remember the last time I'd spoken to Robert. "You know, I haven't." I searched through my messages with Robert and found I hadn't heard from him in a few weeks. "I haven't texted him in weeks, you?"

"No, I sent him a message a few days ago thanking him for the flowers he sent when Techie died, but got nothing back," Carter mumbled, sitting in a chair, his elbow on one of the arms and his ankle crossed over his knee and his thumb rubbing over his bottom lip. I loved that bottom lip.

"You think we should pop over for a visit?" I asked him and his eyes flashed up to mine.

"Really?" Carter asked, surprised.

"Yeah, come on," I said, jumping up and grabbing my purse. "When did you see him last? How did he look?"

"Not great but he was in good spirits," Carter said, following me out of my office.

"Paige, we'll be back in a bit." I called to her with a wave. Carter walked around to the driver's side of his truck and winked at me over the hood. We climbed into his truck and buckled up. "You know, we could have taken your bike."

"Not when it's this cold," he scoffed and I smiled, he was right, it was almost Christmas.

"So, why did you start shaving your head?" I asked, something that I had always wondered but had never asked. Now seemed like as good a time as any. He must have thought I was a little weird, given the look he gave me as he drove but I remember the response to the question of why he'd never had kids and I wasn't sure I wanted to hear about another sex-capade in the mens bathroom.

"It was just easier than getting it cut all the time," he shrugged and smiled. "My hair always grew super fast and it was annoying, especially once I joined the forces so a year or two in I started shaving it, it was just easier and cheaper since my hair is so thick I didn't have to buy shampoo anymore."

"I wish I could see what you look like with hair," I smiled at him and he shrugged.

"I'm sure I could find a picture somewhere," he said and flicked on his turn signal. "Or I could just leave it for a couple of months, I'd have a pretty full head of hair then."

"Is it the same colour as your beard?"

"Mostly, except maybe the gray," he chuckled and I smiled. "Is that what you want?"

"Maybe, honestly I like your bald head so it doesn't matter to me." I shrugged and he smiled again, nodding. He reached across the center console and took my hand, kissing my knuckles. He held my hand as he drove and I twined my fingers with his. "I love you, Carter."

He didn't respond at first, just stared out the windshield with a smile on his face. Then he nodded and turned to look at me.

"I love you, too Carol." We drove for a few more minutes then pulled up to the curb in front of Robert's house. His car was in the driveway and the lawn was mowed and tidy like it usually was. Even since he's been sick he's paid for someone to take care of his yard, his house was always neat and clean. His nurse's car was in the driveway as well so we know he at least wasn't alone.

I sat and stared at the house, worried about what we would find inside. I waited for Carter on the sidewalk then slid my hand into his as we walked to the front door. He squeezed my hand then knocked and we waited. I stared up at his handsome face but he looked straight ahead at the door, a secret smile tugging on his lips. When it opened we were greeted by

Shelley, Robert's nurse.

"Oh hey, guys," she said quietly and stepped back so we could step into the house.

"Hey Shelley," Carter said, bending to kiss her cheek. "We were just saying we hadn't heard from Robert in awhile and thought we'd come see how he was doing."

"It's not good, guys." Shelley said sadly, wringing her hands. "He's really taken a turn for the worse and he made me promise not to call you until after."

Shelley looked to the living room where a hospital bed had been placed so he wasn't stuck in the back of the house in his bedroom. In the living room he could watch the kids ride by on their bikes in the summer or the birds flying by, the sunshine.

"He's got a cold that I think is going to turn into pneumonia or worse." Shelley blinked at the tears filling her eyes. "I think this is it."

I reached forward and squeezed her arm then hurried away to Robert's bed. He was there, his eyes closed and his breathing was laboured. I sat beside his bed and held his hand gently in mine. I sat quietly for a second, just looking at the gaunt, shadowed face of our friend. I sniffed and wiped a tear from my cheek and smiled when I felt his hand twitch.

"Standing out there talking about me?" Robert rasped, harshly. He coughed weakly then opened his eyes slowly. His pretty blue eyes were cloudy and tired but he smiled at me.

"We haven't heard from you, we came to check on you," I told him quietly.

"You brought that giant hunk of man meat?" Robert rasped and wiggled his eyebrows at me.

"You know I did."

"Maybe this will be the day he finally gives me a show."

"Ever hopeful," I chuckled.

"You know seeing all of this would be too much for you," Carter said, sitting in a chair beside me. He cupped his hand over Robert's knee and shook him gently. "How're you feeling, old man?"

"Who you callin' old?" Robert asked, pretending to scowl. "And I'm telling you now it's not all of your hotness that's gonna kill me," he tried to take a deep breath and ended up coughing hard, barking as he tried to clear his lungs. "It's gonna be this pneumonia. It's not just a cold anymore, that was a few days ago."

"You can still fight this," I told him and he scoffed, winking at me.

"Nothing to fight sweetheart. I'm glad you came today and not tomorrow. I would have missed you tomorrow."

"No, Robert," I whimpered, biting my lip and he nodded.

"It's true, and it's okay, I'm tired." He whispered, squeezing my hand. He was so weak I barely felt it. "I thought I didn't want you to come and see me like this, but now I'm glad I get to see you one more time. I'm a selfish man you know. I want you to do me a favour, just one more."

"Anything for you, Robert," I whispered and let the tears slide down my cheeks. I didn't care at this point who saw me or who thought I was weak. This man had become one of my very best friends, my confidant, even the father that I had lost so many years ago. I sat closer, and brushed the backs of my fingers over his temple and he closed his eyes and sighed.

"I want you to stop holding back," he whispered, opening his eyes again and pinning me with a look full of love. "This giant hunk of man meat loves you."

"I know he does," I sniffed and hiccoughed as Carter gripped the back of my neck and I knew he was hurting just as much as I was in that moment.

"But do you understand what his love means?" Robert asked. I blinked at him and shook my head slightly. "It means you are his everything, he gives you his everything, it's time to give him yours."

"Robert, you can't die yet," I whispered, leaning forward even more and smoothing his hair back from his face.

"Sweetheart, it's past time," Robert whispered back with a slight smile. Slowly he lifted his hand and cupped my cheek. He was so weak and I hated seeing him so sick. I cupped my hand around his and kissed his palm. "Say goodbye."

"I don't wanna." I whispered, tears not just tracking down my cheeks, now they full out flowed, unchecked.

"You gotta, I love you girl," Robert said and I huffed a laugh and dropped my forehead to his. Only Robert could remind me of Razz at this moment.

"I'm an old woman," I whispered, with a sob.

"You're a baby to me," Robert smiled and sighed. "Say goodbye, I don't know if I can."

"I love you Robert," I whispered and pressed a kiss to his forehead.

"I love you, girl," he whispered, closing his eyes with a heavy sigh. Carter wrapped his hands around my upper arms and helped me stand then walked with me out of the room. Shelley hugged us both, promising to let us know about funeral arrangements, and then we were on the front step and Carter had me wrapped in his arms.

I sobbed against his chest, losing myself in my sorrow and still he held me tightly. He held me together before I could shatter and fall apart.

"Come on baby," Carter said, kissing the top of my head. "Let's get you home."

By the time we got home I had gotten myself under control enough that I could walk through the main room to the elevator without making a scene or drawing attention. Thankfully there were only a few people there anyway and only Mason noticed me. Carter must have given him a nod or something because he whispered to Jordyn then left her with his kids and followed us onto the elevator.

No one said anything as the car rose and I didn't even notice when we got off on the third floor instead of the fourth. Carter took my hand and led me to his apartment and into his bedroom.

"Give me a minute," he said to Mason who grunted in response. Carter stood me beside his bed and took my purse, dropping it on his dresser and pulling out one of his t-shirts. He pulled off my coat and shirt and tossed them on a chair in the corner then pulled on his shirt and helped me out of my jeans.

"Carter," I whispered but he shook his head.

"It's okay, Carol. You need to rest, today sucked and you need some time, take it. I'll talk to Mason then be right back." He said, pulling the blankets on his bed down and urging me under them. I sighed and crawled into the bed, wrapping my arms around Carter's pillow. He tucked the blanket up to my chin, kissed my forehead and left the room.

I thought about what Robert had said before he told me to tell him goodbye. I thought about him wanting me to give Carter a chance. He wasn't the only one who wanted me to give Carter a chance. I know Paige did, too. She'd mentioned many times that Carter would be so great for me and she wasn't wrong. Carter was great for me. He was gentle and loving and during times of intimacy he was giving and patient.

We hadn't had sex yet, there were too many things that held me back. It wasn't just the scars that replaced my breasts, it wasn't just that I no longer had breasts. It was also that night with Tongue. In a way it helped that Carter had known Tongue, that he'd immediately believed me when we talked about it, and we did talk about it. I told him that I'd thought it was Ghost and he'd laughed and said when Speed told him he'd have thought it was Ghost before Tongue, as well.

I'd been to therapy, regularly, once a month I spoke to someone about all of it. Carter encouraged me to do that, too. He even came once in a while. At one appointment I'd gotten frustrated with his patience. What man would wait five years to have sex with a woman he loved? What few things we did couldn't possibly be satisfying for him and I demanded to know if he was getting sex somewhere else then felt guilty for being angry about it. Of course then I felt angry at myself for feeling guilty.

He'd scoffed at me and told me only with his hand in the shower. I demanded to know if he watched porn or went to strip clubs but he just shook his head. While I liked his answer I was still frustrated with him but he didn't change, he didn't get angry and he didn't demand more than I was ready to give him. The next meeting with my therapist was just as painful because then we had to discuss the previous one without Carter there and I was lost. I was heartbroken thinking maybe he just didn't like sex. My therapist had laughed at me when I said that, shaking her head.

"There is no way in hell that man doesn't enjoy sex," she said pointedly and I nodded.

I thought about Robert again and my eyes filled with tears. I didn't want to lose him, too. I wasn't sure I could deal with that. He was our last link to Razz, the real Razz. Matt was still here, everyone called him Tease now, but he was so not like Razz. He was almost the exact opposite of the man I knew. Razz was gone, Techie had just died, Matt was an idiot and now Robert was dying as well.

It wasn't long before Carter was stepping into the room and sliding onto the bed behind me, pulling me against his chest. Wrapped in his thick arms against his solid warmth I felt safe and cherished. He kissed my ear and smoothed my hair back from my neck.

"Are you okay?" He whispered and I nodded, sniffing.

"I will be, anyway. I'm just going to miss him so much."

"Yeah," he sighed and snuggled his nose into my throat again. "Me too."

Before I could stop myself I shifted onto my back so I could look up at him. He was so beautiful, dark eyes surrounded by thick lashes, his lips were full and soft. His face was masculine and while he shaved his head, his beard was thick and dark. I knew he kept it trimmed and tidy and loved sifting my fingertips through it.

While I studied his face he studied mine and I watched as his lips widened in a small smile.

"What do you see?" He asked gently, his deep voice rumbling out of his chest.

"Perfection," I whispered and he scoffed.

"No, that's what I see," he told me and my gaze snapped to his. I slid my hand up over his shoulder and wrapped it around the back of his neck, pulling his head down to mine. I lifted slightly to meet him part way and gasped at the feel of his lips on mine. His mouth always felt amazing, no matter where he chose to put it on my body.

I wrapped my hands around the bottom of his t-shirt and started pulling it up until it bunched under his arms. He grunted when my hands wrapped around his sides, smoothing down over his abs and back up to his pecs. Carter reached behind his head and pulled the shirt off, tossing it to the floor. When his mouth came back to me he licked up my neck and sucked on the sensitive skin just behind my ear.

I wasn't finished though and attacked the button and zipper on his jeans. He pulled back slightly, watching my hands down the length of our bodies.

"What are we doing, Carol?" He asked, looking up at me, his gaze locking with mine.

"I need you," I gasped and lifted my head, licking his throat and making him groan. Carter bent his head and covered my mouth with his, licking into my mouth and tasting all of me. I moaned and arched, pushing my hands under the waistband of his jeans and pushed them down his hips.

"Caro -" Carter gasped and sat back, pulling the blankets away from me. His hands slid to my hips and pulled my panties off, tossing them on the floor with his shirt. He shoved his jeans and underwear off and climbed back onto the bed, hovering over me. His big palm was cupping my ribs and I knew he wanted to slide it up over my chest but he wasn't pushing me to accept more just yet.

I ran my hands up and down his naked back and shivered, loving the feel of his skin under my hands. His naked legs rubbing against mine and his bare cock nestled against the core of my body. Carter shifted and drew his knee up, pushing my legs wider. I gasped at the sensation, so foreign but at the same time familiar and missed. His hand cupped my ass and the back of my thigh as he stared down at me.

"Carol, are you sure about this?" He asked, breathing hard and holding himself back even though I know he was so ready he was probably in pain.

"Yes, please, Carter," I begged and he dipped his head to kiss me again. Still he didn't move to slide inside of me and I started to worry that he really didn't want this. Then he moved away and reached into the drawer of his nightstand. I thought he was reaching for a condom and was going to tell him not to bother but instead he pulled back a bottle of lube. Sitting back again he flicked the cap open and squeezed a liberal amount out into his hand then coated his huge dick with it.

When he was glistening with the extra moisture he cupped my pussy with his hand and rubbed some of the lube into me as well. He slid two fingers into me and rubbed his thumb over my clit. My eyes rolled back into my head and my neck arched but I didn't stop him. As much playing as we'd done over the years this wasn't something we did often but it felt amazing.

"Carter," I moaned and panted and he pulled his fingers from me, lining himself up and sliding his big cock into me slowly.

"Open your eyes," he demanded, his teeth clenched and my eyes immediately popped open. "You see me." He said, pulling out and slamming back in. "Who's in you right now?"

"You are," I whispered, swallowing hard, having a hard time keeping my eyes open, loving the feel of him over me, between my legs, in me.

"What's my name?"

"Carter ... Sean!" I cried as he continued to pull out and push back in, swivelling his hips on every downward stroke, rubbing his pelvic bone against my clit. His hand drifted down my side again and gripped my hip, holding me tight to him as he pounded into me. I was so close to orgasm I whimpered when he slowed down and leaned back, pulling me with him.

When he'd pulled me all the way up to sit in his lap he continued to thrust up into me gently, slowly and riding him this way was just erotic.

"I want your shirt off," he whispered and I shook my head hard, my eyes wide. "I want to feel your skin against mine."

"Carter, it's ugly," I insisted and instead of disagreeing with me he kissed me hard, mimicking with his tongue what his cock was doing.

"Nothing about you is ugly," Carter declared and slowly lifted my shirt. I froze and tensed, tightening every muscle in my body but he soothed me. "Shh, I got you baby," he whispered, kissing my face, my lips, my neck and when the shirt was gone he kissed my shoulders and my chest, continuing to roll his hips into me. It was just enough friction against my clit and inside me I was beginning to orgasm again. "Unnnhhh, baby."

Carter's hands were flat against my back, holding my chest to his, then they were full of my ass, helping me ride him, then they were gripping my thighs. Never still his hands slid up my front, drifting over my scars but not stopping until they cupped my neck and he was kissing me again. Still kissing me, Carter's hands drifted back down over my chest, his fingertips tickling before sliding back around my back and up over my shoulders.

As he held me to him he continued to thrust his hips up into me, rubbing my clit with his body, his thrusts harder and faster, grunting until I couldn't hold on any longer and I arched my back as my orgasm took over my entire body.

Carter wrapped his arm around my waist and laid me down on

the bed, still thrusting until the last, solid push, locking himself inside me as he exploded, filling me and prolonging my own orgasm.

I gasped and squeezed him with my inner muscles, loving the sound of his low groan as he stretched out over me then fell to the side, pulling me with him.

"I love you," he panted into my hair and I sniffed and nodded. "I love this body, all of it."

"I love you, Carter."

We were silent for what felt like hours but was probably only about ten minutes. Carter had rolled to his back, pulling my front against his chest and pulling my leg over his hips.

"How did you know?" I whispered, not thinking he would misinterpret my question.

"Because I know you," he said, trailing his fingertips up and down my arm.

"You knew I would need lube because you know me?" I asked, confused. "Do I act differently when I'm dry?"

"Oh, that, no," Carter chuckled and smacked my ass. "I did research. I looked up anything and everything about mastectomy's and sex after and a lot of women experience dryness. Having a mastectomy for a lot of women puts them right into menopause."

"Oh," I muttered and settled back down. Then realizing he thought I'd meant something else I sat up again, glaring down at him. "What did you think I meant?"

"Uh, pretty much everything else," he shrugged, smugly and I rolled my eyes at him. "But especially your shirt. We'd never been together before your mastectomy so I didn't know if your breasts were a huge part of your sexual satisfaction or if it was more about the rest of your body."

"I did like it when my breasts and nipples were played with," I said slowly, softly.

"Hmm," Carter nodded and squeezed me to him again. "For some women it's a big deal. Anyway, I figured since you've said before you needed to feel my skin I figured you'd want to feel all of me over all of you."

"Huh, you were right, it was very sensual." I murmured, blinking, thinking about all the things we'd done over the years. "All these years you've been learning me."

"Yup, and it was so fucking worth it," he muttered and I frowned.

"What does that mean?"

"It means, making love to you is a spectacular, momentous thing and I want to do it over and over again every single day, multiple times for the rest of my life." Carter informed me and I was left speechless again.

I pushed on his chest and sat up, looking down at him feeling frustrated.

"How the hell did you wait so long?" I demanded, feeling at odds.

"Because I love you," he shrugged as though the answer were obvious.

"Oh come on, you never had sex with anyone else, you never watched porn, you never went to a strip club. You said yourself the only relief you got besides the little bit that we did was with your own hand in the shower."

"This is true."

"How did you not explode?" I asked, throwing my hands in the air. "You obviously like sex -"

"Yes."

"You're very good at it -"

"Why thank you," he said with a wide smile and a wink, making me roll my eyes.

"Jacking off in the shower could not have been satisfying for you for the last five years!"

"Eight."

"I'm sorry, what?"

"Eight years, not five."

"Eight years?"

"You hadn't had sex in longer than that." He shrugged and I just shook my head.

"Yeah, but I was raped and I'd had my breasts removed and the meds I was on killed my libido!"

"All right," Carter said, pushing to sit up against the headboard. "The last time I had sex was a week before I moved here. I was friends -" he bent his fingers into quotation marks "- with a woman at the Kamloops MC. We knew we weren't going anywhere and we both just needed a release. It was mutually beneficial but we knew it had an end date. When I moved here I met you and was ... intrigued."

"Intrigued?"

"I knew I knew you from somewhere, or at least your name -"

"Tongue."

"Right, but that's not why I held back, when we met you'd just had surgery, that's why I waited. I knew I couldn't just come on to you full force both because of Tongue and because of your mastectomy so I waited. I also thought you were involved with Razz but only for a week or so. Once I knew you weren't with him I started to gentle you into a relationship. Then you were made president and I made it very clear what I wanted."

"But you still didn't get sex."

"No, I didn't and yes it was frustrating but like I said, it was worth waiting for and I knew that all along."

"How did you do it, though? How did you wait?"

"You may have noticed over the last five years, I've put on about fifty pounds of muscle."

"What?" I demanded, looking down at his body and getting lost in the landscape of muscle. Carter had always been heavily muscled but now he had so much more. He used to be built like Chris Pratt from the first Guardians of the Galaxy movie but now he was built like Arnold Schwarzenegger from Conan the Barbarian, only with a nice rug on his chest.

"Seriously, when I wasn't with you or working, I was either working out or running," he said, then shrugged. "Or jacking off in the shower."

"Why aren't you mad?"

"I was," he sighed heavily, reaching out and taking my hand in his. He twisted our fingers together and I had to move closer to him. I had to touch more of him. "I was so angry for so long but not at you."

"Who were you mad at?"

"At first? I was mad at Tongue, actually I'm still mad at Tongue and if I ever see that bastard again I'll kill him slowly. But then I was mad at cancer and that's stupid, it's not a person, it has no feelings, it was doing what it was designed to do by who or whatever designed it. It's destructive and hateful and horrible and I hate it. Cancer is evil and you never should have gotten it, but I can't take my anger out on cancer."

Carter lifted my hand and kissed my knuckles, rubbing his thumb over the kiss and smiling lightly.

"I most definitely couldn't take my anger out on you, I love you, if I took my anger out on you I'd never have a chance with you. So, I took my anger out on dumb bells and weight bags and anyone dumb enough to spar with me. And when I just needed to think I put on my running shoes and I ran."

Sniffing and sobbing again I crawled up into his lap and wrapped my arms around his shoulders. I buried my face in his neck and cried.

I cried for five lost years, I cried for lost friends, I cried for everything we could have had that I hadn't been able to give him. Things that I was too broken to let go.

I could only hope that he forgave me.

CHAPTER 14

Carter

Three days after our visit to Robert his nurse Shelley called us to let us know he had passed away. Carol was heartbroken, as was I, but we couldn't grieve, not yet.

Just as she was hanging up the phone with Shelley a man walked into the office. He was very average looking, light brown hair, brown eyes, clear complexion. He wasn't very tall but he wasn't short, either. On his left wrist he had a very expensive watch and on his right ring finger was a large diamond ring. It was actually pretty tacky. He was also wearing a very expensive suit that probably cost as much as my truck when it was brand new. Even his shoes and over coat were expensive.

"I must speak to your president," he said to Paige who tried to smile but I could tell she was getting the nasty vibe this guy was putting off.

"I'll see if she's off the phone," Paige replied and gestured to a chair. "If you'd please sit?"

This guy sneered at the chairs and turned back to Paige.

"No, go get your president, now. I will not ask again."

Paige blinked at the man but didn't move from her chair. Any other woman would probably have jumped up and scurried away, rushing to do what she was told. Paige wasn't any other woman and she would not be intimidated by this guy. Instead, I watched from my desk as she turned her head and started yelling.

"CARTER!!! THERE'S SOMEONE HERE TO SPEAK TO THE PRESIDENT!"

I smirked as she turned back to the guy in front of her who was probably seething but she just smiled up at him.

"The president should be with you shortly," she said politely and picked up the phone ringing on her desk. Just as the guy was about to swipe the phone off Paige's desk I stepped out of my office.

"Can I help you?" I demanded, drawing the man's attention. Slowly he glared up at me and unbuttoned his over coat, flicking it off his shoulders for his guard to catch. The other man, much bigger than his boss, caught the coat and folded it over his arm.

"Yes, you and I have matters to discuss." The man said haughtily.

"I thought you wanted to speak to the president?" I asked him, quirking an eyebrow. The man now was fuming and I was enjoying this a little too much. "Well come on then."

I turned and walked towards Carol's office giving Trick a chin lift and whistling through my teeth to get Mason's attention. I walked into Carol's office then bent close to her ear so what I had to say wouldn't be heard by the obnoxious little man.

"This idiot says he wants to speak to the president." I whispered, getting her attention. She blinked up at me and frowned but didn't look at the man I was talking about. "I think Slouch should be here but I don't want her seen by this idiot."

"On it," Trick said quietly, having heard the last bit of what I said. He typed a few times on Carol's computer and Slouch, or Rachel, our club lawyer was on the screen. He had also shifted the camera on Carol's desk so Slouch could see the men in the room but they couldn't see her.

"You wanted to speak to me," Carol stated, patting my lower leg to let me know she was okay. I moved away and stood behind her with my arms folded over my chest. Mason stood on one side of me and Trick on the other. We were all three very imposing figures and easily out muscled the little douche and his bodyguards.

"I believe we need to come to an agreement," the man said, blinking at Carol then looking up at me. "You got one of my men arrested and I believe we need compensation."

I blinked at the man then looked down at Carol when she turned her chair to look up at me.

"I thought you said he wanted to speak to me?" She asked me and I had to work really hard to keep the smile off my face.

"I asked to speak to the president of the War Angels MC," the man insisted crossly.

"Then why are you talking to him?" Carol asked, turning back to face him, pointing at me over her shoulder. "Look, you chauvinistic little prick, I can forget that you came in here and tried to push around my employees, that you speak over me like you think I'm too stupid to understand what you're saying. I can even forget the fact that you haven't once told anyone your name but expected every single one of us to cater to you. I already know your name, Reginald Small, and that's really the least of what I know. What I cannot forget is that you sent one of *your* employees after members of *my* family, killing one of them trying to start a turf war that you mistakenly thought you could win."

Reginald Small was getting schooled.

"I know, Reginald, that you are the head of a large organization that makes its money selling drugs and women and children," Carol said, standing slowly and leaning on her desk. "I know that quite a few years ago another such organization tried to take someone very important to me and *my family* not only got that person back but they destroyed that organization."

"Crumbled it into dust," Mason mumbled with a smirk. He hadn't even been there but he'd heard the stories, the same as me and now Trick.

"That organization was bigger than yours so if you think you're going to come in here and push your miniscule weight around you would be mistaken. Here is our deal." Carol continued through clenched teeth. "You and your goons will get out of my office and far away from our property. You will stay on your side of the city and neither you nor your goons, your traffickers or your pick up men will venture past city center. You do that and we leave you alone. Your drugs appear here or children and women start to disappear and the police will be the least of your worries. How does that work for an agreement?"

"I can see you will not be reasonable about this." Reginald said, standing to his feet and sucking on his teeth.

"Damn fucking straight I'm not, Reggie," Carol ground and nodded towards Joe standing in the doorway of the office. Reginald and his guys were surprised to see Joe but the rest of us knew exactly when he'd gotten there.

Trick and Mason walked around Carol's desk and helped Joe usher our guests out the front door.

"Have a nice day now," Paige said cheerfully and I had to laugh. Carol was still angry though so I kept it to a smirk instead of an all out belly laugh.

"Aahhhh," I sighed and sat in the chair douchebag Reginald had just vacated. "That's gonna be a problem."

"How would you have handled it?" Carol snarled and I smiled widely at her.

"Exactly the same way."

She sighed and sat back in her chair just as Joe, Mason, Trick, Bridge and Slouch came into the room.

"What's the plan boss?" Mason asked, sitting in the chair beside me.

"Trick, I know you've gotten us a shit ton of information on Small, but see if there's anything else you can find. Anything at all, family, other businesses, fuck I want to know where he went to play school."

"On it," Trick said and left the room.

"Slouch, check with the police, see where the case is going as far as Dick is concerned. Make sure there's no chance that he's getting out of jail. I have a feeling Reggie was here because there isn't but I want to be sure. Also ask if they know anything about Reggie's organization, make sure they're on top of it."

"You bet," Slouch said, standing slowly. She was still experiencing some pain but she hadn't told me how or why she was injured. I wasn't going to ask either because Carol knew about it and was on top of it.

"Bridge, have you had a chance to go over Reggie's financials yet?" Carol asked our accountant who had a huge smile on her face.

"Oh you bet I did, found some interesting things, too." Bridge said and I thought she was going to start clapping her hands together like a schoolgirl. "If nothing else I know where his money is and Trick can move it easily."

"Excellent, stay on that," Carol said smiling for the first time.

"I'm out," Bridge said and skipped out of the room.

"You three I want on high alert," Carol said now, turning to Joe, Mason and I. "Reggie's whole game, his huge money making business is human trafficking."

"Carol, you said we'd leave him alone as long as he stayed on his half of the city." Mason began slowly, trying to figure out how to question his president without actually questioning her. "You're not okay with him trafficking just on the west side are you?"

"Fuck no," she insisted, shaking her head. "But he doesn't understand honesty and goodness, he only understands corruption and power. He's also not the only one who can tell a convincing lie. Any woman or child goes missing in this city or the surrounding towns and we're on his ass. If those missing women or children don't link back to him right away, we'll find a link back to him because unless there is unequivocal proof that those missing women and children weren't taken by him then they were taken by him."

"Got it," Mason sighed with a nod.

"Don't worry Mase, I don't want any more women turning out like Jordyn any more than you do." Carol said, locking her gaze with the man. "She's a survivor but she shouldn't have had to survive anything in the first place."

"We'll get to warning everyone else, especially the women." I said, changing the subject. "Paige pissed him off so she's going to be a target."

"Sorry, couldn't help myself," Paige said from the doorway. "He just pissed me off so bad."

"Yeah, you're not alone there sweetheart," Carol said to her daughter. Paige smiled and left the room and Joe's eyes stayed on the young woman until she disappeared. "It's been five years, Joe, when are you going to step up?"

"Could ask you the same thing, Carol?" Joe shot back, clearing his throat.

"Carter and I have been together for the last five years, we just haven't said anything to anyone because it wasn't anyone's business," Carol said and I smiled. Joe and Mason just blinked at her, surprised but Joe recovered quickly.

"Well," he said standing, "maybe this is nobody's damn business either."

Then he walked out the door and out of the building.

"Why didn't you guys ever say anything?" Mason demanded, confused.

"Like Carol said," I told him, watching her even though I was talking to him. "It was none of anybody else's business."

"Whatever," Mason said as he, too, stood to leave. "Either way, I'm happy for you both."

"Thanks man," I said as he left and closed the door, then turned to look at Carol. She was tired, weary and sad. "So, what was the phone call before I came in here?"

"Robert," she said softly as her eyes filled with tears.

"Oh fuck, I'm sorry babe," I sighed and she nodded.

"Me too." She sighed and rubbed her fingers over her eyebrows. "Shelley said his funeral is this weekend, said she'd text the details, and afterwards we're supposed to meet with his lawyer."

"Why would we need to meet with his lawyer?" I asked, confused.

"I don't know," Carol said, shaking her head. "Shelley didn't say, just that Robert didn't want a reception but his lawyer said we needed to meet with him immediately after."

"All right," I said, nodding.

Two days later Carol, Shelley and I sat in a lawyers office still very confused. The funeral service had been short and sad. There were a few people there but it seemed that Robert didn't have many friends and none of his family showed. When I asked Shelley about it she just shook her head.

"When he called his brother to tell him that he was dying Roger told him he was sorry but it was Robert's problem. Their parents were old and infirm and didn't want or need to hear about Robert's problems and their sisters, Roberta and Regina, were good upstanding, God fearing women who didn't need to be sullied by Robert's transgressions. Roger's words, not mine. I don't know if he ever told you, but his parents disowned him when he was still a teenager. He hasn't seen his twin brother, Roger or his two little sisters since."

"Wasn't Robert in his sixties?" Carol asked, dumbfounded.

"Wait, Robert, Roger, Roberta and Regina?" I asked incredulously but Shelley and Carol ignored me.

"Yes, that's why John was so important to Robert and then you two and Lyle. You all accepted him without reservation and he was even more touched that you accepted him and spent time with him after you found out he was the one to give John HIV, knowing that Robert had AIDS you didn't desert him like so many others did." Shelley shrugged like it was no big deal but obviously to Robert, and her, it was.

I sighed and wrapped my hand around Carol's just as the lawyer came into the room.

"Sorry to keep you waiting," the man said, sitting behind his huge desk. "I'm Leland Carlyle, Robert and I were friends for years, and this is probably a conflict of interest, being his lawyer now but he begged me to do this."

Carlyle sat behind his desk and opened a file. He handed Carol and Shelley each a disc.

"Those are messages that Robert made for each of you." Carlyle said, looking at each of us. "Robert said I only had to make one copy for the two of you but if you'd prefer I can make another."

"No," I said, shaking my head, looking down at the disc. "This is just fine."

"All right," Carlyle murmured, nodding. "You three are here because you are the only family remaining of Robert's. At least the only family who would accept him and acknowledge him. He has left everything he has to the three of you. His assets and financials will be divided evenly between the three of you except for the house that will go to Shelley and her husband."

"What?" Shelley demanded, tears in her eyes. "Why?"

"I believe Robert explains everything in his message to you." Carlyle explained with a shrug. "He didn't tell me the why of things, just how it was to be."

The lawyer went through a few more things and Carol and I sat almost completely confused the entire time. When he was finished explaining the stocks and shares and that Robert had almost ten million dollars in his accounts combined we were left shocked. We knew Robert was well off, but we were shocked to find out how well off.

The three of us sat in shock for the next five minutes, staring down at the discs in our hands and then at each other.

"Did you have any idea?" Carol asked Shelley and she shook her head.

"No, Robert, I mean, I knew he had money, I knew that besides smart investments and other things his grandmother had left him some money and his family had tried to contest her will, but didn't win. He never talked about money. He paid me really well, like better than any other job I've ever had, but he never talked about money."

Shelley broke down then as tears flowed from her eyes unchecked. Knowing her husband was in the waiting area I stood up and went to get him. Worried, the poor man rushed to his wife and hugged her tightly.

"Let's go home, sweetheart." He said and she nodded. He gave us each a nod then they left.

"Shelley," Carol said just before they left the office. "If you ever need anything, you know where to find us."

Shelley nodded and then they were gone. I thanked Carlyle and then Carol and I left as well. When we got to the compound we went straight up to her apartment. She went to the kitchen and I went to the bedroom, pulling off my tie and suit jacket. I came out again with the top three buttons of my dress shirt unbuttoned and untucked and the sleeves rolled up to find a glass of Jack on the counter.

As I was tossing back my whiskey there was a knock on the door and Paige walked in.

"Hey guys, how was the funeral?" She asked, walking into the kitchen and wrapping her arm around Carol's waist. When she saw the whiskey she smirked. "That good, huh?"

"He left us each a third of everything," Carol told her and Paige frowned. "Just under ten million in his bank account alone and that doesn't include investments and shares and stocks."

"What the hell did Robert do for a living?" Paige demanded and we both shrugged.

"I actually don't know," I frowned at Carol who shook her head. "He never did say and by the time we met him he was already sick. I don't know if he really worked after that."

"I have no idea," Carol agreed with another shrug. She slipped her hand into her purse and pulled out the disc. "He made us a message, want to watch it with us?"

"Really?" Paige asked, her eyes filling with tears. She had met Robert a few times and I knew she wished she could have known him better. "I'd love to."

We sat in the living room with Carol's laptop on the coffee table in front of us and watched the video Robert had made for us. He'd filmed it quite some time ago as he looked much healthier than the last time we'd seen him. He was also sitting at the desk in his home office and he was smiling, his eyes were clear of pain and fatigue and his skin was still full of colour.

"If you're watching this then I'm dead," Robert began dramatically, making us all laugh. "Just kidding," he chuckled, laughing at his own joke like only Robert could. "But all kidding aside, you two were the light of my life. If I had been blessed with kids I would have hoped they were just like you two. Only without the romantic relationship because incest is," he shuddered delicately, "ew."

"Oh my God, Robert," Carol murmured with a smile, tears in her eyes. I shifted on the couch so I could wrap my arm around her and tap Paige's shoulder with my fingertips.

"However, since I couldn't find a woman to have my babies and I spent far too much of my youth catting around, I've decided to claim you, Carol as my daughter. I know, you had amazing parents but when John brought you into my life, even once he'd taken himself out of it, I knew you were something special. I might have broken it off with John out of guilt but I loved him to my dying day. There was never anyone like John, just like there will never be anyone like you, Carol."

I squeezed her shoulder and kissed her temple as the tears slid down her cheeks.

"Carter, you gorgeous hunk of man meat," Robert said suddenly, making Paige laugh. "Now that I've gone to my eternal reward I'll be watching you from the great beyond so feel free to put on a show every night, muwahahahaha!"

"Carter!" Paige gasped and Carol laughed but I just rolled my eyes and chuckled.

"I know, all that you are would stop my heart, but now I don't have to worry about that," Robert said with a cheeky smile. "Just kidding, I'm sure I'll be too busy hanging out with River Pheonix and Robin Williams to engage in a little voyeurism. It's time, Carter, in fact it's past time. Take that woman and press her against a wall with all that manly muscle and lay one on her, show her who's boss and that you're not going to wait any longer."

"Mom?" Paige asked and I looked down to see Carol blushing and I barked a laugh.

"Paige darling, I'm sure you're sitting with your mom right now." Robert said from the computer, dragging her attention from her mother. "I just wanted to say to you that I hope you understand what an amazing person she is. That she loves you unconditionally and that is something so rare and it should be cherished."

Paige sniffed and wrapped her arms around Carol. "I know," she murmured and laid her head on Carol's shoulder.

"Anyway," Robert continued, taking a deep breath. "I'm sure you just spoke to Leland, he probably dropped a bomb or two on you. Yes, I was loaded but the money didn't make me happy, you two and Shelley made me happy. And because you told me stories of Paige, she also made me happy. John made me happy so while I can't be with you any longer, take my money, enjoy it, go on vacation, enjoy life to the fullest. Leland will also be sending you a few things. Things that were important to John and I that I kept for safekeeping. Originally they were kept for Matt but I know now that can never be, unfortunately. John would want you, Carol to have them. Cherish them like I did, throw them away, donate them, do what you want with them, though I hope you cherish them.

"Well, this is my final goodbye. Please keep in touch with Shelley, I left her this monstrosity of a house and I know she'll put it to good use. Her and her husband foster a shit load of kids and they need the space. Be kind to each other, love each other, take care of each other. I love you both so much, thank you for being my friends."

Then Robert walked off the camera and the video ended with a picture of Robert and John smiling at each other.

"Oh my God," Paige sighed and hugged Carol as the two of them cried together. I even had tears in my eyes as I rubbed Carol's back and stared at the picture of Razz with Robert. "Sooo, I think Robert also dropped some bombs in there," Paige sniffed, looking at Carol and I. "Something you want to tell me?"

"Carter and I are -"

"We've been seeing each other for five years," I said, cutting Carol off. "That wall pressing thing happened a couple of years ago . . . and multiple times since."

"Ew," Paige murmured, making me smile. "But I'm glad you're finally admitting it. It was painful watching you two sneak around."

"We weren't sneaking around," Carol insisted, looking up at Paige as she stood from the couch. "We just didn't feel it was anyone's business."

"Uh huh, but I'm not anyone, mom," Paige told her, rolling her eyes. "I'm your daughter, I know you better than anyone except for maybe Carter. I know you kept him a secret at first because you were worried about being president. It's okay, mom but you should have known that I could keep a secret for one, and for another I would never have considered you weak or needing a man to support you. You wanted the man but you never needed him."

"You're right," Carol sighed and rubbed her forehead. "Apparently I'm hearing all over the place that I'm not actually doing that good a job."

Carol stood, patting Paige on the shoulder and walked into her bedroom and closing the door. Paige watched her go, confused then looked back at me with a scowl.

"What the hell is that about?" She hissed, moving over to sit with me on the couch.

"Tease," I mumbled, watching the bedroom door.

"That was hardly her fault," Paige insisted, shaking her head.

"Oh, I know, and her and Trick have figured it out, but she still feels really bad about Heather getting hurt and not knowing that Tease was as bad as he was."

"No one told her, how could she know? And what? She's supposed to give up her entire life to this MC? She can't have a relationship because she's president? That's bullshit, if she's at fault then so are you and so is Mason because he spends so much time with his kids and with Jordyn. And hell, while we're at it, let's blame Bridge because she spends all her time with Grinder when she's not in her office and Slouch because she's injured and doesn't hang out in the main room and party. We should spread it around a little more and blame Joe since he was out with Elli all the time then mooning over me. I could be blamed, too because I didn't say anything to anyone about the way Tease treated me."

By the time she was done her rant Paige was pacing the living room in front of me, breathing hard.

"I don't disagree with you, Paige, but your mom took the whole thing really hard and then with Techie and Small and Robert on top of it all, she's having a hard time."

"Yeah well, I think some people need to back the fuck off," Paige snapped and left the apartment. I sighed and pushed up off the couch, walking into Carol's room. She was curled up on top of the bed, wearing one of my t-shirts and panties and nothing else.

I knew she was crying and trying to keep silent so no one knew she was crying but she could never hide her tears from me.

I stripped off my shirt and dress pants and tossed them onto the pretty armchair she had in the corner then crawled onto the bed behind her, pulling her into my arms. She resisted at first but I wouldn't be denied. I rolled her to face me and pulled her against my chest and held her while she cried. I let her cry and get it all out. I didn't shush her or tell her it was alright because at that moment it wasn't. At that moment nothing was alright.

Eventually Carol cried herself to sleep and I knew she would probably wake up with a killer headache. No matter what I would be the one to take care of her, forever and always.

CHAPTER 15

Carol

"Oh God, Carter," I moaned as I arched my back, rubbing my chest against his. He hovered over me, gliding in and out of me, touching every sensitive bit of my flesh. His big hand cupped my ass and pulled my leg higher then pressed his palm to the inside of my knee and pushed my leg out, opening me even more to his thrusting hips.

"Fuck Carol," he gasped when I squeezed my inner muscles, my hands clenched around his shoulders and I dragged my nails down his chest to flick my thumb nails across his nipples. He groaned again then pulled back just as my orgasm was starting to take over.

"No!" I cried, so close to exploding. Carter wasted no time flipping me onto my stomach and pulled me up on my knees before slamming back into me and setting me off again like fireworks. I screamed into my pillow as every muscle in my body clenched and relaxed, rippling with sensation.

Carter thrust hard and fast into me three more times before exploding inside me with a grunt and a heavy groan. As he slowly pulled back I felt his cum slip out of me and I moaned, hating the feeling of it mixed with the lube we'd used. Carter of course loved it and chuckled, slapping my ass. He left, going to the bathroom to get a wet washcloth to clean me up.

"I know you hate it, babe," Carter said, tossing the washcloth at the hamper and flopping on the bed beside me. "But I think it's fucking hot."

"It's not that," I said sliding to my stomach and curling up against his side. "I don't have a problem with you dripping down my leg," I mumbled into his chest as he chuckled. "It's the lube, it's slimy and gross."

"Then maybe we should try a different kind." He yawned and I shrugged. "Or maybe we should try to use less of it, I usually apply pretty liberally so I don't hurt you."

Carter rolled toward me and buried his mouth in my neck, his beard tickling me and making me laugh.

"Mmm," he hummed, kissing and licking his way up to my ear.

"You're not finished?" I asked, smiling, rubbing my hands up and down his broad back.

"I'm never finished with you." He rasped, rolling me to my back and smoothing his palm across my chest and belly, up my throat then down the center of my torso to my core. I bit my lip and arched my hips into his hand while he watched his fingers slipping around my clit and into my pussy.

Growling Carter shifted and replaced his hand with his mouth, lashing my clit with his tongue. He pushed my legs wide and gripped my hips, holding me to his mouth as he devoured me. Every nip, lick and suck took me closer and closer to the edge until he pushed three fingers inside me, crooking them and rubbing against my g-spot. I arched so hard into his mouth I almost bucked him off but he laughed and continued to torment my clit until I just couldn't take it any longer.

"Carter!" I cried, pushing him away and twisting my hips. He just laughed again and licked all the way up my body until his mouth met mine as he thrust hard into me again. The feel of his cock so hard, filling me and the taste of me on his tongue thrusting into my mouth sent me over the edge again and I was floating and incoherent.

When I could think again Carter was laying beside me, holding my knee cocked over his hip, his legs entwined with mine and he was kissing me gently everywhere he could reach without moving. I turned my head and kissed him, wrapping my hand around his head and holding him close, rolling into him.

"I'm sorry," I whispered when I'd finally pulled away, locking my gaze with his.

"What are you sorry for?" He chuckled gently, slipping my hair behind my ear only for it to pop out again.

"I'm sorry I made us wait five years for this," I told him, biting my lip. "I'm sorry I was too scared and I made us miss this for so long."

"Oh baby," Carter murmured and kissed my forehead, burying his hand in my hair. "I've already told you, I meant it then and I mean it now. You and this, were totally worth the wait. I love you Carol. I don't love you because the sex is off the charts, even though it totally is. I love you because of you."

"I love you, too Sean Carter." I whispered and kissed him again. "I really do wish we could have kids. I would love a little Sean running around here."

"As much as I would love a little Carol I am happy to claim Paige," he said with a snort. I laughed, knowing she'd started calling him dad which he absolutely loved. "It's not just you who probably can't have kids you know."

I nodded, tracing his eyebrows with my fingertips.

"After I was shot I had that infection, the doctor said I most likely couldn't have kids."

"I know, and I don't need to have kids with you to love you. I will always love you completely no matter what," I murmured, cupping my hand around his cheek.

"If you want we could always look into it." He shrugged and kissed me.

"Look into what?" I asked, confused.

"Whether or not we can have kids."

"Carter," I laughed, shaking my head. "I'm forty-four years old, even if I could still have kids I'm way too old for that."

"You are not," he scoffed, scowling down at me. "Forty-four is not old. You'd be at higher risk but you could do it easily. I'm serious, though. Think about it, if you want to look into it that doesn't mean that we will have a kid, it just means it's still a possibility."

"And if we look into it you won't be disappointed if we definitely can't have kids? I mean, my mastectomy most likely put me into menopause."

"Not completely, you still get periods once in a while, which means you're still ovulating."

"True," I shrugged, petting his arm. "But that doesn't mean I can get and stay pregnant."

"No, but that's why we would look into it."

"And if you don't have any swimmers?"

"Then I don't," he shrugged and kissed me again. Conversations with Carter, no matter how serious, always involved a lot of kissing. That is conversations that weren't about the MC. "And we move on and are happy exactly how we are."

"You're serious about this?"

"Are you? You're the one who brought it up. I'm just saying let's rule it out completely before we say we can't or won't do it."

"You want me to get pregnant?"

"I want you to be happy." Carter explained gently. "Yes I want to share that with you, and if we decide when all is said and done that we don't want to have a kid then that's not going to change how I feel about you. If we decide that we try to have a kid and it doesn't happen that's not going to change how I feel about you. If anything, I can only love you more."

"And if I don't want to do it at all?"

"Then we don't do it," he shrugged and kissed me, running his palm up and down my side.

"Can I think about it?"

"No," he laughed, his eyes dancing. "You have to decide right this second."

"Shut up," I scoffed as my phone chirped on the bedside table. I turned away from him, still laughing and looked at the screen. "It's Paige, she says we have guests."

"Small?" Carter asked, concerned. Quickly he stood and started getting dressed. It had been months since we'd heard from Reginald Small at all, but we'd kept him on our radar. He had kept his drugs out of our side of the city and the few times there had been women or children go missing we had found them and pulled them out of his clutches, putting a stop for the most part to that part of his business. We also kept him on the radar of the RCMP so his movements were limited.

"She didn't say but she said it's important." I told him and rolled out of bed as well, pulling on clothes. I finger combed my hair and pulled it back with an elastic, knowing that without a shower I wasn't going to tame the curls. I didn't have time, though so the elastic would have to do.

Carter and I rushed down to the main room but didn't find

anyone there so we continued to my office. I hoped to find Bull standing in my office. Lo had kept all the chapter presidents up to date on Bull's run through the country, trying to keep his girlfriend safe from some organization that was trying to kill her. Lo had said to keep our eyes open and be aware that Bull and the girl could show up on our doorsteps at any time.

There was no one but Paige in my office, though and I turned to look at Paige.

"Sorry, Bull texted to let me know he was coming in, thought you would want to be here when he got here." She shrugged and I rolled my eyes.

"You're right, but maybe next time don't make it sound so urgent." I told her and she smirked.

"Not all of us can sneak away in the middle of the day for sex," Paige told me and Carter chuckled.

"You could if you had someone to have it with."

"Don't remind me," she snarled, her gaze shifting to the hallway behind me, then handed me a slip of paper. "Also, Karl called, wants you to call him back."

"What the hell does he want?" I demanded, frowning down at the message.

"I didn't ask, I don't care." She said, holding her hands up. Growling I stomped to my office and called my ex husband, leaving him on speaker phone. The same ex husband who got Paige kidnapped by possible sex traffickers, the same ex husband who refused to pay child support, the same ex husband who quit working all together so the government couldn't find him and make him pay child support. He was damn lucky I didn't need his money. I didn't even want it, but on principle I was still going to make him pay it if I could.

The phone rang four times before Karl answered.

"Yeah?" He sounded old and strung out.

"What do you want Karl?" I demanded angrily, getting straight to the point because talking to Karl always made me angry and I really did not want to deal with him at all. Joe slid into the room and sat in a chair in the corner. He always loved being around for these conversations, said they were incredibly entertaining.

"Carol, I just wanted to talk to you about the child support stuff," he said, clearing his throat.

"Karl, the papers I had sent to you most recently don't even mention child support or money of any kind." I informed him and he was silent. "Obviously you didn't read them or you'd have known that."

"Carol, Paige is eighteen now, I shouldn't have to pay child support anymore."

"Paige is twenty-four now, dumbass, you don't have to pay child support anymore and haven't had to for the last six years. What you've been having to pay is the child support you refused to pay when Paige was under eighteen. Also, half of her college tuition you were supposed to pay -"

"Carol," Karl tried, but I cut him off while Joe sat in the corner, unsure if he wanted to laugh or kill someone if the look on his face was any indication.

"I'm not asking for money, Karl! I don't want your damn money! I just want you to sign the damn papers! Read the papers Karl!"

"Carol, honey, I don't want a divorce."

"Karl you idiot! We haven't been married for twenty years! You cheated on me and gambled away all of our money! I had to move in with my mother! Just sign the damn papers!" I yelled again.

"But Carol," he whined and Joe scoffed, Carter sighed heavily.

"Get it the fuck done or I'll have your dick and balls stuffed and mounted on my office wall!" I yelled then picked up the phone and slammed it back into the cradle before looking up at the young man standing in my doorway and smiling.

Willis!" I exclaimed, rushing around my desk and hugging him. It had been far too long since I'd seen him even though it had really only been a few months.

"Who are you threatening now?" He asked looking down at me with a smile.

"Promising, not threatening," I told him and went back to my desk. "And that was my ex husband."

"Is dad still not signing the divorce papers?" Paige asked and I sighed.

"He thinks if he drags his feet I won't ask for as much money just to get rid of him. He's wrong, he owes me a lot of back child support and he owes me for half of your college fees." I told Paige who held her hands up in surrender. "However at this point I just want him to sign the damn papers so we can actually be divorced. This has been the longest damn divorce in history."

"I'm not arguing with you," Paige insisted and turned to leave the room. I noticed Willis was not alone and there was another handsome young man, about his age and a young girl with him. The man's eyes followed Paige as she walked away.

"Don't do it man," Willis warned quietly. "She's the pres's daughter and she's already claimed by a member."

"That member just needs to pull his head outta his ass and tell the girl he's claimed her." I said, glaring at Joe.

"Good to see you, Joe." Willis said and Joe grunted but shook his hand.

"Have a seat," I said and slumped into my own chair with Carter standing behind me.

"Come on baby," Willis said to the girl and pulled her into his lap. "Lora sweetheart, that crazy woman behind the desk is Carol, she's the boss here, you don't have to be afraid of her unless you were married to her at some point."

Joe snorted and Carter and I laughed.

"Caro, this is my girl Loralei," Willis said with a proud smile as Lora blushed prettily. He kissed her cheek and gestured to the man sitting beside him. "This is Master Corporal Jace Montgomery."

"Ma'am," Jace said, nodding slightly and touching two fingers to his forehead.

"None o' that bullshit here," I said, waving away his polite greeting. "Caro is just fine. So *Bull*, what's brought you and your merry band of misfits here to my clubhouse?"

"Need to hide out for a bit," he said and I nodded, slowly. "I know it's a lot to ask -"

"Oh, maybe for anyone else," I scoffed and Carter chuckled. "You know I served a tour with your dad and he saved my life way early in my career, how on earth am I gonna repay that if I don't hide his kid now? Not to mention you were my friend when I needed one most."

"I'll always be there for you Caro," he said and I nodded.

"Lo called all the club presidents," I continued. "Even if I wanted to turn you away I couldn't, not if I don't want to lose my club."

"So that's how it is, hey?" He chuckled and I shook my head, smiling.

"Not hardly, boy."

"I know," he sobered with a slow nod. "I would never ask this of you if I had a choice. Hunt is killing innocent people -"

"Fucking Damien Hunt!" Joe growled angrily and I felt Carter tense behind me but I wasn't sure why.

"That's almost as good as Hunt the cunt," Jace said.

"Who are you again?" I asked even though I knew exactly who he was. I probably knew more about him than anyone realized thanks to Trick and Seether doing a little digging.

"I'm the godfather," Jace said, pointing two fingers at himself then turning them to point at Lora's stomach.

"Jace is my best friend, he's a pilot with the air force, he was injured not long ago in a blast and has forgotten how to act like a regular person." Willis murmured dryly.

After talking for a few more minutes, I sent Willis, Lora and Jace with Joe to get them settled in a couple of rooms then turned to look up at Carter.

"What's going on?" I asked him, reaching out to touch his hip.

"Nothing," he said, shaking his head. "I'm gonna go for a run."

That was a dead give away that there was actually something going on. Carter often went for runs, and they weren't always about clearing his head and heavy thoughts. His early morning runs were just that, early morning runs to stay fit. But it wasn't early morning, it was mid afternoon and he had just heard something that bothered him and he was going for a run.

For now I would leave him to his thoughts, but I wouldn't let him shut me out. He would talk to me eventually, he just had to get his thoughts in order.

That night, though, Carter didn't come back to my apartment. We hadn't exactly moved in together but we did spend every night together at my place. Mostly Carter just used his place for storage but it was still his apartment. When I looked up at the clock and saw it was nine pm I got worried and was about to go and find him when there was a knock on my door.

I frowned, thinking Carter wouldn't knock so it obviously wasn't him. I walked over and opened the door, finding Slouch crying in front of me.

"Oh shit, come in here," I said, pulling her through the door and sitting her on my couch. I wrapped a blanket around her then went and made a pot of tea. I knew Slouch, or Rachel, didn't drink coffee and she wasn't big on alcohol but given the way she looked at that moment she probably needed it.

I made up a tray with a couple of mugs, a bottle of Jack, milk and sugar and carried it into the living room. When the kettle boiled I went back to the kitchen and poured the water into the tea pot and carried that back to the living room. I poured a finger of Jack into Rachel's mug but before I could add the tea she picked up the mug and slugged back the whiskey, hissing and gasping at the burning sensation of the alcohol.

She placed the mug back on the tray and I poured tea into it before adding another shot of whiskey. Taking a deep breath she wrapped the blanket tighter around her shoulders and sat back on the couch, pulling her knees up.

"What's going on?" I asked her after a moment, after her tears had slowed just a little.

"He's here," she murmured, sniffing.

"He?" I asked and she nodded. "The guy you fell in love with? The guy who promised you he wouldn't take advantage and then did, leaving you pregnant? That he?"

"Yeah," she whispered, dropping her head to the arm of the couch and blinking slowly, the alcohol apparently starting to take effect.

"Who is he? Bull?"

"No, not him, his friend, Jace."

"Oh hell," I muttered, tipping my head back with a groan. "He's got a story."

"I know, he told me a little bit." Rachel nodded and sighed. "He was so sad, Caro. I could see in his eyes, he had no idea who I was but he was destroyed."

"Did you tell him about the baby?"

"No, I didn't have a chance."

"Are you going to?"

"I don't know, what difference does it make? He doesn't remember anything. Everything I believed for the last three years was a lie."

"It wasn't a lie, it just wasn't what you thought," I told her gently, rubbing her back. Rachel was a certifiable genius. She had graduated high school early, graduated college early then gone into the Canadian Armed Forces because she needed to be stimulated to keep her over intelligent brain from going crazy. She joined JAG and in less time than anyone else she had finished the program and become a lawyer.

A few years ago she'd met a young pilot who everyone knew was a playboy. He was the hit it and quit it kind of guy and while he intrigued Rachel she wasn't about to be one of his conquests. Only something was different this time around. He promised her, swore to her that he wouldn't do that with her. He worked hard just to get a date and a kiss on the cheek.

Eventually they did have sex and then he was deployed for a year. She got pregnant and lost the baby at eighteen weeks.

Rachel hemorrhaged and almost died and still years later had issues with her reproductive organs. She just had to have a partial hysterectomy at twenty-five because of the scar tissue in her uterus causing her problems.

"How do I tell him everything? He doesn't remember me anyway, what difference does it make?" She asked me now and I sighed, shrugging.

"Sweetheart, even if he doesn't remember he's still the father of that baby, he deserves to know." I told her softly and she nodded. She sat up slowly and reached for the tea, blowing over the top of it. We sat quietly and sipped our tea and she told me about her time with Jace. Even after all this time and all the hardship she'd experienced she still loved him, or at the very least cared about him.

Eventually she finished her tea and her eyes were drooping. I took the mug and urged her to lay back down on the couch. After everything she'd just told me I didn't want her to be alone at her place. Plus after two shots of whiskey she was probably more than a little drunk. I covered her up and looked up at the clock, realizing it was after midnight and Carter still hadn't come home.

Sighing I went to bed, alone and fell into a fitful sleep. I got no rest at all and woke up feeling hungover even though I'd only had one drink last night.

When I finally saw Carter again he was looking just as rough as I was feeling and it didn't look like his run had done him any good.

The confusion and anger swirling in his dark eyes told me he hadn't gotten anything figured out and there was probably not a run long enough that would clear his thoughts.

CHAPTER 16

Carter

A few days later we were all back in Carol's office. I hadn't been able to clear my mind of the turmoil, hearing that a man I had looked up to when I was much younger could be the monster we were hearing about.

Going for a run, or multiple runs hadn't cleared my mind. Working out to the point of exhaustion didn't clear my mind. I had gone to bed late every night, except for that first night cuddling up to Carol, hoping to find peace. There didn't seem to be peace to have, though and I laid in bed every night, wide awake, staring at the ceiling. Carol stayed snuggled up to my side, sleeping peacefully through the night but my head wouldn't stop.

"What's up with you and my lawyer, fly boy?" Carol asked Jace as him and Bull walked into her office. Joe and I were already sitting there, waiting for the two of them to come in and tell us what the hell was going on.

"You're forgetting something, Carol," Jace murmured as he sat in a chair in front of her desk, not breaking eye contact with her. "I don't remember the last ten years, so if there's something between me and your lawyer you're gonna have to ask her about it."

Carol grunted and leaned back in her chair, her eyes locked on Jace. Jace was Bull's best friend, they had served together in the Armed Forces and Bull and Lora had just been staying at

Jace's condo until they were found and the condo, as well as the two on either side of it, were burnt to the ground. Jace had an accident on his last deployment that wiped out his memory of the last ten years, which apparently included Slouch. "I don't like to see my people upset."

"I promise you, upsetting Rachel has never been my intention." When Jace used Slouch's real name Carol's gaze shot to Joe and me sitting to the side of the room then back to Jace. "Once all this shit with Hunt is taken care of or it's time for us to move on, whichever comes first, I'll be gone and Rachel can forget about me."

"Like you've forgotten about her?" I snapped, the lack of sleep and peace of mind making me cranky.

"So it would seem." Jace shrugged, but I doubt he was as nonchalant as he was trying to look.

"All right," Carol sighed and sat forward in her chair. "Tell me everything that's going on with Hunt."

"You've got your boys here but not your lawyer?" Jace asked, his eyes narrowing and Bull kicked him.

"My boys are here because they've met Hunt, Joe was recruited by him after and Carter worked with him before he went dark. Slouch isn't here because even if you don't remember, you must have noticed that she's a gentle soul. Hearing the things Hunt has done won't help her and I'd rather keep her in the dark if at all possible. Ignorance is bliss and all. Besides, this isn't a legal matter for the MC, Slouch being here isn't necessary."

Jace grunted again but said nothing else.

"Don't make me explain myself again, fly boy, once was more than anyone else ever gets." Carol was pissed but she was holding back her anger and I had a feeling it was more for Slouch's benefit than Jace's. I needed to pull my head out of my ass and find out what all was going on. "I'm only doing it now because I'm taking account of your infirmity."

"Well," Jace said, planting his hands on the arms of his chair and pushing to his feet. "I can see I'm not needed here, I'll just go visit with my godchild."

"I'm not sure I like that guy," Carol murmured, rubbing a finger under her jaw.

"You get used to him," Bull shrugged and I snorted. "You wanna hear it all or not?"

"Shoot," Caro said and Bull nodded. He started telling her about the things they knew Hunt had done. The things that I couldn't bring myself to accept. None of this made sense in my mind.

We stayed in Carol's office for more than an hour, talking about everything that had happened since last November. It was the middle of September now, it was almost a year since this all began for Bull and his girl.

Carol, Joe and I were mostly silent except for some colourful cursing from myself, pacing the floor behind Bull's chair.

"When I knew Hunt he wasn't like this," Carter said, sounding tortured. "He was a decent guy, I just don't understand what happened to him."

As I paced Carol stood from behind her desk and walked to the door. She locked it then stepped in front of me. Breathing heavy I almost couldn't control myself. She slid her hands into mine as her gaze locked with mine. She looked just as heartbroken as I felt.

"Come on," she said softly and pulled me behind her. She positioned me in front of her big chair and pushed me into it then climbed onto my lap, her knees straddling my hips. With her hands cupping my cheeks she kissed me sweetly. I returned the kiss, sipping from her, taking the comfort she was offering. "I like this."

She was playing with my moustache and I snickered. I had been shaving his morning, trying to tidy up my beard but not paying close enough attention. I'd ended up messing up my beard and having to shave it. I'd left a goatee but I didn't like the way it looked so I shaved my chin as well, leaving a dark fu manchu.

"I fucked it up, I had to fix it somehow." I muttered, leaning my head back against the chair.

"I like it," she smiled gently, tugging on the ends. Carol leaned forward again, pressing her lips to mine, licking my bottom lip then licking into my mouth. I opened readily for her, loving her taste and immediately realizing I had been stupid. With her in my lap and her mouth on mine my soul began to settle. "It's very Sam Elliot."

"Mmm," I sighed, pulling back slightly and pressing light kisses across her lips before touching my forehead to hers. Carol loved old Westerns and Sam Elliot was one of her favourite actors. "I'm sorry."

"What are you sorry for?" Carol asked, her thumbs gently rubbing up and down the sides of my face.

"I wasn't trying to shut you out," I began, my hands flat on her back. I tipped my head and pressed my mouth to the side of her neck. "I tried to do what I always do and run but my head wouldn't clear. I worked out to exhaustion but I would lay down with you and as exhausted as my body was my brain just wouldn't settle."

"I noticed," Carol murmured, petting my head.

"I kept you up."

"No, you didn't. You woke me up a couple of times because your breathing wasn't settled and deep like it usually is. But I was more worried about you and I just tried to do what I could and wrap myself around you tighter."

"Hmm," I hummed again and sat back against the chair so I could look up at her. "I know now I should have just come straight to you, talked to you, held you."

"Are you feeling better now?" She asked, her hands smoothing up and down over my chest.

"I'm calmer," I agreed with a sharp nod. "I can think clearly about this. I'm still in a bit of shock that Hunt is this bad, I still need to know how he turned so bad, but I can actually talk about it now. Next time I'm feeling at odds I'm not going for a run, I'm gonna take you to bed instead."

"Please do," Carol smiled, her hands still moving. "Tell me about Hunt."

"I worked with his team for a couple of years early in my career," I said, clearing my throat. "He was a good guy, solid, you know? Ghost and Tongue goofed around a lot back then but Hunt kept them under control. I was the new guy to the team so I didn't get a lot of the inside info, I went in, did what I was told, did my job, blew shit up. Or stopped it from blowing up. Shortly after I was reassigned so was Hunt and I never really saw him again. I worked with Ghost and Tongue and Speed a couple more times and I was assigned to a team with Speed when I was shot but that was ten years ago."

"You haven't kept in touch with Speed?" Carol asked, frowning.

"We were JTF 2, Caro," I told her, my hands resting on her hips. "If I knew where he was or how to get a hold of him I would but who the hell knows where he is?"

"We should ask Trick, he might know how to find him."

"Speed wouldn't work with Hunt on shit like this, he wasn't like Hunt and Tongue. Tongue I could see working with Hunt doing this shit but Speed kept himself apart from the others to a certain extent. Ghost was all in but he was a genuinely good person. I honestly believe if he'd known about what Hunt has been doing he'd do what was right."

Carol tipped her head to the side and frowned.

"I know, I agreed with you that it was him I would have thought would be a rapist and not Tongue, but not really. You yes because he talked about you a lot, he even talked to me about you once, I remember it because he was with Hunt at the time. Tongue though would have thrived with what Hunt's been doing now."

She nodded and sighed.

"I promise you, baby, Ghost really was a good guy. I do understand if you don't believe me, though."

"It's not that I don't believe you," she said, shaking her head. "I just knew Ghost to be pushy and he tried to use his higher rank against me."

"Yeah," I chuckled and shook my head. "Ghost could be a dick for sure, but he wasn't a bad person."

"I get it," she said softly with a nod. Lifting her hands, Carol smoothed them over my bald head and smiled. "So, Hunt is a truly horrible person."

"Yeah, I guess he is. I can't tell you anything specific because he lost his way after I knew him."

"We may never find out what it was that made him turn like that. Are you going to be okay with that?" She asked, cupping my cheeks again. I closed my eyes and sighed heavily.

"I'm gonna have to be right?" I said, opening my eyes and pinning her with my gaze. Her eyes were sad but full of understanding and I knew she wished she could make this better for me. Unfortunately she couldn't and I would have to learn to live with it.

"Are Bull and Lora safe here?"

"Yeah, I think so. No one here would let the cat out of the bag. And unless Hunt or one of his men followed Bull they wouldn't assume he would come here. They'd assume Saskatoon or back to Kamloops."

"Okay," Carol sighed and kissed me again.

"Can you tell me what's going on with Jace and Slouch?"

"Ugh," Carol muttered, tipping her head back. She sighed heavily and looked back at me. "All right, but I only know Slouch's side, I don't know Jace's side of the story."

"From the sounds of it no one actually knows Jace's side of the story, not even Jace."

"True," she sighed again. "A couple of years ago Slouch and Jace met at the base in Ottawa. He came on strong like he apparently always did. Liked his women he did. Slouch put him off and put him off and put him off until he finally broke her down and she agreed to go out with him, but with the condition that he promised he wouldn't ghost her when it was all done."

"He ghosted her."

"Yeah, eventually he did, but he doesn't remember any of it and he swears that if he ade the promise that he wouldn't then he wouldn't and Bull agrees with him. Problem is, they had sex, she got pregnant he disappeared. His records show that he was deployed twice and was injured on the last deployment."

"So it's possible that he's not lying, that he didn't actually ghost her."

"Right," Carol shrugged. "Until or unless fly boy remembers we may never know."

"So where's the kid?" I asked and Carol frowned, tipping her head to the side. "You said Slouch was pregnant, where's her kid?"

"Oh, she had a traumatic miscarraige, like she almost died. Last year when she was off for a while, she'd gone to get a hysterectomy. She had so much scar tissue that every month her periods were off the charts. It was safer for her to just have it removed."

"God you women go through some horrible shit," I sighed and she nodded.

"Yeah, sometimes we do." Carol replied sadly. She bent forward and kissed me again, smiling against my lips. "You ready to go back to work?"

"Yeah, I guess," I sighed heavily, pretending to be depressed about going back to work, making Carol laugh. I kissed her again, deeply, loving her taste.

I helped her off my lap then walked over to the door and unlocked it. I walked to my office, passing Paige as I went and she looked up with a smile.

"All good, dad?" She asked, concern in her voice.

"All good, girl," I told her and hugged her to my side. She patted my belly and walked back to the file room at the back. It was amazing how Carol had changed things around here.

Razz had his way but Carol ran the MC like she would a business. She considered the MC a conglomerate and she ran it accordingly. She definitely dealt with MC stuff, the member's issues and complaints but she also had to oversee all the other businesses attached to the MC. With Bridge's help Carol had saved the MC and the individual members a lot of money and made us more money through investments and smart spending.

I never thought for a second that Carol wasn't the best person for the president's position but after almost six years it was more than obvious that there was probably no one better.

Carol and I had never talked about marriage, neither of us bringing up but I wanted that. I wanted her as my wife. Probably we had never talked about it because she was technically still married to that idiot Karl, but I wanted that with her. Even if when all was said and done we never had kids, which would be fine with me, neither of us were all that young anymore, she was forty-four and I was forty, it was Carol I wanted for the rest of my life.

CHAPTER 17

Carol

"Mom!" Paige hollered from the front of the office.

"Paige, we have a phone system for a reason!" I called back but she appeared in the doorway of my office.

"Heather's in labour, Trick's taking her to the hospital."

"Second baby, this one will probably come pretty quick, you staying or going?" I asked her before moving.

"I'll stay, I think you need to go."

"Are you sure? You and Heather are friends."

"Yeah, I'll be there after, I'm just waiting for Joe to get here so he can answer phones." Paige assured me and I nodded, grabbing my purse and cell phone. "You really need to be there. You and Trick have history over the last year and I think you need to be there for him."

"Why did you take business admin and not psychology?" I asked my daughter who just shrugged with a smile. I shook my head and kissed her cheek then rushed out of the office.

"I'll make sure everyone knows!" Paige called after me as the door closed behind me.

"Where we goin'?" Mason asked, jumping in the passenger side of my SUV.

"Heather's in labour." I replied as I backed out of my spot.

"Crap," Mason mumbled and I laughed.

"Don't wanna hang out at the hospital?" I asked and he sighed.

"Don't wanna hang out in labour and delivery with a bunch of women in labour," he replied and I laughed again.

"It's not that bad," I promised him but he just snorted. "Seriously, second babies always come faster than first ones. You can take my keys and take my car home. Paige will be there soon enough, I can catch a ride home with her."

"You're a lifesaver," Mason sighed with relief and I laughed again.

"Where are your kids?"

"With Jordyn, like always. I should've known when Trick dropped Gray off with her and took off." He shrugged and I eyed him out of the corner of my eye.

"What's going on with you and Jordyn?" Mason didn't answer right away. In fact I thought he wasn't going to answer me at all he took so long.

"I care about her," he said softly and I nodded, waiting for more, wondering if I would get more. "She's fragile though."

"Yeah," I agreed and he sighed.

"I don't have a problem going slow, moving at her pace and I know that pace is going to be super slow and I'm totally okay with that. I'm having trouble with her not trusting me." Mason finally said, his voice full of frustration. "She's spending more time with just me, though."

"Are you sure she doesn't trust you?" I asked as I turned onto the street leading to the hospital. "I know trust is hard for her and it probably always will be, I know more about that then most people know. I just mean, is it possible she trusts you but reacts in a certain way because that's how she's been trained to react?"

"What do you mean?" He asked, frowning.

"I mean, if you move quickly does she flinch?"

"Everytime, no matter how often I promise I won't hurt her, especially not like that."

"Has she been flinching less than when you first met her, or less visibly?"

"Yeah, I guess so," Mason said with a shrug as I pulled up in front of the hospital.

"So, over the years she was trained to expect to be hit," I continued, putting my SUV into park and turning to face him. "She was trained for that a lot longer than she wasn't. It's re-training, she needs to get used to you and your movements and you need to get used to moving a little slower. For women like Jordyn you'll need as much retraining as she will. She won't believe you're a great guy just because you and every-one else around her says you are. You have to prove it to her and keep proving it to her, probably for the rest of your lives."

I left the SUV running and got out, rushing inside. Mason didn't want to stay and I certainly wouldn't make him.

I ran up to the labour and delivery floor and asked the nurse about Heather.

"She's here," the nurse said with an excited smile. "The doc-tor is just in with her and her hubby now. I'll let them know you're here when the doctor comes out."

"Thanks so much," I said and went into the waiting room. I pulled out my phone and sent a message to Paige and Carter, letting them know I was there waiting. It wasn't long before more of the MC members arrived and I had someone to wait with me. Mostly it was women but there were a few men as well. Grinder had come with Bridge and Joe had arrived after the office had closed for the night. I don't know what he'd done to piss Paige off but she spent the majority of the time we waited either glaring at him or ignoring him.

When Paige did finally arrive with Carter right behind her Trick stepped into the room. He didn't look like his usual easy going self, now he looked stressed and worried. When I saw him I stood up and moved closer. It had been over two hours since I got here but hadn't heard anything about how Heather was doing.

"What's going on?" I asked, touching his arm.

"They're taking her in for a c-section. They said she's not moving along the way she should and the baby's heart rate is off or something. I don't think I got it all, I was too freaked out." Trick replied, swallowing hard.

"Hey, they'll both be just fine," I assured him and he nodded. "The doctors know what they're doing."

"This doctor is an idiot, I don't like him at all. He's not her usual doctor and he treats her like she's stupid." Trick insisted, his hands on his hips and shaking his head. "I'm pretty sure he only decided on the c-section because I almost killed him."

"Well, he won't be the one doing the c-section, right?" I asked, rubbing his upper arm. He nodded, biting his lip and I knew he was super worried for Heather and their baby. "Gray is at home waiting for his mom and dad and his baby brother or sister. In another hour you're gonna come out here and tell us how beautiful your baby is and Heather is doing just fine."

Trick nodded again and sighed. "I gotta go, I gotta change into scrubs and shit."

"We'll be here waiting for the good news." I said and he nodded again.

"Thanks Carol," he murmured and walked out of the waiting room.

"I'm not the only one who should have gone into psychology," Paige said, nudging my shoulder with hers.

"Whatever," I mumbled and turned to sit beside Carter. He wrapped his arm around my shoulder and pressed a kiss to my temple. I blinked when I saw everyone in the room watching us. "What?"

"It's just weird," Grinder shrugged and I cocked an eyebrow at him. "Good weird, though."

Bridge elbowed him in the side and I snorted at him. Carter chuckled, hiding his face in my hair but I just rolled my eyes. Joe came in with trays of coffee for everyone while we waited and a few went for walks to stretch their legs, but I wasn't going anywhere. I promised Trick I'd be right here and this is where I would be when he came back. I had just finished the last sip of my coffee when Trick rushed into the room, a huge smile on his face.

"Boy! It's a boy!" He crowed excitedly, hopping on the balls of his feet. "He's fuckin' perfect!"

A big whoop went up in the room among the members, high fives and hugs and congratulations were passed back and forth.

"How's Heather?" I asked him, gripping his lower arms.

"She's good, they're just cleaning her up and then she'll be in a room."

"Baby's name?"

"Coal Keith, after my brother, and Heather has a thing for colour names."

"How big?"

"Just over eight pounds," Trick exclaimed, his smile so wide I thought his face might crack.

"Go back to your family," I said, patting his cheek then squeaking when Trick bent and hugged me hard. Then he was running out of the room to find his girl and their baby.

Carter and I stayed just long enough to see baby Coal and check on Heather then went home. Holding hands we walked together through the parking lot to Carter's truck. I didn't say anything and he seemed to be deep in thought. That's the only excuse I have for what happened next.

Neither of us were paying attention to what was going on around us. I looked up at Carter to ask him a question and suddenly he was ducking away from me, pulling me to the ground.

"Carter!" I cried, my hands and knees hitting the concrete before he dove over me, rolling us behind a car and covering me. "What the hell?"

"Shot," Carter groaned, rolling over me, crushing me to the ground.

"You're shot?" I demanded, staring up at him with wide eyes. "Where are you hit?"

"Fuck," he cursed and rolled off of me, pushing me under the car we were hiding behind. Carter slowly lifted up on his feet with a groan.

"Where is she?"

"Who?" Carter asked, bending at the waist, his hands on his knees.

"The bitch, boss wants to talk to her." From under the car I watched Carter shake his head and stand up straight and pulled out my cell phone, texting a 9-1-1 to every guy still in the hospital, letting them know we needed help in the parking lot.

"Don't know what you're talkin' bout man," Carter mumbled and I watched as blood dripped from his fingertips to the ground.

"Don't be stupid man, we saw her with you, she under the car?"

"Dude, I don't know what you're talkin bout," Carter gasped and I could hear him swallow. He had been shot, he was in pain and our guys had better get their asses out there fast. I wasn't stupid, Carter had shoved me under the car for good reason. I didn't know if there was one guy or more than one, I knew at least one of them had a gun if there was more than one and I was not going to get my ass out from under that car until our guys came to save us.

"Hey!" I peeked out from under the car where I was hiding and saw Joe and Grinder running towards us with a couple of security guards.

"Don't move!" The guard yelled and I heard Carter sigh.

"Stay," Carter said and I knew he was talking to me. I knew this guy would shoot me if I came out even though there were multiple witnesses. He wouldn't care about that, he would only care that he did what he was ordered to do.

It didn't take long before the gunman was subdued and his gun retrieved.

"Carol," Carter groaned and I knew he was hurting and bad. I crawled out from under the car and fitted myself against his side, under his arm.

"Come on, let's get you back inside." Slowly we trudged back to the hospital and the security guard made sure we got right back to see a doctor.

Carter had been shot and the bullet had lodged itself in his shoulder. Because he had turned at the last second the bullet had entered the back of his shoulder and gotten stuck before exiting out the front. On top of that, he'd lost quite a bit of blood while standing and talking to the gunman. After two hours in surgery he ended up staying over night and I refused to go home without him.

It wasn't long after Carter got out of surgery and was resting somewhat comfortably in a room that the police showed up in his room.

"Constable Dawson," I said with a slight smile. "Nice to see you again."

"You too, Ms. Wilson, though we need to meet under better circumstances." Dawson chuckled and I nodded.

"Carol, please. And I thought you were going to come and talk to me about hanging out with us more?"

"I was, and I am, I've just been swamped at work." He shrugged, rolling his eyes. "I did contact Lo Winters, though. Good guy."

"He is that," I agreed.

"So, you wanna tell me what's going on?" Dawson asked, pulling a chair closer and sitting down.

"You remember Trick?" I asked and he nodded with a smile. Dawson had been one of the constables who had been called out to deal with Tease when he'd beat up Heather. "Him and Heather just had their baby."

"No kidding?"

"Yeah, little boy, that's why we were all here."

"Well I'll have to go and say hi before I leave."

"For sure, anyway, Carter and I were walking out to his truck to head home, we were probably the first to leave and the parking lot was deserted. I admit though I wasn't paying very close attention. I happened to look up at Carter just as he ducked away from me then pulled me to the ground and rolled me under a car."

"You didn't hear or see anything?"

"No," I sighed disgustedly. "I didn't even hear the gunshot."

"Okay, Carter rolled you under the car and then what?"

"I figured he'd put me there for a reason so I stayed. He'd told me he'd been shot so I pulled out my phone and messaged the members who were here in the hospital. Carter stood up slowly and started talking to someone. The guy asked where the bitch was and the boss wanted to talk to her. Carter just kept saying he didn't know what the guy was talking about."

"Do you know what the guy was talking about? Do you have any enemies?"

"Not really," I shrugged and Carter grunted beside me.

"Small," he rasped and cleared his throat. I jumped up and got a cup and filled it with water, sticking a straw in it. After a quick drink Carter continued. "The gunman was one of the goons Reginald Small brought with him when he came to the office."

"Reginald Small the drug dealing sex trafficker?" Dawson asked, frowning, his gaze jumping between us. "That Reginald Small?"

"One and only," Carter whispered. I smiled down at him and

smoothing my palm over his forehead.

"Okay, what's your connection to him and his organization?" Dawson asked.

"One of his men killed Lyle Connor, one of our members," I began and Dawson nodded, remembering the incident last year. "He came into our office a month or so later and demanded compensation for us putting his man in jail. I pretty much told him to go fuck himself and stay on his side of the city and we would leave him alone."

"And have you left him alone? Has he stayed on his side of the city?" Dawson asked with his eyebrows raised.

"No, and yes, however we can't stand by while the man kidnaps and sells people so we've been disrupting his supply. We kind of know who his main guys are and we sometimes follow them to keep an eye on them." I shrugged and Dawson nodded.

"Vigilante justice?"

"Not at all," I disagreed, shaking my head. "If our guys see Small's men showing too much attention to any one person we'd make sure that person knew they were a target if it was an adult or tell the target's parents if it was a kid. If we saw Small's men actively trying to take someone we made sure the police knew and found a way to stall them."

"From what I've heard you've been pretty successful with this." Dawson murmured and I shrugged. "You think this is what Carter getting shot is all about?"

"It's possible," I shrugged again looking down at Carter. "If he says the man who shot him was one of Small's then he was one of Small's. It's not like I have a ton of enemies."

"What about Robert Panone?" Dawson asked, looking down at his notes.

"What does Robert have to do with this?" Carter rasped, just as confused as I was.

"Just that he died recently and he was a friend of yours." Dawson shrugged.

"Robert was a friend of ours, he was Razz's partner until they both got HIV. Razz killed himself over it and Robert just recently passed away from pneumonia related to the virus." I explained, feeling his loss all over again. Dawson nodded and scratched the back of his head.

"I have to ask, so please bear with me, but you received quite a large inheritance when Mr. Panone passed away."

"We did," I nodded, frowning. "Robert's family had disowned him when he came out so he left his estate to Carter, myself and his nurse Shelley."

"His brother has been looking into contesting the will." Dawson explained, looking up at us from where he still sat.

"Why now? Robert died almost a year ago," Carter said, grimacing as he pushed himself up in the bed.

"He said he only just found out that Robert had died. The brothers had a falling out but he believes that Robert's death was suspicious."

"The falling out they had was Roger refusing to acknowledge his brother because he was gay. Robert called Roger to tell him he was dying and Roger basically said he didn't care and neither did the rest of the family. I don't know if there was an autopsy but we visited Robert the day before he passed away. He had pneumonia, he said himself he was glad we came that day and not the next because he knew he'd miss us if we had waited."

Dawson nodded sadly and sighed.

"Why hasn't our lawyer been notified about all of this?" I asked and Dawson shrugged.

"I honestly don't know. I would think that if your lawyer, Rachel, right?" I nodded and he continued, "If she wasn't the one who handled the case in the first place then she wouldn't be the one to know about it being contested now. You should probably contact that lawyer."

"You're right," I said and looked down at Carter. "Do you remember his name?"

"Leland Carlyle," Carter murmured, wincing again when he shifted his shoulder then groaned. "I remember because it was such a strange name for a guy who really wasn't any older than you and me."

"Right," I nodded.

"I know Carlyle," Dawson said. "He's a good guy."

"I should talk to Shelley, too and see if she's heard anything about it since she did get Robert's house." I said and Carter nodded. "I'll do it tomorrow."

"When are you out of here?" Dawson asked.

"Tomorrow," Carter said, reaching up to scratch his chin.

"Isn't that a little early?" Dawson asked, frowning.

"Don't care, I'm not staying here any longer than I have to," Carter grumbled. "Last time I was in the hospital after getting shot I ended up sterile."

"Uh -"

"He was shot in the leg, the bullet hit his femoral artery, he got an infection and that's what caused the *possible* sterility," I explained and Dawson nodded his understanding with a smile.

"Well, I think I'm good for right now," he said standing and tucking his notebook into his pocket. "If I have any questions I'll give you a call."

"Thanks Dawson," I said and Carter lifted his left fist for a bump. When he was gone I turned to Carter with a glare. "You lost a lot of blood, if you have to stay another night you're staying."

"Carol, I'm going home tomorrow."

"I watched blood drip from your fingertips, Sean!" I never used his first name, or at least rarely, so he should know how serious I was. "If your doctor says you're not leaving the hospital tomorrow you're not leaving the damn hospital."

"We'll see." He said and I grunted at him. We would see.

Unfortunately I lost that round and Carter did go home the next morning. It helped that we had opened a clinic in the one remaining space of our strip mall and we had a doctor onsite if we needed one. I still wasn't happy about it but Carter was adamant so I gave up.

While he was recuperating in my bed, though I moved all his stuff up to my apartment and there was nothing he could do about it.

"All you had to do was say so," he grumbled later as we lay in bed, talking like we usually did. "I would have moved all my shit in here years ago if you had just said so."

"I know," I sighed and kissed his chest.

"You know what I was thinking? When I got shot?"

"What were you thinking?"

"I was thinking those five years we were doing our thing I should have gotten a piercing."

"What?" I demanded, sitting up to stare down at him.

"Seriously, not like I didn't have time to heal and shit," he shrugged then winced and I rolled my eyes. "Okay, for real, I was thinking we should get married. I want to get married."

"You want to get married?" I asked, quietly, watching his face.

"Absolutely, I love you, I want the world to know it."

"Is this you asking?"

"No, I'll ask properly when I'm not in a sling, I'm just saying that's what I want."

"Okay, I'll get Slouch to check the status of my divorce first thing in the morning. Karl swore he signed the papers over a month ago."

Thankfully my divorce was almost final and I didn't have to send Joe and Mason over to Karl's house to *persuade* him to sign them.

CHAPTER 18

Carter

Groaning, two weeks later, I tried to roll out of bed. My shoulder had stiffened up and I was having to use every other muscle in my upper body to sit myself up on the edge of the bed. The stitches had come out a couple of days ago, the sling was gone and I was about to start physio. I was frustrated to say the least, not being able to work out except for my legs. Even running hurt.

"Hey," I turned to see Carol walking through the door of our room. Yes, *our* room. After everything that had happened in the last couple of months Carol had been telling everyone that we were together and had been for years. "How's your shoulder?"

"Stiff," I muttered and leaned back against her as she crawled across the bed and wrapped herself around my back.

"You want me to rub it down, loosen it up?"

"Would you?" I asked, looking at her over my shoulder. "I'd really appreciate it."

"Absolutely." Carol smiled and kissed my cheek. She reached behind her and pumped some of her lotion into her hand and rubbed her hands together. When her warm hands cupped my shoulder and started rubbing her thumbs into my stiff muscles I sighed heavily. Her hands moved up my neck and down my left side.

I groaned again, dropping my chin to my chest, feeling goose-bumps flash across my skin. I always loved having Carol's hands on me and even now with the pain in my shoulder I was thickening and hardening. When Carol started kissing across my shoulders, still digging her thumbs around the scar in my shoulder I knew she wasn't unaffected by what she was doing either. Her fingertips started brushing across my back and around my side, making me shiver.

Now her hands weren't massaging so much as rubbing, her palms flat. I was breathing heavily then gasped when her hand slid down and cupped my hard cock, squeezing tightly. Groaning again I dropped my head back as Carol kissed and sucked up and down my throat, then licked up to my ear. Her hand squeezing and pumping my cock through my underwear.

Slowly Carol shifted on her knees and crawled around me, stepping off the bed she sunk to her knees in front of me. Lifting both hands she curled her fingers around the top of my underwear and pulled them down, releasing my cock to her view.

"Babe," I whispered as she leaned forward and licked me from the base to the tip, swirling her tongue around my crown. Sucking just the head of my cock into her mouth she poked her tongue into the slit before sliding her mouth as far down my length as she could go.

"Mmm," she hummed, swallowing around the head.

"Fuck," I gasped, leaning back on my uninjured side and sliding my left hand into her soft hair. Carol had been working at getting more of me into her mouth, relaxing her throat muscles. She was close, her nose almost touching my stomach before she pulled away, sucking hard. "Stop, stop, stop, stop," I panted, my hand tightening in her hair. "Come here, take your pants off."

Carol stood quickly, shoving her pajama pants down her legs as I leaned over and pulled the bottle of lube from my night stand.

"I don't want it," she said, batting my hand away.

"This is a different one," I told her, gripping her hip. "I don't want to hurt you."

I knew she hated how thick the lube was so once again I'd done some research to find one that was thinner and not as slimy. I took her hand and poured some in her palm then wrapped her hand around my cock again.

"Better, right?" I asked and she nodded with a slight whimper. I shoved my underwear down farther and pulled her closer. "Come on, ride me."

Carol lifted her knees to either side of my hips. I held my cock up, my other hand wrapped around her hip, gripping her ass as she lowered herself over me. Moving slowly she slid down, her head tipped back and a heavy sigh slipping through her lips. We both moaned together once I was seated fully inside her and she swiveled her hips, rubbing her clit against me. Her inner muscles clenched around me with every movement.

"I think I could come like this," she whispered, panting as she lifted up slightly and slammed herself back down.

"Do it, I'm so fucking close, I'm almost there," I growled, my hands gripping her hips tightly. I slipped my hands up and under her shirt, cupping her ribs as she swiveled her hips again and clenched around me. "Keep going, don't stop."

I leaned forward and licked her throat, kissing and sucking her sensitive skin as she moved. She moved faster and harder, tightening her inner muscles around me, milking me as she rubbed her clit against me, panting and breathing hard. As I felt her climax starting I gripped her hips again and started lifting her and pulling her down over me, thrusting my hips up to meet her.

"Carter!" She cried, her fingers digging into my shoulders as her head fell back and her back arched.

It only took two thrusts before I was emptying inside her with a grunt into her throat. Carol sighed as I fell back onto my back, taking her with me and holding her against my chest. Still panting she tucked her lips against my neck, her pussy rippling around me with the aftershocks of her orgasm.

"Holy fuck," I groaned and kissed her temple. "We should start every morning like this."

Carol giggled and kissed under my jaw then sighed happily then groaned unhappily when her cell phone chirped.

"That was Slouch's ringtone," she told me, sitting up and crawling off my lap with a whimper. "I asked her to look into the mess with Robert's family."

"Mmm," I hummed and sat up, my muscles much looser now than they had been.

"You're right, that lube was much better." Carol said, bending to grab her pajama bottoms and going to shower. I chuckled and pulled my underwear back up before going into the kitchen to make a cup of coffee. There was a knock on our door just before Paige walked in. I turned and put another pod in the Keurig and made her a cup of coffee.

"Whoa dad, put some clothes on," she teased, sitting on a stool on the other side of the counter. I smiled at her and shook my head.

"Just got out of bed, kid," I told her and set her cup in front of her before handing her the flavoured creamer from the fridge.

"Thanks, and I don't want to hear about your bed fun," she

smiled as she poured a bit of creamer into her coffee.

"Morning, Paige," Carol said as she walked through the apartment to our room wrapped in a towel.

"Mornin'," Paige called back and sipped her coffee. "What do you guys have planned today?"

"Nothing that I know of," I shrugged and drank my own coffee. "Your mom just got a message from Slouch so I'm sure we'll be in the office for a bit. What about you?"

"Hanging out with Heather and the babies," Paige smiled and I nodded.

"How're they doing?"

"I think it's taken Heather a little longer to recuperate after the c-section and she's frustrated about it but they're good. Coal sure is a cute little bugger, and so good. Heather said he sleeps really good, and Gray absolutely loves being a big brother."

"I don't know shit about kids, but I imagine sleeping is a good thing," I chuckled and she nodded. I turned and started making another coffee for Carol just as she came out of her room, dressed for the day and combing her fingers through her wet hair. I poured just a bit of vanilla creamer in her coffee and handed her the cup.

"I'm going up to see Heather, you want to come with?" Paige asked her mom who shook her head as she sipped her coffee.

"Got a meeting with Slouch first," she replied then patted my ass. "Go get dressed, you have to come with."

I bent and kissed her lips then moved out of the kitchen, messing up Paige's hair as I passed her.

"Dad!" She yelled and I laughed. I took a quick shower and went to our room to get dressed, thankful I had thought to wrap a towel around my hips since Paige was still sitting at the counter when I walked through. "Not lookin' dad!"

"Thanks little girl!" I told her and closed the bedroom door. When I came back out Paige was still talking about Heather.

"She said to tell you thanks for the bonds for Coal and Gray but I told her she should tell you herself." Paige said and Carol nodded. It was something Carol had started doing now that there were a couple more kids in the clubhouse. When Coal was born she had sat down with Bridge and bought a savings bond for each of the kids, just a hundred dollars but it would gain a lot of interest over the years.

"It was no big deal," Carol shrugged but I knew it was actually a big deal. She had wanted to do something for all the kids and she wanted to make things easier on their parents once they got older. If they decided to go to university or trade school they would have some money to help. "It was a tax right off anyway."

"Whatever," Paige scoffed and finished her coffee. "I'm out, see ya dad!"

"Bye little girl." I smiled and wrapped my arm around Carol's shoulders and kissed the top of her head. "You need to just say you're welcome when someone thanks you for your generosity."

"It's really no big deal," Carol insisted, shaking her head.

"Carol, you're a good person, you do good things and you can accept praise once in a while." I told her and turned her to face me. I cupped her cheeks and kissed her. I hadn't planned on more than a gentle touch of my mouth to hers but as always that little taste just wasn't enough. I opened my mouth and pushed my tongue past her lips and devoured her.

Carol whimpered and gripped my t-shirt at my waist, holding

me close. She kissed me back eagerly, pressing as much of her body against mine as she could.

"Come back to bed," I whispered and she moaned into my mouth.

"We can't," she whined and I snorted a laugh. Her eyelids were lowered but I could see in her eyes how much she really wanted to go back to bed. "We have to meet Slouch in a couple of minutes, we're probably going to be late."

"Ugh, this better be an important meeting," I growled and nipped her bottom lip.

"We'll meet with Slouch, visit Heather and the babies, come back here and go back to bed, lock our bedroom door and not come out until morning."

"That sounds like a spectacular plan," I agreed and kissed her hard then let her go. "Come on, the sooner we get to Slouch the sooner we get back here and naked."

"You know, I like this look you've got going on," she said, plucking at the short sleeved t-shirt I was wearing over the long sleeved one.

"It's too cold for a t-shirt but not cold enough for a sweater." I shrugged. Carol laughed and grabbed her phone, slipping it into the back pocket of her jeans and we left the apartment.

We rode the elevator down, waved to a few people in the main room then left, hurrying through the cooler air of late fall to the office. No one should be here since it was Saturday but Carol said Slouch would be in her office. I was surprised to find the door locked but glad for it. Slouch was always all about safety and I liked it.

"Here," I said, pulling my keys out, knowing Carol hadn't brought hers. I unlocked the door and pulled it open then locked it again once we were inside. We walked back to

Slouch's office but she wasn't there.

"Slouch!" Carol called but there was no answer. We frowned at each other and went to check the rest of the office. The entire space was empty so Carol pulled her phone out of her pocket and texted Slouch. I turned when I heard a jingle coming from Slouch's office and found her phone sitting on her desk.

"What the hell?" I demanded, holding it up to show Carol. Instead of answering she called Paige.

"Hey, you see Slouch at all today? No, she's not here but her phone is. No, she's not in the bathroom, I checked." Carol paused and listened to what Paige was saying then nodded and ended the call. She opened her mouth to say something just as her phone rang again. "Hello?"

Carol looked up at me with a frown and then her eyes widened. She quickly pulled the phone away and put it on speaker so I could hear what was being said.

"- she's awfully pretty this little one," Small's voice came through the phone. I pulled out my phone and started recording. "All this blond hair on such a small frame, she could easily pass for much younger than she is."

"What do you want, Small?" Carol demanded and he chuckled.

"You know what I want, I want you to stay away from my people and my business."

"You know we can't do that, Small." Carol told him, shaking her head. "We can't allow women and children to be exploited that way."

"Then you owe me a lot of money, how do you propose to make up for my loss of revenue."

"I don't propose anything, there is no market here for your business, you need to find another way to make your money. I would suggest branching out into more legal means."

Small chuckled and I could hear the evil in his voice through the phone.

"I have your girl, I will just use her to make up my loss, or maybe I'll keep her, she's very pretty." Small paused and we heard a muffled scream through the phone. I worked hard to keep control of my anger but I could hear the plastic of my phone creaking in my hand. "This one and one more will recoup my losses, there are some very pretty pieces in your clubhouse. Your daughter is one of them, isn't she?"

"You can't have any of them and we will be taking the girl you have back." Carol snarled. "When we come to get her, if there is even a hair missing on her head you won't be able to hide from us, we will find you and slaughter you."

"We will see," Small said and ended the call.

"Fuck!" Carol yelled and pushed her hands into her hair. She looked up at me with tormented, tear filled eyes. I reached forward and cupped my hand around the back of her head and pulled her into my chest.

"Fuck is right," I growled and kissed the top of her head. "We'll get her back, you call Jace, I'll get the rest of the guys down here."

"Why Jace?" She asked, looking up at me confused.

"What do you think he's gonna do if we don't call him? Slouch told him what happened, he has feelings for her even if he doesn't remember her. Call him."

Carol watched my eyes for a moment then nodded once and dialed Lo. I sent out a mass text to all the members to be on alert and letting them know what was going on then sent another one calling Trick, Joe and Mason to the office. We had work to do and we weren't resting until it was done and

Slouch was back here and safe. And Reginald Small was possibly very dead.

Carol was still on the phone with Lo so I called Dawson, knowing we weren't doing this alone, we needed a police presence so Small didn't get away in the end because we hadn't crossed all our 't's and dotted all our 'i's.

Carol was still on the phone with Lo when Trick, Joe, Mason and Grinder appeared at the door. Trick yanked on it but I had forgotten to unlock it so it didn't budge. I stepped over and flipped the lock then went back to Carol's office where she'd disappeared with her phone. Trick went immediately to his office and the rest of us followed Carol. We sat around her office and listened to her talking to Lo on the phone.

"You got video yet?" Lo asked and Carol looked up at me.

"Trick's doing it now," I replied and she nodded.

"Get video calling up."

"Let's go to the conference room, it'll be easier." Mason said and we were all on the move again. Once in the conference room Trick joined us and hooked up the video call with Lo and the guys in his office. Trick had his laptop with him and was typing quickly.

"Got it?" He asked and we saw Seether nod. "Watch."

We all watched a square on the screen and watched the surveillance video of two guys slipping in the back door of the office and hiding until Slouch came in. We saw her lock the door and walk into her office, tossing her phone on the desk but she didn't get around to the other side. One of the guys rushed in after her and covered her nose and mouth and held her until she went limp in his arms.

The man tossed her small form over his shoulder then both were leaving out the back door again. Slouch was tossed into the back of a waiting SUV and it quickly drove away.

"No plate," someone said and Trick growled.

"Lo, I need to get there," Jace said, his voice sounded tortured.

"You and Bull are on the next flight out," Lo assured him and we all nodded.

"What are we thinking?" Lo asked and I sighed.

"I called Dawson, he seems to be the guy most often assigned to our cases when we need the police," I began and Lo nodded.

"I talked to him, he seems solid."

"I think he is, he's a good man," I agreed then continued. "He should be here any minute but given what Small is into we need to get Slouch out of there fast."

"Rachel," Jace snapped, pushing to his feet. "Her name is Rachel."

"Sorry man," I said gently and he sighed, beginning to pace.

"What's our time table here?" Mason asked, folding his arms over his chest.

"I think our time is up," Carol said looking up at him. "I think if we don't get her back in the next twelve hours we'll never see her again."

"Fuck!" Jace snapped.

"I agree," I nodded, ignoring Jace for the most part. "The way he was talking I'd say he's going to sell her for a huge amount of money, or he's going to use her as quick as possible. She was alive and awake when he called if that was her screaming in the background but I think she's out of time. He said he's trying to recoup lost revenue so we might have a little extra time but I wouldn't count on him planning on selling her."

"I would agree with you on that," we all looked up to see Dawson standing in the doorway.

"Come have a seat, Dawson," Carol said, waving the constable into the room. Once he was sitting she pointed to the guys on the screen, introducing them quickly then turning back to Dawson. "What have you got?"

"Not much other than the guy who shot Carter has asked for a deal if he squeals." Dawson sighed.

"With one of our people missing I would vote for the deal." Trick muttered as he typed.

"I second and third that!" Jace exclaimed as he continued to pace.

"I called the DA about Rachel being missing and in Small's hands. Given the amount of help you guys have given us to shut Small down it looks like you're going to get your vote. We all want Rachel back in one piece." Dawson nodded.

"I got a ping on a cell tower," Trick said suddenly and we all turned to look at him. "Either Small is really stupid or he's really full of himself. He didn't even use a burner phone. I can tell you the general area where he made the call from."

A map of the city appeared on the monitor on the wall with a red flashing dot.

"If it's not a burner phone can you pinpoint where it is now? Is it moving?" Carol asked, sitting forward.

"Why can't all the bad guys be this stupid?" Trick asked with a snicker. "The phone is not moving so either he's still there or he's ditched it."

"Go get it! Him! Her! Go!" Jace yelled at the screen.

"Dawson, call my phone, I'll hook up to CCTV," Trick said

and Dawson jumped up, rushing out of the building with Joe, Mason and Grinder hot on his heels.

"Sean," Carol said softly and I nodded. I jumped up, too and ran after Dawson, sliding into the front seat of his car just as he was putting the vehicle into gear.

"I haven't called Trick yet," Dawson said and I pulled my phone out of my pocket and made the call.

"I'm with Dawson," I said into the speaker when Trick picked up.

"CCTV shows nobody in or out of that location. It's an old warehouse that seems to be abandoned." He told me and I looked at Dawson who nodded.

"Regardless we've got back up coming, you see any vehicles around there?"

"No, especially not a dark coloured SUV with blacked out plates, but it could be parked inside."

"Or it could be a trap and the whole building is set to blow," I said and Dawson nodded.

"Eh," Trick said and I could just see him shrugging. "Then I guess it's a good thing you're an explosives expert hey?"

"Fucker," I muttered and he snickered.

"Hey guys," Carol said, getting our attention. "Jace and Bull just left to catch a charter, they'll be here a lot sooner than we thought. Also Lo's got some guys through Diagraphic on the line. We were in luck, they've got a team in Ontario training so they're relatively close, they're coming out to help."

"Fuckin' A," I heard Mason muttered and I knew Carol had an open line to the other vehicle on her phone while Trick was on with Dawson and me.

With lights and sirens we made it to the warehouse in record time and parked a few blocks away. As Dawson called in his position I got out of the car and walked over to the driver's side of Mason's SUV.

"See anything yet?" He asked and I shook my head.

"I could go check but my range of motion is still fucked," I said, shrugging my shoulder a bit.

"I'm going," Joe said quickly and slid out of the back of the SUV. "Small's never seen me, it makes sense."

"Be careful." I told him and he waved his middle finger over his head at me as he jogged up the street. Looking both ways he quickly crossed then walked in front of the warehouse with his head bowed and his hands swaying. It was almost as if he was talking to himself, trying to look like he was out for a stroll and not there to look at the warehouse.

He stopped right in front of it and turned to look up at the building across the street, standing with his hands on his hips. Then he turned and looked up at the warehouse we were looking at. He looked around like he was lost then stepped towards our warehouse and stepped inside. Just as quickly he stepped back out and turned his back to the wall and leaned against it. Joe stood, looking completely nonchalant with his shoulders leaning back on the wall and one knee bent, his foot pressed flat against the old bricks.

Looking around he bobbed his head as though he were listening to music then flashed two fingers.

"We got two inside," I mumbled then watched as Joe grabbed his crotch and I snickered. "I'm guessing that means it's two men."

"That would be my guess," Mason muttered, chewing on his thumb.

Surprisingly as we stood watching the two men walked out of the building and right past Joe.

"Hey," we heard him call as the first stepped just past him. The other reached for something under his jacket and Joe slammed his fist into the guy's face, dropping him with one punch.

"Fuck!" I yelled and started running as Joe took a punch to the stomach from the other guy then blocked another flying towards his head. With two quick swings he had the guy on his knees but still conscious. "Holy shit, Joe!"

"It happens," Joe shrugged as he pushed the guy he was fighting to the ground on his stomach as Dawson joined us.

"I haven't seen a guy taken out with one punch since I watched Hammer fight," Grinder said with a huge smile. "I think we've got another Hammer on our hands, like a sledgehammer, man."

Dawson quickly handcuffed the guy Joe was sitting on and read him his rights but didn't move him. We only waited a couple of minutes before another police car arrived and the constable jumped out and cuffed the guy napping on the sidewalk.

"Can you check this out?" Mason asked me, peeking through the door.

"We know for sure these guys belong to Small?" Dawson asked before I walked away. I pointed at the one still conscious.

"That one is, I'm sure if you searched the other one you'll find a gun of some sort under his jacket."

"Got it," Dawson said and started moving the two guys to the police cruisers as I walked over to Mason.

"What are we looking at?" I asked, following his gaze.

"Just wanted to make sure nothing was wired." He said and I nodded. I began checking all points of entry but with the main door sitting wide open I doubted there was anything there.

"Get your lights out, check for trip wires," I said, pulling out my phone and turning on the flashlight.

"You think she's here?" Grinder asked as we moved slowly through the huge main room.

"No, but we've still gotta check," I murmured. Since Carol had been voted president Grinder and I had come to an understanding. I wouldn't say we'd become buddies in the last few years but we certainly didn't hate each other, either. I knew when push came to shove that I could count on him when I needed to. The four of us moved slowly through the warehouse then stopped when I heard Dawson call my name. "Come in slow, straight line to me, there's nothing between us."

"You haven't found anything at all yet?" He asked once he'd gotten to my side, pulling out his own flashlight and turning it on. Dawson's police issue mag light was much more powerful than our cell phone flashlights and it lit up a much larger area.

"No, but I wasn't really expecting to. At least I wasn't expecting to find Slouch." I told him, looking around the room.

"Don't let Jace hear you call her that," Mason snickered and I sighed.

"Hey guys, there's a door over here," Grinder said suddenly and before I could stop him he pulled it open.

The explosion of sound had us all hitting the floor but the blast knocked Grinder back and off his feet.

"No!" I yelled and belly crawled across the floor towards Grinder. He lay motionless on the floor, a pool of blood growing around him. I heard Dawson call for EMT and backup on his mic as Mason and Joe called back and forth to each other. "Grinder!" I yelled in his face but his stare was already blank. "No Grinder, come on man."

I crawled up on my knees and tore open the front of his shirt, finding a huge bullet wound in his chest, blood bubbling out. I tore off my own shirt and pressed it into the wound, trying to slow the flow of blood.

"Come on Grinder, don't do this," I muttered through clenched teeth. "Stay with me man."

Dawson slid up to Grinder's other side, slipping in the pool of blood and checked for a pulse in his throat.

"Fuck, he's gone man," Dawson gasped, swallowing hard.

"No he's not," I insisted, shoving Grinder's chest, trying to get a response. "Wake up Grinder! Open your fucking eyes!"

"Carter!" Dawson yelled in my face, grabbing my shoulders and shaking me. "He's gone!"

"No!" I screamed in Dawson's face but he didn't back off. Instead he locked his gaze with mine and I could see the sympathy in his eyes. "He can't be."

"I'm sorry," Dawson whispered and shoved against my shoulders, shaking me again and I fell back on my ass.

"Carter, check it out," Mason called from the room Grinder had opened. Panting I looked over, knowing my job wasn't done yet. Slowly I got to my feet and righted the long sleeved T I was still wearing and shuffled over to the doorway. "Look," he said, pointing around the room and I followed his finger. "It's set up to fire when the door was pulled open."

I looked around, seeing the wire that was strung through pulleys and tied around the trigger of the rifle. A Browning single shot rifle and I would bet a hundred bucks there was a 30-06 in it.

I stood looking around that room, seeing the weapon that had killed my friend and cursed.

Then I looked at Joe and Mason who were looking at me expectantly and I shook my head.

"No," Mason said, shaking his head and I looked away, unable to keep eye contact as my eyes filled with tears. "FUCK!"

"That son of a bitch is dead," Joe snarled and stormed out of the room.

From somewhere out in the main area my phone rang with Carol's ringtone. Now I had to tell her we had lost a man. I had to tell her that she would have to tell Bridget that Grinder was gone. The man she had finally agreed to move in with. The man she had planned on marrying and possibly having kids with in the near future.

Fuck, I didn't want to do this.

CHAPTER 19

Carol

I stood in the hallway in front of Bridget and Grinder's apartment door and sighed, burying my face in my hands.

"Babe," Carter whispered and I nodded. I sniffed and took a deep breath as he cupped my shoulder and squeezed. I lifted my hand and knocked on the door. It didn't take long before Bridge had opened the door and she smiled at us.

"Did you find her? Is she back?" Bridge asked excitedly. She looked from my face to Carter, Mason and Joe behind me then back to me. "You need to come in."

I nodded slowly and she stepped back, holding the door. We all filed in and waited for her to follow us to the living room.

"So, what's going on?" She asked, swinging her hands in front of her and clapping her palm against her fist lightly, biting her lip.

"Bridge, hon, have a seat," I said pointing at the couch.

"I need to sit down," she said softly and nodded. Mason sat beside her and I sat on the coffee table in front of her. Joe sat on the far side of the couch and Carter stood just behind me, and I knew he was still hurting after watching Grinder die. I knew he would be for a long time.

"Bridge, hon -" I started and she frowned.

"Where's Grinder?" She looked around at the other guys but

none of them could meet her eyes.

I sighed and dropped my chin.

"Sweetie, Grinder didn't make it," I murmured, reaching forward and taking her hands in mine.

"What, like he missed the bus?" Bridge asked with a smile that didn't reach her eyes. Eyes that were beginning to fill with tears and look hysterical. "He needs to come home, Caro."

"Bridget, Grinder was shot, the autopsy isn't done yet but the EMTs said the bullet went straight through his heart, he had no chance," I whispered, my own eyes filling with tears.

"I tried, Bridget," Carter murmured, swallowing hard and sniffing. "I tried to bring him back."

"I - Grinder, Paul, he has to come back, he just moved in here, with me," Bridget insisted, looking up at Carter then over at Mason and Joe. When she looked back at me her lips turned up slightly and she shook her head. "We just moved in together, I - we haven't even put all his things away."

Bridget blinked quickly as tears slid down her cheeks and I bit my lip, trying not to cry with her, not yet and squeezed her hands again.

"He said when he got back today he had a surprise for me, o-only he was really horrible at keeping secrets," she looked up at Carter with a smile and I saw him nod. "Did you know that? He couldn't keep a secret to save his life. I found it," she reached behind her and picked something up off the table behind the couch and showed it to me. It was a small ring box and when I opened it I found a gorgeous engagement ring.

"It's beautiful," I whispered and swallowed hard.

"Isn't it?" Bridget nodded with a whispered sob. "It's exactly what I would have picked out. You know, he was really worried about our age difference?"

"He is quite a bit older than you Bridget," Mason murmured, his hand on her shoulder and she nodded.

"Thirteen years, but I didn't care," she whimpered, her face crumpling. "I know you guys had your differences," she said to Carter who shook his head. "But he really was a good man."

"He was a very good man, Bridget," Carter agreed, nodding slowly. "I saw that, we had our differences, you're right, but once we got to know each other we were good, he was solid."

Bridget sobbed again and turned her face into Mason's shoulder. He held her tightly, his hands rubbing up and down her back. After a minute she sniffed and cleared her throat, trying to take a deep breath.

"I had a surprise for him, too." She whispered but her eyes were staring blankly, her temple still on Mason's shoulder. She sniffed and rested her hand on her stomach. "I just found out a couple of days ago." She whispered again and looked at me, no expression in her gaze. "I'm pregnant with Paul's baby and now he's not here to raise it with me."

"Oh God, Bridge, I'm so so sorry," I murmured as her whole body crumpled and she cried even harder into Mason's chest.

"I'm gonna kill him," Joe growled and stood, storming out of the apartment.

"I got him," Carter murmured and followed the much younger man.

"I'll get Paige and Jordyn," I told Mason as he held Bridget while she cried. "I'll take the kids to Heather."

Mason nodded and just continued to hold Bridget. I squeezed her knee and left her apartment. I needed to take a break before I went to find Paige, Jordyn and Heather and tell them about Grinder, ask Paige and Jordyn to help Bridge, ask Heather to watch all the kids. I leaned back against the wall beside the door and bent in half, bracing my hands on my knees. I took a couple of deep breaths then straightened quickly when the doorway to the stairs opened and Carter and Maker walked through.

Maker ignored me but I saw the devastation on his face. It was the look of a man who had just lost his best friend. As Maker walked into Bridget's apartment Carter pulled me into his arms and held me tightly against his chest. As much as I didn't want to cry standing in the hallway where anyone could see me I couldn't stop the tears.

As I cried, the door opened again and Mason stepped out. When he saw us he stopped, patting Carter on the shoulder and rubbed my back then bent and kissed the top of my head before turning and walking away.

"I have to go get Paige and Jordyn," I said quietly, pulling away and wiping my face with the heels of my hands.

"Joe already went to find Paige," Carter said, pressing his lips to my forehead. "I'm sure Mason just went to find Jordyn."

"He needs to die," I whispered and Carter nodded. He was about to say something when his phone chirped and he shifted to pull it out of his pocket.

"The Diagraphic guys are here," he said and kissed me again then took my hand and led me to our offices. When we were all sitting in the conference room again a grim looking Trick had called up video calls with Lo and the Diagraphic offices.

"Carol," Lo began slowly, "I am so sorry for your loss."

"Thanks Lo," I sighed and sniffed. "It's worse that you think, though. After the guys left today Bridget, our accountant, her and Grinder were together, she found an engagement ring with his things, he'd told her he had a surprise for her when he got back."

"Fuck," someone in the Diagraphic office snapped.

"She had a surprise for him, too." I continued. "She's pregnant."

There was some shuffling in the background on Lo's end and he watched whatever was going on almost dispassionately. When his gaze came back to mine I could see the sadness in his eyes.

"That was Hammer," He murmured, clearing his throat. "Him and Grinder were close when Grinder was here, they kept in touch."

"I'm sorry," I whispered and Carter caught my attention when he scoffed. "What?"

"I just think it's funny that shortly before he died Grinder said Joe hit like Hammer. Joe knocked a guy flat with one punch and Grinder said he hadn't seen anything like it since he saw Hammer fight." Carter murmured and Joe growled from the doorway. He came in just before Mason walked in. They both took a chair around the table and Joe sneered at everyone, his bad attitude firmly in place. "He said Joe hit like a sledge-hammer."

"We didn't know your friend," one of the security guys said calmly. "But we would love a chance to stop the man who killed him."

"And get your girl back," another of the guys said and I nodded. There were only four guys here from Diagraphic but they were all big and all well trained.

"Do we know where she is yet?" Lo asked and I looked to Trick.

"I've been working on it," he said without looking up from his computer. Within a second there was a map of the city up on the big screen, splitting the picture of Lo and Mitch from Diagraphic. Apparently the reclusive owner of Diagraphic felt the need to get in on this mission. "I've narrowed it down to two places. Small has a large mansion on the south side of the city. The security is top notch and I've been watching camera feeds, there are guards everywhere. If you want to go in there with stealth it'll be tough."

"What's the other place?" Mitch asked, sitting forward to study the map.

"The other place is another warehouse on the north side of the city. More security, more guards and fewer cameras." Trick said.

"Where's Dawson on the information from the guy who shot Carter?" I asked and Mason sat forward.

"The last time I talked to him he said they had some pretty good information."

"Good enough for a warrant?" Micah, one of the Diagraphic guys asked.

"I don't know, I'll call him and ask," Mason said standing and leaving the room.

"We don't know which building she's in, shouldn't we wait until we know?"

"What are you thinking, Micah?" His partner Hudson asked.

"I'm thinking we go in stealthy, we just have the warrant to back us up." Micah shrugged and I nodded. "There's four of us, we're sanctioned to work with the police, we split up though, two at the house and two and the warehouse. We coordinate to hit it at the same time."

"It makes sense," Kelly said with a nod. I looked at him closely for the first time since he sat down and was surprised. He had such dark black hair it looked like he had blue highlights. But what was really striking were his piercing blue eyes. Hudson and Micah both had brown hair and brown eyes. Both men were handsome but not striking like Kelly was. Then there was Bhodi who looked like the quintessential surfer with his longer blond hair, five o'clock scruff and light blue eyes. He actually looked like Patrick Swayze from Point Break only bigger, much bigger.

"Here," Mason said, coming back into the room with his cell in his hand. "I've got Dawson on the phone."

Mason set his cell in the middle of the table and sat down.

"Dawson, we've got a few extra people in the room," I said then told him who all was there and who else was listening in. "Can you tell us what you've got?"

"We have ERT ready to roll, we're just waiting for those warrants before we start to roll out." Dawson replied. ERT stood for Emergency Response Team, Canada's version of SWAT.

"Can you include a couple of guys?" I asked, looking up at the Diagraphic team. "I've got four guys here who work for an R&R team that are sanctioned to work with the RCMP."

"I'm sending their info to your captain now," Mitch said from Vancouver.

"Fuckin' A," Dawson murmured and we heard him talking to someone else in the background. "Can they get here in the next half hour?"

"We just got word that Bull and Jace will be landing in an hour," Lo said from Kamloops and Carter stood.

"I'll take these four to Dawson then pick up the other two at the airport," he said and the five men left the room.

"I need to do something Carol," Joe said standing.

"Go with, Sledge," I said. He looked at me for a second then grunted and ran out. "Stay out of trouble!"

"Good luck with that," Lo muttered and I snorted at him. "He pulled his head outta his ass yet?"

"Did you expect him to?" I asked and Lo shook his head with a slight smile. "Bull said there was something going on with him and Paige so it can't be that bad."

"Yeah well, now Paige is pissed off because he had his head stuck up his ass for so long. He claimed her, told everyone else to stay the fuck away from her but never stepped up. She's rightfully pissed."

"We're men, Carol," Mitch mumbled with a shrug. "We're all stupid at some point in time."

I couldn't disagree with him but I knew it wasn't just men, women could be stupid, too. It was just more rare, a lot more rare.

"What do we do now?" Mason asked, looking from me to Lo and Mitch and Dawson still on the phone.

"Now we wait," Lo said and I sighed. "Mason you any good with computers?"

"I get by, I'm not as good as Trick by any means." Mason shrugged.

"Trick, can you set Mason up with a computer, between the two of you keep your eyes on both the house and the warehouse?" Lo asked and Mason frowned.

"Good idea," I said, nodding. "If Trick's got eyes on the house and Mason's got eyes on the warehouse then we're not missing anything because one of them is dividing attention."

"Exactly," Lo agreed and Mason nodded, catching on.

"Let's do it," Trick said, picking up his laptop and walking out of the room, Mason right behind him.

"How're you doing Carol?" Lo asked and I sighed.

"Definitely been better, Lo." I tapped the table and he nodded. "I've got one member kidnapped and God knows what's happening to her, one member dead and another member having a baby without the father." I shook my head and sighed. "Not sure I'm doing that great a job here, Lo."

"None of that is your fault, Carol," Lo reminded me and I shrugged.

"I'm the one that challenged Small, I'm the one who kept my guys on his case so he couldn't grab any girls or kids. You sure it's not my fault?"

"Positive Carol," Lo assured me and I sighed.

"I don't know, Lo."

"This is a horrible situation, I'm not gonna lie to you," Lo murmured, rubbing his fingertips over his bottom lip. "What would be worse, the situation you're in? Or knowing you did nothing and multiple women and little kids went missing, were sold into slavery, used by degenerates."

"I know what you're saying, Lo and tomorrow I'll agree, hell later tonight I'll agree, but right now I'm feeling pretty shitty."

"I get it, Caro, I really do." He watched me through the camera and I felt my eyes fill with tears. "It's not an easy job we've got, Caro."

"You know, it hasn't been a super easy six years." I murmured and cleared my throat. "First Razz, that was hard enough and I didn't even have the job yet," I huffed a laugh and Lo smirked.

"Then Techie and Tease and Trick on my case but damnit he was right. It's 'T' names."

I stopped and sniffed and both Lo and Mitch nodded and smiled. Mitch had kept quiet I had almost forgotten he was there.

"I remember the first time I lost someone," Mitch said with a nod then shook his head. "Fuckin' sucked. You ever hear how I met my wife?"

"No," I frowned, confused how this was relevant.

"I almost died, just barely made it out, had another officer save my ass and I wanted like hell to repay his family but I never had the chance. Not until almost twenty years later when that officer's wife was kidnapped in Columbia. Normally I wouldn't have taken my team down there for a woman who by all accounts was just some woman. The job definitely paid but I was still resistant, until I saw what her name was. She was the wife of the man who had saved me so I had to go and get her.

"Fell in love with her in the middle of the Columbian jungle." Mitch said and I still wasn't sure what he was telling this for me. "The decisions we made as leaders are never easy ones, Carol and if they are it means you don't care. If I had gone with my gut I wouldn't have met my wife, I wouldn't have three great grandkids and another two on the way. Sometimes we make mistakes and sometimes we don't but making mistakes doesn't mean we're not good at our jobs, it's what we do about fixing our mistakes that makes us good at our job."

I nodded slowly, understanding completely what Mitch was saying. I looked up at him and took a deep breath. Blinking tears out of my eyes I smiled slightly.

"Thank you, Mitch."

"I'm gonna sign off, I'll get the particulars from my guys, talk to you both later." Mitch said and before either of us could say anything more he was gone.

"He's right you know," Lo said as the door of his office opened and Hammer walked around the computer and sat beside him.

"Hey Hammer," I said smiling sadly. "I'm really sorry about Grinder."

"You know how he got that name, Carol?" Hammer asked me and I shook my head. Grinder was here before I had gotten here and already had his name. "Did you know he liked to box? Used to beg me to get in the ring with him."

"And then you'd hammer him into the ring?" I asked with a snicker.

"Sometimes," Hammer agreed with a nod. "For sure at the beginning it happened a lot, but not for long. Grinder, or Paul back then, would get into the ring with anyone, he'd train outside the ring with anyone for hours, he'd grind away at something until he got it, until he had it perfect. Then when he got back in the ring with me he'd grind away at me until I ran out of steam. See, I can hit hard and I'm relatively quick, but Grinder would work his ass off, he had stamina for days and then he'd get you down on the mat and keep grinding."

"I see it," I smiled again. "He said Joe hit like you, called him a sledgehammer."

"You called him Sledge earlier." Lo reminded me and I nodded.

"I think that's a good way to remember my friend." Hammer murmured and I agreed.

"Thanks guys." I whispered.

"Keep us posted." Lo said and ended the call.

Now, alone, I folded my arms on the table and dropped my forehead to them. I wasn't sure how I was going to get through the rest of the night. It could be so much worse though.

Sighing, I stood up and walked into Trick's office. Trick was at one desk and Mason at another, one set of monitors showing a fancy mansion and the other a rundown warehouse.

"How's it going?" I asked them but neither of them answered, not right away anyway.

"We're thinking the guard changes are on the same cycle," Mason mumbled to me, his eyes on his screen. "New one."

"Same," Trick replied and I blinked. "So here's how it goes, they've got two guys patrolling at all times. Each guy is replaced every four hours so that every two hours there's a new guy."

"So we've got a window of two hours to get in," I stated and both men nodded. "Good job guys, I'll let Dawson know. Keep it up, I'll have someone bring you something to eat."

"Thanks Carol," Mason mumbled and I left the office.

I went to the clubhouse to see who was around. I knew my best bet to get good food for Mason and Trick was either Heather or Jordyn, but I knew Heather wasn't cooking as much now that she'd had her baby and last I heard Jordyn was with Bridge. I had just decided I would just have to make something myself when I walked into the kitchen and saw Jordyn stepping out of the pantry. She froze for a second then kept walking to the counter.

"How are you, Jordyn?" I asked her and she smiled sadly at me.

"I think I should ask you that," she murmured and continued making whatever she was making.

"Today sucks," I shrugged and she nodded.

"You're doing a good job here, Carol," the woman told me and I tipped my head to the side. "I've been where Rachel is, no one bothered to even try to get me back. It's good to know Rachel has people who care so much about her . . . and that those people like me just a little bit."

"Jordyn, the people here more than just like you. We all care about you, a lot and not just because you keep us fed, though we really do appreciate that. You're a good person Jordyn, you take care of all of us, we all see that and I'm sorry it took us all so long to really welcome you."

"That's not your fault," Jordyn said, shaking her head. "I'm as much at fault for that as anyone else. I wasn't ready to come out of my head, for good reason, but I was still stuck there because I was scared. Hell, I'm still scared."

"You have reason to be scared."

"Not anymore I don't." She insisted, shaking her head again. "The gang I was with in Kamloops has been taken down, Tease is gone, Small's organization will be taken down tonight. Mason will always keep me safe."

"You sound so sure that Small is done."

"Of course I am," Jordyn assured me with a small smile. "The War Angels MC is involved, they'll definitely get the job done."

I smiled at her and nodded. "You're right."

"Will you do me a favour?"

"Absolutely, Jordyn."

"Will you take this up to Bridget and Maker?" She handed me a plastic bag with wrapped sandwiches, cookies that looked homemade, some apples and oranges and cut vegetables.

"Absolutely."

"I'm going to take this to Trick and Mason," she said holding up a similar bag. "Then I'm going to come back and I'm going to get the twins and Gray from Heather and I'm going to take them to Mason's and put them to bed."

"Jordyn, you are a valuable and necessary part of this family. Thank you."

"Thank you for letting me be here, Carol." Jordyn smiled then left the kitchen.

I wasn't sure I wanted to see Bridget again, or rather I didn't want to see her grief, but I knew I had to at the very least stop in and see how she was doing. I didn't do well with grief and while I had experienced quite a bit of my own over the last six or seven years I still had a hard time with it. I wasn't normally an emotional person and I always felt feelings like sadness and grief were a private thing.

Now though all of our hearts were laid bare and we were all wearing our grief and our loss for all to see.

CHAPTER 20

Carter

As I pulled up to the arrivals door at the airport Bull and Jace pushed through the glass doors and climbed into the SUV. Bull got in the front and Jace in the back and we were driving away before I even had a chance to put the vehicle in park.

"Where we going?" Jace demanded and Bull turned slightly in his seat so he could see us both.

"Relax man, we already talked about this," Bull told him and he growled back. "Seriously, you don't need to piss Carter off, you're gonna get punched and left in the back seat while we get shit done."

Jace slumped back sullenly and scowled, staring straight ahead out the windshield. Bull turned to me and sighed.

"What do we know so far?" He asked and I nodded.

"I don't know a shit ton," I told them slowly. "I dropped the four Diagraphic guys off and came to get you. I knew that within ten minutes of me dropping them off they were splitting up and hitting both locations. It would take each team about half an hour to get to each location. By the time we get back to the detachment where Dawson is waiting he should have some news for us."

"Fuck," Jace muttered in the back seat and I nodded.

"We don't know if Sl - uh Rachel is at the house or the warehouse. If I had to guess I'd say the house but we'll have to wait and see." I said as I drove.

"Why do you think the house?" Bull asked and I bit my lip, looking into the mirror and catching Jace's gaze, worried about how he'd react.

"Just say it," he grumbled and I sighed again.

"The way Small was talking when he called Carol, he sounded far too interested in keeping Rachel for himself. If that warehouse is where he keeps his merchandise then we'll find a shit ton of other things there, possibly more women, definitely drugs, probably guns. But I think Rachel will be at his house where he can keep an eye on her himself."

"Right," Bull agreed and Jace nodded.

"I wanna be there." Jace said just as my phone rang. I pushed the bluetooth button and answered the call, Joe's voice coming through the speakers.

"Just got word from the leaders of both teams they're set to go in," Joe, Sledge, informed me.

"Got Bull and Jace with me," I told him and he grunted in reply. "We'll be back there in the next five minutes or so."

"Yup," he said and hung up.

"He seems cheery," Bull muttered and I sighed. I had forgotten that while Grinder was getting shot, these two were in the air.

"I've got some bad news for you guys," I began and Jace sat forward. "It's not about Rachel, specifically. Trick found a ping for Small's cell phone in an old warehouse where he called me and Carol from right after Rachel was taken. We went to check it out, knowing she probably wasn't there. Joe went in first to make sure no one was there and took out two guys. The rest of us went in to check out the warehouse and Small's guys had rigged up a rifle to shoot when a door was opened and ..."

"And what?" Bull asked, his gaze jumping from me to Jace and back again.

"Uh, Grinder was shot, he didn't make it." I finished and Jace slumped back again while Bull turned away with a curse. "His girl found an engagement ring in his stuff and she just found out she was pregnant."

"For fuck sakes," Jace snapped from the back seat. I nodded, silently agreeing with him. This whole situation fuckin' sucked. Six minutes later I was pulling into the parking lot at the detachment. There wasn't a lot of public parking in the lot and it was a tight fit for my Yukon XL. Still, I was trained to drive a Humvee so the Yukon wasn't too difficult.

Again before I even had the thing in park Jace was bailing out and running to the front doors.

"Dammit," Bull muttered and bailed after him. I turned off the SUV and got out, slamming and locking the door, knowing there was really no reason to rush. Hurry up and wait was the plan for the next couple of hours no matter what happened.

When I got inside I found Joe with his fists full of Jace's shirt, holding him against a wall while the other man struggled and Bull and Dawson trying to pull them apart.

"Enough!" I bellowed and all four men froze. "Back off!" I told Joe, Bull and Dawson and slowly they stepped back but Joe kept a hand pressed to Jace's chest, holding him against the wall. I stepped forward between Joe and Jace and got into Jace's face. "You freaking the fuck out isn't helping anyone, least of all Rachel. You will behave yourself or you will leave."

Jace glared at me, breathing heavy. "Is that understood?"

"HUA," he growled, snarling at me. I shoved him hard and turned to Joe.

"Keep it together, Sledge."

"We've got camera feeds," Dawson said from across the room. We all hurried over to see multiple screens set up with what looked to be body cams. Each feed showed a ton of movement as the men ran across open space then sidled up against a wall. Some showed the men stalking through trees or around corners. When each man was in place they checked in and we saw each man look at his watch.

When their second hands hit the twelve they all started moving. Some were stealthy, some were yelling for targets to drop their weapons and lay down on the ground. It was hard to split my attention between the warehouse team and the house team but I wanted to see what was found at each location.

It took half an hour at the warehouse to get every guard out and into the yard, laying on their stomachs with their hands cuffed behind their backs. Then the hunt was on to see what was stored there. The team only found three women and they all looked like they needed a shower and food. There was a ton of heroin and cocaine found as well as a few crates of guns. There was one crate of semi-automatic pistols but there were also multiple crates of semi-automatic H&K MP5Ks, small enough to hide under a jacket but still had the ability to fire multiple rounds a second.

"The target is not here," came the team leader's voice once the warehouse had been completely searched. We all turned our attention to the team at Small's mansion and waited. It took another twenty minutes to get all of the guards and staff at Small's house out of the house and handcuffed. Small was with the group but he wasn't talking. The team searched every inch of the house but found nothing.

"Where the fuck is she?" Jace demanded angrily, his fists clenched at his sides. I was listening to the team leader at the house question Small when Dawson's phone rang. He pulled it out and put it on speaker and Mason's voice filled the room.

"He's got a safe room," Mason said quickly. "I was watching through his cameras, in his office behind the bookshelf."

"It's so cliche," Jace muttered and leaned forward with his knuckles on the desk as he watched and Dawson relayed the information to the team leader at the house. Quickly I saw it was the Diagraphic guys who rushed to the office and started searching the bookshelves, trying to find one that will open.

"Tell them the shelf with the bust of Mozart," Mason said and Dawson once again relayed the information. "Pull the head forward and twist it to the left."

"Got it," Kelly said through his mic and stood in front of the shelf in question. "Does this feel too easy to anyone else?"

"Remember what happened at the other warehouse with Grinder," Dawson told him and he nodded.

"Unless something was set up way beforehand then there shouldn't be anything there," Mason said. "When the police showed Small just shoved Rachel in the room."

"You know for a fact it was Rachel?" Dawson asked as Kelly paused, him and Bodhi standing back as the door slowly began to open.

"Yeah," Mason insisted through the phone. "I didn't have eyes on her until just before Small tossed her in that room. She was in rough shape though, I don't know how long she'll last if you leave her in that room too long."

"What kind of rough shape?" Jace demanded, not taking his eyes off the screen that showed Bodhi and Kelly.

"She was fully dressed if that's what you're asking. Beaten and bloody, though." Mason replied, sounding clinical, as though he were speaking about someone he didn't actually know and know well. "She's definitely going to need an ambulance and a hospital."

Dawson picked up a phone and made sure there was an ambulance on the way to the house.

"Go into that room slow and careful," I said through the mic that was set up in the room and Kelly and Bodhi gave each other a thumbs up so we could see their agreement.

With their H&K MP5s at the ready they slowly made their way into the room. At first it was pitch black but Kelly flicked on the light attached to his helmet and looked around. The room was small, but it had a mini fridge, a sink, a bed, shelves of canned food and a toilet in the far corner behind a thin wall. On the wall beside the door was a keypad and a computer.

On the floor beside the bed was Rachel, curled up in a ball and shivering.

"Rach," Jace gasped, his eyes wide and fearful.

"We got her," Kelly said, turning to Bodhi and I saw him reaching for a light switch.

"Don't!" I yelled into the mic and both men froze. "Don't turn on the light, you were right, it was way too easy getting in there. That room has to be rigged somehow and it might be the light switch."

"Good point," Bodhi said, slowly pulling his hand back from the switch.

"In fact, get her and get out, the door might be rigged with a timer."

"We could hurt her worse if we move her." Kelly said and I nodded even though they couldn't see me.

"You could, or you could all end up dead." I told him as he

secured his H&K to his vest and crouched beside Kelly. "Bodhi, look around, specifically at the keypad on the wall."

Bodhi did as I asked and when the camera feed cleared I saw numbers counting down on the keypad.

"See the numbers on the keypad?" I asked him and he said yes. "I wouldn't be surprised if they were counting down to a detonation or something. I would guess that until or unless a code is punched in once that countdown hits zero that room is set to blow."

"Just the room?" Bodhi asked as Kelly lifted Rachel in his arms. She cried out in pain as he carried her out of the room with Bodhi fast on his heels.

"Hell, for all I know it could be the entire house." I turned to Dawson and saw him pick up the phone again, ordering a fire-truck out to the mansion.

"EMTs are here," Bodhi said and we saw that an ambulance had just pulled up in front of the house. "We're putting her in and sending her to the hospital."

"Good work guys," Dawson said with a sigh and bent at the waist, finally able to relax.

"Come on, let's go," Jace said, pushing away from the table and walking to the door. "We've gotta get to the hospital."

His last words were cut off by a loud explosion at the mansion. The explosion was followed by a lot of swearing and yelling as guys started running around moving the men they had hand-cuffed away from the now burning house.

"What's going on?" Micah demanded from the other site and Dawson explained what was going on but that they'd found Rachel and she was on her way to the hospital.

"Let's go," I said, leading Sledge, Jace and Bull from the room.

"We'll call Carol on the way to the hospital."

It was just after three in the morning when we all pulled up to the hospital. I called Carol and she said she knew. Trick and Mason had called her to the office when the ERT teams were ready to go in and she had watched a lot of it going on through Small's own cameras.

Since we were closer to the hospital at the detachment we actually beat the ambulance getting there, but only by a couple of minutes. Jace looked lost so I went to the registration desk and let the woman there know why we were there. She nodded and made a note on her computer then smiled at me.

"I'll make sure you know how she's doing as soon as the doctors have seen her." The woman said and I thanked her. I went and sat in the waiting room where Sledge sat in a corner, nursing his bad attitude and Bull sat in a chair in the middle of the room watching Jace pace.

"You all right, Sledge?" I asked Joe, sitting in a chair a couple down from him and leaning my elbows on my knees.

"Why do you keep calling me that?" He asked with a sneer and I smiled.

"Something Grinder said, that you hit just as hard as Hammer, that you've got fists like a sledgehammer." I shrugged and he scoffed. "I think it suits you."

"Sure," he muttered then sighed. "If I have to be called something other than my name I suppose a nickname given to me by a man I respected who gave it to me right before he died is a good one to have. Sledge."

"Well, we can't call you Hammer, that's already been taken." I replied and Sledge snorted again. We all sat in silence until Carol and Paige rushed into the room with a tray of coffees. Paige went right to Sledge who stood and pulled her into his arms, burying his nose in her hair. Carol handed Jace and Bull coffee from her tray then came to me and sat in my lap.

"You doing all right?" She asked me quietly and I nodded then kissed her lips. "Trick and Mason were right behind us."

"Any word on the women from the warehouse?"

"Yeah, we decided they would be better off going to the club-house and seeing our doctor there instead of coming here." Carol said and I nodded again. "Jordyn's there waiting for them, since she's been through what they have she wanted to be there to help."

"Makes sense," I agreed just as Trick and Mason walked in. Trick went straight to Bull and gave him a manly, back slap-ping hug then shook Jace's hand.

"We got her, man." Trick said, squeezing Jace's shoulder. "She's beat up but she's tough, she'll make it through."

Jace nodded and bumped Trick's shoulder with his.

"We came in the same time as the ambulance," Mason said, grabbing a coffee from the tray Carol held and sat beside us. Sledge sat back in his seat in the corner, only now with Paige in his lap, facing the rest of us.

"Family for Rachel Gibbons?" We all looked up as a doctor stepped into the room.

"I'm her fiance," Jace said, stepping forward with the bald faced lie. No one corrected him, though, knowing the doctor would be more likely to give us information this way.

"Rachel has a dislocated right shoulder and a broken elbow. We've set both and her arm should heal with no issues. She was beaten severely, though and has a concussion and broken ribs. We believe there might be some internal bleeding so she's going into surgery now to make sure she's okay. I would guess her kidneys and liver are bruised and we may have to remove her spleen. She's got multiple shallow cuts on her left arm that don't need stitches but should be watched closely for infection. It looks to me as though she was tortured. Two of the fingernails on her right hand were torn out and her right ankle was also broken.

"Rachel has a long road to recovery and she'll need a lot of help." The doctor continued with a heavy sigh. "We're optimistic, though that she will make a full recovery. She's still young, we'll get her body back to where it should be but be aware that she will need therapy. I can't imagine anyone being tortured the way she was and being completely sane afterward, man or woman."

"Thank you doctor," Jace rasped, his hands on his hips and his head hanging.

"Talk to the registration desk, they'll let you know where you can wait while Rachel's in surgery." We all nodded and the doctor left again. Jace took a deep breath and lifted his gaze to the ceiling then blew the breath out slowly. Mason left the room then came back and told us we needed to head up to the third floor to wait. We all trudged out of the waiting room and into the elevator, probably straining the weight restrictions.

When we stepped off the elevator Mason went to the desk and let the nurses there know why we were suddenly arriving en masse.

"Can you call Maker and let him know what's going on?" Carol asked me and I nodded, pulling out my phone. "Bridget will want to know that we have Rachel safe."

"Absolutely," I said and opened Maker's contact information. I hit dial and stepped away from the group a few steps.

"Yeah?" He said when he answered.

"Hey, how's Bridge?" I asked first and he sighed heavily.

"Man, she either sleeps or she cries, I'm lost." Maker replied and I could hear how much his best friend's loss weighed on him.

"I know man, it fuckin' sucks. She eat anything?"

"A little bit, but only because Jordyn forced her to then made her feel guilty about the baby."

"Shit," I murmured and ducked my head.

"Any word on Slouch?"

"Yeah, that's why I'm calling. We're at the hospital now, she's in surgery. Dislocated shoulder, broken elbow, ribs and ankle, possible internal bleeding, bruised organs." I lifted my hand and rubbed my palm over my head. "Doctor believes given her injuries she was tortured, definitely beaten but it doesn't look like she was raped."

"Well, I suppose we should be thankful for that," Maker mumbled and I grunted. "I'll let Bridge know, she'll want to know that Slouch is safe. What about Small and his group?"

"Small has been arrested as have all the guys who were on his grounds and at the warehouse. I haven't heard yet from Dawson about all of that but I'm sure there was enough evidence found at both locations to put him away for a very long time. The team also found three other women who have been taken to the clubhouse. Jordyn is with them now."

"Good, she'll be the best one to stay with them and keep them calm."

"Yeah, when we know more about Rachel I'll give you a call. Spread the word, yeah?"

"Yeah, absolutely." Maker said then ended the call without

saying goodbye.

"How's Bridge?" Carol asked, stepping into my arms as I slid my phone into my back pocket.

"Maker said she's sleeping and crying. Jordyn had to guilt her into eating something but he thinks she'll be happy to hear about Rachel." I told her and she nodded.

"Both of them have a long road of healing ahead of them." Carol sighed into my chest and I nodded, rubbing my cheek over the top of her head. We stood in the hallway for a few minutes, just being together. We didn't know how long Rachel's surgery would take and I for one wanted to give Jace enough room to pace. I had a feeling that if we didn't he'd lose what little control he had. "Have you talked to Jace?"

"Not about Rachel, no." I replied, rubbing her back. "We didn't really have a chance to talk."

"If you're wondering if he remembers her, the answer is no," Bull said, stepping up beside us. Carol reached over and rested her fingertips on his upper arm. "He's remembered a few things that he had forgotten but all he remembers about Rachel is going to her barracks between the two deployments and not being able to find her."

"At least he remembers something," Carol sighed again and I nodded.

"It's really tearing him up, though that he can't remember anything else. He even tried hypnosis but couldn't come up with anything more." Bull explained sadly.

"He may never remember," I said slowly and the other two nodded.

"He does remember some other things," Bull said, turning as Jace stepped out of the waiting room to pace in the hallway. "He's always done that, too. Not often because he's usually pretty even keel, even overly cheerful, always joking. But when shit hit the fan and he couldn't figure it out, which was rare cause he's so damn smart, he'd pace."

"That should be his name," Carol muttered and I agreed.

"Between Sledge and Pace it seems to be the day for new names." I said and squeezed Carol tightly.

It was two hours later that a doctor finally came to tell us that Rachel was out of surgery and resting in a room. They didn't think she needed to be in ICU but they did want to limit the number of visitors she had.

"We didn't have to remove her spleen, thankfully," the doctor said with a heavy sigh. "Her spleen along with her kidneys and liver and intestines are bruised from the beating she took. There wasn't much we could do for her ribs, but they aren't in danger of puncturing her lungs and her heart is healthy. Her shoulder is back in place and her elbow is set but it can't be casted because of where it was broken. She'll be in a sling for quite awhile while that heals."

"Can we see her?" Jace asked, desperately.

"Yeah, just two at a time, though," the doctor said and left the room.

"Paige, you go with Jace," Carol said, taking charge like she was so good at doing. "I'm sure Jace will want to stay the night, I'll stay with him, when Paige comes out the rest of you go home and get some rest."

"I'm staying," I told her and she looked up at me with gratitude in her eyes. "I'll stay here or in the hall though."

"Now that Rachel's found I've gotta head home," Bull said, clapping Jace on the shoulder. "I'll stop in and say goodbye before I leave tomorrow though."

"Yeah," Jace nodded, slowly.

"When I get home I'll ship all your stuff out."

"Thanks."

"Let's go," Paige said, touching Jace's arm and pointing to the nurse standing in the doorway, waiting to show them to Rachel's room. They weren't gone long before Paige was back with tears in her eyes.

Sledge pulled her into his arms and held her while she cried then they were all gone and Carol was gone to sit with Jace for the night.

Bull promised to bring real food and coffee when he came the next morning and I made myself as comfortable as I could, knowing I would probably get little to no sleep in the uncomfortable waiting room.

CHAPTER 21

Carol

I don't know what woke me, but I was definitely stiff and uncomfortable. I blinked and slowly sat up, looking around the dimly lit room. The door was closed and there was no nurse in the room but Jace was standing beside Rachel's bed, talking quietly to her. He was bent all the way over her as though he was protecting her, his arm wrapped around her injured shoulder.

She looked upset, like she was crying, and he looked like he was trying to calm her down. I got up and left the room, going to find a nurse to let her know Rachel was awake, then to find Carter. The nurse smiled at me then rushed around the desk into Rachel's room and I went to see Carter.

"Hey," I said softly, sitting beside his chair in the waiting room. He looked incredibly uncomfortable.

"Mornin' babe," Carter rasped, throwing an arm around my shoulder and pulling me close. He kissed my temple and snuggled up with me. "You get any sleep?"

"Some, but I hurt, hospital chairs are not very comfortable." I sighed and he nodded. "You?"

"Ugh," he groaned and shifted, stretching his back. "Same as you but I also didn't sleep much anyway keeping an eye out."

"You think you need to keep an eye out?"

"Nah, probably not, but you never know. I haven't heard anything from Dawson so we don't know that all of Small's guys were caught. I would like to think with the head of the snake gone the worker bees will scatter."

"Isn't it a queen that runs a beehive?" I chuckled, rubbing my cheek on Carter's chest.

"Given the cost of Small's outfit the last time we saw him I'd say he could be a queen." Carter muttered and I laughed. "Don't get too close baby, I can't smell good."

"Like I care," I whispered and stretched up to kiss the underside of his jaw, his beard growing in around his fu manchu. "Rachel was awake when I came out, she looked pretty freaked out so I thought I should give them a moment."

"Mmm, good plan," Carter hummed, closing his eyes and tipping his head back against the wall. Movement at the door caught my attention and I looked up to see Jace walking through it.

"Hey, how's she doing?" I asked and he sighed, slumping into a chair across from us.

"She had a nightmare, that's what woke her up," he mumbled, scrubbing his hands over his face. "Of course she's physically a mess so when she woke up and started freaking out it just hurt her more."

"That's not good," I sighed and he nodded then shook his head.

"I don't know what to do," Jace mumbled, his elbows on his knees and his head bowed, his hands clasped over the back of his head. "I don't remember her enough to know how to help her."

"Why are you here Jace?" I asked him gently and he looked up at me with a scowl.

"Where else would I be?" He demanded and Carter chuckled.

"Back in Kamloops? In Ottawa?" I said, giving him the obvious answers. "You don't remember Rachel, you just said so yourself. You don't remember your relationship with her, you don't remember what you felt for her, you don't remember her so why are you here with her now?"

"I . . . I need her," he rasped, his eyes tortured. "When I saw her again the last time we were here I knew she was mine, even before she slugged me," he scoffed and I smiled. "I was so drawn to her, she settled something in my soul, I don't know what it is."

"Okay," I nodded, completely understanding what he was saying because Carter did the same for me. I knew Carter agreed because he squeezed my shoulder. "Then when the time comes I'm sure you'll know exactly what to do and what to say. You're a genius, remember, you'll figure it out."

"Jace?" We looked up to see the nurse standing in the doorway. "Rachel is asking for you."

"Thanks," he said and jumped up, rushing from the room.

"Who's taking Bull to the airport?" I asked and Carter sighed.

"Probably Trick," he shifted and looked at his watch. "Probably be here in the next little while."

"Mm, hopefully with coffee," I mumbled and kissed Carter again. "I'm gonna go to the bathroom."

"Sounds good sweetheart," Carter said and shifted in his seat again. I figured besides his back, his shoulder also had to be stiff and I decided I would give him a rub when I got back. I did my business, washed my hands then swished my mouth out with some cold water.

I was sure I had gum in my purse though and was looking down, digging around in my purse, I walked out of the bathroom. Of course with my head down, not paying attention to where I was going I ran right into someone going the other way.

"Oh!" I said, looking up quickly with a smile. "I'm so sorry."

"Don't be," the man in front of me said, his hands gripping my upper arms. "You're just who I was looking for."

"I, what?" I asked, looking up at him. I had no idea who this guy was but I certainly didn't think there was any reason for him to be looking for me. "Sorry, I need to get back."

"No no, there's someone looking to speak to you," the man said, gripping my bicep hard.

"No!" I yelled, trying to tear my arm away. "Carter! Help!"

I fought harder and yelled louder, lifting my knee, trying to slam it between the guy's legs but he was expecting it and shifted so I got his hard thigh muscle. He grunted and shook me, trying to grab me with the other hand but I wouldn't stop fighting, I couldn't let him take me off this floor. I needed to get Carter to come get me, I needed Carter.

"Carter!"

"Shut up!" The guy snapped and punched me in the face. I was fighting too hard, though and his fist grazed my cheek, stunning me instead of knocking me out like he'd intended.

I shook my head, trying to clear it as the guy pulled me towards the stairs.

"Carol!" Carter called and I fought harder, trying to pull away.

"Carter!" I cried, whimpering and fighting, digging my heels in. I could feel the guy's fingers digging into my muscle and bruising my arm. Twisting as the guy pulled me through the door I grabbed the railing over the balcony of the stairwell and held on, pulling my arm back as hard as I could. "Carter!"

"Carol!" He yelled again, shoving the door to the stairwell open wider and I ducked just in time so I didn't get the door in the head. The shock made the guy's grip slip off my arm. His momentum sent him falling back against the cement wall hard, knocking his balance off and he tumbled down the stairs. "Baby!"

"Get him," I gasped when Carter stopped to see if I was okay. "I'm good, get him."

I wasn't sure how good I actually was, I felt super stretched out and my shoulders and cheek started to ache. I curled up into a ball and crawled to the top of the stairs to look over the edge at Carter and the guy. Carter was crouched over him with his fingers pressed to the guy's throat then shook his head.

"Carol!" Trick yelled, rushing through the door.

"I'm good," I mumbled, holding a hand up. "Call Dawson and get a doctor in here."

"Yup!" Trick turned and rushed away as Carter slowly walked up the stairs. He bent when he got to me and helped me to my feet. Slowly I got my feet under me and stood, backing up a step so Carter could step up higher. He pushed me back a little farther and bent, lifting me into his arms and carrying me back to Rachel's room.

"What the hell's going on?" Jace and Bull demanded when Carter walked through the door.

"I walked out of the bathroom," I said, swallowing hard. "Was stupid and wasn't paying attention, walked right into the guy and he dragged me into the staircase, said someone wanted to talk to me. He almost got me down the stairs before Carter got there."

"Fucker fell down the stairs and broke his neck." Carter finished and I swallowed hard again, grimacing when I shifted in

Carter's lap and my shoulders and arm started to ache even more.

Rachel moaned softly from the bed and Jace immediately bent over her, talking quietly. The doctor stormed in the room looking harried.

"What the hell is going on here?" He demanded, throwing his hands in the air. "This is a damn hospital!"

"Hey, you can blame the crazy drug dealer in the stairwell," Trick told him, walking in behind him.

"Whatever, let me check her over," he said pointing at me. "Then I'll check my actual patient."

After having my eyes checked for concussion and my joints poked and pulled, I was told I was fine but would probably be stiff. Ice and heat and some anti-inflammatories were what the doctor ordered. Then he checked Rachel over, not bothering to kick us out of the room even though he was uncovering sensitive areas. Rachel winced and whimpered, gripping Jace's hand and refusing to look at the doctor.

The doctor left and Trick handed me a coffee and an egg sandwich. I took a couple of bites then handed it to Carter.

"You eat it babe, I had mine," he murmured, holding his hand up. "I'm gonna share your coffee, though, I spilled mine when you started yelling."

"So what are we thinking here?" Trick asked as I handed Carter my coffee cup.

"He said there was someone looking to speak to me," I told them as I chewed slowly.

"Who is? Are we thinking Small isn't the head of the snake?" Bull asked, scowling his arms folded over his chest. I noticed his prosthetic had a few new scratches along the forearm.

"It's possible someone else is pulling his strings," Trick shrugged, rubbing his fingers over his jaw. "Could be Small was the top dog here in the city but there's gotta be someone else he answers to, right?"

"You're probably right," I agreed and Carter nodded, handing me my coffee back. I took a sip then handed it back. He needed it more than I did since I'd actually gotten some sleep.

"We gotta head out if I'm gonna make my flight," Bull said looking at his watch. He stepped up to the bed and clapped Jace on the shoulder. Rachel was turned into Jace's side, curled up as much as she could be, hiding her face from the room. "Unless you need me to stay, I'll delay my flight."

"No, we're good, Lora needs you," Jace told Bull, holding his hand out. It wasn't quite a hand shake since Jace's arm had to cross his body with Rachel holding the other hand so tightly. Bull lifted his fist and they bumped then Bull clapped Jace on the back. Before he left he bent over Rachel's ear and whispered something to her then patted her hip as she nodded and he left. "Take care of my Godchild!" Jace called and we heard Bull laugh.

We heard him and Trick talking to someone in the hall then Dawson stepped into the room.

"Hey guys, how's it going?" Dawson asked quietly, walking over and stopping at the end of Rachel's bed but looked right at me. "I hear you had some excitement this morning."

"I prefer my mornings excitement free," I told him with a slight smile and he nodded. "Sean is all the excitement I need."

"Who's Sean?" Jace asked and Carter lifted his hand with a two fingered wave. "Oh."

"Tell me what happened?" Dawson asked and I told him everything. He took some notes but didn't put his little book away. "Here's what we know so far, he didn't have any ID on him but when we questioned Small he didn't have a whole lot to say, about anything. Actually looked pretty sure he was getting out of all of this. I have a feeling he was expecting this guy whoever he is, to get Carol or even Rachel to whoever the boss really is."

"That's what we were just thinking," Carter said, rubbing his palm over my knee. "Someone else is pulling the strings on Small."

"Yeah, Small's not talking but his guys are. The ones from his house had no idea what his business was, just that he was a really rich guy who wanted professional security and lots of it." Dawson told us and I shook my head. "They did see when Rachel was brought in and thought it was strange, there had never been women at the house before. Then a few of the other guys from the warehouse show up and disappear for a day and the security company has to wonder."

Rachel whimpered and shivered and Jace bent over her a little farther, wrapping his free arm around her shoulders.

"The guys at the warehouse, though are a different breed of security, they're not talking, at all."

"And this guy at the bottom of the stairs is probably one of theirs," I murmured and Dawson nodded.

"Rachel, I know this sucks, but can you tell me anything?" Dawson asked her gently. She sniffed and nodded slightly, rolling away from Jace as he helped her sit up a little. "Sweetheart, I don't need details on how you got your injuries, okay?"

Rachel sniffed and nodded and I hated the sight of her pretty face so bruised and swollen.

"They didn't want me," she whispered and swallowed hard. Jace turned and poured a cup of water with a straw then held it for her to take a few sips. "They were in the office when I got there, I don't know how they got in."

"It's okay, hon, we know." I told her, moving off of Carter's lap and stepping forward to cup my hand over her knee.

"They kept asking how to get Carol," Rachel rasped. She looked up at me and frowned. "Small was really mad at you, he kept screaming about how you ruined his plans."

I nodded and she looked back at Dawson.

"Take your time," he said but she shook her head.

"That's all he wanted to know, how to get to Carol and how to get the MC off his back." She swallowed hard again and Jace held the cup for her. She took it from him, her fingers bandaged all the way up to her elbow. The bandages hid the cuts on her arm and the missing fingernails but we still knew what was there. "He told me he was going to do all sorts of horrible things to me and if I wasn't dead when he was finished he would sell me."

"I need to know, Rachel, did Small ever say anything about his business, not to you specifically but just while he was in the same room as you? Did any of his guys?"

"The two who were there the most kept talking about the girls they had at the warehouse, that they couldn't wait to get back to the warehouse and, you know."

"I do know Rachel, but I need you to say it." Dawson urged gently and she closed her eyes.

"One said he couldn't wait to get back to the warehouse to fuck the little girl, she was tight and strangled his dick perfectly." Rachel whispered, panting. "The other one agreed but said she was too young for him and he liked the red head because she fought and she had great tits."

"All right hon, that's all I need," Dawson said, finishing a note in his book and closing it.

"Small gave the two of them hell, said to use the other girl more because the buyer for the other two girls was on the way to get them." Rachel continued, looking up at Jace who bent and pressed his lips to her forehead.

"What are the chances no one told this guy his merchandise had been seized?" Carter mused, catching all of our attention.

"Can we get one of the first guys we caught talking about that?" I asked Dawson and he shrugged and nodded. "The one who asked for a deal?"

"Worth a try, he swore to give us all the information we asked for," he agreed and waved as he left the room in a hurry.

"You did really good, Rachel," I told her, rubbing her leg. She sniffed and tears slid down her cheeks as she turned into Jace again. "We're gonna head out," I said looking at Carter who nodded. "Someone else will come by a little later to see if you need anything all right?"

"Thanks Carol," Jace murmured, all signs of the joker gone.

Carter and I left the room and made our way into the elevator then to the SUV he'd driven the night before. It was still somewhat early so we decided to go back to our place, shower and go back to bed for a little while.

When I got up again Carter was in the kitchen standing on one side of the kitchen island talking to Paige sitting on a stool on the other side, both of them sipping their coffee. It was the same scene from two days ago when I'd walked out of the shower the day all of this had started. Was it really only two days ago? It was hard to believe that in two days so much had happened.

As I walked into the kitchen Carter put a mug under the Keurig and made me a cup of coffee. I smiled up at him and stood beside Paige, rubbing her back.

"So," I said to my daughter and she groaned, knowing I was about to get nosy. "What's up with you and Sledge?"

"Sledge? Who the hell is Sledge?" Paige asked, frowning at me.

"That's what Grinder called Joe right before he died," Carter explained as he poured a slurp of creamer into my coffee then handed me the mug.

"Oh, I suppose that makes sense, he hits really hard." Paige nodded slowly.

"How do you know he hits really hard?" I asked, frowning and she looked up at me with wide eyes.

"Because I've seen him fight."

"Where the hell has he been fighting?"

"Uuhhh, just, you know, working out in the gym," she hedged and I scowled at her.

"Why are you lying to me? What is he doing that he doesn't want anyone to know about?" I asked and she paled. Paige never lied, she never felt there was any reason to and it was always too hard keeping track of all the lies. It was always easier to either tell the truth or say nothing at all.

"It's not my story to tell and I shouldn't have said anything to begin with," Paige said, holding her hands up. "He swore me to secrecy and I really shouldn't have said anything, he'll kill me if he finds out I let it out."

"You know who else will kill you if you don't keep talking?" Carter asked her then pointed at me when she looked up at him.

Paige sighed heavily and tipped her head back.

"I can't!" She exclaimed, looking torn, upset. "I promised him I wouldn't say anything. I can't tell you!"

"Paige, is Joe in trouble?" I asked carefully.

"No, I don't think so," she said shaking her head.

"Okay, here's the deal, I won't bug you about this, I won't ask questions and I won't demand answers, for now. At any point in time if you think he's in any kind of trouble you need to come to me. Got it?"

"Got it," she nodded, sharply and looked at her watch. "I gotta go, Maker is still with Bridge but I think he needs a break, I'm gonna go and see Rachel and Jordyn's got the other three women from the warehouse in a room on the second floor. At least for now. Trick is looking into their families to see if they're safe to go home then he's contacting the families to come and pick them up. They're all in the same room, they refused to be split up and I think Jordyn's been taking them food."

"Thanks Paige," I sighed and rubbed my forehead as she got off her stool. "I'll go see the women, take Jordyn with me then go see Bridget, give Maker a break then go and see Heather. We should probably set up a schedule for someone to be with Bridget until she's doing a little better and set up a schedule for Rachel so Jace can take a break if he needs it."

"Good plan, I'll start on that when I get to the hospital, I'll send out a mass text and get volunteers and set it up." Paige said and kissed my cheek, waved to Carter and left the apartment.

"We need to figure out what's going on with Joe." Carter said and I nodded with a sigh.

"Yeah we do," I agreed. "How do you suggest we do that?"

"You leave it to me, you've got enough going on right now, I'll take care of Joe and make sure he's not doing anything stupid."

"Thanks," I nodded and walked around the counter to hug him. "I love you Sean Carter."

"I love you Carol Wilson soon-to-be-Carter." He kissed the top of my head as I giggled and hugged me to his side. I loved this man, so much.

CHAPTER 22

Carter

I sat in the main room of the clubhouse two days later, shooting the shit with Mason as I waited for Joe to make his move. It was pretty late and Mason's kids were with Jordyn up in their apartment. When Joe made his way through the room and out the door I watched him out of the corner of my eye then turned to look at Mason.

"You wanna do a little investigating?" I asked him and he raised his eyebrows.

"What kind of investigating?"

"A little tailing and stealth," I told him with a slight smile and his eyes became intrigued. "Information gathering."

"Let's do it," Mason said standing. "What's the background here?"

As we walked out to my truck I told him about what Paige had said and how she had been evasive and adamant she couldn't say anything more. How she said Joe had sworn her to secrecy about something that she'd actually spilled the beans on. Just not enough beans to tell us the whole story. I was surprised when Joe climbed onto his bike considering it was late October and damn cold to be riding a motorcycle.

Staying well back from Joe's bike we followed him out of the city and out to what looked like an abandoned warehouse. Or at least it would have looked abandoned if there weren't so many cars, trucks and motorcycles parked in the lot in front. We sat in the truck looking at the building and wondering what the hell could be going on inside then looked at each other and shrugged.

As we slid out of my truck we were assaulted by the loud music coming from the building as the front door opened then closed quickly, dulling the sound but not blocking it out completely.

"What the fuck is this place?" Mason demanded but I shook my head.

"Only one way to find out." I murmured and started forward. When we got to the door I yanked it open and walked through, stopping just far enough inside for Mason to enter behind me. Looking around I was shocked by the number of people in the space, all of them yelling, dancing and most definitely drinking. On either side of the huge space was a huge bar with three bartenders behind each, all six running like crazy to keep up with the orders of the crowd.

"Hey," Mason yelled, tapping my arm. I looked at him then followed his pointed finger to the center of the huge space and saw a cage. Not like a dog cage, but like a giant ring surrounded by chain link fence and inside the cage were two men beating the hell out of each other. When one would land a particularly vicious hit or kick the crowd would cheer even louder.

The two men were naked from the waste up and barefoot and covered in sweat. One of them had a cut over his eyebrow and was bleeding while the other one was laughing and his teeth were red with blood. As we watched he spit the blood and possibly a tooth out onto the mat then attacked his opponent with fists, feet and knees, taking the other man to the mat and not backing off until a bell rang. He stood and backed away, hopping on the balls of his feet while the man on the ground was examined and the ref pointed to the man standing who threw his hands in the air, making the crowd cheer even louder.

Over a speaker system someone announced the winner's name and the amount of the pot he had won for winning the fight. The ref waved something under the other man's nose and roused him to get him out of the ring. The announcer told the crowd to back off so the ring could be cleaned for the next fight and another cheer went up through the crowd.

I looked around, trying to see if I could find Joe but his wasn't the familiar face I saw.

"Aw fuck," I groaned and hit Mason on the shoulder. When he turned to me I pointed then started walking. I knew he'd seen who I saw when he, too, swore and followed after me. I stepped up to one side of Paige and he stepped up to the other, surprising her.

"Shit!" She exclaimed, scowling up at us. "What the hell are you two doing here?"

"We could ask you the same thing," I snapped at her, glaring down in her face. "There is no way it's safe for you here."

"I am actually probably one of the safest people in here," she informed me belligerently.

"How do you figure that?" Mason demanded, looking around us. This was a rough crowd and there were very few women there. Definitely none of them were standing alone like Paige was. I pulled her into my side as a fight broke out between two random guys a few feet away, proving Mason's point.

"So safe." I muttered angrily.

"I am safe because I'm here with the champion. He's made it very clear that if anyone comes anywhere near me he'll kill them and since they've all seen him end a fight with a single punch then come to my rescue -"

"He had to leave a fight to come to your rescue?" I demanded, scowling down at her and she rolled her eyes.

"It was no big deal!" She insisted, throwing her hands in the air. "He was about finished with the fight anyway, he was just taking his time finishing it because the longer he's in the cage the more money he makes so he drags it out. When he saw a guy coming on to me, not touching me, who wouldn't take no for an answer he punched the guy he was fighting, knocked him out then came down and made it very clear I was off limits."

"Paige, what the hell are you doing here?" I groaned, scrubbing my hands over my face. "Like really, why are you here?"

"Honestly, I found out about this the same way you guys did." She said with a shrug. "Joe was acting strange and disappearing at night then reappearing most mornings with bruised knuckles. He never lets anyone hit his face but I'd seen his body after a fight and he's always all bruised to hell. One night I followed him here."

"Holy fuck," Mason groaned, turning to look at the cage as the announcer came back on to announce the next fight. Cheering began as the challenger was announced and a big guy wearing padded gloves and boxing shorts came out of some back room. And by big I mean he was huge, he was probably my height and weighed at least what I did, if not more. He hopped around on the balls of his feet, swinging his fists in short, hard jabs, every muscle in his body tight and hard.

Then the announcer was talking again, announcing the champion of the cage, now fighting under a new name and the second the voice said 'Sledge' I knew exactly who it was. Joe came out much like the challenger did, barefoot wearing only a pair of shorts and gloves. The challenger must be a professional fighter, though because his shorts looked like an actual boxer or fighter would wear while Joe's were just a pair of navy blue basketball shorts, the kind we all wore when we worked out, the kind you paid fifteen bucks for at Walmart.

Joe was only a couple of inches shorter than I was and I'd seen him work out, he was ripped and covered with muscle. He could also outlift me on the bench press which was saying something because no one else even came close to what I lifted. When Trick had first moved here and I'd asked him to spot me I'd seen the disbelief in his eyes.

As we watched, Joe walked into the ring, not bouncing on the balls of his feet, not punching the air or lifting his arms. He stood on one side with his arms hanging by his sides and his head bowed. I even thought his eyes might be closed. When the bell rang to start the fight Paige turned around and faced away from the cage.

"What are you doing?" Mason asked, frowning at her.

"I can't handle this, I hate it but I understand why he does it so I come to support him anyway." Paige explained, folding her arms over her chest. "I just can't watch him get beat to hell."

I grunted and watched as the challenger bounced into the center of the cage and Joe slowly moved forward. The challenger yelled at Joe to make a move, taunting him to do something but Joe waited and watched. When the challenger was finally sick of waiting he lashed out and caught Joe in the ribs but instead of fighting back Joe just smiled, and then the fight was on. For the next twenty minutes the two men beat the hell out of each other like Paige said and the challenger even got a shot into Joe's face which seemed to piss him off.

Then the fight was really on and it was obvious the challenger had no chance of winning this fight. Joe punched, kicked, kneed and ended the fight with an arm hold that probably hurt like hell. The challenger tapped out and the crowd exploded with noise and the announcer came back to crow through the speakers that Joe was still undefeated.

"Come on," Paige said, grabbing our sleeves and pulling us behind her. "Let's go see him."

"So why does he do this?" I asked her as she walked but she shook her head.

"You'll have to ask him, and if he tells you great, but if he doesn't you need to leave it alone. He's going to be so super pissed that you guys are here right now." She said and pushed through a door into a locker room. She walked around a wall of lockers and over to Joe where he sat panting on a bench, drinking a bottle of Gatorade. His gaze followed her with heat in his eyes as she walked over and sat beside him then he looked up at us and scowled.

"For fuck sakes, Paige!" He yelled, sitting forward so he could turn and glare at her.

"Don't look at me, they followed you!" She told him and he scoffed, sitting back against the wall.

"It's true," I told him as Mason and I stood in front of them with our arms crossed. "She was already here when we got here, we followed you from the clubhouse."

"Yeah well, go back to the clubhouse and forget you ever saw this place," Joe said and finished his drink. He was even still wearing his gloves from the fight and after throwing the Gatorade bottle in the can across the room he started pulling them off. Paige stood and walked over to a locker and pulled out a first aid kit.

"Let's get you cleaned up," she said gently as she set the open kit beside him on the bench. "This one doesn't look like it'll need stitches at least."

Joe grunted and his angry gaze shifted from Mason and me to

behind us as the door to the locker room opened and closed again. Joe's face completely shuddered so there was no expression at all in his eyes. Mason and I shifted as the challenging fighter walked around the wall of lockers behind us.

"How many is that, *Sledge*?" The man asked through heavy breaths.

"Too many to count, Titan," Joe smirked and the other man chuckled.

"One of these days I'm going to beat you." Titan said, shaking his head.

"And one of these days I'm going to take you up on your offer."

"Since you keep telling me there's not a snowball's chance in hell of that ever happening I guess I won't hold my breath," Titan snickered then looked at us and back to Joe. "Friends of yours?"

"Sort of," Joe said, locking his gaze with mine then looking back at Titan.

"They fight?"

"No," Joe replied shortly, almost growling. "Not if you want to walk out of the cage and ever fight again."

"Like that is it?" Titan asked, eyeing Mason and I.

"Like that it is," Joe replied and Titan nodded then walked away, whistling.

"What the fuck, Joe?" I demanded and he pinned me with a glare.

"Shut the fuck up, Carter," Joe rasped just as angry. "I just told him you two fight to the death, you don't stop because someone taps out or is knocked out. Unless you'd like to prove me right or wrong, shut the fuck up."

"You've got a lot of fuckin' explaining to do," Mason mumbled and Joe sighed.

"Yeah, I know."

"Tomorrow morning, first thing in Carol's office." I told him through clenched teeth. He nodded and I looked at Paige. "You, too."

"Aw fuck," Paige muttered, her shoulders slouching.

"Damn straight."

"Here you go Sledge," a barely dressed woman said, sauntering into the men's locker room like she belonged there. She didn't come in the main door and seemed to appear out of nowhere. Joe watched her as she walked through the room, her hips swaying in her very short shorts but there was no emotion or acknowledgment in his eyes. He noticed the woman was barely wearing a bra and what might as well be denim panties but his eyes never left her face.

"Don't get caught in here, Jewel, you know what happened last time." Joe told her and she shrugged slightly.

"Nothin' I can't handle," she said and handed him a thick envelope. "It was a good take tonight. Good fight."

Paige watched the other woman cautiously as she flirted with Joe but said nothing. It seemed the two women had an understanding but Paige wasn't letting anything get past her. Jewel might be flirting but she didn't make the mistake of reaching out to touch Joe. If that was because of Paige or because of what happened last time, I didn't know. I wanted to find out, though.

"Thanks Jewel, now get gone before he finds you in here." Joe said and Jewel pouted prettily but sauntered out of the room. Interesting, maybe 'he' was the reason she was keeping her hands to herself.

"Where's it going tonight?" Paige asked quietly as Joe handed her the envelope and she tucked it into her purse, waiting until she was sure that Jewel was gone.

"Same place as last time," Joe said, looking up at her and she nodded. She finished doctoring him up and then he went to have a quick shower.

"I'm out of here," she said, packing up the kit and Mason shifted.

"I'll go with you," he said and she shook her head. "It's not negotiable, Paige, I'm going with you."

"Fine, but I'm not talking about this with you," she heaved a sigh and shoved the first aid kit into the locker she'd gotten it from then stormed out of the locker room with Mason hot on her heels. Before long Joe came out of the shower with a towel wrapped around his hips and started getting dressed.

"Where's she taking the money?" I asked as Joe pulled his shirt on over his head. His eyes shifted around the room but he shook his head.

"I'll explain it all tomorrow, this is not the place to talk about any of this." He said softly and pulled out his leather jacket and led me from the locker room. As we walked through the still packed warehouse he received pats on the backs and high fives but he didn't stop. I looked around as I followed him and found Jewel wrapped around another man who seemed to be holding court on the far side of the room, his gaze on Joe the entire way.

The look in the man's eyes was calculating with a bit of maliciousness but he made no move to intercept Joe and when we were out in the cool night air he walked away from me to where he'd parked his bike. I sighed and shook my head, knowing I would get nothing from him tonight and walked to my truck.

Tomorrow would have to be soon enough.

The next morning when Joe and Paige walked into Carol's office, hand in hand, Mason, Trick, Carol and I were already there waiting. Carol watched the two of them as they sat down across the desk from her and waited. It didn't take long for Carol to lose her shit, I'd told her a little of what went on last night and she hadn't slept much all night worrying about what Joe would tell her today.

"What the fuck is going on?" Carol demanded angrily. Joe was sitting, completely relaxed, slouched slightly with his knees spread, taking up as much space as he could while Paige sat with her legs crossed, her body turned towards Joe, her hand still in his, resting at his hip. It looked like Joe was the one not letting go, though, not Paige.

"You don't want Bridge here?" Joe asked, watching Carol, looking lazy when he was anything but. "I'm only explaining this once so if she needs to hear it you'd better get her here."

"She's planning Grinder's funeral with Maker, Jordyn and Heather," Carol snapped, still scowling. "If you tell me anything she needs to know I'll tell her."

Joe grunted, then took a deep breath and sighed.

"Seriously Joe, what's going on?" I asked quietly.

"What would you all prefer? That when I need an outlet because I'm losing my shit I do it here? And hurt someone? Or wreck something? Or I go to some underground fight and hurt someone who's expecting it and is there for the same reason?" Joe asked, his eyes full of pain, anguish.

"What do you mean, Joe?" Trick asked, frowning.

"None of you know about my past, except maybe Carol, you probably know some of it," Joe began and shrugged. "I'm not explaining it now, just know it was shit, growing up I never had a chance to be a kid and I fought every single day just to get by. I went into the military to get out of a shitty situation and for the most part it worked. I got out of a bad situation but lost a lot that mattered to me. Like all of you I saw shit overseas and there are times that I can't handle the anger and it has to come out somehow."

"You're not doing it for the money?" Mason asked, his eyes squinting and Joe shook his head. "Where did we go last night?"

"It's a women's shelter," Paige said quietly.

"What the hell were you doing there in the first place?" Carol demanded of Paige but she just shrugged.

"It's better that I deliver the money than Joe," Paige explained, licking her lips. "The money always goes to a shelter in the city, sometimes the same ones sometimes new ones. Sometimes it goes to half-way houses for troubled kids. It's never a good idea for a guy looking like Joe to make the deliveries. He tends to scare the residents."

"How much was it last night?" I asked and Joe shrugged.

"Last night was ten grand," Paige said, supplying the total. "Joe takes twenty-five percent of the pot -"

"That's forty grand!" Trick exclaimed and Paige and Joe shrugged.

"You never keep the money?" Mason asked and Joe shook his head.

"I'm not doing it for the money," he said, his voice low. "I do it for the outlet so I'm not hurting anyone here. I could spar here but sometimes the anger is too much and I can't control it, not completely. When I was in Kamloops I would fight with Bull or Hank but they didn't hold the same anger I do. It's hard to explain, but I don't go very often anymore. It used to be every night, now it's once a week. I work off the anger, make a little money that someone can use and then relax for a while. Mostly now I only fight when I get word that there's someone who wants to challenge the champion."

"That guy last night, Titan," I said, watching Joe. "He's a professional fighter."

"Yuh, he hasn't been able to beat me and it grinds his gears. He's a good guy and a good fighter but he's not angry like me. He fights for the money, the glory, but he's got something to lose, I don't."

I had to disagree with Joe, since he was sitting in that chair, in a room full of people who cared about him, holding the hand of a woman who loved him. Who he loved even if he refused to admit it. "What offer does he keep making?"

"He wants me to train with him and get a few pro fights in, see where it goes." Joe shrugged. "He's even had his manager and a few coaches come out and watch me fight and they offered me a lot of money but I don't want it. Every time I see Titan he offers, sometimes he comes out to just watch fights so I see him more often then when I actually fight him."

Carol hadn't said much once Joe had started talking but she had watched him closely.

"So what? Is this like fight club?" She asked now.

"More or less," Joe shrugged with a snort.

"And it's illegal?"

"Probably," Joe nodded. "The fights themselves maybe not but the gambling for sure and I wouldn't be surprised if there were drugs being passed around, even some prostitution."

"The bars?" I asked and Joe laughed.

"I highly doubt they've got a liquor license."

"Who was the guy Jewel was wrapped around when we left?" I asked and Joe blinked slowly.

"He's the boss. He's not overly fond of me because I take such a big cut of the profit, but I don't care. He made forty grand on one fight last night, ten percent goes to another organization and Angel gets the rest."

"Angel?"

"Angelo, don't know his last name, don't care to," Joe shrugged.

"He the one who would be mad about Jewel being in the men's locker room?" Mason asked and Joe snickered.

"Yeah, but she's a little kinky, she likes his kind of punishment," he explained with a shrug.

"So she's not in danger?"

"Oh, she's in danger, but it's nothing she can't walk away from. She chooses to stay there because Angel takes care of her, protects her from certain people. They'll both tell you he bought her and owns her but their relationship is more than that now."

"He bought her?" Carol sneered and Joe shrugged.

"He gave me shit once for looking at her, said to keep my eyes off his property, that he paid far too much for her for me to make her dirty with my eyes." Joe told her and she scowled harder. "She's not really in any danger, Carol. Technically money was exchanged but Angel probably saved Jewel from something far, far worse. And in his way he cares about her and does protect her."

"This is a fucked up situation, Joe." Carol snarled. "And you got my daughter involved in it."

"Yes, it is fucked up, but no I did not get your daughter involved. She did that to herself." Joe corrected and Paige stiffened. She had yet to make eye contact with Carol and I could see that she was worried. "Like Carter and Mason, Paige followed me one night. When I told her to mind her own business and stay the fuck away from there she refused to listen. I had to come up with some fancy excuse as to why she was there and off limits to keep her safe. Now if she doesn't show up Angel wants to know why. Make no mistake, Carol, Paige got herself into this, I'm just doing everything I can to keep her safe."

"Fuck, Paige," Carol sighed, resting her elbows on her desk and pushing her hands into her hair.

"It's one night a week, mom," Paige muttered, still not looking up. "And like Joe said, I'm completely safe there as long as he's there. I don't go if he's not, ever."

"It's illegal, we can't have this associated with the MC," Carol insisted and Joe shook his head.

"No one there knows about the MC," he assured us. "They don't even know my real name or where I'm from. As far as any of them know I don't even live in the city."

"You could be followed at any time," Carol told him but he shook his head.

"I followed you and you had no idea," I reminded him but he shook his head again.

"I had no reason to worry about someone following me there from here, I'm always more alert when I leave. I never come straight here and more often than not I go to a motel for the night."

"And Paige? Does someone follow her?"

"They're really not interested in her, Carol." Joe said, shaking his head again. "Once I claimed her there and made her off limits she had no value to them. They all know if anything happens to her their money maker is gone for good and they're not going to chance losing me over her."

"I still don't like this, Joe," Carol sighed, rubbing her fingertips over her forehead. "In fact I think this is a really fucking bad idea. I can't force you to quit, though. I'm asking you to pull back, get out of it as much as you can."

"It's kind of like the Hotel California, Carol. You can check out but you can never leave."

"Did you sign something? Do you owe them money?"

"No, it's just an understanding." Joe sighed, shaking his head. "Unless I end up with a major injury and can't fight anymore I'm expected to fight any challenger. If I lose to that challenger it'll be easier for me to get out but at this point me winning means a lot of people who need help get it."

"Ten grand is a lot of money," Trick said, rubbing his jaw.

"Slow night," Joe shrugged and I scoffed. "I'd already fought Titan and won, the crowd wasn't as into it as they are when I'm fighting someone they've never seen me fight before. I usually make double what I made last night."

"This is absolutely insane," Carol sighed, slumping back in her chair. She watched Joe watch her for a few minutes, neither of them saying anything. "Do you want to stay there? Do you still need to fight the anger?"

"Not so much anymore," Joe replied shaking his head, his gaze sliding to Paige then away again. "But like I said, you don't just walk away and I don't have it in me to throw a fight. I also don't want to be injured to the point that I can't fight and I'm not the only one who benefits when I win."

"What would it take?" I asked, curious.

"Something that can't be rehabbed," Joe shrugged and I nodded.

"We could always fake it," I told Carol who blinked at me and nodded slowly. "We have our own doctor now, we can fake a bike accident and wrap you up in a few casts, give you a cane, fuck we could put you in a spinal collar if we had to."

"That might be the only way to do it." Joe agreed and I sighed.

"Do we need to take these guys down?" Carol asked Joe and he shrugged again.

"Honestly, we probably should. Angel isn't really a bad guy, he's not the one running the drugs or the girls, he's just not putting a stop to it. Pretty sure I've seen a couple of Hells Angels there a few times."

"Are there fights every night?"

"Don't know. When I started a couple of years ago it was every other night, now they don't need the revenue as much and it's every few nights. I only know for sure about a fight when I get a call about a challenger, otherwise I stay the hell away."

"You said you fought every night, but there's only fights every other night?" Trick asked, sitting forward.

"Angel's isn't the only place in the city to fight," Joe shrugged.

"We need to talk to Dawson," Mason mumbled and we all agreed.

"All right, go," Carol said with another heavy sigh. "Carter give Dawson a call, I'm gonna go and check on Bridge, see how things are going with Grinder's funeral, then I'm going to the hospital."

"Do we know when Slouch is coming home?" Trick asked, rubbing his hand over his chin.

"Next couple of days, Jace said. Her internal injuries are mostly healed, she's just sore now and her ribs will take at least another four weeks to heal, her shoulder is probably good but her elbow still needs to be in a sling. The cuts on her arms are healed and her concussion for the most part is cleared up. Her ankle is still in a boot but it's a walking boot." Carol explained and we all nodded.

Carol stood and left the office, not waiting for anyone to follow. Everyone else probably thought she was pissed but I knew it was so much more than that. She was honestly worried about her daughter first of all, and the MC second.

"God, she's so mad at me," Paige sighed and everyone nodded.

"Serves you right," Joe told her and she scowled at him. "I told you to stay the fuck away but you didn't listen."

"You could have just told me what you were doing, then I wouldn't have had to follow you."

"Or you could have minded your own business like most people do when they're told to mind their own damn business!" Joe snapped.

"The only people who mind their own damn business when they're told to are the ones who don't care!" Paige snapped back and Joe growled. This was obviously an old argument that they'd had many times.

"She's not mad so much as she's worried, about both of you, and the MC." I told them, ending the argument for now. "You've both put her in a tough spot and now she has to figure out how to get you out, keep the MC out of it and keep you both happy. She could have easily ordered you to get out, Joe, given you an ultimatum, but she didn't. She asked you to get out for the good of the MC and her daughter and is willing to help you do that so there's no blow back on you."

I stood up and stretched muscles that were still sore.

"I'm gonna go call Dawson, see what he has to say about all of this." I said and left the room.

If the others stayed in the office talking I didn't know about it. I also didn't care. Right now all I cared about was Carol, just like I'd told Lo so many years ago, the only thing I cared about was Carol. Of course, caring about Carol meant caring about Paige and keeping Paige safe, too.

I hadn't been here when Paige had been kidnapped by her dad's bookie, I hadn't arrived here until a few years later when Carol had her surgery and Paige was older. I did consider her my daughter now but I couldn't very well tell her what to do. She was a grown woman and I hadn't helped her become the amazing woman she was now. I was just around to witness how great she was and it was all because of Carol.

With a heavy sigh I picked up my phone and called Dawson to see what the deal was with Angelo and his underground fight club.

CHAPTER 23

Carol

When I left my office I didn't go straight to Bridget's apartment. Instead I took a walk around the clubhouse, taking my time, cooling down, getting control of myself.

I didn't want to go up to Brigdet's feeling like I was. After a few minutes of pacing and kicking at stones on the ground I slowly walked back to the clubhouse, going in the back door.

I waved to the few people in the main room as I went through and took the stairs up to the third floor. I knocked on Bridget's door and smiled at Jordyn when she opened it.

"Hey Carol," the younger woman said softly and stepped back so I could enter. "You just missed Heather."

"Oh? I was hoping to see her before I went up to the hospital." I said, walking into the living room where Bridget was curled up on the couch.

Maker was sitting at the far end of the couch, slouching in the corner watching a hockey game on the TV.

"Gray needed a nap," Jordyn shrugged. "She took Max and Dax with her to make them lunch."

"How're you doing, sweetie?" I asked Bridget as I sat beside her on the couch. I rubbed her hip as she blinked and shifted her gaze to me with a sigh.

"I could do without the morning sickness," she murmured and

I smiled.

"Yeah, that was the worst part of being pregnant for sure." I agreed. "How's everything else?"

"The funeral is planned, it was nice of the funeral home director to come here instead of me having to go there."

"Is there anything you need?"

"No," she sighed, shaking her head a bit. "Just Grinder but we can't get him back, can we?"

"No honey, if I could bring him back to you I definitely would." I replied as her eyes filled with tears. "I'm gonna go see Rachel at the hospital, anything you want me to tell her?"

"Just that I'm thinking about her and I'm glad she's safe." Bridget sniffed and swallowed hard.

"All right, I'll come see you again later, okay?" Bridget nodded and I patted her hip then stood and walked to the door with Jordyn.

"I'll get you the information for the funeral tonight," she said softly and I nodded, squeezing her shoulder.

"Thanks," I said and left, walking down the hall to Heather and Trick's apartment.

I knocked on her door quietly, knowing at least Gray was sleeping and possibly Max and Dax, I didn't want to wake them up. It didn't take long for Heather to open the door with a smile.

"Hey, how are you doing Carol?" Heather asked, stepped back so I could come in.

"I'm good, I can't stay, I just wanted to say hi before I went to the hospital to see Rachel." I said, rubbing Heather's shoulder. "And I wanted to see that beautiful boy of yours."

"Come on in, he's sleeping but he's out here since the other three are passed out in Gray's room." Heather led me into the living room and we oohed and aahed over the baby sleeping in the bassinet.

"He is so beautiful, Heather," I told her and she smiled proudly. "How are you feeling?"

"Okay, but I'm really not liking the recovery time after a c-section. I never want to do that again."

"Trick said your doctor was not really on the ball, hopefully if there's a next time you'll have a better one."

"Well, I can't really blame the doctor since Trick was kind of being a jerk." Heather smirked and I smiled. "I think the doctor was scared of him more than anything."

I snickered and shook my head. "That's the thing about these alpha males, they really can't handle when their women are in pain. It freaks them out, especially when they can't fix it."

"Isn't that the truth?" Heather laughed.

"He's beautiful sweetheart, when I have more time and he's not sleeping I'll stay longer and cuddle the little guy. I don't want to lift him up and wake him, though." I turned towards the door and Heather followed me. "You should have a nap, too while you have a chance."

"I just might." Heather agreed.

"Thank you for all your help with Bridget, I really appreciate everything you're doing for her."

"After everything everyone here has done for me, it's the least I can do." Heather said, reaching out and squeezing my elbow. I didn't tell her it was the one Small's guy had hurt in the stairwell, I sucked up the little bit of pain. "You guys welcomed us, gave us a home, I can never repay that."

"There is nothing to repay, Heather. You and Trick have given us just as much as we've given you, if not more." I patted her hand and left the apartment.

I went first to mine and Carter's apartment and grabbed my keys and my purse then pulled out my phone and told him I was on my way to the hospital.

He wasn't the one who met me at my car, though. Paige was.

"You coming with me?" I asked as I climbed in and started it.

"If I'm allowed to," she replied, buckling her seatbelt then looking at me expectantly. "Unless you're so angry with me you don't want me around."

"I could never be that angry with you, Paige. I'm upset yes, but I'm not actually angry with you. Or Joe even." I said as I left the clubhouse and drove towards the hospital.

"That's what Carter said."

"Well, Sean is very good at being right," I told her and she chuckled. "I'm worried about you. I'm also worried about what Joe might have to do to keep you safe."

"What do you mean?" She asked, frowning.

"You said the first time you were there he ended a fight early with one punch then came to your rescue. What did he do?"

"He punched the guy who was talking to me," she shrugged and I nodded.

"Just once?"

"He picked him up and punched him a couple of times I guess."

"Right and I bet that guy left the fight with at least a concussion, possibly a few broken bones." I said, glancing at her sideways. "What happens when someone else shows up who doesn't know the situation and Joe has to do it again? Will he get away with a couple of punches? Or will he have to go farther?"

"I don't know, I never thought about it I guess." Paige replied, frowning again.

"Right, so if it happens again and Joe has to go after another guy and maybe that other guy isn't just some low level drug dealer, but someone important to the Hells Angels or in Angel's organization and Joe does some real damage.

"Then you're both in a whole lot more trouble and while Angel's guys will stay away from you I guarantee the Hells Angels won't."

"Okay, I understand, mom."

"Are you sure? Because if you get lucky and that guy isn't a Hell's Angel but he's a cop and Joe loses his cool and ends up arrested for assaulting an officer?" I shook my head as I slowed at a red light. "A biker and you're dead, a cop and Joe is in jail for a very long time."

Paige didn't say anything else, but stayed silent for the rest of the ride to the hospital, obviously deep in thought. When we pulled up to the hospital I found a parking spot and we walked in together, going straight up to Rachel's room. We knocked and Jace called for us to go in.

Rachel was sitting on the side of the bed, breathing heavy with tears in her eyes. Jace was standing right in front of her, ready for anything, his hands cupping her elbows gently.

"Hey, you getting up? Walking around a little?" I asked Rachel and she swallowed hard. Her face wasn't as swollen as it had been the last time I was here and the bruising was starting to yellow but she still looked like hell.

"Th-the doctor said th-the more I walk around and th-the

more I move th-the faster I'll be able to go home." Rachel replied and it didn't escape my notice that she was suddenly stuttering when she never had before.

"Well that's good, honey," I said, with a smile. "We really want you to come home, you think you're ready?"

"I th-think I want a decent meal and to sleep in my own bed," she sighed. Her breaths were still shallow and I imagined her ribs still hurt a lot.

"I don't blame you even a little bit." I patted her shoulder gently, knowing it probably still hurt and I didn't want to jar her elbow in the sling. "Bridget said to tell you she's glad you're safe, and she can't wait for you to come home."

"Where is Bridge?" Rachel asked with a slight frown. "She's th-the only one who hasn't come to see me."

"Well," I hedged and looked up at Jace who shook his head slightly. "Damn, Rachel honey, when we first found out you were missing we got a call from Small. We pinged his phone and a few of the guys went to check it out.

"Grinder was with them and he opened a door at the ware-house they were searching, not knowing there was a rifle rigged to fire when the door was opened. He was shot, he didn't make it."

"Oh my God," Rachel gasped, reaching out to grab Jace. "Grinder was killed because of me!"

"No," Jace insisted, shaking his head, cupping her jaw in both hands. "Grinder was killed by Small because of Small. You have done nothing wrong, baby."

"But, if I had done someth-thing, if I had fought harder or someth-thing, Grinder, th-the guys wouldn't have gone look-ing for me and Grinder wouldn't be dead."

"Rachel," Paige said, sitting on the other side of her bed behind her and squeezing her arm. "This is not your fault, there was nothing you could have done. We all watched the video of those guys taking you. You were unconscious before you even knew they were there, you can't fight if you don't know you're supposed to."

Paige actually hadn't seen the video, but I had told her what had happened. I didn't think anyone but the police really needed to see the video but we did need to see how they got in the back door in the first place.

"I should have known th-they were th-there!"

"Why? Both the front and back doors were locked, or should have been. Those guys somehow got past our security and no one knew about it." I insisted, making her look into my eyes. "Trick fixed it. No one is getting past our security again, but there was no way whatsoever that you could have known those men were in the office."

"Is Bridget okay?" Rachel asked, the tears in her eyes flowing over and spilling down her cheeks.

"She will be," I promised and gently wiped a tear from her cheek. "Grinder left a little piece of himself for her to love. She found out just over a week ago that she's pregnant. She was just saying today the morning sickness has been pretty horrible."

"I don't know if th-that's better or not," Rachel whispered. "Grinder's gone but she has his baby to raise by herself."

"She's not alone, she never will be and neither will you." I told her and she nodded. "Has the doctor said when you might go home?"

"If I can prove th-that I can walk okay and get around a little he said tomorrow morning." Rachel sighed and looked at Jace.

"Jace says he's just fine being here but I know he wants to go home."

"I'm not going anywhere without you." Jace assured her and she shook her head.

"I'm sure Bull wants you back in Kamloops, and th-the CAF needs you for someth-thing."

"Those aren't home," Jace told her, shaking his head. "You're home. If you're here in Winnipeg then so am I as long as Carol doesn't kick me out."

"I don't understand."

"I'm not going anywhere, Rachel," Jace told her and I could see the confusion in her eyes. "I'm here with you for as long as you'll have me. I'm hoping that's forever but I'm not letting you make the decision to say goodbye until you're at a hundred percent and I don't just mean physically. As long as you keep having these nightmares I'm staying with you."

"Jace, you can't mean th-that, you don't even know me," Rachel sighed, shaking her head.

"I know enough. Maybe what I need to remember is to be here with you. Being away from you didn't help, I'd rather try this."

Rachel sighed, knowing arguing with him wasn't going to get her anywhere so she didn't bother. Paige and I stayed with Rachel and Jace for a while as she slowly walked up and down the hall. When we got back to her room she was exhausted so we said goodbye and left her to nap.

Once Paige and I were back in the SUV and on our way home I drove to a McDonald's instead and got us both and Carter a coffee. Paige smiled her thanks but didn't say much. I was just pulling into the parking lot when she did finally start to speak.

"I know you're right about the fighting," she said softly and

I nodded, letting her get it all out. "I'm going to talk to Joe about it. He doesn't need it like he did before."

"Why did he need it so much before?" I asked as I parked in front of the office.

"He was so angry, mom." She sighed, shaking her head. "I think a lot of the anger is left over pain and guilt from his childhood, but he really hasn't told me much about that so I don't know for sure. He had to let it out somehow, like he said, but didn't want to hurt anyone here or get kicked out for any reason."

"We would never have kicked him out. Made him go back to Kamloops for more therapy maybe, or see someone here at the very least, but never kicked him out." I told her, squeezing her hand and she nodded. "That's still an option, if you think he should. I was planning on talking to Doc and seeing if we could use her office once a week for a psychologist for anyone who wants to talk."

"That's a really good idea," Paige nodded with a smile. "Or we have the conference room in our office, the psychologist could set up there. I don't mind taking on extra work as his or her receptionist."

"I'll talk to Carter and the guys about it, see what they say." I smiled and she nodded again. We got out of the SUV and she went to her desk while I went to Carter's office and handed him his coffee.

"Hey baby," he said with a smile and I closed his door then walked around his desk and crawled into his lap. "Mmm," he hummed, wrapping his arms around me and kissing the top of my head. "I missed you."

"I missed you," I smiled, snuggling closer. "Did you send Paige out when I texted you that I was going to the hospital?"

"I might have mentioned it to her," he murmured and I

chuckled.

"We're good, she's gonna talk to Joe about quitting the fighting."

"That's good."

"We also talked about having a psychologist come in once a week, either use an office here or a room at the clinic."

"Another great idea," Carter agreed, rocking his chair slightly. "Though I wonder if here is the best place for it."

"What do you mean?" I asked, sitting up to look him in the eyes and he shrugged.

"Just that some people might be more open to it if it were more anonymous. Maybe certain people wouldn't want their boss or coworkers to know they're seeing a head shrinker."

"Good point," I murmured, biting my lip. "I'll think about it, you think about it. We'll talk to the guys and see what they say."

"We should also do some research about the head shrinker we want. We don't want just anyone, it should be someone who has experience with guys like ours."

"You're right," I agreed and leaned forward to kiss him. "I'll get on that. How did it go with Dawson?"

"He's looking into it. He said they already have a file on Angel but as far as they can tell he's not specifically doing anything illegal."

"Seriously? He allows prostitution and drug distribution."

"They can't prove that he knows about it." Carter shrugged and I sighed. "He actually does have a liquor license and he is licensed to run his fights and if there's illegal activity he doesn't know about it and they can't prove that he does."

"Ugh," I groaned and Carter smiled. "What about the gambling?"

"According to Dawson it's all above board," Carter shrugged again and I frowned.

"All right, I suppose all we can do is just keep an eye on it. Paige said she was going to talk to Joe about getting out altogether so that's something. I don't really have a problem with Joe fighting, I just have a problem with illegal activities being linked to the club."

"I get it, I'm behind you a hundred percent. And it's good if Joe gets out. Maybe we can give him a job setting up a fighting gym here. We've got some land where we can build another strip of businesses. I overheard Patsy saying she would like to expand the cafe and add a bookstore and actual restaurant but she doesn't have the room.

"If she could move into a new space that's bigger than Maker could take over the old cafe and add the custom paint shop he was thinking about."

"Huh, you're really good at this reconnaissance, information gathering thing."

"It would also give us somewhere to put another office just for the head shrinker."

"What else could we put there?" I asked, getting comfortable on his lap, knowing he had more ideas and was just waiting for someone to ask for them.

"Trick and Heather talked about a daycare, we could put that in the end unit, and for now we could leave a few units empty until someone comes up with an idea."

"Why don't we put the word out, see if anyone else has any ideas?"

"That's an even better plan," Carter nodded and smiled.

"I was also thinking about the money that won't be going to the shelters and such when Joe does stop fighting. I wonder if there's a way to keep at least a little money going in that direction."

"Hmm, good point, we'll have to consider it, fundraising or something." Carter agreed thoughtfully. I leaned down, cupping his face in my hands and kissing him deeply.

"Are you finished here?" I asked, panting as I licked down his jaw to his ear.

"Mmm, no," he growled, squeezing my hips in his big hands. "I have at least another hour of work before I can bug out."

"Dammit," I sighed and kissed him again. "Me too."

Carter chuckled against my lips and kept kissing me, his hand coming up to cup the back of my head and hold me to him. I could feel him thickening between my legs, straddled on either side of his thighs and I moaned.

"We're not doing this here," he groaned, fisting his hand in my hair. "There are too many people here right now."

"Dammit," I moaned and kissed him again. "Get your work done, I need you naked, very soon."

"Nnnn," Carter groaned biting his lip as I kissed up his jaw and bit his ear. "You have an hour, then I'm coming for you and we're getting the hell out of here."

"Yes please," I whispered and kissed him again. I pushed off his lap and righted my clothes and hair as I walked around to the front of his desk. "Hurry up, I don't want to wait much longer."

Carter chuckled as I reached for the door and pulled it open.

"I'm gonna go and research those doctors, see what I can find."

I smiled at him and he nodded. "I think I'll contact the CAF and Lo, too. Maybe they have someone who wants a change of scenery."

"Good plan," Carter said looking at his watch. "You've got one hour."

"I'll be timing you."

Forty-five minutes later I was on the phone with a psychologist when Carter walked into my office just as I was finishing my conversation. I promised the woman I would be in touch then ended the call and leaned back in my chair.

"You're early."

"Do you care?"

"No, let's get out of here."

CHAPTER 24

Carter

"Mmm," Carol hummed above me as I pushed her thighs wide and licked between her folds. I had just made her come once but it wasn't enough. I wanted another one from her, at least one more. "Carter!"

I opened my mouth over her and sucked her clit, flicking my tongue over it as Carol writhed under me. I hummed against her, letting the vibrations send even more sensation over her sensitive flesh. Her hands were gripping my shoulders and I knew I would have crescent moon shapes dug into my skin from her nails but I loved it.

I pulled back a bit and licked her again from her opening to her clit and swirled my tongue around her clit in tight circles.

"So close," Carol sighed and I dipped my mouth lower, pushing my tongue deep inside her. My hands gripped her hips and my thumbs pulled her apart, giving me more room to get deeper. Carol's hips arched up off the bed, trying to get more contact so I moved up again to lick and suck her clit. I pushed both thumbs into her channel, filling her with them and making her scream.

I chuckled darkly and crawled up her body, kissing my way over her skin, licking across her scars until I could reach her mouth. I kissed her deeply, pushing my tongue into her mouth and letting her taste her release on me as I lifted her knee and wrapped her thigh around my waist. Slowly I thrust my cock into her, making her she was wet enough to take me.

The entire time I pumped in and out of her, slowly, she lifted her hips to meet me and we kissed. I refused to pull away from her lips except to take a breath and then I needed to taste her again. When I finally felt Carol start to tighten around me, her pussy milking me gently, I began to move faster and harder, keeping my mouth hovering so close to hers until I felt my balls draw up and a tingle in the base of my spine.

When I emptied into Carol a second later I grunted my release, holding my hips tight to hers, jerking and groaning. I dropped my forehead to her shoulder with a heavy sigh. Carol shifted under me, widening her thighs and wrapping her legs around me, her fingers tickling up and down my spine. I shuddered with a chuckle and kissed her neck, nibbling under her ear.

"Hmm," Carol giggled and shifted under me, making me groan again before I slid to the side, pulling her with me. We lay side by side, facing each other, still kissing. I smoothed her hair back with my fingers, loving the way it felt like strands of silk. I kissed her forehead and she sighed, snuggling into me.

"What are you thinking about?" I asked her a couple of minutes later.

"Mm, kids." Carol said, her palm sliding up and down the back of my arm.

"Oh?" I asked, leaning back so I could see her face. She smiled and pressed her palm to my chest, cupping her hand around my pec and flicking her thumb across my nipple. I grunted and she smiled wider. "What are you thinking about kids?"

"I'm thinking I don't want to have any more." She said gently, blinking up at me and biting her lip nervously.

"Okay," I said and kissed the teeth marks on her lip.

"That's it?" She asked, confused.

"I would like to hear your reasons, but yeah, that's it." I shrugged a shoulder and she sighed.

"I just think we don't have enough time," she began, scratching her nails through my chest hair, making me growl. "I mean, first we need to find out if we can even have kids, right? That could take a few months, then we need to actually try, maybe I have to take meds, maybe you do, maybe we need to do IVF and that's super expensive. How long will that take? I'm forty-five next month, it could be a couple of years before I even get pregnant, if I even get pregnant. And what if I don't and we do all of this and it doesn't happen? I don't know that I could handle that."

"I see what you're saying and you're right," I nodded and she smiled sadly.

"I want your baby more than anything, and I hate that we probably could have done all of this when we first got together six years ago and I kept putting you off-"

"That's not on you," I insisted, shaking my head. "I really believe that if we'd jumped into all of this before either one of us was completely ready we wouldn't be solid like we are."

"I'm good with being everyone's favourite aunt and eventually grandma to Paige's kids whenever she decides to have them."

"As long as I get to be grandpa," I chuckled and bent my head to kiss her neck.

"Damn straight you do, Papa," Carol laughed and pushed me onto my back, crawling over me and reaching into the drawer and pulling out the bottle of lube. She tossed it on the bed beside me and scratched her nails through my chest hair again, pinching my nipples with an evil smile. She bent and kissed me, licking into my mouth as she reached between her legs and cupped me in her hand.

It didn't take long with her ministrations to get me hard and aching again and she smiled wickedly. She got me ready then slid over my cock, filling herself slowly. Carol tipped her head back with a groan, squeezing me tightly deep inside her. Sighing heavily she leaned forward, cupping her hands over my chest and lifted her hips, sliding me out of her almost all the way then dropping down until I filled her again.

"Ungh," I grunted, gripping her hips and pulling her up then slamming her down on me again. Panting Carol didn't move, just let me take what I needed and I could tell by the look in her eyes that she was as close as I was. I slid my thumbs to her center and pressed them into her clit, gritting my teeth, trying to hold on until she came before I let go.

I shifted my thumbs slightly, rubbing in a circle and sending her over the edge, relaxing and exploding inside her as she clenched and rippled around me. Slowly Carol collapsed over my chest and panted, her breaths hot against my throat.

"Mmm, I love you," I murmured, and kissed her forehead.

"I love you, too." She sighed and snuggled deeper against my chest, reaching up to kiss my throat.

"Sleep baby, we've got nothing going on right now." I told her and she sighed happily. We napped then I had to get up and stretch stiff muscles and pee. I was making a sandwich in the kitchen when Carol came out wearing my t-shirt.

"Did Dawson say anything about Small?" She asked, squeezing my shoulder.

"He's still not talking but I don't think it matters," I shrugged, bending to kiss her. "From what was found in his house and the warehouse he's done."

"What about the other guy? The buyer?"

"Don't know about that, I'm sure Dawson'll have something to tell us in a day or two."

"Hm, can't happen soon enough. Rachel's supposed to come home tomorrow."

"That's good, what's Jace's plan?"

"He's staying."

"You alright with that?"

"Why wouldn't I be?" She asked, frowning and I smiled.

"You two don't exactly get along."

"Eh," she shrugged and took my beer bottle, sipping some before giving it back. "I don't not like him, he's just snarky and his sense of humor rubs me the wrong way."

"Hm," I nodded and took a bite of my sandwich before sharing it with her. Carol took a bite then went to the fridge to grab her own beer just as a knock sounded on the door.

"Are you decent?" Paige called from the door. "I'm not alone!"

"Close your eyes!" Carol called back and walked to our room to put on some pants. I had luckily pulled my jeans on when I got up so I wasn't worried about it. Once Carol was gone Paige and Sledge walked into the apartment and sat on the stools at the counter.

"So, this is a thing now?" I asked, flicking my finger back and forth between them.

"We're working on it," Sledge mumbled and I nodded. Paige rolled her eyes and reached across the counter to steal the other half of my sandwich. I grunted at her but she just gave me a cheeky grin.

"You're only working on it because I didn't give you a choice,"

Paige mumbled around her mouthful. Sledge ignored her and kept his eyes on me. "Freakin' took you long enough, too. I had to make the first move."

Sledge snorted and looked at her. "Your first move was getting yourself picked up by a drug dealer."

"Worked didn't it?" Paige asked with a shrug.

"Yeah, like that was your plan," Sledge scoffed, shaking his head. I smiled at the two of them then reached in the fridge for two more bottles of beer just as Carol came out of our room wearing pajama pants under my shirt. She didn't say anything about Paige and Sledge being together but took the half eaten sandwich out of Paige's hand and finished it.

"What's up?" She asked, ignoring Paige's scowl.

"I want out but I need help." Sledge said, watching her. Carol nodded and swallowed.

"What do you need?"

"I've got one more fight scheduled that I can't get out of but I've made sure Angel knew it was my last one. His response was we'll see which means he's going to keep scheduling fights for me." Sledge explained and I nodded. "I need a good reason to not fight after next weekend."

"You can't throw the fight," I said and Sledge shrugged.

"I'd rather not. It would be pretty obvious now." He replied and I nodded again then sighed.

"They follow you from the fight?"

"Sometimes, they probably will that night since I've said it's my last."

"Then we stage an accident," I said, sipping my beer. "We'll get Dawson there, make it look real. You might have to total your bike."

"Ugh, that's fine, I wanted a new one anyway," Sledge shrugged and I rolled my eyes.

"All right then, we'll plan it for right after your next fight. We'll put you in a HALO and doctor some records to make it look like you've got a spinal injury that'll keep you out of the cage indefinitely."

"Sounds good," Sledge shrugged again. Him and Paige finished their beers then left and Carol and I cuddled on the couch watching TV.

The next morning as we walked into the office Dawson was close on our heels.

"You got news?" I asked him, motioning for him to follow us into Carol's office.

"Damn straight I do," he said, clapping me on the shoulder. "He's done."

"What do you mean, done?" Carol asked, sitting behind her desk as Paige brought us all cups of coffee.

"I mean he's done. There is no coming back from the shit we found in his office and in his warehouse." Dawson explained with a shrug. "Rachel will still have to testify, but her testimony and that of the other three women won't bear as much weight, it'll just be the nail in the man's coffin."

"Well that's good."

"He's looking at life in prison and so are the majority of his guards from the warehouse. The guards from the house have all been cleared of any wrongdoing, at least we can't prove that they were involved at all."

"I'm okay with that," I said, looking at Carol who nodded.

"I'm just glad he's out of our city." She agreed.

"Since I'm here, would it be all right if I went up to talk to Bridget? Small is being charged with Grinder's murder, too." Dawson said and Carol nodded.

"I'll text Jordyn and have her meet you at the elevators and take you up," Carol said and he smiled.

"Thanks a lot for all your help with this." Dawson said standing.

"Hey, stop here on your way back, we have something we need your help with." I told him and he nodded then left the office. I looked over at Carol as she tossed her phone on the desk and sighed.

"It's done." She said and I smiled.

"It is done," I agreed. "So when are you going to marry me?"

"As soon as you say you're ready." She replied and I nodded.

"How about a month after Grinder's funeral?"

"Done," Carol smiled, tipping her head back against her chair.

"Tell Paige, tell her to get planning." I said, standing and leaving the office.

"Where are you going?"

"I have some shopping to do!" I called back, going to my office and pulling up jewelry sites on my computer.

I needed the perfect ring for my perfect woman.

Epilogue
Carol

Today sucked. Funerals were always hard, but today's was the worst. I stood beside Bridget and Maker in the front row of chairs at the cemetery and watched as Grinder's casket was lowered into the ground. Bridget cried and turned her face into Maker's chest while he held her tight. Maker's wife stood behind us, her hand on Bridget's arm, offering her support. The entire MC was here and even Dawson was standing in the crowd.

Rachel was there, sitting at the end of a row with Jace beside her, seemingly staring into space. I knew she wasn't though, she was working really hard to not break down. I knew she still felt guilty and probably would for a while. Even though Bridget had told her many times it wasn't her fault that Grinder had died. The two of them would always be friends but for a little while their relationship would be strained and that sucked even more.

Afterwards we all went back to the clubhouse and had a toast to Grinder. Bridget stuck around for a few minutes but couldn't stop crying so Jordyn and I took her back up to her apartment. She stood in the middle of the living room, looking around with tears in her eyes.

"I can't stay here," she said as those tears tracked down her cheeks. I blinked at her and nodded.

"We'll move you into another apartment," I told her but she shook her head.

"No, I need to get right away from here." She insisted, wiping her tears away. "I can't stay here at all."

"Bridget, are you sure?" I asked, standing and taking her hand. Jordyn moved to the door when there was a knock and Dawson stepped inside quietly.

"I'm sure, I need space, everything here reminds me of Grinder, I need to get out of here completely."

"Okay, then tomorrow we'll find you an apartment in the city," I told her and she nodded with a sniff. "You'll still have a job with us, right? We still need you to do our books. When you're ready we have some pretty major plans."

"I can still do that, just, not right away." She whispered and I nodded, hugging her.

"Uh, if it helps, I have a spare room and a pretty big house," Dawson said from the hall leading to the door. "Then you don't have to look for an apartment and you're completely safe if there's any blow back with all of this shit. There shouldn't be but you never know."

Bridget looked over at him and then back at me.

"It's up to you," I said shrugging. "I trust Dawson, but it's completely up to you what you do. I'll support you either way."

"Thanks Dawson," Bridget said softly, nodding. "Do you mind if I pack a bag now?"

"No, go do it, I just came to say I was headed out but I can wait a few minutes while you pack."

It happened quickly, but I had a feeling it was probably for the best. Dawson was a good man, he would take care of Bridget and she would get the space from the MC that she needed.

Once she was packed and on her way I went back to my own apartment to find Carter.

"What's going on?" He asked, confused.

"Bridget went to stay with Dawson for a while," I told him with a heavy sigh. "She said she needed space."

"Mm," Carter nodded then pulled me into his arms. "How are you doing?"

"I'm okay, you?"

"I'll live." He said, pulling back and looking down into my eyes. "We'll all miss Grinder but life has to keep going, right?"

"It does."

"So, are you going to be Mrs. Carol Carter? Or Mrs. Carol Wilson-Carter?" He asked, dipping his head and kissing my lips.

"Mmm, I kind of like the sound of Mrs. Carol Carter. Very alliterative," I smiled and he chuckled. He pulled his arm from around my waist and dug in his pocket then stepped back and knelt in front of me. Holding up an open, black ring box he smiled up at me.

"Carol Wilson-soon-to-be-Carter, will you marry me?"

I looked down at the ring box and smiled. There were three rings in the box. One men's solid band with a single diamond and a matching women's band. The other was a solid band of square diamonds that sparkled in the light.

"Yes, Sean Carter, I will marry you." I chuckled and sniffed. Carter stood, smiling, pulling out the band with the diamonds all the way around and slipping it on my finger. "It's perfect, Sean."

"Just like you," he said softly and bent to kiss my lips. "I love you."

"I love you."

Bending, Carter lifted me into his arms and carried me to our room. Laying me gently on the bed he hovered over me and nuzzled my neck.

"You were well worth the wait."

"I am grateful every single second of every single day that you loved me enough to wait for me." I whispered, cupping his head then sliding my hand down to his jaw.

"I couldn't not wait for you," he said, kissing me. "You're the greatest thing that's ever happened to me."

"Make love to me Carter, then we have a wedding to plan."

"Gladly!"

Printed in Great Britain
by Amazon

86280203R00193